DIVIDED
WE FALL

DIVIDED
WE FALL

TRENT REEDY

SCHOLASTIC INC.

ISBN 978-0-545-54368-2

Arthur A. Levine Books hardcover edition designed by Christopher Stengel, published by Arthur A. Levine Books, an imprint of Scholastic Inc., February 2014.

12 11 10 9 8 7 6 5 4   15 16 17 18 19 20/0

Printed in the U.S.A. 40

This edition first printing, January 2015

This book is dedicated to
Staff Sergeant Ryan Jackson
and Staff Sergeant Matthew Peterson,
whose leadership and guidance
helped me understand what it
means to be a soldier.

"No armed police force, or detective agency, or armed body of men, shall ever be brought into this state for the suppression of domestic violence, except upon the application of the legislature, or the executive, when the legislature can not be convened."

Constitution of the state of Idaho
Article XIV, Section 6

I am Private First Class Daniel Christopher Wright, I am seventeen years old, and I fired the shot that ended the United States of America.

When I enlisted in the Idaho Army National Guard, I swore to support and defend the Constitution of the United States and the state of Idaho against all enemies, foreign and domestic. I swore that I would obey the orders of the president of the United States and the governor of Idaho, as well as the orders from officers appointed over me, according to the law and regulations.

But what could I do when my president and my governor called each other domestic enemies and both issued me lawful orders to fight against the other? When both claimed to support the Constitution? When the Army was ordered to fight against the Army and no place was safe?

I swore to obey the orders of my president and of my governor. I swore to defend the Constitution. I swore these things before God.

May God forgive me. May God in Heaven forgive us all.

Sweeney gave me a little too much lead on the pass. I had to kick up the speed and reach like crazy. Damn near fell, but I caught the football before Cal could get his hands on it. I ducked to dodge his try at a one-armed tackle, turned upfield, and ran, snapping each foot down fast as I could. Our safety, Travis Jones, was the only guy who might stop me. TJ was the fastest guy on the team.

Well, he used to be fastest.

He had a good pursuit angle, so I knew I couldn't run right by him. I juked left and made him stutter-step. Then I figured, *What the hell? Jones is a total jackwad.* I gripped the ball tightly, put on a burst of speed, dropped my right shoulder, and crunched into his gut.

He groaned and I shoved him away with my left hand. His shoulder pads clicked as he hit the dry practice field. Then I bolted toward the end zone. I felt so fast, so powerful, I swear I could have run all the way up Silver Mountain to the west of town.

Coach Shiratori blew his whistle when I had like twenty yards to the goal line. No way was I stopping. Drill Sergeant McAllister would hang right behind me on five-mile runs in basic, shouting, "Private, you will run faster or I will *kill* you!" After that, I could always find more speed.

"Wright! Get back here!" Shiratori called as I crossed the line into the end zone.

"Moving, Coach!" I shouted. I tossed him the ball on the way back to the offensive huddle.

Sweeney slapped me a high five. "Nice one, man."

"Wright!"

"Yes, Coach!" I shouted as loud as I could. Coach Shiratori always tried to act like a cold-hearted badass, but I could see amusement cracking through his hard shell when I treated him like a drill sergeant. Truth was, after having the Army mentality beat into me all summer, I don't think I could have acted any other way.

"When I blow the whistle, you stop the play. You wanna run extra, we can figure it out after practice."

"Yes, Coach!"

"Wright!"

"Yes, Coach!"

"What's harder, the Army or football?"

"Coach, this *is* the Army!"

Assistant Coach Devins laughed. "That's the best answer I've ever heard."

But I wasn't sucking up. I meant what I said. I loved this.

Shiratori looked at his watch. "Right! We gotta wrap it up for the morning. Get on the goal line. Time for conditioning!"

Some of the freshmen groaned quietly, but us senior and junior guys cheered like running was the best possible thing. That's how Coach liked it. Complain about it: Run longer. Yell and cheer for more, what Sweeney called "faking the funk": Coach would let us go earlier. Maybe.

Coach put us on Idaho drills: sprint fifty yards, drop down to do ten push-ups, bear-crawl on hands and feet to our right for about twenty yards, and then sprint back to the goal line. Five rotations. They were killer, even though I was in awesome shape.

Cal puked. He always puked. That's how hard he pushed himself. An animal, that guy.

Coach let us go after his usual end-of-morning-practice lecture:

drink lots of water, be on time for the evening practice, don't do anything stupid. Our cleats thudded and scraped on the sidewalk back to the locker room. The light breeze felt good on my sweat-soaked shirt. Good thing this was our last two-a-day. I needed this coming weekend.

Cal elbowed me. "The Army issue you new moves this summer?" He rubbed a bruise that wrapped from his big bicep to his stacked tricep. "What d'you think you're doing showing up the starting defense like that?"

"Riccon, who says you're starting defense, you slow bastard?" Sweeney smiled.

"Sweeney, you little bitch, I'll crush you." Cal dropped his pads and locked his hands over his cut belly, flexing the huge traps in his shoulders. Sweeney grinned and then pretended to yawn. Cal picked up his pads. "Seriously, though, Wright," he said. "Nice moves, especially burning TJ. The guy looked pissed."

"Good," I said. I had no patience for TJ. The guy was an asshole, and I knew for a fact that he had tried to put the moves on my JoBell backstage at last year's spring play. "He's not coming tonight, is he?"

Sweeney looked around. "Dude, chill. I told everybody that I've got no action tonight."

"We gotta do something," Cal said. "This is the last weekend of summer. The last summer before senior year."

"Yeah, no kidding," I said. We always partied the last weekend before school, plus I'd just spent a miserable two months at Fort Leonard Wood down in Missouri at basic training for the Army National Guard. I needed to relax.

Sweeney pulled me and Cal off to the side and spoke quietly. "My mom and dad took the ski boat down to Coeur d'Alene. I got the keys to the pontoon. I told everybody there was nothing going on so we can take a small group out on the boat after practice tonight. Jet Ski too. Grill some steaks. Throw back some beers."

"I'm in," Cal said.

"Yeah," I said. "I'll be out later. I gotta check in with Mom after practice."

Cal sighed. "Come on, man. Really? Can't you —"

"Shut up," I said. We'd been over this a thousand times. Mom had this thing, like a kind of panic attack she'd get sometimes. She didn't like her routine interrupted, and it wouldn't be good if I wasn't there to greet her when she got home. Cal didn't know how bad she could freak out because only JoBell and Sweeney had witnessed it, but he should have been used to the drill by now.

We stowed our gear in the locker room and went out to the parking lot.

"Anyway," Sweeney said, "give me a call when you get to the lake and I'll pick you up on the Jet Ski." He elbowed Cal. "You need a ride right now?"

"Naw, I'm good. Got my motorcycle. I have to get to work. Lot of tourists on the lake. They'll be wanting to rent every kayak and paddleboat we got. I'm hoping those hot blond twins come back." He cupped his hands in the air. "You know, the ones that got great . . . um . . . twins."

Sweeney laughed. "Hmm. Sounds good. I might have to bring my Jet Ski over that way today."

Sweeney's parents had struggled for years to have kids of their own. Finally, they adopted Sweeney from Korea as a baby. They must never have gotten over how happy they were to have him, because they bought him all the best stuff.

Cal took off and Sweeney looked over my shoulder. "Hey, Timmy!" he shouted at Tim Macer behind us. "You still need a ride?" The kid nodded. "You're with us in the Beast. Hurry up."

The Beast was my awesome cherry-red 1991 Chevy Blazer. She was way older than I was, but I'd spent a ton of money and worked my ass off to get her fixed up good as new. Better than new. With a four-inch lift kit and the thirty-six-inch super swamper tires, she drove like a tank. The dual three-inch-diameter electric exhaust cut-out let me flick a switch to run right off the headers with no muffler. Then the Beast would roar louder than a jackhammer. Since it was summer, I'd taken her hard-shell top off in back, so she was basically an old-style pickup truck, with no wall behind the cab, a handy bench seat in back, and plenty of cargo room under the roll bar.

"My truck ain't no taxi," I said to Sweeney. "It's bad enough I got to be your shuttle, now you're making me drive some little sopho-more around?"

"Chill. Anyway, you have room, and he might be coming with us tonight." He held his hand up before I could complain. "As long as he brings his sister Cassie."

"Your new girl?"

He shrugged. "One of them, anyway."

I shook my head. That was Eric Sweeney. Always the go-to guy for the parties. Always scamming on another girl. Sometimes I thought it would be cool to get with as many girls as he did.

But those thoughts were swept aside when my JoBell led Becca Wells and a bunch of other girls out of the school from volleyball prac-tice. JoBell wore a faded blue-and-white Freedom Lake Minutemen T-shirt and little gray shorts. Her blond ponytail bounced behind her as she ran. I stared at her. I couldn't help it. She tossed her duffel bag in the back of the Blazer, then opened the passenger door and pushed the lever to flip the seat forward. "Hey, babe. Becca's mom needed her car."

"Okay if I ride?" Becca said as she climbed in and moved to the back. She spread a towel out on the bench seat. "I promise I won't sweat your truck up."

I acted upset, even though Becca was JoBell's best friend and a girl I'd been friends with my whole life. "Do I have a choice?"

"No," JoBell and Becca said at the same time.

Sweeney stepped on the right rear tire, grabbed the roll bar, and swung into the backseat. Timmy Macer did the same thing on the other side, but he was clumsier.

"Whoa!" I shouted as he was about to sit down.

"The hell you think you're doing!?" Sweeney yelled at him.

Timmy stood up straight and about fell out of the truck when he tried to take a step back. "What did I do?"

I shot Sweeney a look. I'd *told* him I didn't want to give this kid a ride. "You damn near sat on my hat." I held out my hand and waggled my fingers until the kid handed it over. It was a golden-white fur felt cowboy hat with only a couple dingy spots that I'd been meaning to clean for a long time. I curled the sides of the brim a little.

"No bull has ever bucked him off while he was wearing his lucky rodeo hat," Sweeney said. "And you almost crushed it."

I held the hat over my heart. "I would have had to kill you, Timmy."

"And that'd be a shame," said Sweeney.

"Sorry," Timmy said. He looked so serious, like he'd just shit his pants. "I didn't know."

JoBell reached over and squeezed my knee. "I love you," she said with amusement in her eyes. "But sometimes you're too much."

We all laughed, and I flipped my hat on my head. Even the kid relaxed and forced himself to chuckle with us.

"What are you laughing at!?" I shouted, eyeing Timmy in the mirror.

"Danny," Becca said. "Leave the poor kid alone."

I turned the key, and my truck's three-hundred-forty-horsepower 350 V8 roared to life. I closed my eyes for a moment, feeling the torque of the engine shake my body. She growled like a chained animal waiting to be released, with the power to claw through anything. I'm not gonna lie. She was the most badass truck in Freedom Lake. She was the Beast.

JoBell leaned forward to switch on the radio.

> *That's country! When I lay it all down*
> *I work hard for my money and I love this little town*
> *When them city slickers come, asking what it's about*
> *I pick up my guitar and I sing and I shout*
> *That's country!*

"Ugh, how can you listen to that crap?" JoBell said.

"That's a good song!" I said. "Hank McGrew's newest."

JoBell fiddled with the dial until she landed on the news. Her old man was a lawyer with a small private practice in town. I'd had supper a bunch of times at their house, and he passed every meal by bringing a current topic up for discussion. The two of them could get pretty intense when they debated, so JoBell liked to go in prepared.

> *Overnight violence and vandalism have marred the second*
> *day of protests in downtown Boise as police struggle to*
> *maintain order. Dozens have been arrested, and several*
> *officers have been reported injured, including one in serious*
> *condition after sustaining a head injury.*

As I pulled out of the parking lot, JoBell switched stations.

> *From NPR News, this is* Everything That Matters. *I'm David*
> *Benson. The Federal Identification Card Act would provide a*
> *high-tech replacement for flimsy paper Social Security cards,*

saving millions of dollars by streamlining and simplifying access to federal services and providing easy proof of legal eligibility for employment.

"So, Timmy," Sweeney said. "We were thinking that tonight —"

"Shh, quiet!" JoBell said. "For a sec, anyway. I want to hear what's going on."

It was a hard-reached compromise, a rare spark of unity in an otherwise deeply divided nation. Now, as NPR's Molly Williams reports, the law faces bipartisan, but not necessarily united, criticism from both progressive and conservative groups.

Sweeney leaned across the center console and spun the radio dial until he found some music. "Enough of that already. So boring." He flopped back into his seat. "So, Timmy, we're taking my parents' pontoon boat out on the lake tonight. You and Cassie want to come?"

Becca groaned. "Oh, come on, Eric."

Sweeney held his hand up. He had tried to get with Becca for years, but she wouldn't go for him. That was unusual, since most of the time when Sweeney had his eye on a girl, he'd find a way to make it work out. Still, I'd seen Timmy's little sister, and part of me hoped Sweeney wouldn't be her introduction to high school and high school guys. I caught Becca's eyes in the mirror and shook my head.

"She's just a freshman," Becca said. "She's a nice girl."

Timmy must not have heard Becca, or else he didn't understand or care what she meant. "Sure! If our parents will let us. But you really want my sister to come?"

"Oh yeah," Sweeney said. "She's friends with JoBell on the volleyball team and all."

"Leave me out of this, Eric," JoBell said.

"Okay, kitten," Sweeney said.

She turned around in her seat to face him. "Call me any more sexist names, Eric, and I'll make sure you never ride in this truck again. I have some pull with the owner."

Sweeney grinned and put his hands up in surrender. JoBell really didn't like the nicknames that Sweeney often made up for her, but at this point her anger and even Sweeney's sexism was mostly an act, a game the two of them had been playing for years.

After we dropped Timmy, Sweeney, and Becca off, I pulled the Beast over in front of JoBell's big brick house. She squeezed my hand. "Wish you didn't have practice again tonight."

"Yeah," I said. "It's the last two-a-day, though." I looked down. "Last two-a-day of my whole life."

She put her fingers under my chin and made me look at her. "You sound all sad, like one of the old-timers at the coffee shop who sits around reminiscing about the 'good old days' of high school." She leaned forward and we kissed. I could taste her favorite spicy gum on her tongue. She kissed my cheek and then my neck, and tingles rippled all the way down my body. "But these *are* the good times." She gave me a quick kiss on the lips again and kept her face close to mine. "And they are never" — kiss — "going" — kiss — "to end."

I looked into her warm, happy eyes. "I love you," I whispered.

"I love you more." She unbuckled her seat belt. "This is senior year and, yeah, lots of things will be changing. But this" — she pressed her hand over my heart for a moment and then held my hand over her own — "is forever."

I laughed a little and gently slid my hand up her neck and around the back of her head to pull her close one last time. Then she climbed down out of the truck and pulled her duffel from the back. I watched her jog up to her porch. She stopped at the door and waved, then went inside. My chest ached the way it did whenever JoBell left, but I started the truck and drove to the shop.

I parked off in the grass like I usually did to let customers use the driveway. The faded sign squeaked as it swung in the breeze. I could hardly read SCHMIDT & WRIGHT AUTO on it anymore. It probably hadn't been painted since before Dad died. I dropped three quarters into the old pop machine that sat between the two open garage doors, hit the button, and pulled a Mountain Dew out of the slot.

"Look who finally shows up!" Schmidty said. I laughed. He spun away from the desk in his dusty old swivel chair. My dad's longtime business partner — now my partner — was taking his lunch break with his daily ham sandwich and iced tea. He took a drag on his cigarette. "How was practice? Coach still bustin' your balls about not being in his precious weight room this summer?"

Coach had been kind of a dick when I first started practice because he had this idiot idea I hadn't worked hard enough at Fort Leonard Wood. "Naw. I've been blasting right by all the best guys."

Schmidty raised a bushy eyebrow as the Buzz Ellison talk show music came on the radio. "Is that right?"

"I even laid out TJ today. You should've seen —"

"Hang on now." He flicked his cigarette ash in an old coffee can. "Shut up, and let me enjoy my show in peace." He pointed to the Honda Civic GXE in the far bay — a natural gas/electric hybrid with solar assist. Someone had some money and really cared about cutting emissions. "You want to get started?" Schmidty said. "Oil change and tire rotation." He called cars like this "dirty hippie cars." Wouldn't touch them.

I went over to the far bay as Buzz Ellison returned from a commercial break.

Welcome back, all of you true patriots. You're listening to the one, the only, Buzz Ellison, the last bastion of truth and freedom in a very troubled America, broadcasting live coast to coast from Conservative CentCom in downtown Boise, Idaho. The number to call if you'd like to be on the program today is 1-800-555-FREE, that's 1-800-555-3733. More reports are piling in from across the nation about people who just aren't buying El Presidente Rodriguez's party line about these government surveillance cards. We have protests on campuses in Florida, Texas, Iowa, and, of course, a chaotic situation right here in Boise.

Buzz faded into the background as I went to work. Schmidty and Buzz got all fired up about politics and how Democrats, liberals, and the government were supposedly destroying America. JoBell sometimes argued the exact opposite. I mostly let them all spin on. Politics weren't my thing.

"Yeah, Buzz! That's exactly what I've been saying!" Schmidty spat out bits of his sandwich as he yelled at the radio. I had to laugh. I'd told him over and over that he should have his own show. "Are you listening to this?" he asked me.

I hadn't been, but I paid attention now.

These are sad days for America. First, terrible unemployment at 18 percent. Federal debt off the charts, a federal government shut down over budget disagreements earlier in the year. Now this. I don't even want to think about what's next. Well, but I already know. More big government. Remember what

Ronald Reagan warned us about, patriots, when he said, "Government big enough to give you everything, is also powerful enough to take it all away."

"Yeah! Give 'em hell, Buzz!" Schmidty shouted. Buzz rolled on.

People might ask me, "But Buzz, if everyone hates these new cards, why did the bill pass?" Well, that's the problem! There are people out there . . . I have people on my phone lines right now waiting to disagree with me, people who are willing to overlook all the drawbacks in this boneheaded idea. These idiots are out protesting in the streets too. It's an absolute mess.

Schmidty stood up and stretched, his stained T-shirt rising to expose the bottom flap of his big sagging belly. He downed the rest of his iced tea and then wiped his mouth with the back of his hand. "I don't know why you signed up with the National Guard. This ain't the same country that your father died defending."

This was like the hundredth time he had said something like that. I don't know why he didn't get it. As soon as I'd heard that a kid could join the Army National Guard at seventeen, I begged Mom to sign the permission form so I could enlist right on my birthday and ship out to training two days later. It was the perfect deal. The Guard would pay for all the auto tech classes I needed to really expand the business, even the advanced tech stuff for working on these newer hybrids, compressed natural gas vehicles, and second-gen solar-assist systems that Schmidty couldn't stand. With my Guard pay from the summer and the money I'd been saving, I'd be able to buy Schmidty's half ownership of the garage when he retired in a couple years and set up a real future right here in Freedom Lake.

More than the money, though, it was an honor to be a soldier and serve my country like my father had. Standing straight at basic training graduation, saluting the flag while the national anthem played, I knew I was part of something important. I loved my home and I loved America, and I was willing and ready to fight to defend them, to defend freedom and protect the people I loved.

I went back to work on the oil change. Buzz Ellison went on arguing with callers and complaining about the president. Schmidty worked on a pickup and argued with the callers as well. "Dumbass hippie protestors!" he yelled once.

That was classic Dave Schmidt, never happy unless he had something to be mad about. Still, he seemed worse than usual. Business had been bad lately. With gasoline prices so high for so long, the people who couldn't afford to switch over to electrics or to cars like this Honda were actually driving less. Less wear and tear on cars meant less repairs meant less money. But that was pretty much the same story everywhere, and this old shop had never made Schmidty or Dad rich.

I sighed. No time to worry about this stuff now. All I could do was get a little good car work done before I headed back to school for afternoon practice.

Practice that afternoon was rough. It was like Coach Shiratori was mad that he couldn't have practice on Saturday and Sunday, so he worked us extra hard to cram three days into a couple hours. TJ made sure to pair up with me for tackling drills, trying to get even for the way I'd smoked him that morning. I wouldn't say I beat him in the drills. I fought him to a good draw, though.

After practice, at home, I hurt everywhere while I showered and dressed. Then I drank a huge glass of cool water, trying to get hydrated for the night's party. Leaning back on my bed, I picked up a photo from my nightstand. It was taken last summer after I'd won first place in the senior high school division for bull riding. In the photo, me and JoBell were leaning against a white wooden fence, my arm around her. I'd been riding so much that summer that my brown hair was bleached nearly blond. I was sweating a little and there was a streak of dirt on my cheek, but JoBell just smiled at me.

I carefully put the photo down and opened the drawer to my nightstand, reaching all the way to the back until I found the little black box. For about the millionth time, I looked at the golden ring with its single diamond. It was a whole quarter carat, and it cost a fortune, but JoBell was worth it. I knew we were way too young to get married, but maybe in a year or so we could get engaged. Then, when I had enough money to buy the shop from Schmidty, I'd be making enough for us to live on. It could work. It really could. I ran my finger down the glass over JoBell's image.

Hank McGrew cut into the silence from my COMMPAD, an older Samsung Cloud II. *"Hey, partner, you got . . . a text coming in from JoBell."* Hank's digi-assistant app didn't run so well on a measly three gig and cellular. I picked up the comm.

"Hank, put it up."

In the window at the lower right corner of the screen, the image of Hank McGrew gave a thumbs-up and then disappeared. The text blinked on-screen: Hey babe. Becca and me are at the lake. Where are you?

From outside came a high-pitched noise and the crunch of tires on the gravel driveway. I hoped that wasn't Mom's car. From the squeaking sound, it needed something. Hopefully it was only belts.

I looked out my window and sighed, then tapped the TEXT button and said, "At home. Mom just got here." I tapped SEND.

Yeah. Hurry up. I want to have fun tonight.

I grinned. Keep your panties on. I'll hurry.

Her text came back. No panties tonight. Only the bikini. Come get it.

"Danny?" Mom called from downstairs. Nothing to calm hot thoughts about JoBell like Mom shouting. "Danny? Where are you?" The shadow, that panicked disconnect from reality, was creeping into her voice worse than it had in a long time. Mom didn't handle stress very well, especially when she was away from home. I always helped her relax when she got here. I'd have to move quickly.

"Yeah, Mom —" I started to yell when Hank came back on my comm.

"The National Guard's calling, buddy. Thanks for ser . . . ving your country."

What could the Guard be calling about? Drill wasn't until next month.

"Danny!" I heard a glass break downstairs.

"Mom, hang on! I'm here!" I shouted as I tapped in to the voice call. "Hello?"

"Danny!" Mom was nearly to shriek mode. The shadow almost had her now.

A deep voice came from the comm as I reached the bottom of the stairs. *"Private First Class Wright?"*

"Yes," I said. Mom had her hands up in front of her chest, picking at the skin around her fingernails and taking little steps as she shuffled around the living room. The shards of one of her ceramic horse knickknacks littered the floor by the end table. "This is Wright," I said into my comm.

"Oh! There you are." Mom rushed over and hugged me tight. I slipped my arm around her and rubbed her back in the way that sometimes calmed her down. "At first I didn't think you were here, and then I started to get nervous so I accidentally knocked the horse off —"

"PFC Wright, are you listening? This is Staff Sergeant Meyers."

The voice came louder over the comm. I turned away so Mom couldn't hear Meyers and held the comm away from my mouth. "I have a call, Mom," I said to her. Into the comm I said, "Roger that. Go ahead."

"*Rattlesnake. Rattlesnake. Rattlesnake.*"

Rattlesnake. Three times. The phrase was only used for one purpose. It meant our Guard unit was being activated.

My heart thumped heavy in my chest. Getting this code now didn't make sense. My unit, the 476th Combat Engineer Company, was already deployed to Iran. They left before I even went to basic. The only soldiers who drilled at the 476th armory outside of Farragut Falls were new privates like me and prior service transfers from other Guard units — soldiers who had moved to the area and switched to our company after most of the others had shipped out. They couldn't be mobilizing us now.

I slid out from Mom's hug, smiling and pretending I was almost happy, like I was talking to one of the guys. "Go —" My mouth suddenly felt dry. I licked my lips. "Go ahead," I said to the sergeant. I covered the mike on my comm. "Mom, have a seat in your chair. I'll make you some tea." A hot cup of chamomile tea always helped relax Mom's nerves. She shuffled to her recliner as I slipped into the kitchen.

"*Private Wright?*" said Sergeant Meyers. "*You there? Prepare to copy.*"

"Yeah. Go ahead. I'm here, Sergeant."

"*This is your mobilization call.*"

I wedged the comm between my ear and shoulder as I filled the teakettle and put it on the stove. "Iran or Pakistan?"

"*Negative,*" Sergeant Meyers said. "*By order of the governor of the state of Idaho, you are hereby ordered to report to your duty station, 476th Engineer Company armory, no later than eighteen hundred hours this evening.*" He sounded stiff, like he was reading from something. "*Uniform will be MCU — Multinational Combat Uniform. You will receive further instructions upon reporting for duty.*"

I cranked the heat up on the burner and tilted my head back and forth to stretch my neck. "You can't tell me anything about what's going on?"

Meyers didn't answer for a moment. I could hear the faint sound of voices in the background. Then he cleared his throat. *"Listen, Private,"* he said in a quiet, tough voice. *"There's trouble with this protest down in Boise. Stuff getting torn up. At least one police car has been flipped over, maybe set on fire. The governor is sending in the Guard to restore order. But you didn't hear any of that from me. Understand?"*

"Roger that, Sergeant. I guess I'll figure out what's going on when I get to the armory."

"You need to man up and pay attention tonight," said the sergeant. *"This is the real deal. It's going to be a long night. That a good copy?"*

"Roger," I said.

"Hurry up and get here. Do not *be late. Out."* The line went dead. I stared at the "call ended" message on the screen.

"Who was that?" Mom said.

I jumped a little. How had I not heard her enter the kitchen? She wasn't shaking as much. "You okay, Mom?" I tried to act happy. "You had me worried when you came in. Why don't you have a seat?"

The metal kitchen chair scraped on the linoleum floor as she sat down. "I . . . I had a rough day at work. They want me to use this new computer system, even though they're hardly giving me time to train on it, and the old one worked fine. Rita called in sick, so I had to cover a lot more, plus she said she would help me figure out the new system. Then I couldn't find you . . ." Her breathing was getting faster again.

"It's okay, Mom. You're home. You're good now."

She pressed her hands to her chest, closed her eyes, and focused on her breathing. "I . . . I'm fine. That Eric calling?"

She had calmed down a little bit, but she'd freak if she knew I'd been activated and had to go on duty. "Yeah. Sweeney was hoping I could meet him. Take his boat out. You know, fishing and everything."

"Drinking?"

"What? No, Mom. Trying to catch some fish. Maybe play a little poker."

She didn't look completely convinced. "Sure. Okay. If you're staying late, don't be driving."

"Sure." I took a few steps toward the door to the hallway, then stopped. This was the absolute wrong time to be called up. "You going to be okay?"

"Go." She waved me away. "Have fun with your friends. You work too hard taking care of your crazy old mother."

I crossed the kitchen in three big steps, put my arms around her, and kissed the top of her head. "You're not crazy or old, Mom."

"Go on now. I love you." She patted my hand as I pulled away. "Danny?" she said as I reached the door again. "Be careful tonight."

I nodded and headed toward my room to get my uniform. Back in the kitchen, the boiling kettle began to scream.

─•─• As you can see, Tom, I'm quite close to the disturbance, and what began as a protest against Governor Montaine signing the bill to nullify the Federal ID Card Act has quickly expanded into counter-protests about a host of issues. Excuse me, sir, can you tell us why you're protesting today?"

"Yeah, I'll tell ya. Look, I don't care about any stupid ID card law. I'm pissed because the government needs to know we're sick of this, man! Mr. Big Shot Governor so busy talking up new jobs in Idaho, building COMMPADS and electronics in Boise and Idaho Falls. I applied there. Didn't get the job. I can't even afford a comm! Tired of this! •─•─

─•─• Come to the Coeur d'Alene gun show featuring locally manufactured Castle Firearms! Under Idaho law, if you're an Idaho resident and buy locally manufactured weapons, federal gun control laws do not apply to you. So take advantage of this opportunity to purchase an AR15 or other quality, locally made fire-arms. There's even an air rifle range for the kids! This Saturday at the •─•─

─•─• Climbing three positions to number five on the country music charts, here's Hank McGrew with his latest hit, "Rise Up":

Old Merle got home early from the factory today
His wife put on the dinner, said, "It'll be okay
For you and me, six kids in our family"

Well, Ol' Merle's daddy taught him to judge from right and wrong
Said, "Life will sometimes drop you, but don't stay down for long
You're an American, not an Ameri-can't"

And when the next day rolled around, Merle went down to
  the mill
No jobs that day, but he won't give up
And you know he never will

'Cause the Eagle carries the Sword of Justice in her beak
She lands and stands proud on the church steeple peak
As the flag flies over this town . . .
Oh, you can't keep America down •—ᐱ

—ᐱ• *of Democrat senators threatening to filibuster a defense appropriations bill unless their unemployment package is brought to the floor for a vote. The Republican leadership countered, saying the soaring federal deficit would not allow* •—ᐱ

—ᐱ• *With the last of the phase-one pipeline system complete, the New Plymouth natural gas compressor station went online today, making western Idaho's recently discovered extensive natural gas resources commercially available for the first time. A spokesman at the plant says that phase two, scheduled to begin within the year, will focus on distributing natural gas to commercial filling stations for use in cleaner-running natural gas automobiles. Lynette Jatherine, KTVB Boise News.* •—ᐱ

—ᐱ• *As president, one of my chief responsibilities is upholding the law. Nothing is more sacred to me than our rights as Americans as provided for by our Constitution. During my time in the Senate, I worked to limit the warrantless surveillance power of the National Security Agency, begun under President Bush and expanded thereafter. As president, I put an end to the practice started by President Obama and continued until my administration, of using drones or other means to kill American citizens without due process. I did these things because I respect and cherish our Constitutional rights.*

So yes, the new federal identification cards will contain a lot of personal information in order to streamline access to federal services, and it is precisely because these cards will contain such information that they contain a chip allowing their location to be tracked. If one of these important cards is lost or stolen, it can quickly be located. I understand why people, including those in Idaho, might be upset about the federal government's ability to track the location of these cards, but I promise the American people that the location of any federal ID card would never be tracked except at the request of its owner, or with a proper warrant issued by a court of law. •⎯⌄

TWO

JoBell had been supportive, but not excited, about me enlisting. While I was in basic training without my comm or any screen, she wrote me actual paper letters every day, telling me that she hoped I was doing good on my rifle marksmanship or my push-ups and sit-ups for physical training. She said she missed me, and even that she was proud of me, but she never came around to admitting that enlisting had been a good idea. I was pretty sure she'd be mad or at least dump a bunch of I-told-you-so's on me when she found out I had to miss tonight's party because of the Guard.

Driving north on the highway toward the armory near Farragut Falls, I called out, "Hank."

"*Wha'chu need, chief?*"

"Speaker-call JoBell."

"*No problem. I'll put a voice call with JoBell on speaker,*" Hank said. "*You want to listen to a sample of my newest song while you wait?*"

"No thanks. I'm good."

"*No problem. Let me know if you change your mind. Of course you can always add the song to your playlist for only . . . two dollars.*"

Maybe I should have paid extra for the ad-free version of the digi-assistant. Finally JoBell picked up. "*Danny? Are you here? I'll come get you on the Jet Ski.*"

"*Cannonball!*" Cal shouted in the background. I heard a big splash and people laughing.

"I'm not at the lake." I hated lying to JoBell, but if I made her angry over all of this, it would ruin her evening. "Mom's having a rough night. I need to stay home and help her."

"*Oh no,*" she said with real concern in her voice. "*Is she okay? Is it a bad attack? Do you want me to come over to help?*"

Despite how uncomfortable I felt making up this story, I had to smile. A lot of girls would be mad that I was bailing. JoBell was just worried about Mom.

"No," I said. "No, it's cool. I got this. I'm just bummed I'll have to miss everything."

"*Family first, Danny. Your mom is most important. She helped me so much when my mom left Dad and me for that prick dentist. I wish she didn't have to have it so rough like this. Maybe she could see another doctor? Maybe a different prescription would help?*"

Her caring wasn't making it any easier to lie. "She's been to a zillion different doctors, believe me. This anxiety thing is kind of a family curse. Grandma was the same way. Anyway, I don't want to mess up your party. Have twice as much fun for me."

"*You know I won't have half as much fun without you. But I'll try. I love you.*"

"I love you more," I said. "Hank, end call."

"*I'm hangin' up.*"

I drove on through my ruined night toward the National Guard armory.

After I pulled into the parking lot inside the fence, I shut off the engine and sat back in the quiet stillness for a moment. So far, the Guard had been all about training. At basic, we'd practiced marching, shooting, throwing grenades, and we ran battle drills. Everything we'd done had been closely supervised under controlled conditions, with enough safety precautions to take all the danger and fun out of it. It sounded like we were going real world tonight. What would that be like?

By eighteen thirty I was in MCU, helmet, and body armor, one of nineteen soldiers crammed inside the cabin of a roaring Chinook helicopter. I'd been on an airplane for the flight to and from basic training, so this was my third flight ever.

It really sucked.

As I settled into the miserable flight, the sweat rolled down my face and back. It wasn't only the heat in the helicopter under all this gear. Every time the Chinook bumped in the air, I felt like my insides were flipping over. Sure, this wasn't close to as bumpy as bull riding, but at least on a bull I felt more in control, and the fall to the ground was short. If this bird went down, I was helpless to do anything but wait to die.

The drive from Freedom Lake down to Boise took about eight hours. They said this flight was supposed to be about an hour and a half. I checked my watch. We should have been getting close.

"All right, listen up, men!" Staff Sergeant Meyers shouted over the engine noise as he walked down the aisle. I looked to Specialist Sparrow to see if she was mad about being called a man, but she was cool. Meyers went on. "The lieutenant has our orders, so stop your gabbing and make sure you pay attention so you know what's going on!"

Nobody had been saying anything. The nine soldiers in my squad sat on the canvas seats lining one side of the bird, staring across the aisle at second squad. These guys were mostly strangers to me. Besides basic training, all I'd ever done with the National Guard was one weekend drill with my unit. First Sergeant Herbokowitz was usually the NCO, the Noncommissioned Officer, who yelled at us, but he was on the other Chinook with third and fourth squads. Second squad's leader, Staff Sergeant Torres, hardly ever said anything. Lieutenant

McFee was supposed to be in charge of the whole platoon, but the problem was LT McFee was really young, which let Meyers think he could run things. Or maybe Meyers was just kind of a dick.

Lieutenant McFee sat in the middle of second squad. He leaned forward in his seat a little and wiped the sweat from his brow. "Okay. This is your op order." I could hardly hear him over the engine noise, especially with my stupid earplugs in.

Meyers shouted, "Sir, you're going to have to stand up and be a hell of a lot louder!"

McFee nodded. He rose and slid his finger along his Army-issued comm in its thick green case, maybe trying to bring up the right page. The glow from the screen cast shadows above his cheeks, making him look like a zombie or something. "Paragraph One: Enemy Forces. Okay." He held his comm closer to his face and squinted. "The situation is that protestors down in Boise in the vicinity of the capitol building are creating a dangerous or potentially dangerous environment. They have thrown rocks, bottles, or other objects at law-enforcement personnel. Some vehicles have been destroyed and a few businesses have been looted. Probable course of action is that the protestors will continue to cause injury and property damage."

Sergeant Meyers sighed loudly. He leaned forward and pressed his forehead against the side of his M4 barrel.

Lieutenant McFee shot Meyers a quick, nervous look, but went on. "Friendly forces. Okay. Um. We have local law enforcement in the area. State police. EMTs. Also, um, firefighters. Soldiers from the local Army National Guard headquartered at —"

"Sir?" Sergeant Meyers stood up again. "That's a bang-on start of a textbook five-paragraph op order. I think we can skip to the mission. These Joes just need the basics."

Lieutenant McFee took a breath like he was about to say something, but then he blew it out and sat down.

Meyers spit tobacco juice into the empty Mountain Dew bottle he'd been using. "This is a piece-of-cake mission," he said. "The bird puts us down on the baseball fields at Ann Morrison Park, across the river from the real downtown area. Then first squad is going to move to the east to set up a checkpoint on South Capitol Boulevard right north of University Drive. Second squad will be securing Americana Boulevard. Third and fourth squads in the other Chinook will join other soldiers to help shut down I-184. Other Guard units from across the state will be setting up the same kind of checkpoints all over. Basically, we're one part of a big circle of National Guard all around the riot. The state police and local Boise cops will be handling the rioters. We'll be far away from the action. We block off the road. Nobody gets downtown. It's simple. Even morons like you can figure this out. Everybody got it?"

Private Luchen raised his hand. "Sergeant?"

Meyers spun to face him. "What, Luchen?"

Luchen was maybe two years older than me, but he seemed much younger. He was one of those little guys who sometimes had trouble making the Army minimum weight standard. "Sergeant, what about traffic heading away from downtown?"

There were groans and some laughter from the guys. "Damn it, Luchen, the hell you think?" Luchen watched Meyers with his mouth open, as always. "You let them through. We're trying to get people *out* of the downtown area."

"Roger, Sergeant," Luchen said. " 'Cause I was thinking that —"

"Don't think!" Meyers shouted. "You have to remember one thing." He stared down both rows. "And this goes for all of you. You just do whatever I say."

Staff Sergeant Torres and Lieutenant McFee both looked up. Meyers must have seen their questioning expressions because he went on, "Yeah, and Torres and the LT. Do what you're told and you'll be fine. I'm just pissed we won't get to go down by the capitol building and kick a little protestor ass!"

Sergeant Kemp leaned over and said something close to the lieutenant's ear. Kemp was my team leader in the squad. McFee nodded and Kemp stood up, carrying a green rectangular ammo can with him. "Sergeant Meyers makes a good point. This isn't an ass-kicking mission. We're going down there to stop trouble and calm things down. For some reason, we're supposed to get ammo. I'm passing this can around."

Ammunition? Why were we getting ammo to run a simple roadblock? Rent-a-cop security guys did this kind of traffic stuff at the rodeo parking lot and they only had flashlights. Maybe we had blank rounds to scare people, or those cool rubber bullets that were supposed to hurt but not kill.

Kemp held up one thirty-round magazine. "Each man will draw two magazines. Both will go in your ammo pouch on your vest. Do *not* load a magazine into your weapon. I say again, do *not* load a magazine until you are ordered to do so."

My stomach heaved a little as I lightened in my seat. The Chinook was descending into Boise. I closed my eyes and took deep breaths in through my nose, trying to fight the drooly, almost-want-to-puke-type feeling. All I could hear was the loud drone of the engines and the clink of the magazines against the metal ammo can while the guys drew their loads.

Luchen elbowed me. "Dude. Check it."

I opened my eyes as he put the ammo can in my lap. I pulled out my two clips. There were green metal tips on the end of the standard 5.56 rounds. They were issuing live ammunition! No blanks or anything. These were the real deal.

Out the back hatch of the Chinook, I could see buildings and streets below. In the distance, near the white dome of the state capitol building, the streets were full of people. Smoke rose in columns from several fires. Everywhere else, it looked like any other town.

I held my rifle tightly. I'd practiced with an M4 all summer at basic training, but this was the first time this particular rifle had been assigned to me. It felt right, warm and familiar in my hands.

The Chinook set down, and the light above the bay door switched from red to green. The flight engineer gave a thumbs-up and shouted, "Okay."

"Okay, ladies, on your feet! Let's move!" Meyers ran down the length of the aircraft past the helicopter crewman. He jumped down to the ground and crouched-ran at a right angle from the aircraft through the rotor wash off to the side. Lieutenant McFee, who was in charge and should have dismounted first, waited a moment before following him.

Sergeant Kemp held his hands up to slow us down. "Second squad . . . good luck," he shouted over the roar from the engines and the wind from the rotors. "First squad, you're out first. Follow Sergeant Meyers." Kemp stepped down off the end of the ramp. He motioned for us to follow.

Specialist Stein gave a whoop like he thought this was a party as he ran after Meyers. Luchen hit me in the arm almost like we were heading out of the locker room for a football game. The others were all business. I was the last in our squad to get off the bird. Kemp grabbed me like he'd stopped everyone else. "Duck low and head out straight that way." He pointed in the direction my squad had gone. "Get out there and take a knee with our fire team."

A wave of heat off the turbine engines near the back of the fuselage blasted me in the face. The rotors were kicking up a blinding cloud of dust from the baseball field. As I ran, crouching low and carrying my M4, the stupid gas-mask carrying case kept twisting around to my front side and whapping me in the nuts. When I cleared the dust cloud, I could see where the others were set up. I spat to get the dirt out of my mouth, but the grit was still in my teeth.

"Hurry up! Move your asses!" Sergeant Meyers paced around the soldiers who had taken a knee in a loose group. Lieutenant McFee stood, scanning the area with binoculars. Sergeant Torres led his squad off at a slow run across the park away from us.

The damned mask carrier was hanging down almost between my knees now. There were three different straps on the case and I could never figure out how to get it secured to my leg like it was supposed to be. It was tricky to run, but I put on some speed.

"Private, slow down," Sergeant Kemp said as he caught up to me. "Your mask is all jacked up." He made some adjustments to the carrier's straps. "You don't want to trip while running with a weapon. Calm down. You're fine."

We joined the others. Then the Chinook sped up its rotors, stirring even more dust as it rose into the air and flew off. In the relative quiet, I could hear sirens and honking horns, shouts and chanting in the distance. A bead of sweat ran down the back of my neck. It had been blazing hot at practice earlier today, and even though the sun was low in the west, it hadn't cooled off much yet.

"All right!" Meyers yelled. "If any of you ladies are afraid or missing your little girlfriends, get that shit out of your head right now and focus."

"'Ladies'? Oh, come on," said Specialist Sparrow under her breath.

Meyers heard her. "Hey, Specialist, it's just part of being in a combat unit, so don't make this into some kind of feminist thing. If you want to roll with the men, you gotta toughen up!"

"I passed all events on *my* PT test," Sparrow said quietly.

Some of the guys laughed. Meyers was kind of fat. If he heard her, he ignored her. "Lock and load!" Meyers shouted.

A couple guys slammed magazines up into the wells of their M4s, then yanked back and released the charging handles above the stocks of their rifles to chamber a round.

"As you were! Do not lock and load!" Kemp shouted. That was a gutsy move for him. He was a sergeant, a rank below Staff Sergeant Meyers, so he was outranked and out of line. "We don't need to chamber rounds. This isn't a war."

Meyers turned to Kemp. "I gave you and everybody else in my squad an order, *Sergeant* Kemp. Lock and load."

I had my hand on my weapon's charging handle, but hadn't pulled it yet. A bunch of the guys exchanged glances like, *What are we supposed to do?*

"Maybe the lieutenant should decide," Kemp said. "Sir, we don't need to go into this with rounds chambered. I can't believe we were even issued live ammunition in the first place."

Meyers pulled the binoculars from the lieutenant's face. "LT, if this shit goes bad, we won't have time to be worrying about our weapons. How are you going to feel if one of your men gets hurt because he was still chambering a round when trouble hit?"

"There won't be any trouble," said Kemp. "It's only a checkpoint. A traffic stop."

"Make the call, sir," Meyers said.

The lieutenant looked from one NCO to the other with wide eyes. I knew how he felt. I basically wanted to get out of there as fast as possible. Still, McFee was supposed to be in charge. Some loud shouts and the sound of breaking glass came from somewhere not too far away.

Lieutenant McFee pulled his CamelBak hose around and took a long drink. "Lock and load."

"Good call, sir," said Sergeant Meyers. Kemp shook his head. Meyers smiled. "You heard the lieutenant. Lock and load," he called out to all of us. Then he stepped close to Sergeant Kemp and spoke quietly, but still loud enough for me and the guys to hear. "Sergeant Kemp, if you can't follow orders in my squad, I will find a new alpha team leader."

Rifles clicked all around me. I pulled back and released my own weapon's charging handle.

Lieutenant McFee stood up straight at attention. "Fall in!"

Everybody jumped up and rushed to stand shoulder to shoulder, grouped into their four-man fire teams, facing the officer in formation. Sergeant Meyers was at the far right of the rank. Sergeant Kemp stood next to him in the A team leader spot. I was the last guy in our team, with Specialist Sparrow and PFC Luchen between me and Sergeant Kemp. To my left was the B team leader, Sergeant Ribbon. Next to him was Specialist Stein, PFC Nelson, and finally Specialist Danning.

"Port *arms*!" the lieutenant shouted. I executed the movements I had been taught, bringing my rifle up at an angle across my chest. My right hand moved down low, holding the top of the stock with my left hand high under the end of the barrel. The other guys did the same, but some were pretty sloppy.

"Right *face*!" McFee ordered. Everyone made a one-quarter facing movement to the right.

"Forward *march*!" said McFee. We all started forward. "Your left. Your left. Your left-right." He called out the cadence quietly, better than the loud, stupid, cheery singsong cadences like I'd had to do during drill and ceremony at basic all summer. D&C sucked, and it was worse on a Friday night when I was supposed to be partying with the guys and JoBell.

Even though the sun was going down, the late August heat cooked us in our uniforms. On that hot cement, we were like burgers frying on the griddle. I tried to ignore the sweat running from under my helmet and dripping down my back. Couldn't do anything about it anyway.

We marched around the corner in the park. Across the street ahead, some kids pointed at us as they came out of the Gas & Sip. A little girl's ice cream sloshed out of her cone as she stared. People in the McDonald's watched us through the window. A bunch of people took pictures with their comms. Others clapped and cheered.

I held back my grin. Even though I mostly wanted to go home, I also felt kind of cool. There I was, wearing a real Army uniform, a trained soldier with a rifle. At basic, I'd been a real good shot too. Earned an expert rifle marksman badge. *That's right*, I wanted to call out to the crowds, *the Idaho Army National Guard is here*. The trouble would be over soon.

When we reached South Capitol Boulevard, the situation was different. A couple dozen people stood around the far side of the street. A lot of them were dressed almost as if they were going to the beach, with the guys in ragged, faded T-shirts or shirtless, and bikini-topped women. Could they be from the college? A bunch of them tipped back beers. Some held up signs complaining about police brutality or the wars in Iran or Pakistan. I reminded myself to focus on my duty.

"Group, *halt*!" McFee ordered.

With a final "left-right," we stopped marching. I sneaked a look to my left. McFee had a map up on his comm. He ran his finger along it, then looked up at the street sign before checking the map. He sighed and then came to the position of attention. "Left *face*!" We all quarter turned to the left to face him. "On the command of 'fall out,' you will fall out and take a knee in a security perimeter around me. Fall out!"

"Move it!" Sergeant Meyers positioned his guys in a circle. I took a knee facing the street. Sergeant Kemp nodded at each of us in his team as if checking we were okay. Then Meyers joined the lieutenant in the middle of the circle. After a moment, Meyers called for Specialist Sparrow, our Radio-Telephone Operator, to stick with the lieutenant so he'd be able to use the radio that she carried in her pack.

"Go home, pigs!" a hot redheaded girl in a tank top and tiny, tight jean shorts shouted.

"Get out of here! We don't need no Army here!" someone called from the middle of the group.

"Hey hey! Ho ho! All these soldiers got to go!" They took up the chant.

What was their problem? We were just coming to fix things downtown. A guy with a beard and those nasty, white-boy, wannabe dreadlocks stepped away from the crowd, halfway out in the street. "What's the matter? You lost? Go home!" he shouted at us. The crowd cheered and started moving to join him. Dreadlocks Guy locked eyes with me. I tightened my squeeze on the pistol grip of my rifle. He pointed at me. "This isn't the war in Iran. If we didn't waste so much money on you military people, maybe the university would be funded better and tuition wouldn't be so high!"

"Bring it in close, men!" McFee called. I was glad to get away from the crowd as I went to join the others. "Okay, listen up."

"That's right! Run away!" Dreadlocks shouted.

"Pussies! I'll kick their asses!" Luchen elbowed me as we came up near the lieutenant.

"They never lifted a finger to defend this country," said Specialist Sparrow. "We fight to protect their freedom of speech, and they wanna give us trouble?"

"I said listen up!" McFee shouted. His eyes flicked from us to the protestors in the street.

"At ease on that tough-guy stuff," Kemp said to us. "We're professionals. We have a job to do."

Sergeant Meyers glared at the crowd. Lieutenant McFee wiped his hand down over his face. "Okay. Um." He pointed toward the street. "So our mission is to secure this road right out here. We're going to move out to the middle of South Capitol Boulevard and move in an, um, kind of diamond formation north above University Drive. We'll stop all traffic and, ah, people who are trying to get to the riot downtown that way."

"Remember your military bearing," Kemp said. "Do not say one word to those protestors."

"And stay alert!" Sergeant Meyers said. "They may start getting violent. Watch to see if they have weapons. It's called situational awareness."

Sergeant Kemp shook his head. "Yeah, yeah, but try to calm down. Keep under control. These people out here are just mad about a lot of different things. They're probably harmless."

"But don't be complacent," Meyers said.

Watch for weapons? What did these guys think was going to happen? I hoped the other Guard units around the city were having a better time than us. From the shouting and sirens coming from downtown, I was glad I wasn't one of the police officers assigned to break up whatever was happening down by the capitol building.

We formed up into two tight wedges. Alpha team was in the forward wedge. Sergeant Kemp had point. Me and Luchen were staggered back at an angle to his left and right. Bravo team marched behind us, forming a diamond with Staff Sergeant Meyers, Lieutenant McFee, and Specialist Sparrow in the center.

"Group, *halt*!" Lieutenant McFee ordered when we approached the crowd. He stepped up until he stood right behind Sergeant Kemp at the front of the diamond. "Okay, listen," he shouted to the crowd. "Our orders are to secure this road out here. I'm going to have to ask you to please step back."

"What if we don't want to?" the hot girl said.

McFee tried again. "Okay, folks, you're going to have to move."

"He didn't say please this time!" Dreadlocks called out.

Sergeant Meyers stepped up next to the lieutenant and shouted at the long-haired guy, "Get the hell out of the way, you hippie piece of shit! You will move voluntarily or we will move your sorry asses for you!"

"Come on, Meyers," Kemp hissed.

The crowd wailed. Instead of moving away from our formation, they came closer. "This is bullshit," Dreadlocks yelled. "We have rights! We got every right to be here."

"Hell yeah!" Another college guy held up his can of beer. He chugged the rest of it and threw it at us. The empty can landed about six feet away. The drinker cracked open another beer and clinked it against his friend's can. "Hell no! We won't go!" he shouted.

Others joined him in the chant. What was their problem? This wasn't a party. Why wouldn't they move?

"Sir, we can't afford to lose control here," Kemp said. "Let's go around them. We have to move up the street to block the road off at our assigned point."

The lieutenant nodded. "Sergeant Kemp, guide the formation around the crowd to the left. We'll move around them. Everybody stay tight. Forward, *march*!" We walked forward, sweeping toward the side of the crowd, but the protestors shifted over in front of us again. "Okay, Sergeant. Straight through the crowd then," said McFee.

"Hold your weapons tight," Sergeant Kemp called out.

There were so many protestors. Some were staggering drunk. Some looked mad. Others laughed. It was chaos, and we weren't even downtown to the real disturbance yet. The tip of the diamond formation reached the crowd. The group parted around us, but they were standing close.

Too close. One of the guys grabbed the end of my M4's barrel. I tried to pull the weapon back, but he had a good grip. "Let go," I said through gritted teeth. What the hell did this guy think he was doing? I wanted to punch him, but I couldn't let go of the rifle.

One of my guys came flying past me in a blur. His butt stock nailed the gun grabber in the face. The crack was so loud, at first I thought the rifle's stock had broken.

The protestor fell flat on his back, both hands to his face as thick red blood gushed out from between his fingers. "You broke my nose, man!" he said.

A couple people crouched down around him. Sergeant Meyers wiped the guy's blood from his weapon. "Never lose control of your weapon, Private. Never," he said to me.

People in the crowd screamed with anger. They had been backing up a little, but now they moved forward.

"Fix bayonets!" Lieutenant McFee called out.

Oh shit. Bayonets? I had never used a real bayonet. In basic training we'd practiced just with fake rifles with little metal rods welded to the end. The drill sergeants had made us shout stuff like "red blood makes the grass grow green." Broken Nose Guy's blood wasn't growing anything. I absolutely did not want to mess with the bayonet.

My hand shook as I reached for the pouch on my vest, but I unsnapped it and pulled the knife out. Then I pushed its little housing onto the catch under the barrel of my M4. Now my rifle was kind of like a sword too.

We moved forward again, holding the ends of our weapons a little higher so the crowd could see the blades. They seemed to get the message this time. They parted and moved out of our way a lot faster. Finally, we stepped out into the middle of South Capitol Boulevard and marched in diamond formation up the street to where it split into two one-way streets.

One of the distant sirens got louder as a police car sped toward us. Half of its lights on top were smashed, and the windshield was spiderwebbed with cracks on the passenger side. They were driving fast, so I didn't get too good a look, but the face of the cop riding shotgun was bright, bloody red. He must have been cut up pretty bad.

The crowd followed us. A rock flew from somewhere behind us and hit the ground a few feet to my left. We turned to face them and spread out at the point where the street split, with no more than a few yards between each of us. We had blocked the road.

The protestors settled down about twenty yards away, still chanting and shouting, cussing us out, and daring us to put down our guns to give them a fair fight. Someone set off what must have been fireworks — little black cats, probably. At the first crack I jumped and tensed up on my weapon. Good thing I wasn't on the firing range. I was shaking way too much to hit any of the pop-up plastic targets.

Specialist Sparrow stepped over to me. "I've been hearing some crazy stuff over the radio," she said. "The police are having trouble keeping the mob from breaking through the barricade around the capitol. Some cops have been injured. I think that last ambulance that went through might have had a cop who was stabbed. There must be four or five platoons in the area, all on this frequency. All bad news."

"So it's not getting any better down there?" I asked.

She shook her head. "Sounds like it's getting worse. One Guard squad called in and said fights are breaking out even between protestors. It's like —" She stopped and pressed the radio handset tighter to her ear, holding up a hand for me to be quiet. She pushed the transmit button. "Last calling station. Last calling station. This is cobra three one. Say again, over." Cobra was the 476th Engineer Company code name, so she was identifying as the first squad of third platoon. "Roger that. Wait one, over." Sparrow shot me a tense look and then called out for the lieutenant. "Sir, we got orders coming in."

The lieutenant rushed over, took the handset, and called up to higher. He typed some things down on his comm. "Roger. That's a good copy. Wilco. Cobra three one, out." McFee tossed the handset to Sparrow, squinted his eyes shut, and pushed his fists against his temples. Then he checked the empty street in front of us. "New mission," he said. "Governor Montaine is ordering the Guard units to tighten the perimeter until we've moved into the downtown area. We're going in to stop the disturbance."

"Finally, we can put an end to this shit," Sergeant Meyers said. "Show these bastards who's boss!"

McFee held a hand up. "Negative. Okay? We're . . . You know, this is probably no big deal here. Heading down there to help the police make some arrests or . . . um . . . for presence. Kind of . . . Okay. Anyway. Squad wedge formation. We're heading straight up this street about a dozen blocks right to the capitol."

"I'll take point," Sergeant Meyers yelled. "Alpha team back to my left. Bravo back and to my right. Sparrow, stay in the middle to keep the radio close to the LT."

The sun was down as we moved off in a big V pattern up Capitol Boulevard. As we moved, the protestors we'd already run into kept shouting and making fun of us. Some of them rushed past, running downtown. We had to let them go. There was nothing we could do about it.

Blocks and blocks away was the dome of the capitol building. In the growing darkness, red and blue lights flashed on the massive crowd with their protest signs. Beyond that, over the tops of the buildings off to the right, a plume of smoke rose up into the sky, with another ahead and far off to the left. We passed at least two burned-out cars on the side of the road. Four or five businesses had their windows busted. Sirens seemed to blare all around us.

We marched closer, coming within a block of the real riot. Now that stuff back closer to where we'd landed looked peaceful by comparison. A huge mob of people pressed against the metal barricades that had been set up around the capitol building. They were all yelling, shoving, and screaming. One man was pushed into a woman. Another guy, maybe her boyfriend, shoved the first man, who responded with a hard jab. In seconds, others had joined the fight. Off to our right, a few squads of police with huge clear plastic riot shields and clubs tried to break up a different fight among the protestors. Some of the crowd had moved on the cops, flanking them. A few of them had stolen some of the riot shields. It was like every pissed-off person in Idaho had saved up their anger for years and decided to let it all out tonight here in Boise. This was pure hell.

The lieutenant finally halted us at the intersection of Capitol and Bannock, right at the edge of the main part of the riot. He held the radio handset to his ear but shouted to us, "Our orders are to hold position here and wait for other units to get into place."

It was a sea of chaos in front of us. People held signs: DON'T TREAD ON ME! OCCUPY IDAHO! NO GOVERNMENT SPY CARD! DOWN WITH PRESIDENT RODRIGUEZ! TIME TO THROW OUT THE TEA BAGGERS! Signs with pictures of donkeys hanging from ropes. MONTAINE SUCKS! Signs with dead elephants.

"What is this protest even about?" I said. "Whose side are these people on?"

PFC Nelson wiped his nose with his hand. "Looks like we got all sides."

Sergeant Kemp stepped up to us. "Both parties, plus maybe some others. Some drunks. Crazy biker-type guys. And enough news reporters to cover it all. This here's real bad."

Other Guard units came in from all directions to set up a perimeter in a circle around the crowd. I drew in a deep breath. It was a relief to see at least a couple hundred Guardsmen and know my unit wasn't alone out here.

An Army Black Hawk helicopter swooped in among the TV news camera drone copters. It flew in circles around the immediate area, shining a bright spotlight down on the chaos below. "ATTENTION!" a voice blasted out of a loudspeaker on the chopper. "THIS IS AN ILLEGAL ASSEMBLY. RETURN TO YOUR HOMES. THIS IS AN ILLEGAL ASSEMBLY. RETURN TO YOUR HOMES. . . ."

"Everybody get your ProMask on. They're going to CS gas the whole area." Lieutenant McFee handed the radio handset back to Sparrow.

"Oh shit," Sparrow said next to me. "I hate this thing."

Everybody hated the gas mask. I pulled open the Velcro flap on my carrier case, yanked the mask out, and pushed it to my face. At once my cheeks and chin began to burn a little. Some idiot hadn't cleaned his mask from a two-week summer training session when the guys must have been in CS. Still, getting a whiff of the tear gas live was worse than any residue left in the mask. I pulled the web of elastic straps down behind my head and tightened the buckles on the bottom two, then put my hand over the front of the mask and pressed hard while blowing out. Then, while my hand covered the filter canister, I sucked in. The mask tightened to my face. A good seal. Now with every breath I took, I sounded like Darth Vader.

Some of the people in the crowd were shouting stuff at us. Getting closer. I watched them through the little blurry windows in my mask. One guy shouted something I couldn't understand. He lit a rag that stuck out of a bottle. Then he took a few running steps before he let the thing fly.

"Get down!" Sergeant Kemp shouted. I dropped to the ground. The bottle crashed on the street maybe fifteen or twenty feet in front of us. Fire and broken glass erupted all around it. Some people in the mob cheered. There were only nine of us in the squad, ten with the LT. If the rioters attacked us, what were we supposed to do?

The lieutenant pulled our two team leaders close and said something to them. Both of them quickly loaded a forty-millimeter gas grenade into the M320 grenade launchers mounted below their rifle barrels. Seconds later, I heard the popping sound of the launchers firing. Kemp had fired short so the gas round would hit the street about twenty yards in front of us and then bounce toward the crowd, spraying white hard-core nasty tear gas. Ribbon fired a second round the same way.

The other Guard units must have had the same orders, because a faint white cloud developed at the edge of the crowd. Weirdly, nobody seemed to notice for a moment. Then more screams and swears erupted out of the crowd. Some people ran away. One guy vomited in the street as he rubbed his eyes. Stupid. Rubbing your eyes in a cloud of CS gas was the dumbest thing to do. It made it burn ten times worse. Sergeant Kemp fired one more gas round. The protestors scrambled to get away, but bumped into each other as they tried to get out of the gas. Then the wind must have shifted, because some of the gas drifted back toward us. The exposed skin of my hands and neck burned like crazy. It must have been terrible for the protestors in the worst of it.

"THIS IS AN ILLEGAL ASSEMBLY. RETURN TO YOUR HOMES."

"Okay," the lieutenant called out. He said something else, but I couldn't hear him over the roar from the crowd and the helicopter.

"What did you say, Lieutenant?" Sergeant Meyers said.

Nobody could hear anyone when we were talking with these stupid masks on. The lieutenant passed the word down the line, like that telephone game they used to make us play in school. Luchen's mask came up next to my face. "The squads are going to start moving forward. We're going to move up in a wedge."

Oh no. What kind of plan was this? We were supposed to march forward into the crowd and . . . what? Stab them with our bayonets? Part them until they closed in behind to surround us?

McFee ordered our squad ahead with a hand motion. Sergeant Meyers, on point, held his rifle up above his head with both hands in a kind of "raise the roof" gesture. We started forward. Kemp looked back at us guys in his team before moving up. I walked after them on the far left. Inside my mask, I could hear my every breath heavy and loud. I kept my thumb on the safety switch of my weapon with my finger right next to the trigger.

Oh God, I prayed. *Please help me get out of this one. This stuff isn't cool anymore. I just want to —*

Something smacked into my mask and my weapon went off. Through the cracked plastic of my mask's eyepieces, I saw the flash out of the end of my barrel.

"Hold your fire!" someone shouted.

"Oh shit," I said. How had that happened? Someone threw a rock and hit me and I was surprised. Must have accidentally —

Another gunshot went off. Wasn't me. A third shot.

"Who the hell is shooting!?" Sergeant Kemp yelled from somewhere.

Our formation had stopped now. A rock hit me in the chest. Screams came from the crowd. The cracked lenses in my mask blurred my vision. When I closed my left eye, I could barely see around the white cracks in the right lens. I started to pull my mask up, but someone grabbed my wrist.

"Keep that mask on, Private," said Sergeant Kemp. "You don't want —"

Another shot.

"The protestors got guns!" Sergeant Meyers called out. "Shoot 'em! Aim for the ones with guns!"

"No! No! No!" Sergeant Kemp pushed Luchen's barrel down. I didn't even try to shoot, but went down on one knee.

Protestors scrambled to get away. Another Guardsman, far enough away to be from one of the other Guard units, raised his M4 and fired. One, two, three rounds. Blood sprayed from some guy's neck, his head snapped back like a yo-yo, and his Broncos hat went flying. Another round sliced through a man's chest and cut into the belly of the woman behind him. Both dropped. Another guy's hip shattered as he was hit. He screamed as he fell, his leg at a wrong angle. I hoped it was just the way my lenses messed up my vision.

Another soldier fired. I couldn't tell who. One, two. Three, four. Four more people fell as they ran. Screaming people trampled a teenage girl in their rush to escape. A bullet cracked through a storefront window behind us to our right. Someone inside screamed. Some dumbass reporter kept shouting at the cameraman who was filming him and the shooting.

The Black Hawk finally silenced its loudspeaker and flew away. The capitol square was mostly empty now. Except . . . Out where the protest had been, there was blood. There were bodies.

"Let's go! Let's get some field dressings on these wounds," Sergeant Kemp yelled. "Casualty treatment. Move it!" He ran forward and I followed. Some of the other guys might have been with us. I think Lieutenant McFee stayed in the intersection, sort of waiting there on his knees.

We reached the first person on the ground. "I can't see shit. I'm taking this thing off!" I said.

Sergeant Kemp grabbed my mask and held it on my face. "Private! Private, listen to me. There are cameras all over the place — TV news crews, comms. You do *not* want them to see you. Keep your mask on. Keep your armor vest on to hide your name tape. You do *not* want to be identified. Got it?"

I nodded. Sergeant Kemp went to his knees next to the body on the ground. He put his ear over the person's mouth. Then he rose up and put his fingers to the neck. He shook his head and ran off.

But I stayed. It was the redheaded college girl from before. The angry girl who had been so beautiful and alive. But now her tank top was ripped down the side, and meat and bone stuck out from below her left breast. Her blood spread out in a pool beneath her. Her mouth was open like it had been when she was shouting at the protest. Like she was screaming at me now.

But she was silent, and the breath was gone from her. She'd never shout . . . or speak or laugh, ever again. Her lifeless eyes were open and the way her head was tilted . . . she was . . . staring right at me.

I dropped to my knees, holding my weapon across my stomach. Her sticky blood was still a little warm as it soaked through the knees of my pants. I gagged once and then puked, hot and sour-sweet. It filled the bottom of my mask. Burned up in my nose. I had to pull the thing off my chin to let the vomit run out on my chest. Then I put it back on and tried not to barf again with the taste and smell filling the air I was breathing.

I wished I'd never been called up for this mission. Wished I'd never enlisted. I wanted to get up and walk away. Go and never look back. But I couldn't move. This girl wouldn't let me.

She looked at me like she knew. She was dead because of me. I'd fired the one shot that spooked everybody else. I might as well have killed her myself.

↲• High and outside. Ball two. Two and one is the count. . . . It may be worth pointing out that this season the Mariners have only been able to make a comeback three times whenever they have trailed in the •↲

↲• This is a CBS Special News Report. From the CBS newsroom, here's Simon Pentler."

"Tragedy has apparently struck tonight in downtown Boise, Idaho, where a number of shots were fired outside the state capitol building, the site of an ongoing and increasingly violent demonstration. National Guard troops dispatched by Idaho governor James Montaine to augment the state police are alleged to have fired into the crowd of protestors, with some reports indicating that as many as sixty or seventy gunshots were fired. Now, we do not have any official word on the number of casualties, but some raw video shot by a CBS aerial camera drone would seem to confirm soldiers have fired their weapons, and we should perhaps prepare for terrible news from Boise. Taking you now to that video •↲*

↲• another video angle sent to us via the CNN Citizen Reporter app. We should warn you the footage you're about to see is very graphic and may not be suitable for sensitive or younger viewers, but it reminds one less of a police action and more of an all-out battle, with •↲

↲• word yet on whether any arrests have been made, Tom. Everything here on the ground is still very chaotic. I'm standing about a block away from the heart of the riot. As you can see, the situation behind me is one of total panic and devastation. Moments ago, hundreds of shots rang out. Then my camera crew and I were nearly trampled as the protestors rushed to escape the •↲

RICK ABERNATHY ★ ★ ★ ★ ☆

Soldiers shooting us now! Maybe now you liberal Democrats will understand why the second amendment gaurantees our right to own weapons. The soldiers (thugs) who did this better be punished! All my peeps in Boise, please check in and let me know your OK.

★ ★ ★ ☆ ☆ This Post's Star Average 3.06   [Star Rate][Comment]   5 minutes ago

ALLAN FITZKIRK ★ ★ ★ ☆ ☆

I'm a liberal Democrat, and while I'm sickened by what these soldiers have done, I know the situation would have been much worse if the crowd had all been carrying M16s. You mindless Republican/NRA drones need to come up with something besides "Get More Guns!"

★ ★ ★ ☆ ☆ This Comment's Star Average 3.00   [Star Rate]   4 minutes ago

HEATHER CHIPLEY ★ ★ ★ ★ ☆

Maybe we should wait until all the facts are known before we start arguing about all this again. Right now I'm just praying for the victims of this tragedy.

★ ★ ★ ★ ☆ This Comment's Star Average 4.25   [Star Rate]   3 minutes ago

BETH PHILSOM ★ ★ ★ ★ ☆

Rick (and everyone else), I want to let you know that I'm fine. My boss let us off work early when it was getting crazy downtown. I'm so sorry for the people who were down there though. This is so terrible.

★ ★ ★ ★ ★ This Comment's Star Average 5.00   [Star Rate]   30 seconds ago

⌁• *No word yet from Governor Montaine or the president, but certainly we can expect a response from authorities very soon. We will continue to bring you updates as they come in. Until then, we're going to go to Dr. Timothy Hemand of Princeton University, an expert in crisis situation management. He's studied these types of mass shootings and has served as an advisor on numerous panels, including* *•⌁*

CHAPTER
THREE

Sometime later I felt hands on my arms. Kemp, maybe. Sparrow too. They stood me up and led me away with the rest of the squad.

Somehow we found ourselves alone in a windowless boardroom somewhere in the basement of the capitol. The room was dimly lit and empty except for a long wooden table surrounded by cushioned swivel chairs. The walls were stark white and blank except for a row of framed photographs. Military guys. Some generals. A colonel. They were the Idaho Army National Guard chain of command photos. There was a set like this in the 476th armory, showing who was in command all the way up to the governor and the president. I stared at them, not able to look at my squad.

Officers came in and confiscated our gas masks, weapons, and comms. Then they left us alone again. After a while, most of the guys sat down.

"What the hell were you thinking?" Sergeant Kemp said. I jumped and spun around to see the sergeant slap his hands down on the table. His face was bright red and there was sweat on his brow, even though it was cold in the air-conditioning.

I shook my head. "Sergeant, I didn't —"

Kemp waved his hand as though brushing my comment aside. He leaned over the table toward Meyers. "Why the hell did you fire?"

Meyers's face twisted into a kind of snarl as he stood up. "You talking to me, Sergeant Kemp?"

"Damned right I am!" Kemp pushed himself away from the table and paced the room.

"Well, you better check that attitude right now, Sergeant Kemp, because —"

"What are you going to do? Court-martial me?" Kemp threw his hands up. "We're probably already headed to prison for that colossal screwup out there!"

Meyers circled the table in four long, fast strides. "We didn't do anything wrong!"

Kemp ran at Meyers and grabbed him by his uniform coat. "Why'd'ya shoot!?"

"There were shooters in the crowd. Self-defense!" Meyers shoved Kemp back.

"Bullshit!" Kemp drew back his fist.

"Luchen!" I dove for Sergeant Kemp, caught his arm, and pulled him clear. Luchen knocked his chair over as he rushed for Meyers, dropping his shoulder into Meyers's gut and doing his best to push the big staff sergeant back.

"Let him go," Kemp said. He threw his elbow into my stomach to break away. He held up his fists for a fight, but the other guys had rushed between them both now. Everybody except Lieutenant McFee.

"You shouldn't have fired," Sergeant Kemp growled.

Meyers backed away from the guys, holding his arms out from his sides as though he was so stacked that he couldn't put them down. He made a big show of breathing real loud through his nose and staring at Kemp. The quiet settled. "We took fire from armed protestors in the crowd. I called Lieutenant McFee for instructions. He ordered us to fire."

"That is not what happened!" Kemp said.

"Yes it is!" Meyers stepped up to the lieutenant. "LT?" McFee did not look up. Meyers grabbed his shoulder and shook him. "LT! You told us to fire, right? You gave the order. Tell him."

"I don't care what he says," Sergeant Kemp said. "That is not what happened!"

"Listen to me, you dumb sons of bitches!" Meyers shouted. "It doesn't matter what *really* happened out there. Okay? I don't know what really happened. Neither do you." He pointed at one of the generals on the wall, at the picture of Governor Montaine. "But these guys are going to want to know. They're going to bust in here any second and we better have an answer for them."

Was he talking about cooking up a story? A cover-up? When people were dead? How did I get stuck in the middle of something like this? I couldn't let them lie for me. Dad always used to say that a man should never lie to avoid responsibility for the wrong he's done.

"I'll tell you what happened," I said quietly.

Specialist Stein sat back in his chair. Everyone but me sat down too. "They did have guns," said Stein. "I swear to God there was more than one guy shooting at us from the crowd. That's why —" He swallowed. "That's why I fired. Shooting at them."

"I'll tell you what happened," I said louder.

Kemp glared at Stein. "There was no way that —"

"I shot first!" I shouted. "I got nailed in the middle of my mask by a rock and I . . . I don't know . . . I jerked the trigger or something. The weapon fired. It's my fault."

Sergeant Kemp slouched in his seat. He put his face in his hands. "It's okay, Wright. It might have happened to anyone."

"Yeah," said PFC Nelson. "But the Army gets real pissed about accidental discharge."

"Yeah," Meyers said. He looked hard at Kemp. "One of the guys in your team —"

"In your squad!" Kemp said.

"In my squad," Meyers agreed, speaking calmly. "In the lieutenant's platoon. We're all in this. And we better figure out what we're going to say because when they start asking —"

Sergeant Ribbon sprang to his feet. "Atten-*tion*!"

We all stood up and snapped to attention as an officer in a dark blue Army service dress uniform opened the door. He stood for a moment in the shadows at the end of the room. I couldn't see him all that well, because at the position of attention I couldn't move my head, but out of the corner of my eye I could tell he wore a ton of ribbons on his chest. He took three even steps forward until he stood in the glow cast by the lights over the table.

"At ease," said the officer. We all shifted so that we stood with our feet shoulder width apart and our hands behind our backs. Now that I was allowed to move my head, I saw he was a short man, broad in the chest, with his little remaining gray hair buzzed short to Army regulations. "I'm Brigadier General McNabb, Commander, Idaho Army National Guard." The general looked at each of us in turn. "You soldiers can relax. Have a seat."

We all sat down. General McNabb remained standing. "We've secured your weapons and counted the rounds. Eight rounds are missing from this squad's initial load, one from one rifle, three from another, and four rounds from a third. Now I want to know what happened out there."

All of us except for the lieutenant exchanged nervous glances around the table. Sergeant Kemp stood up. "Sir, I respectfully request that I be allowed to speak with an attorney before —"

"You don't need a lawyer, Sergeant. No charges have been filed. I'm trying to find out what happened."

"Nevertheless, sir, I think that under the circumstances —"

"This isn't open to negotiation, Sergeant! This isn't a happy, peaceful civilian world. There are twelve people dead out there. Nine more have injuries from gunshots, including two of my soldiers. I am ordering all of you to tell me what the hell happened!"

Silence fell on the room. Twelve people dead. Twenty-one people had been shot. My mouth felt watery, my stomach cold and hollow. I put my hands to my face for a moment until I smelled the blood. The redheaded girl's blood was still caked in my fingernails, still sticking my pants to my knees.

I took a deep breath. I didn't want to throw up again.

The door opened at the end of the room, but I didn't move or look to see who it was. Luchen grabbed my arm and pulled me up.

Governor Montaine approached the table, wearing a blue suit and tie with a white shirt. His graying brown hair was sticking up funny. He reached into the inside pocket of his jacket and pulled out a pack of cigarettes, a lighter, and a small plastic ashtray. He placed the cigarette in his mouth, flicked the lighter, and lit up, holding out the pack toward our squad. "Smoke?"

I would have loved a cigarette right about then, but nobody else was taking, so I kept my mouth shut.

"It's a government building, sir," said Sergeant Kemp.

The man removed his jacket. "That it is. I'm Governor James Montaine." He hung his coat on the chair, rolled up his sleeves, and loosened his tie. "Sometimes I think we can bend stupid little rules, especially on nights like tonight. Relax. Please sit down."

We took our seats. The governor flicked a little ash into the ashtray. He pulled another long drag on his cigarette. "I'm not going to lie to you boys. I'm all about straight talk in my campaigns, and believe it or not, I believe in straight talk. And the simple fact is that we are in a world of shit. I have phone calls from everyone all the way to the Pentagon. That guy in the White House will probably be calling soon enough. The press is going crazy, naming this the Battle of Boise. Everybody wants to know what really happened. Why don't you start by telling me?"

Sergeant Meyers stood up at attention. "Sir, our squad was ordered to go downtown to hold position near the riot. The protestors were out of control, sir."

"I know that, Sergeant. That's why I called in the National Guard in the first place. Why did you start shooting?"

I saw Meyers's eyes dart my way for a second. "Sir, there were armed civilians among the protestors. We took fire. At that point Lieutenant McFee gave the order to shoot those protestors who had guns."

McFee sat up in his seat and opened his mouth like he was about to speak, but then stopped. The governor looked his way for a moment as if waiting for him. When he stayed silent, the governor raised an eyebrow and took a drag on his cigarette. The cherry flared brightly. After a moment he let the smoke roll out. "You're telling me that some of the protestors had guns? You say they shot at you?"

"Yes, sir," said Sergeant Meyers.

This was all wrong. Meyers was trying to pass it all off on the lieutenant. I couldn't let that happen.

The general cleared his throat. "Why am I only hearing from NCOs? Lieutenant McFee, is this true? Did you give the order to fire?"

The lieutenant's eyes were wide open.

"Pull yourself together, Lieutenant," said the general.

McFee licked his lips and swallowed. "Sir, there were a lot of people. Um . . . protestors. Okay. I'm not . . . I mean, I don't —"

I stood up. "Sir, I fired the first shot."

Everything was quiet. I remembered the feel of the little recoil in my M4. The surprise. How bad I wanted that bullet back.

"What did you say, Private?" the general said.

I thought I saw Sergeant Meyers shake his head a little as if telling me to shut up, but I'd gone this far. I had to tell him now. "Sir, someone in the crowd threw a rock. It hit me in the face. In the gas mask. The shock of it." My eyes were stinging. No. I couldn't cry. Not here. I wiped my eyes. "I don't know. I was surprised. My fingers jerked. I accidentally fired my weapon. I don't know if I hit . . . anyone. My lenses in my mask were cracked and I could hardly see. I'm so sorry."

Governor Montaine sighed. "How old are you?" He sounded different now. Sad.

"Seventeen, sir."

"Seventeen? You still in high school?" the governor asked.

"Yes, sir," I said.

"And how old are you, Lieutenant?"

"Twenty . . . twenty-three, sir."

The governor snuffed his cigarette out in the ashtray. "Why do I have kids doing missions like this, General?" He spoke slowly and quietly.

If General McNabb noticed the anger in the governor's voice, he didn't show it. "Sir, most of the Idaho Army National Guard is deployed to Iran. Our forces here are limited. You asked for enough troops to effectively assist the state police. Young soldiers like this PFC would never deploy without having completed their training for their military occupation specialties, but to accomplish the mission, I was forced to resort to activating almost all of our remaining soldiers, certainly all who had completed basic training and were slotted to a combat unit."

Governor Montaine walked to the end of the room, looking away from us. He didn't say anything for a long time. Finally he turned back to me. "Son, I want you to listen to me for a second —"

Something in my chest tightened up. "Don't call me 'son,' sir."

General McNabb cleared his throat. "Private," he said in a warning tone.

"Sorry, Governor, but I'm not your son." It had been me and Mom on our own for a long time now, but I did have a father once. The hell if I was going to let some politician or anyone else call me "son." "My father was killed in the war," I said to the governor. "In Afghanistan."

"He was in the Army?" the governor asked.

"The Idaho Army Guard, sir."

"Why'd you sign up?"

"Sir?"

The governor sighed again. "You're only seventeen. Why did you enlist?"

"I signed up because . . . Sir, I just . . . I love my home. Wanted to serve my country. Do my part." I had really believed that when I enlisted. I wanted to believe it now, but after what had happened tonight, my words sounded fake, rehearsed, too polished, like Montaine doing one of his speeches.

The governor shook his head. "The bullets from all the soldiers who were called on this mission have been counted?" He looked at the general, who nodded. "And your squad is the only one missing rounds. Something's not adding up. Some of the men must have reloaded or fudged their initial round count."

"Or someone besides my soldiers was firing," said General McNabb.

"Some of the people in the crowd did have weapons, sir," said Sergeant Meyers.

Was that true? There was a lot of gunfire, but how could anyone tell where it was coming from? Twenty-one people had been hit, but only eight of my squad's bullets were gone.

"Of course we'll know more when we recover the bullets from the . . ." The governor rubbed his chin. "When we recover the bullets. I doubt anyone in the crowd was firing five-five-six rounds. We'd have spotted a rifle like that on one of our videos. A bullet that wasn't standard military issue would seem to prove that someone else was shooting."

"I swear we were being fired on," Meyers said.

General McNabb nodded. "There was a casualty in the café behind your position, a fifteen-year-old girl. From the limited information we've gathered so far, you would have had to turn around and fire away from the crowd, deliberately targeting the café."

"We didn't!" Specialist Stein said.

The general held up his hand. "I know. You couldn't possibly be responsible for that casualty."

"They're not responsible for any of the casualties," said the governor. Everybody watched him. "Maybe there were guns in that crowd. Maybe not. All the video footage I've seen so far is mostly a confused and garbled scramble, partially hidden by smoke and tear gas by the time the shooting started. Can't tell what's going on. We may never know the truth. But we do know that the numbers aren't adding up. You soldiers couldn't possibly have caused all the casualties.

"As governor, I'm responsible for all of this. I should have called in more law enforcement earlier so the situation didn't get so bad. Maybe that would have prevented this. I don't know. But I do know that I gave the National Guard a lawful order to stop an unlawful and dangerous riot. That's what they did. They carried out my orders. That's the end of the story."

He took a moment to look us all over. Either he was a great politician, or he was being really honest, because I believed him. He pulled a chair out from the table, sat down, and leaned forward.

"Listen to me, because I promise you this. I will not sell you out. Things are going to get ugly for a while. People are already upset about what happened. But so far, nobody knows which units were there to stop the riot. We're going to keep it that way." He looked toward the general. "I'm ordering this whole thing classified. Nobody will ever know the identities of the soldiers involved in this. Nobody will know which officers gave what orders. Any matter of investigation on this issue must come directly to me, General."

"Understood, sir." The general snapped to attention. "With your permission, I'd like to begin carrying this order out immediately."

"Do that, General McNabb. Also, get some helicopters ready to take these men home. The faster we get them back, the fewer people will know they were here." He motioned to us. "Do not talk about this event with anyone. Not even your family. This is for your protection and theirs. I'll do everything I can to make sure you aren't punished for carrying out my orders, but you have to help by keeping your involvement in this a complete secret. If anyone does know you were activated tonight, you will tell them that you were simply on standby in case the situation worsened and you were needed. You flew down to Boise where you sat in an armory all night."

I checked my watch. A quarter to one in the morning. I hoped they'd hurry up and get us back. I'd told Mom I was going to be out late with the guys, but if she'd seen the news about this and got the idea I was involved . . . I tried not to think about how bad she'd be freaking out.

"I'm sorry this happened," said the governor. "I'm sorry about the deaths and injuries. Sorry you're caught in the middle of it." His jaw seemed to tense. "If that . . . president hadn't passed that . . ." He held his hands up. "Sorry. This isn't the time for politics." He stood. "I have a lot of work to do. Stay here and try to relax. Someone will be here soon to get you once your transportation has been arranged." He looked us over again. I felt his eyes stop on me, but I couldn't meet them. "You did your jobs tonight. You are soldiers, and sometimes soldiers have to do . . . unpleasant things." There was a long pause. "Thank you for your service."

I kept my eyes fixed on the table until long after he'd left. Eventually some officers arrived, giving our comms back and escorting us to the helicopters that waited to take us home.

I had felt proud to wear my uniform on the way home from my first weekend drill at the beginning of the month. I'm not gonna lie. I even made an extra stop at a gas station to buy pop and beef jerky, just so I could walk around in public as a soldier. I didn't feel proud about anything tonight. As soon as we returned to the 476th Engineer Company armory, I changed into some old sweats that I found in my locker. I crammed my MCUs into my duffel bag and drove home in silence, leaving my comm and radio shut off. I didn't want to hear any news.

At home, I breathed a sigh of relief when I saw Mom asleep in her recliner, covered up with Dad's old Army blanket. The living room screen was on with a reporter in Boise. *"You can see that behind me, some sort of canvas barricade has been put in place, and we can only assume that this is to keep us from seeing the cleanup after tonight's tragedy. Although the protests here have been crushed, outrage is already building in cities across —"*

"Living room screen, off," I said. The stupid thing blinked out. Then I stood in the dark, listening to Mom's slow, deep breathing. Would I ever feel peace like that again? Would I ever get the images of blood, of that girl's torn body, out of my head? I bit my fist as my eyes stung.

"Danny?" Mom's voice was quiet in the dark.

"Yeah, Mom. It's me."

"What are you doing?"

I swallowed. "I got home a second ago. I was about to wake you so you could go to bed." I turned away from her so that in case she switched the lamp on, she wouldn't see the tears on my cheeks. "You know you always have a sore neck if you sleep all night in your chair."

"Ah, you worry too much," she said. "Did you have a nice night?"

"Yeah, Mom." I swallowed. "It was just great."

⌄—• Welcome back to Sunday on Fox News. *A nation mourns the tragedy at Boise. While details of what actually happened remain sketchy at best, we have now received word that the families of all the victims have been notified of their injuries or deaths, and the victims' names are now being released. We do not yet know much about those who were killed or injured, but we will be bringing you that information as soon as it is available. The list of those confirmed dead after the shootings: Nineteen-year-old Allison Danter of Twin Falls, Idaho. Twenty-one-year-old Damarcus Washington of Boise. William Seiffert, nineteen years old, from Bozeman, Montana.* •—⌄

⌄—•

timlutzman: Angry about Battle of Boise! A 15 y.o. girl killed too? WTF #angryamerica #BoB

1 day ago   Reply · Shout Out
                                                                    •—⌄

⌄—•

shootstrue: Watch kneejerk reaction to BoB. Protect our gun rights! www.nra.org

1 day ago   Reply · Shout Out
                                                                    •—⌄

⌄—• Sandra Schneider, a twenty-year-old nursing major at Boise State. Jeffrey Markinson, also twenty, who was studying to become a teacher. Brittany Barker, only fifteen years old, was a bystander in a café well behind the soldiers. Her parents say she dreamed of being an actress. Three of the twelve who were killed in Boise Friday. More on this when Sunday with the Press *continues* •—⌄

⌄—• Weekend from NPR News. I'm Renae Matthews. I'm here with Craig White, author of Sixty-Seven Bullets: Understanding the Kent State University Shootings. *Craig, your book focuses not only on*

May 4, 1970, when Ohio National Guardsmen were responsible for the deaths of four young people on the Kent State University campus, but also on the aftermath of that tragedy. There are obviously some similarities between Friday night's shootings and those at Kent State. What do you think we can expect to see unfold from these events?"

"Well, Renae, first, I think it's really quite inaccurate to refer to the murder of twelve innocent people as 'The Battle of Boise.' That implies that the twelve dead and nine wounded had some chance of fighting back. Just like at Kent State, these innocent people had no chance once the National Guardsmen began firing. This is really a massacre, and if Governor Montaine gets his way, this could all work out a lot like it did at Kent State, when nearly every legal authority agreed the Guardsmen were unjustified in killing the students, but that somehow killing the students did not interfere with their civil rights. •—⌄—

Thinker85: I stand with the soldiers. Don't judge before U have the facts. #loveitorleaveit

1 day ago   Reply · Shout Out

CoffeeJill: Demand justice for BoB victims! Soldiers must be punished. www.battleofboisejustice.com #BoB

1 day ago   Reply · Shout Out

OEFVet78: Proof Boise rioters had guns!
http://www.butchersofboise.com

about 8 hours ago   Reply · Shout Out

$\rightsquigarrow\!\!-\bullet$ and nine wounded, and the president is calling for calm pending his investigation? What kind of leadership is that? Americans want unity, and they want answers. And he's offering none."

"Speaker Barnes, don't you think it's appropriate to grieve? Does this situation have to be reduced to party politics already?"

"Grief and mourning are important, Kathy, but President Rodriguez should know that he doesn't get a break. He has a job to do. He's not doing it. Were I president, I'd have more to tell the American people about this tragedy."

"Mr. Speaker, is this an announcement of your presidential candidacy?"

"Whoa there! I'm flattered, but we just had an election. It's too early for that kind of talk. I'm merely pointing out the president's obvious indecisiveness and ineffectiveness. $\bullet\!-\!\rightsquigarrow$

FOUR

I spent all weekend trying to avoid the news on the living room screen. It wasn't too much of a lie to say I was sick, and except for going to church on Sunday, I hardly left my room.

I left the radio off Monday morning when I went to pick up JoBell for the first day of school. Music wasn't what I needed, and I damn sure didn't want any more news. Parked in the street in front of her house, I still felt miserable about Boise. I closed my eyes and let the Beast's low growl rumble up through my body to soothe me. Apart from JoBell, nothing felt better than a tough motor.

"You got yerself . . . a text from JoBell."

I reached over and grabbed my comm, tapping the screen to silence Digi-Hank, and checked JoBell's message.

I'll be out in a second.

Finally she came out onto her porch wearing little jean shorts and a brown shirt that fit just snug enough. Her long blond hair blew back off her shoulders in the breeze, and sunlight glinted off my class ring, which dangled from a chain around her neck. The chain was new and had cost a ton of my basic training money. For probably the first time since Friday night, I smiled.

"Feeling better?" JoBell climbed up into the Beast. She closed the door and strapped herself in.

"Yeah, I guess so," I said. The acidy feeling deep in my stomach had made me wonder if maybe I really was sick. I could have stayed home from school, but I needed to get out of the house and think about something besides Friday night in Boise.

JoBell ran her soft hand down my face. "You sure you're all right?" I nodded. She leaned toward me and kissed me, hungry and wet. No simple "good morning" kiss. "Mmm." She licked her lips. "I missed you this weekend, Friday night especially," she said. "But don't worry. That bikini will be back."

Any other day, it would have been pretty hot to see JoBell all worked up like this. Today, though, I couldn't focus, especially knowing the news I had to give her. The governor had ordered us all not to say anything about the . . . disturbance . . . in Boise, but JoBell was different. We'd grown up together, been dating since freshman year. She knew about my mom and her fits. She knew everything about me. The hell with the governor's orders. If I didn't tell my JoBell about something this big in my life, what kind of relationship did we have?

I put the truck into gear and hit the gas hard. The tires spun out in the gravel at the side of the road.

"Danny!" She giggled, leaning forward. "You know my dad hates it when you do that."

"Listen, JoBell, about Friday night —"

She waved my words away. "It's okay. I understand. Your mother needs help sometimes." She slid her comm out of her bag. "Eleanor?"

"*Good morning, JoBell. With the new day comes new strength and new thoughts.*" JoBell had chosen the Eleanor Roosevelt digi-assistant.

"Will you pull up my updated news feeds?"

"*It would be my sincere pleasure to do that for you.*"

JoBell squeezed my arm. "So it's okay if you need to take some time to help her. You and your mom are two of the most important people in my life, and I love you both for the way you look out for each other."

"No, it's not that." I was picking at my dry lips before I realized what I was doing and forced my hand back to the steering wheel. "I mean, I really wanted to be with you at the lake."

"If you're worried about TJ, you can relax. Ugh, I spent way too much of Friday night trying to stay away from him. You'd think he could keep his eyes off my chest for five seconds."

"TJ was there?" I hadn't been thinking about that jackwad, but I was now.

JoBell tapped at her comm without looking at me. "He showed up at Eric's pontoon on his own Jet Ski with a whole case of beer. The guys couldn't send him away after that."

I'd deal with TJ at football practice. "Actually, I have to tell you something else about —"

"Geez, would you look at this? Can you believe it?"

I almost crashed the Beast into a tree. Her comm showed CNN's prime image, a photo of me in my gas mask, holding my M4, crouched over the dead redheaded girl as she lay bleeding in the street. The headline over it read MASSACRE!

"This is disgusting," JoBell said. "I wish more than that guy's gas mask had been broken. All of these murderers should be in jail right now." She flipped through news feeds until she settled on her favorite, the NPR site. "Not even one of the soldiers has been arrested!"

My throat felt like it was closing up. "You know . . ." I swallowed and cleared my throat. "We don't have the whole story and —"

"Shhh, hang on, baby. I want to hear this. That scumbag governor is speaking live right now." She tapped into the feed. I kept my eyes on the road, wishing I could avoid hearing the governor's speech too.

"Cynthia, you've got the first question," Montaine said.

"Governor Montaine, you've made it clear that you do not plan to prosecute any of the soldiers involved in the shootings regardless of the results of the investigations. What do you say to reports that President Rodriguez has asked for disclosure of all the shooters' identities, and to widespread speculation that the federal Department of Justice may arrest the shooters on charges of civil rights violations?"

"First," the governor said, "the 'shooters,' as you call them, are American soldiers, Idaho National Guardsmen. And let me make one thing absolutely clear to you and to the rest of America, including the president. As governor of the state of Idaho, I was well within my rights to activate the National Guard soldiers under my command. I gave them a lawful order and they followed it. I will not, under any circumstances, allow my soldiers to be punished for following my orders. When I spoke with President Rodriguez on the telephone Saturday morning, I made it clear to him that I will absolutely not provide the identities of any soldiers involved in Friday night's incident. I'm Governor James Montaine, and I never abandon the soldiers under my command."

I gripped the steering wheel tight. The president wanted us arrested? Montaine hadn't said anything about that. Maybe he didn't abandon soldiers under his command, but how could he protect us if the president of the United States came after us?

"Ugh," JoBell said. She tapped out of the feed. "I can't believe that asshole Montaine is going to let those murderers get away with this!"

I closed my eyes for a moment. "What?"

"What happened to freedom of speech? Right to assembly? The government can have soldiers shoot American citizens now and nothing happens to them?"

"I . . ." I felt like throwing up again. "I don't think it's that simple."

JoBell patted my arm. "I know it's not. Of course, not all soldiers are bad. I'm glad you weren't in the middle of this. It makes me sick."

"You and me both." I hammered down on the accelerator to get to school faster.

I'd never felt so relieved to be in school, even if I was sitting in what everybody always said was the toughest graduation requirement for seniors, Mr. Shiratori's American Government class. Coach Shiratori paced the front of the room, carrying what he called his "Stick of Power," a piece of well-sanded wood a little longer than a yardstick, and just over half an inch wide. The end of the stick tapped the gray tiled floor with every step he took. Each tap echoed in the quiet.

He put the Stick of Power in its holster on the side of his podium, then picked up an actual paper version of our textbook. With all the pages crammed between two thick covers like that, the book was huge. The handful of books I'd read in the last few years were all on my comm. Not too many people bothered with the old, clunky paper books anymore.

"One key difference between this course and the American History class that most of you took as freshmen," Mr. Shiratori said, "is that we will not be using the textbook nearly as much in Government. The whole first quarter of the book recounts the American Revolution and the events surrounding the drafting of the Constitution. It's all material we've already covered.

"So." He dropped the textbook, letting it slap loud on the podium. "We're going to try something you kids never do anymore, now that you're always texting on your comms. We're going to actually talk to one another, face-to-face, voice-to-voice."

He yanked the Stick of Power out of its holster and threw it up in the air, swinging his arm to snatch it in his other hand before it started to fall. "The Freedom Lake High School Board of Education requires all seniors to pass American Government in order to graduate. The board obviously believes this class is important. So . . . Why?" The room was silent for a moment. "Why is it important to study your government?"

Mary Beth Reese, the only girl challenging JoBell for valedictorian, reached to switch on her comm. Shiratori tapped her desk with the Stick of Power. "Comms off! Don't look it up. Don't quote the book or report what the Internet has to say on the subject. Tell me what you think."

TJ raised his hand and Coach Shiratori pointed the stick at him. TJ flashed his big stupid-ass grin. "So we know who will be sending Wright to war."

A couple of the guys over on TJ's side of the room chuckled. I leaned toward Sweeney and whispered, "Remind me to knock his teeth out at practice." He nodded.

"Well, that might be a bit of a stretch," Coach said. "But yeah, we should be aware of who is making important decisions like sending our troops overseas." He saw JoBell's raised hand and smiled. "Ah, Miss Linder. Never one without an opinion. Let's hope you haven't mellowed out since your freshman year. Why do you think it's important to study government?"

JoBell leaned forward in her chair. "Because people need to know that our governor thinks he doesn't have to listen to the president of the United States, that it's perfectly fine to violate the First Amendment rights of hundreds of people, and that he lets soldiers get away with murder!"

"Does anyone know what JoBell is talking about?" Mr. Shiratori asked. "Hmm? Have you been keeping up with the news?"

I sank lower in my desk as my cheeks flared hot.

"Some kind of shooting?" Caitlyn Ericson said.

Coach tapped the stick on the floor. "A tragic shooting in Boise Friday night."

He told the class all about it. He got most of it right. I don't know. I was reading the stupid "soar with the eagles" motivational posters on the walls, trying not to have to hear about it all over again.

"Pay attention, Wright!" he said. I sat up a little bit. "Now, it's a complicated issue about who had the authority to do what. Miss Linder mentions the First Amendment to our highest law, the United States Constitution. The First Amendment guarantees us, among other things, the right to freedom of speech and the right to *peaceably* assemble."

"That's the problem!" I blurted out. "The rioters, the protestors. Whatever. They weren't peaceful at all."

JoBell glared at me. "That doesn't give our soldiers the right to kill them."

"I don't get it," TJ said. I wasn't surprised. "Why were these people even protesting?"

"Ah." Mr. Shiratori held up the Stick of Power. "This is another example of the importance of studying our government. As we'll learn in greater detail when we study the Constitution in its entirety, Article Six, Clause Two states, in part, 'This Constitution, and the Laws of the United States which shall be made in Pursuance thereof, shall be the supreme Law of the Land, and the Judges in every State shall be bound thereby, any Thing in the Constitution or Laws of any State to the Contrary notwithstanding.'"

"Whoa," said Cal.

"Whoa indeed, Mr. Riccon. Can you tell me what that means?"

"Uh, Coach, I don't —"

"Mr. Riccon, as I've told you before, on the football field or even in the halls, you are free to call me Coach, but here in my classroom you'll address me as Mr. Shiratori or sir. Now do you know what that clause means, Mr. Riccon?"

"I was just impressed that you had all that memorized, sir." Cal didn't say anything more, but Mr. Shiratori kept looking at him. The silence stretched on. "But . . . I mean . . . it's . . . supreme, you know. So, really powerful. Powerfuller than the states, even. Maybe," Cal said. "I don't know, Coach. Er, sir."

Mr. Shiratori didn't move. " 'Powerfuller than the states, even.' Mr. Riccon, your unconventional grammar notwithstanding, I think you pretty much understand the clause. It's the part of the Constitution that says the Constitution and the laws passed by Congress and the president are more powerful than laws passed by states. So Idaho can't pass a law that says, 'There is no US president.' "

"Idaho has to listen to what the president says," said JoBell.

"What does this have to do with the protest?" TJ asked.

Mr. Shiratori tapped the stick on the floor. "I'm getting to that. In addition to the First Amendment and Article Six, Clause Two, otherwise known as the Supremacy Clause, there is also the Tenth Amendment, which states, 'The powers not delegated to the United States by the Constitution, nor prohibited by it to the States, are reserved to the States respectively, or to the people.' "

"Whoa," Cal said again. "Mr. Shiratori, how do you memorize all —"

"I study, Mr. Riccon, and I've been teaching this class here for fifteen years. The Idaho state assembly and our governor recently voted for what is called the *nullification* of a law passed by the US Congress, a law that would require us all to carry a national identification card. Idaho basically said that requiring people to carry ID cards is a power reserved to the states. They say certain features of the new federal ID cards, such as the fact that they'll carry all our medical records and contain a chip allowing the location of the card to be tracked by satellite, constitute an illegal invasion of our privacy."

JoBell could hardly stay in her seat. "But the Supremacy Clause —"

"Only counts" — Mr. Shiratori spun to face JoBell, pointing the Stick of Power at her — "when the law the US Congress passes is constitutional. The Idaho state government said that the law was not constitutional, so the federal government didn't have the power to pass it, and that Idaho will refuse to enforce it."

"Can Idaho do that?" Samantha Monohan asked.

"That's the question, isn't it? *That's* what people were arguing about in Boise, and *that's* why we need to understand our government and how it works. Because what I've described to you are only the basics of the case. Nullification, or the right of a state to, on its own, declare federal laws unconstitutional, goes all the way back to some of Thomas Jefferson's ideas, and most especially to the 1830s, the state of South Carolina, and the vice president at the time, John Calhoun. Calhoun and his supporters opposed certain tariffs, or taxes, on the importation of foreign goods, and they argued that any state in the union had the power to declare any federal law to be unconstitutional for the entire country."

I couldn't believe it. The whole disaster in Boise had happened over a stupid argument about ID cards? How could people be dead as a result of something so unimportant?

JoBell couldn't remain silent. "But —"

Mr. Shiratori held up the Stick of Power to cut her off. "South Carolina argued that once a state had nullified a law, it would take a constitutional amendment passed by three-fourths of the states to make the law constitutional. President Jackson believed that everything Calhoun and South Carolina were proposing was dangerous and illegal. He said, 'Nullification means insurrection and war.' So the federal government did two things. They passed a law that would allow President Jackson to use the military to force South Carolina to obey the federal tariff laws, and they also reduced the tariffs that South Carolina had been mad about in the first place. In a way, both sides won."

"So are we going to have a war?" TJ asked.

"Don't be stupid," I said. "This is America. There's no way —"

"Mr. Wright, you're free to debate in this classroom, but you will not insult people."

Did TJ really count as a person? I decided to let that issue rest. "Fine. Sorry. But that stuff you were saying about South Carolina is totally different from what Idaho is doing, right? Idaho is only saying that the federal law is not allowed in Idaho. It's still allowed in the rest of the country."

"It's allowed in the rest of the country for now, Mr. Wright," said Mr. Shiratori. "But the states of Texas, Oklahoma, and maybe even New Hampshire are already considering nullifying the law as well."

"People need to calm down and talk this out," I said. "Find a way to get along and then come to an agreement. That President Jackson guy is from way back. Things are different now."

"Yeah," Sweeney said. "No way is anyone going to fight over this. No way could a president get reelected if he launched a war on a state, if he killed people just over stupid ID cards."

"Exactly," I said. "This isn't old pioneer times or whatever. We're a united country. We're all one big Army. Soldiers all go to the same basic training, wear the same uniforms."

"Maybe you and Sweeney are right about all that," JoBell said to me and the class, "but the bottom line is Idaho doesn't get to decide which federal laws to obey and which to outlaw."

iratori tapped the stick on the floor. "It's a hot controversy, now that people have died, now with Governor Montaine refusing to even release to the federal government the identities of the soldiers involved, it's more contentious than ever."

JoBell switched Eleanor back on and held up the photo of me leaning over that dead girl. "Whatever they decide with this ID card law is one thing, but our governor should be in jail along with this guy who murdered those people Friday." She held up the image of me on her comm. "I hope the president gets them!"

Mr. Shiratori pointed at JoBell with the Stick of Power. "Miss Linder, I think the situation is a lot more complicated than you think."

I sank down lower in my seat. Mr. Shiratori had never been so right.

‑√‑• *Warning, you are about to enter the Truth Zone. Here comes . . . The O'Malley Hour!*

Let's get right to the talking points tonight. The president has danced around the issue with the Idaho Guardsmen for an entire week. If the federal Department of Justice has enough evidence to indict the Idaho Guardsmen for this incident, then those men should be arrested. Negotiating with the Idaho governor is a waste of time. It's not up to Governor Montaine to make this decision. Unfortunately, so far, he's the only one deciding anything. •‑√‑

JANE PINKLETON ★ ★ ☆ ☆ ☆

THERE'S BLOOD ON THOSE CAPITOL STEPS! SHAME ON YOU, IDAHO!

★ ★ ★ ★ ☆ This Post's Star Average 4.15   [Star Rate][Comment]   12 hours ago

‑√‑• *With us today on* Viewpoints *is Senate Majority Leader Laura Griffith! Thanks for being here, Senator."*

"It's a pleasure, Belinda!"

"Well, we'll get right to business because I have a bone to pick with you."

"Uh-oh!"

"I think I speak for most of the women here on Viewpoints when I say that we are generally supporters of President Rodriguez, and so we're concerned, I think, with the way you've been very critical of him lately."

"To be fair, Belinda, most of my problem is with Governor Montaine, but this isn't merely party politics. Look, what Idaho is doing is. Completely. Illegal. It's unconstitutional. The shooting incident is a tragedy, and I hope a full investigation is finally allowed, but the shooting and Idaho's nullification attempt are two separate issues. Nullification is tantamount to secession, and it must be dealt with immediately. I'm disgusted with Governor Montaine and certain members of the Idaho legislature, and rather than being critical of the president, I'm merely strongly encouraging him to take immediate action to rectify this dangerous situation. •—⌄

⌄—• is willing to examine Governor Montaine's claims that some bullets recovered from Boise shooting victims were not military issue, seeming to substantiate reports that at least one civilian involved in that protest was armed. White House spokesperson Kelsey Santos says that the president will not be satisfied until a full federal investigation has taken place.

Governor Montaine said in a written statement this morning, quote, "There is conclusive ballistic evidence suggesting fifteen-year-old Brittany Barker was killed by someone other than Idaho soldiers. One of the Guardsmen was wounded by a non-military weapon. It is almost a certainty that some of the rioters were armed. However, although shots from rioters would certainly justify the Idaho Guardsmen's decision to fire, my legal and proper order to disperse the dangerous riot was all the justification they required."

In the meantime, the federal government is doing its best to proceed with its own investigation into the Boise shootings. The FBI is asking anyone who has photographs or video of any aspect of the protest, particularly images of the National Guard soldiers, to please send those photos and videos to the website listed at the bottom of the screen. They are looking to get as many angles on this tragedy as possible, and we have not seen the FBI enlist the help of the public like this since their investigations in the wake of the bombings of the Boston Marathon and the Mall of America in Minneapolis. ●⎯⋏⎯

FIVE

Friday brought the first football game of the season. Coach posted the starting roster on Thursday, and I was glad to have my shot as one of the starting wide receivers.

In the locker room Friday night, Sweeney had some of his screaming, thrashing metal music blasting from the new high-powered speakers that he'd bought for his comm this season. TJ and Dylan traded fierce licks on pretend guitars. Cal wore all his gear except his helmet and cleats. He walked back and forth with his fists pressed to the side of his head, his biceps bulging. He was whispering something so fiercely that he looked like he could literally kill someone. Timmy Macer wasn't watching where he was going and only stepped out of Cal's way at the last second.

"I want to *hurt* somebody!" Our starting center Brad Robinson threw fake punches at his locker door. "Rip their guts out!"

This was what it was all about. The intense concentrated rage, the anticipation. Football was half the reason I bothered showing up at school. JoBell was probably the other half. Tonight, though, with everything that had happened, I couldn't get myself into it. I sat there in my football pants and shoulder pads, holding my helmet and shoes.

Mike Keelin walked by me on his way to his locker. "You ready to rock, Wright?"

I couldn't take it. I heaved myself up off the bench and headed out of the locker room into the gym. Sweeney was playing catch with our tight end, Randy Huff, and with TJ, who had somehow snagged the other starting receiver slot.

"Dude, where you been?" Sweeney fired a perfect pass right to me. "We need to get warmed up."

I caught the ball.

"We've been waiting for you forever," said TJ. "Some of us actually want to win this game."

I whipped a hard pass straight for TJ's head and kept on walking through the gym out to the school lobby and drinking fountain. The door to the gym closed behind me, and I ducked down to get a drink. A moment later I heard someone slam into the door, throwing it open.

Sweeney walked up and leaned against the wall by the fountain. "Okay, Wright, it's game night. Time to get focused. So tell me. What's your problem?"

I stood up and wiped my mouth. "Nothing. I just can't stand when TJ —"

"Cut the bullshit. This isn't about TJ. You've been weird all week."

"You want to warm up?" I said. "Fine. Let's go throw the football around." I started back for the gym, but Sweeney pushed himself off the wall and grabbed my arm.

"We've known each other since we were both shitting our diapers. Something's wrong. You have to tell me."

"I can't get into it tonight. Into football, the zone, whatever."

Sweeney stared at me. He wasn't going to let this go. I tried to get past him to the gym, but he stepped in front of me.

Fine. The governor could stuff his orders. I needed someone to know what was going on. I checked the hallway to make sure nobody was around. "The other night when you had your pontoon party? I didn't stay home to take care of my mom."

"What? That was a cool party. You should have been there. Where did you go?"

"I went to Boise with the Guard."

Sweeney almost always kept his cool, but now his jaw dropped right open. Before he could start asking a million questions, I told him everything that had happened, swearing him to secrecy when I was finished.

"Of course I won't tell. You know you can trust me. But dude, JoBell is *pissed* about this. You have to talk to her."

"I know she's mad! Why do you think I can't tell her? She's taken this up as her personal . . . political . . . whatever. She set that stupid photo of me as her comm's background. Every time I almost work up the guts to tell her, she cuts in with the latest bad news or some rant about how terrible I am for what I did."

Sweeney held his hands up. "Whoa, whoa, whoa. First, she doesn't know it was you. Second, she doesn't know what really happened. Third, and most importantly —" He grabbed me by the shoulder pads. "Danny, we have a game tonight. We've waited for this forever. Plus you had to work extra hard to prove you were good enough to start at receiver after missing all the summer workouts. You know how Coach is always telling us to leave it all out on the field? Let's do that tonight. Right now . . . forget all that other stuff. Just put it all to the side and let's play some football."

"I don't know if I can. That's what I'm trying to tell you."

Sweeney shook me. "Sure you can. It doesn't matter anyway." He put his arm over my shoulder and led me back toward the gym. "Since I'm the quarterback, I'm telling you right now, you better get open, because I'm gunning for you."

"Don't," I said. "I'm really not up to it."

"Then we're gonna get our asses kicked tonight, because the ball is coming for you whether you like it or not. So be ready."

★ ★ ★

Our team got off to a strong start, marching down the field with a bunch of seven- and eight-yard gains along with a couple quick passes to Randy. Then Cal broke open a crazy thirty-eight-yard touchdown run. I made it downfield to block one safety. I thought the other one had him, but Cal ran him right over.

Our defense slipped up, though, and the Sandpoint Pirates did much the same as we had, driving downfield a little at a time, until their tailback weaseled his way in past us for a forty-eight-yard touchdown.

Our kickoff return brought us to our thirty-five-yard line. We were huddling up waiting for TJ to run the play in from Coach Shiratori. Sweeney leaned over and tapped his face mask against mine. "Coach is probably going to call for a pass play. Run the first part of your route and then get deep. I'm bombing it to you."

"Don't do it," I said.

"It's coming to you. Get in the game or not. Your call." Sweeney heard the play from TJ and then called it out. He was right. The play called for both receivers and our tight end to run pass routes.

The huddle was broken and I went to the line, split off from our offensive tackle. I looked over to the middle to see if I could get Sweeney's attention, but he was all business. "Damn it, Sweeney," I whispered. The ball was snapped and I shot out ahead, faking inside and then dodging outside of an outside linebacker. Then I cut a slant across the middle, feeling the Sandpoint cornerback right on my six.

TJ was wide open on the out he'd run. Sweeney could have connected with him for at least twenty yards. For a second I thought he would, but he pump-faked and looked back to the left. A defensive end tore through our line, but Cal knocked him out, giving Sweeney more time. Randy scrambled and escaped his coverage. Any sane quarterback would have thrown to him, but Sweeney moved to dodge another defender. That one hooked an arm around his middle, but Sweeney held on to the ball and twisted free.

"Damn it, Sweeney," I whispered again, and then shot off downfield. The Sandpoint safety had screwed up, thinking our quarterback had a brain and was going to pass to Randy. He slowed down, and I sprinted back behind him into the open field.

Sweeney cranked back his arm. I kept running, checking back as I went. The ball was sailing toward the end zone. I sped up. Checked again. Reached out and caught the ball on the tip of my fingers. It bobbled for a second and I was sure I'd drop it, but in the next instant I snapped it in close to my chest.

The other safety crashed into my side out of nowhere. I spun to my left, but kept my feet pumping toward the goal line, high-stepping backward with the safety hanging off of me. When the strong safety nailed us both, I fell back and hit the ground.

I groaned against the dull ache in my ribs and looked down to make sure I wasn't imagining that I still had the football. Then I saw the ref throw both hands straight up in the air. Touchdown. I stood and tossed the football to the other ref right before Cal smashed into me.

"Hell yeah!" He hit his face mask against mine. "That's the way we *doooooo* it, Wright!"

Cal and I ran back to the huddle to get ready for our extra point attempt. Sweeney just held his hands out down low and flashed me that stupid sly smile of his. I slapped him in the side of the helmet. "Thank you, Sweeney."

Then I tipped my head back and screamed like a maniac up at the lights. Maybe this touchdown and this game didn't fix everything that was screwed up in my life. It didn't erase what had happened last Friday night. But I was back in the game! It felt great.

We ended up winning the game twenty-one to thirteen. Afterward, a bunch of us drove out to the old steel truss Party Bridge. Years before I was born, Highway 41 looped around the north side of Silver Mountain and came down to Freedom Lake farther to the west. It turned east, crossed Freedom River north of the lake, and continued through some low woodlands before coming out into open fields and heading south through town. Eventually the bridge over the Freedom River became unsafe for cars, and someone decided to reroute the highway to avoid it altogether. Some people adopted it as Party Bridge, and the crumbling section of forgotten road between the ROAD CLOSED sign and the river was called the Abandoned Highway of Love. Me and JoBell had made some good memories on this road.

Out on the bridge, music played from Sweeney's comm over by the cooler, where Dylan, Chase, and Cal hung out. Cal was tracing out lines on his hand, no doubt reviewing some play from the game. JoBell was talking with Becca, Caitlyn, and Samantha in folding chairs by the fire, though I think Sam, who hadn't even changed out of her cheerleading uniform, was vid-chatting with someone else on her comm. Rumor said she was making it with some guy from Sandpoint, but rumor said a lot of things, and I didn't care what the word was. Sam was cool.

I leaned against the railing off to the side, happy to watch my people having fun. Happy to be with them. To belong. My whole body was stiff and sore with new bruises from the game, but the pain felt like a reminder that I was alive, that we'd won an awesome game, that I had the best friends in the world, and that maybe things would get back to normal after what went down in Boise.

TJ stepped out of the shadows into the faint glow from the fire-light. "Hey, Wright," he said stiffly. "Nice catch."

I'd only made the one, but at least I'd scored, which was more than TJ could say. I could afford to compliment him back. "Yeah, you had a couple good grabs yourself."

"Three," he said as he walked by me, heading for the cooler. "I had three receptions."

"I know that, jackass," I said under my breath. By "a couple" I didn't mean exactly two. I took a deep breath. No way would TJ ruin my night.

"Hey, Wright, you should come down here! The water's great," Brad called up to me. Him and Randy and that weirdo Skylar Grenke were down in the river. Brad's head and shoulders were the only part of him above water.

"Thanks, man," I said. "I'm good here."

"At least chuck me a beer?" Randy said.

"Me too," said Brad, holding his hands up.

"Yeah, hold on," I said.

Sweeney stepped to the railing, carrying two cans in each hand. "Way ahead of you." He tossed two cans down to the guys before handing me one and cracking open his own. I popped the top on mine, and me and Sweeney clinked our beers together. He held his up in salute and then drank.

I chugged down half of my beer right away. "Nice pass." I spoke through a belch.

Sweeney flashed his million-dollar smile. "What did you expect, given my superior Asian coordination and athletic prowess?"

"You've lived in Idaho since you were two weeks old. I doubt you mastered too many skills in Asia."

"Yeah, then explain how else I got the ball to you."

"I don't know." I laughed. "But you need new material besides the stupid jokes about your race."

Sweeney shrugged. "It was actually a stupid pass too. Coach was kind of pissed about it. If you hadn't scored on that play, he'd have killed me."

I looked upriver at the moonlight sparkling on the water. One of my favorite Hank McGrew songs came on Sweeney's comm. "Hey, crank that up," I shouted. Dylan did, and the chorus came around:

> It's the roar of the crowd
> You and the boys standing proud
> You score a touchdown
> To win the game for your town
> Forget the bruises and cuts
> You'll never give it up
> 'Cause nothing feels so right
> As those Friday night lights

I took another drink. The beer was perfect, ice cold. "You were right."

"It's fun, isn't it?" Sweeney said. "Football."

"Yeah. But also . . . I needed . . . I've been dreaming about that night. Nightmares about the redhead in that photo with me. I needed a break from all that, you know?" I swept my beer around to take in our friends down in the river and over around the fire and the cooler. "Needed all this too."

"Don't sweat it with that Boise stuff. In a week or so, some politician will screw up, or some dizzy nineteen-year-old singer-actress will do something or some*body* stupid, and people will have other stuff to post about on FriendStar." He took a drink. "It'll blow over."

Becca came up to us. "What are you two moping about over

here?" She touched her butterfly hair clip, and her big silver "Cowgirl Up" belt buckle sparkled in the firelight.

"Oh, nothing," Sweeney said too quickly.

"Yeah, sounds like nothing." Becca rolled her eyes and sipped from whatever fruity wine drink she'd brought. "Whatever it is, let me hang out with you?" She leaned in so close that I could smell her perfume. "Caitlyn is on the warpath, ripping on whoever's not here like she always does. She was complaining that Cassie Macer doesn't set her up right, but Cait couldn't nail a spike if the net was half as high."

"Hey, where is Cassie?" Sweeney downed the rest of his beer and crushed the empty can in his hand.

"That's my point," Becca said. "She's not here, so Caitlyn thinks she can —"

"Timmy Macer!" Sweeney shouted. "Damn it, Timmy, you had *one* job to do tonight! *One* damn job!"

"What?" Timmy asked from where he sat on a log on the other side of the fire.

Sweeney headed in his direction. "Where's your sister?"

Me and Becca laughed. "Want a drink of this?" she asked.

I tipped back the bottle. "Ugh. It's too sweet. Like Kool-Aid."

"Anything's better than beer," she said.

We watched Randy down in the river spread his arms and flop face-first into the dark water. He came up sputtering and shouting.

"You okay?" Becca asked, turning to me.

"I'm great. Why?"

She looked at me. "Danny, we've been friends for as long as I can remember. I think I can tell that you've been pissed off or whatever. Don't tell JoBell I told you this, but she's been worried about you too."

"I'm fine." She raised one eyebrow. "Well, I'm going to be fine now," I said. "I promise."

She squeezed my shoulder. "Cool. Just remember. I'm your friend. If you want to talk about whatever it was, about anything. You know where to find me."

"Thanks," I said. She went back to the girls. I hadn't been fooling anyone. They all knew something was up with me. I put my hands over my face and shook my head, wondering what I was going to do about all this.

Then I stopped. That kind of crap was exactly why everyone knew something was wrong. I had to act normal, so I went to get another beer and talk football with the guys.

The game and this party had shown me that it might be possible to get back to my normal life. The only other part of it I still needed to fix was JoBell. I missed out on that bikini last Friday, and I wanted to make up for lost time. After a while, I found her by the fire and gently pulled her out of her chair, slipping my arms around her and hooking my fingers through the belt loops of her jeans. "Hey, let's go back to the Beast," I said. "I want to talk to you about something."

JoBell pressed herself against me and kissed me quick. "You want to talk?"

"Um . . . Not really," I said.

"Then what are we gonna do?"

"I'll show you." I started to unbutton the top button of her shirt, but she laughed and pushed my hands away.

"Dan-neee," she said in that cute way where she held my name for a long time. Then she took my hand and led me through the darkness down the Abandoned Highway of Love.

⌁• Governor Montaine has called a second special session of the state legislature today in hopes of passing what he is billing as another round of emergency legislation, this time creating a new employment initiative known as the Idaho Civilian Corps. The governor describes it as an unarmed supplement to the Idaho National Guard, where the Corps could be called out to work in emergencies such as flood or wildfires. Keep it tuned to Idaho's news station, AM 1430 KGLR. •⌁

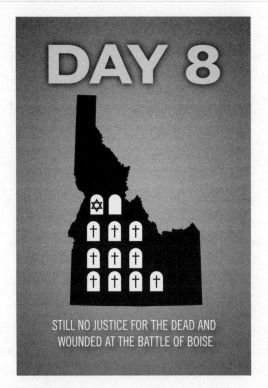

JAMES HAMILTON ★ ★ ★ ☆ ☆

That's only a week. Real and fair justice takes time. We don't want to rush to any unfair conclusions.

★ ★ ★ ☆ ☆ This Comment's Star Average 2.80   [Star Rate]   47 minutes ago

RACHEL BECKLEY ★ ★ ★ ★ ☆

I've seen the videos. They may not be very clear, but I can see soldiers shooting. Those innocent people didn't kill themselves.

★ ★ ★ ★ ☆ This Comment's Star Average 4.25   [Star Rate]   43 minutes ago

GARY FINLEY ★ ★ ★ ☆ ☆

The fifteen-year-old girl at the cafe damn sure didn't kill herself!

★ ★ ★ ★ ★ This Comment's Star Average 4.75   [Star Rate]   22 minutes ago

ISAAC SIMPSON ★ ★ ★ ☆ ☆

Hey, those soldiers were under attack from rioters and looters. I'm supporting the troops! You don't like it? Then get out of America!

★ ★ ★ ★ ☆ This Comment's Star Average 3.86   [Star Rate]   19 minutes ago

⌐• statement from the White House today was the first indication of Washington's growing impatience with the Idaho situation. When asked if he would issue Idaho an ultimatum for compliance with federal demands, President Rodriguez said only that state officials did not have unlimited time.

Protests have intensified on several campuses around the nation. Almost all of these have been peaceful demonstrations calling for the arrests of the Idaho Guardsmen involved in the shooting in Boise last week. Police and campus security were on heightened alert at the University of Wisconsin–Madison, when a growing group calling itself "Citizens Supporting Soldiers" showed up with a counterprotest in support of the Idaho Guardsmen. Hostile words were exchanged between the groups, but no violence or injuries were reported.

General Mills reports another round of layoffs. A little over one thousand employees will be let go, mostly line workers in Ohio, West Virginia, and Tennessee plants. The company is citing lower than expected third-quarter returns and improved production methods as the reason for the cutbacks. You're listening to ABC News. ●—⌄—

CHAPTER
SIX

As many problems as Mom had, me and her talked a lot, about everything. Well, not everything. We didn't discuss things me and JoBell did together. That would be gross. So far she hadn't brought up Boise, but I worried all the time that she would, and I dreaded all the ways that conversation could go bad.

"Tea?" I said that Saturday morning.

"Mmm." She nodded and I poured her some. "Forgot to tell you." She took a sip of her tea and closed her eyes, rubbing her temple with her free hand. She had headaches a lot. "I have to go to this nursing conference in Spokane for recertification. It starts the last Monday of the month and goes all week. You'll be on your own. I'm going shopping sometime soon. Leave me a list of the stuff you want me to get for you to eat. Canned soup. Frozen stuff."

"Okay," I said, but the idea worried me. Mom didn't always do so well with stress or new situations. How would she handle a whole week away from home? "Mom?" I said. She opened her eyes and looked at me with a frown. "Mom, are you sure you'll —"

"I'll be fine." She shrugged. "Work."

I wasn't convinced, but I went back to my breakfast. "Speaking of work," I said after I'd finished my toast, downing the last of my tea and rising from the table.

"Love you." She reached out, and I leaned down for a quick hug, but she held on and squeezed me tight for a long time. When she let me go, she kept hold of my hand and looked me in the eye. "Be careful, Danny."

She said that a lot, but somehow today, there was something in her words — more weight, more feeling. Instead of rolling my eyes and mumbling "Yeah, yeah," I nodded.

I was in the Beast on the way to the shop when Digi-Hank said, *"You got a video call coming in. He ain't in your contacts list. Don't reckon I know who it is."*

Who would be vid-calling me that would come up unknown? "Put it up," I said.

"You got it."

It wasn't really safe to be vid-chatting while driving, but I risked a look at my comm sitting on the passenger seat.

"Oh, shit!" It was Governor Montaine. I'd just sworn at the governor. "Sorry, sir. I didn't realize it was you. Kind of surprised. Can you give me a second to pull over?"

"No problem," said the governor kindly.

I parked the Beast and then, making sure I was off-camera, knocked my head back against the headrest again and again. I was beyond tired of dealing with this stuff. I just wanted my life back.

I picked up my comm and held it in front of me. The image of the governor was at a weird angle, looking up from below. *"Then they'll have to move the luncheon,"* he said to someone offscreen. Someone answered, but I couldn't make out the words. *"Then get Darlene to help them schedule someplace else. The banquet hall is a barracks now. I'll not have those men sleeping in tents out on the grounds."* He looked down at me. *"Sorry, Private Wright."* He frowned and waved someone away. *"Things are busy here. This situation is moving fast. In one week, it's become a lot worse. I hope you're holding up okay."*

"I'm fine, sir. I had a little trouble focusing on football last night, but I figured it out."

"Ah, play a little high school football, do you?"

"Yes, sir. We won twenty-one to thirteen." I stretched my sore arms.

He threw his head back in a big, loud politician's laugh. *"Good man!"* Then he leaned forward and looked into the camera so that his whole face filled my screen. *"Listen, I'm sorry to mess up your morning, but I'm sending a helicopter to your armory. I'm calling everyone in the rest of your squad next. I want you all down here in Boise for a meeting this morning. We need to discuss strategy and some other issues. No uniforms or anything. Come as you are."*

"I was on my way to work," I said before thinking. Annoying as all of this was, he was still the governor. "I'm sorry, sir. I mean —"

"Not at all. I understand this is difficult for you. Believe me, I'm on your side. I'll see that you're all put on state duty pay for this meeting starting right now, and I'll make this as quick as I can. You should be back home shortly after noon."

"Yes, sir," I said.

"Good man," he said again. *"See you then."*

The connection ended. I fired up the Beast and then turned around to head out of town toward the armory.

I always hated flying, but as flights went, the trip to the governor's mansion was at least better than my last flight to Boise. Even Staff Sergeant Meyers was quiet, sleeping off a hangover the whole way. We all basically agreed to say yes to whatever the governor wanted — whatever it took to get out of there as fast as possible.

As the Chinook descended, I could see the governor's mansion out the back hatch. It was an enormous house at the top of a hill above Boise. One of the largest American flags I'd ever seen fluttered in the wind on a pole that must have been at least a hundred feet high. Even before the helicopter landed on the massive brick circular driveway, a ring of soldiers had set up a security perimeter around it.

"Is all this really needed?" Luchen asked next to me. I hoped not.

We exited the aircraft and followed Lieutenant McFee, who had dark circles under his eyes and chapped lips. He looked like he hadn't slept much lately. A different lieutenant led McFee toward the house. The Chinook took off again as soon as we were clear.

"Classy," Specialist Stein said as we were led through the double front doors with arched tops. We entered a room with a carpet version of the Idaho state flag on the floor. In the center of a dark blue field was a circular image with food, some kind of miner or pioneer guy, and a woman in a white dress. The picture was framed by a gold band with the words *Great Seal of the State of Idaho*. Straight ahead, between an American flag standing on the left and the real Idaho flag on the right, a fancy stone staircase rose halfway up to the second level, stopped on a landing, then split into two stairways for the rest of the way.

Governor Montaine came to the second-floor railing and looked down at us. "Great. You're here." He took the steps two at a time to join us on the flag carpet and shake all our hands. "General McNabb is upstairs in the office. Follow me."

Sergeant Kemp shot me a look like, *Is this for real?* Staff Sergeant Meyers only yawned and led the way after the governor. Lieutenant McFee was supposed to be our leader, but he trailed behind us and faded into the background like a ghost. The guy had hardly said a word this morning and wouldn't meet anyone's eyes. I tried to act the way everyone else seemed to be handling all of this — like it was no big deal to be following Governor Montaine around his mansion to meet with the commander of the Idaho National Guard — but I couldn't get over how crazy this whole situation was.

We entered a busy office with officers and civilians sitting and standing around half a dozen tables. People worked on big screens at the tables or stood around typing things into their comms. Montaine pushed aside a comm and took a seat on the edge of a desk. "Darlene, can we get some chairs for these soldiers, please?"

"Right away, sir," said a dark-haired woman at a table in the corner. She started pulling every free chair in the room for us. We sat down. General McNabb remained standing, speaking quietly to an officer whose three large screens all showed different maps of Idaho's borders.

"Thank you for coming," said the governor. "I know you probably have other plans today, so I'll get right to the point. We're concerned that we're not going to be able to keep your involvement in the Boise incident a secret. The general and I have been discussing contingency plans in the event that someone leaks your identities to the Fed or to the press, or in case new evidence links any of you to the shooting. In that event, what I'm concerned about is safety and security for you and your families." The governor frowned a little when General McNabb's comm rang, and the general hurried out of the office with his comm to his ear. "I'm assigning local law enforcement to step up patrols near your homes, to keep a closer eye on you and your families to make sure you're all safe. What I'll need from you today are the names and addresses of any extended family we should be concerned about protecting. Grandparents. Siblings. That sort of thing."

Wait a minute. What was he saying? Did he really think someone was going to hurt or arrest our families? It was just Mom and me on our own. I think she had like one sister who lived in Arizona or New Mexico or something, but they hardly talked to each other. "Excuse me, sir," I said. "The federal government wouldn't go after our families to get at us. That's illegal, right?"

The governor smirked. "It seems like the Fed changes what's legal and illegal whenever it suits them. But I'm also worried that if your names are discovered, regular angry citizens might try to take revenge of some kind."

As soon as I was starting to think life could get back to normal, now I had to worry about people coming after my mom? What if they tried to take it out on my friends? On JoBell?

Sergeant Kemp leaned forward in his chair. "Sir, do you know of any credible threats? Has anyone found out we were there that night? And what about the other units involved in the incident?"

"We don't have specific information on any leaks yet, but people are poring over all the photographs and video footage, so it's a real possibility. I'll be meeting individually with each of the units who were at Boise that night, including the rest of the squads in your platoon. That way, any soldier who might disobey my order to keep quiet can only sell out his own unit, not all the others."

My cheeks grew hot when I thought of how I'd told Sweeney about Boise. Well, the governor would never find out I'd told him. I trusted Sweeney more than just about anyone else.

"Also on Monday," said Montaine, "I'll be issuing a call for volunteers among all Idaho Guardsmen, asking any interested soldiers to come work full-time for the state. You all would be most welcome and encouraged to take advantage of that opportunity. We're going to take some steps to make sure the federal government can't launch any surprise incursions into —"

"Excuse me, Governor!" General McNabb burst back into the room. "Code red!"

Six men in black suits poured into the room, all of them carrying handguns. They took up positions around the governor. My squad and I jumped to our feet.

"Sit rep!" said the governor.

"The situation is two Chinook helicopters are flying in from Hill Air Force Base in northern Utah," said the general. "They've ignored our request for identification and mission and are headed directly for us."

"Maybe they're on the way to Mountain Home?" the governor asked.

"The base isn't answering our calls and the birds have already passed it. They'll be here in about ten minutes," said McNabb.

The governor's comm went off, playing "Hail to the Chief." "That'd be the president calling," said Montaine.

"All right, everybody, let's clear the room," said the general.

"No, that's okay, General. I have nothing to hide. I want everybody here to know exactly what we're dealing with." The governor tapped his comm. "Good morning, Mr. President."

"James Montaine, I need you to immediately begin enforcing the federal ID card law, and I need you to give me the names of all those soldiers involved in the shooting at Boise. I need you to do those things right now."

"Well, *President* Rodriguez, I didn't realize we were on a first-name basis now, or that you had become so disrespectful that you no longer address me by the title of the office to which I was elected. But to make this easy for you, I'll get to the point. The answer is no. And 'no' is something that you boys in Washington better get used to hearing."

There was a pause. *"All right, Mr. Montaine, then you leave me no choice. By the authority vested in me as president of the United States of America, I am hereby placing you under arrest on the* charge of obstruction of justice. Two helicopters are on their way to your location at this time, both carrying soldiers from the 78th Special Forces Group. You will be taken into custody and moved to Washington, DC, where you will likely face additional charges before you stand trial for your crimes."

The governor stood up a bit straighter. His eyes narrowed. "I've committed no crime. It is *you* who are breaking the law with your unconstitutional mandates and your efforts to prosecute innocent soldiers whose only crime is doing their duty."

"*We've been over this! It's too late for talk. My men will be there soon. This ridiculous standoff is over.*"

"No, Mr. President. You will turn those helicopters around, or I will. This doesn't have to escalate to violence, but if people do get hurt today, it will be your fault. Goodbye, Mr. President. We can resume a productive discussion of our problem after you remove the threat of attack."

The president had started to speak, but Governor Montaine tapped out of the conversation. "General McNabb, scramble our Apache gunships. Intercept and repel those federal birds. Tell our pilots not to fire until I give the order."

"Right away, sir." The general picked up his comm and passed on the orders. Then he said to his captain, "Are the men ready?"

The captain, a little older than our Lieutenant McFee, nodded. "Quick Reaction Force is suited up and standing by. Snipers are in position."

"Good work," said McNabb. "Same orders to the men. Nobody fires unless ordered to do so. Make it happen, Captain."

"Yes, sir." The captain jogged out of the room.

"Sir, what's happening here?" I asked. They were seriously getting ready for a firefight with our own guys? With other Americans?

McNabb spun to face me. "Private Wright! You and your squad will stay here and remain silent! Do you understand? Lieutenant McFee, control your men!"

McFee barely seemed to hear the general.

The governor's assistant, Darlene, stood up from her desk and pointed out the window. "My God, there they are."

She was right. The Chinooks were small in the distance, but closing fast.

"Where's our camera drone?" the general asked.

A major at another table tapped the large screen in front of him a few times and brought up a close image of the two helicopters. "Sir," he said to the general. "Our Hummingbird is in range. We have visual."

"About time." General McNabb motioned to the governor. "One of our newer rotary-blade surveillance drones is in position, Governor. We'll be able to control the situation from here."

I wanted to do something, anything, to try to stop this. Sending Idaho National Guard attack helicopters and soldiers up against US Army helicopters and soldiers? This was madness. I looked to Lieutenant McFee, who seemed even more useless than he'd been last week in Boise. Sergeant Meyers was watching everything around him with a big smile, like he was happy to be in the middle of some action or spy movie. Sergeant Kemp wore his serious look, a crease between his eyebrows. At least I wasn't the only one who knew this had to stop.

On the large screen at the major's table, the image zoomed back to show the approaching Apache helicopters, with thirty-millimeter machine guns between their wheels and Hellfire missiles and rocket launcher pods under their wings. I could hear the rotors as the birds drew closer.

Then the federal Chinooks dove toward the ground, banking to the right and left to split formation as they put on speed. The Apaches whipped around and bolted back to regain their position between the Chinooks and the governor's mansion. It looked like they were all getting ready for a firefight.

I said a silent prayer, begging God to make the Feds go back. I didn't think I could handle being stuck in the middle of another shooting crisis.

"They're making their move!" said the major.

Governor Montaine folded his arms. "General McNabb, have those gunships fire warning shots across their bow to stop them."

I didn't care what General McNabb said. He could court-martial me if he wanted. I had to do something. "Governor Montaine, you can't make them fire! Those are Americans!"

McNabb didn't waste time. "Lieutenant McFee, get him out of here right now!"

"No, wait," said the governor. "That's okay." He looked me in the eye. "I know how you're feeling, Private Wright. Believe me, I respect and honor all the members of our military. I've been a soldier too. But I have to stop these men from doing what they've been sent here to do. We cannot keep giving in to the federal government's expansion. I promise, I'll do everything I can to keep all our boys from being hurt."

I had to give Montaine some credit. He was maybe the most important guy in the whole state of Idaho. He was in the middle of a crisis, and yet he took the time to talk to me, Private First Class Nobody. I still didn't want any of this to happen, but I believed what he said.

McNabb must have given the order, because red blips of tracer fire, almost like little lasers, ripped through the air about a dozen feet in front of the Chinooks. Puffs of dust shot up from the dry, empty hillside in the distance as the rounds hammered into the ground.

I moved to watch the helicopters through the window. One of the Chinooks had stopped, and the Apache had flown around to block it from moving ahead. The Chinook that had banked down to the left swooped back to the right and cut altitude, coming in fast about sixty feet above the governor's lawn at the edge of the property.

The other Apache banked to chase it, but it was too late. Black ropes fell out of the Chinook, and seconds later, soldiers fast-roped down. A whole nine-man squad hit the ground, rushing toward the mansion with M4 rifles drawn.

General McNabb tapped his comm. "Captain, deploy QRF. Detain the approaching squad on the south hill."

Below us out the window, an entire platoon of four squads rushed out in one wall of soldiers. Two armored Humvees with men in the turrets behind .50-caliber machine guns sped after them.

"It's like it's all happening again," Luchen whispered. Specialist Sparrow nodded.

Moments later, two lines of soldiers faced each other with weapons drawn.

"Come on now," Luchen whispered as he stared at the standoff. "Don't nobody do nothing stupid here."

I'd never agreed with him more.

Outside, there looked like there was a lot of shouting from both sides. One federal soldier jerked his weapon, like he was about to fire, but another quickly pushed the gun down.

"If the Feds shoot, they're dead," Luchen whispered.

"At least one of them understands that," said Sparrow.

The second Fed pointed out the machine guns on the Humvees. He must have known the Feds were outnumbered four to one. He motioned for the rest of his squad to lower their weapons, but they didn't put them down.

A bunch of soldiers shouted back and forth from both sides. The Idaho guys tensed up on their weapons.

"Come on, give it up," I said quietly.

One Fed took a couple steps forward, but the leader of his squad rushed toward him, pointing at him "blade hand" with his fingers and thumb locked together vertically. The angry Fed wasn't about to be silenced that easily. He calmed down a little bit, but kept arguing with his leader.

"Nobody fires unless I give the order!" the governor shouted to McNabb, who relayed the order through his comm.

"These special forces guys aren't used to getting stopped by the National Guard." Sergeant Kemp spoke at nearly a whisper. "They're pissed."

"If the Feds were smart, they'd have fast-roped right down onto the roof," Sergeant Ribbon said.

"Must not have been expecting trouble from Apache gunships and a whole platoon of Guardsmen," I added.

The captain who had been up in the office with us stepped out in front of the Idaho soldiers. He said something to the Feds, then motioned with a sweeping gesture toward his own men and all their guns. Lastly, he pointed up toward the mansion.

"What's he doing?" Specialist Stein asked a little too loudly.

Sergeant Ribbon elbowed him. "I think he's pointing out sniper positions, trying to prove to the Feds that they have no chance."

"Which they don't," said Sparrow.

"I know," Luchen whispered. "Why don't they give up already?"

Almost as if they'd heard him, the Fed soldiers lowered their weapons.

General McNabb looked satisfied. "Governor Montaine, I think we've stopped this."

I heard sighs from all over the room.

Montaine closed his eyes and bowed his head a little. "And no one hurt," he said after a moment.

"Should we bring the federal soldiers in, sir?" asked the general.

"For what? All they've done is follow orders. I won't punish them for that. Allow one helicopter to land and pick them up. Have the Apaches escort them out of Idaho airspace."

Everyone in the room snapped to life, placing calls, giving orders, working their stations. Outside, one Chinook landed and the squad of federal soldiers that had made it to the ground boarded. The helicopter joined the other Chinook in the sky and then flew off, with the two Apache gunships trailing close behind.

The governor, the general, and their staff continued their flurry of business. Me and my squad sat in the corner out of the way, surfing the wire or watching shows on our comms.

After about an hour, the governor finally seemed to remember we were there. "Gentlemen, I'm sorry, but obviously the situation has changed, and we're not going to be able to do the nice sit-down meeting like I had hoped. Look for more information on your comms. I'll have a flight coming to get you soon. Meanwhile, I've got this press conference to do down in the entryway in a few minutes. You're welcome to watch on the screens in here."

He left the room. A few moments later, the image on one of the larger screens in the office switched to show Governor Montaine stepping up to a podium in front of the stairway. He held up his hand for quiet. *"By now, you have all heard the reports about the president's unlawful and failed attempt to arrest me a short time ago.*

"I want to be absolutely clear. My actions today were not

motivated by my own self-interest. On the contrary, I have acted so that the will of the residents of Idaho, through its legislature, will not be suppressed by the federal government. I have acted to protect the dutiful soldiers under my command. I could not allow the federal government to arrest me — first because I have done nothing wrong, but more importantly, because to do so would jeopardize or sacrifice the will of the residents of Idaho and the safety and freedom of Idaho soldiers, who are also blameless.

"Today the president contacted me and repeated his demands. I repeated my refusal, and I will say this to the president and to the nation. Any attempt by the federal government to kidnap me or any other elected Idaho official or to detain any innocent soldier of the Idaho National Guard is illegal and will not be tolerated. At this time, I, Governor James Montaine, do hereby invoke Article Fourteen, Section Six of the Constitution of the state of Idaho, which reads, 'No armed police force, or detective agency, or armed body of men, shall ever be brought into this state for the suppression of domestic violence, except upon the application of the legislature, or the executive, when the legislature can not be convened.'

"That means I will not allow any further armed federal incursions into Idaho with the exception of normal flight operations at Mountain Home Air Force Base southeast of Boise. No armed active duty military personnel from Mountain Home will be allowed to leave the base unless he or she is an off-base resident of Idaho. Any other armed federal agents in the state have twenty-four hours to surrender their weapons or leave.

"I hope that this confrontation is resolved quickly, but make no mistake. We will not be governed by unconstitutional laws, and the soldiers involved in the shootings in Boise will not, under any circumstances, be prosecuted for their actions in stopping the Boise riot. I'm Governor James Montaine, and I stand by my soldiers."

He motioned to the crowd. *"Any questions?"* He pointed at someone quickly. *"Yeah?"*

A blond woman stood up. *"Governor, how will you enforce this decree of yours?"*

"First of all," said Montaine, *"this isn't my decree, okay? This isn't something I just made up. Article Fourteen, Section Six has been a part of Idaho's constitution since it was first ratified. We have not had a need to enforce this clause until now. Secondly, this will be enforced by any means necessary. Right now, I am working with Idaho law enforcement and the Idaho National Guard to deploy checkpoints at all entries to the state. Idaho airspace is being monitored and will be patrolled by our own air assets. I urge the president and the federal government to take us seriously and respect the law."*

Another reporter flagged his attention. *"Governor Montaine, how do you answer critics who would say that by voting for nullification of the ID card law, Idaho is, in effect, seceding from the Union? And aren't your actions today, coupled with the establishment of these checkpoints, a clear sign that Idaho is a rebel state?"*

Montaine pounded his fist on the podium. *"That is absolutely untrue! I have been in close counsel with the leadership of the Idaho legislature, and they assure me that both the Idaho house and senate stand with me in opposition to the new federal ID card law. The law is unconstitutional. The Idaho state legislature and I don't care if the nine people on the US Supreme Court uphold the law or not. It is time we moved past the idea that* only *the federal government gets to decide whether or not its own actions are constitutional. We ourselves have read the Constitution and studied the issue, and we will not have the federal ID cards in Idaho."* He held up one finger. *"And that is only one law. That's it. One. We're still obeying constitutional federal laws. We're still paying federal taxes. Right now, over a thousand Idaho Army National Guardsmen are serving in Iran, fighting to protect America from the threat of an Iranian nuclear weapon. I myself proudly served in the United States Army years ago in Iraq. The people of Idaho are 100 percent American, and in no way does the refusal to implement this one unconstitutional ID card law, or my refusal to allow the federal government to arrest my innocent soldiers, equal the state of Idaho withdrawing from the Union."*

Some of the officers in the room with me cheered. Sergeant Meyers clapped. On the screen, more people called out questions, but I couldn't take it anymore. I popped in my earbuds, put a country music station on my comm, and waited until the helicopter finally came to take us home.

It was after two in the afternoon when I pulled up to the shop in the Beast. I sat for a couple minutes in the still quiet after I shut off its rumbling engine. At last, I climbed down out of the truck, hobbling a little bit from the bruises the Pirates had stamped on me last night and the stiffness from that uncomfortable flight.

"Look who finally shows up. You want to explain where you been?" Schmidty walked out through the bay door to join me in the gravel parking lot.

I knew something like this was coming. "Sorry," I said. "I, um . . . My alarm, I set it wrong and —"

He blew smoke in my face. "Cut the bullshit. I called your house already. Your mom said you left bright and early this morning. She started to panic a little, wondering why you weren't here, so I had to tell her some story about how you'd been here, but then went to pick up some parts, and I was wondering if you'd stopped at home." He spit into the gravel. "I don't like lying for you, so maybe you could stop lying to me."

"I . . ." What could I tell him that he'd possibly believe? Even if I told the truth, he might not buy it. "I had to go to the armory."

"This ain't your drill weekend." Schmidty frowned as he drew on his cigarette. "This have something to do with that mess down in Boise?"

"It was . . ." I was scrambling to think of a story, but I could never explain why I'd been gone all morning. I looked down and kicked a rock across the lot. Schmidty's wife had ditched him years ago, and from what I could tell, his life was a lonely stretch of cigarettes and cheap beer. I could probably tell him the truth. He'd keep it safe just because, in general, he hated talking to people. I looked up at him and held out my hand. "Give me a cigarette. There's something I got to tell you."

I told him the whole long stupid story, coughing a little as I tried to smoke. While I described the Battle of Boise, I kept waiting for him to start cussing me, the protestors, the governor, or the president out. He stayed quiet, though, watching me with his eyes sharper than I remember them being in a long time. I explained how I'd been at the governor's mansion for the troop standoff. "So yeah," I said when I finished. "Seems like everybody has it out for me these days."

"Not everybody. Buzz Ellison's been talking all week about how the soldiers did nothing wrong, about people jumping to conclusions and assuming you were all guilty." He almost smiled. "Lot of people on Ellison's side. On your side."

"I . . . I felt so helpless there today. Our own soldiers about to fight against each other, damn near shooting down helicopters, and there was nothing I could do."

"Something you can do. And you better get to doin' it real quick." Schmidty jerked a thumb back toward the shop. "Back your truck in. We need to get it ready in case something happens."

"What's going to —"

"Just go get your truck!"

I did as he said, and when I climbed down from the Beast, he was waiting for me with a big black metal toolbox. Inside he'd packed a couple lighters, a serious bowie knife, a hatchet, a length of rope, a blanket, a dozen military meals ready to eat, and some bottled water. "We'll bolt this to the back of your truck so nobody can steal it and so it don't rattle around." He pointed up to the loft where I kept the Beast's hard-shell cover for the back. "We'll put that on today too." I opened my mouth to complain, but he held up his hand while he lit another cigarette. He puffed smoke. "No, don't give me no back talk. You'll need the cover on that thing. It'll be cold soon anyway. Keep that truck fully fueled at all times, and check the spare tire. Run a full maintenance check on it every week."

"Geez, Schmidty," I said. "You sound like this is the Army. We're not at war, you know."

"I don't know what's going on." He pointed at me with his cigarette. "Neither do you. But shit's gettin' bad, Danny. Real bad."

We started bolting the heavy toolbox down in the back of the Beast.

⌁● *The Dow plummeted 6 percent today. The NASDAQ and S&P also suffered another decline. Investors are worried about the increasingly troubling situation in Idaho and how that might affect the nation's industrial and agricultural production, while currency traders are dumping the dollar, resulting in a spike in dollar-based commodities. Oil and gas prices are on the rise, bringing bad news for an already struggling transportation sector. Market analysts predict ●⌁*

⌁● *From NPR News, this is* Everything That Matters. *I'm David Benson. While a shocked nation waits to see President Rodriguez's response to Idaho governor James Montaine's forcible defiance of the federal government, the American public is not waiting to respond with their opinions. The newest poll figures released this morning show the president's approval ratings plummeting to a mere 33 percent, the lowest by far during his entire presidency. Nationwide polling also shows considerable disapproval for Governor Montaine, with only 39 percent of Americans polled supporting the governor.*

Montaine is polling much higher within the state of Idaho, but there may be serious signs of trouble for the governor and some of his supporters in the Idaho legislature. The Idaho secretary of state announced today that Montaine opponents have gathered enough support to begin an official petition for the governor's recall. The opponents now have seventy-five days to collect a sufficient number of signatures. Under Idaho law, if the petitioners succeed, a special recall election would have to take place this November second. The secretary of state also recognized the start of recall petitions for many of the governor's allies in the legislature. Even if Governor Montaine survives the recall attempt, recalled seats in the legislature would remain vacant until the next general election, making it difficult for the governor to pass his initiatives in special sessions, as he has twice this year. If enough Idaho voters choose to recall the governor, the post would be filled by the lieutenant governor until the next general election.

While the president's Republican opposition might be expected to take advantage of these poll numbers, Speaker of the House Jim Barnes said this morning that, quote, "unity and understanding are more important than ever in light of the current crisis."

On the other hand, support from Democrats is beginning to cool. Senate Majority Leader Laura Griffith said, quote, "I fully expect the president will finally engage with this issue to lead us to a solution to this problem. Delay only worsens the situation." ●—⩘

CHAPTER
SEVEN

Once during our junior year, I overheard Sweeney talking to his girl-friend at the time — a girl from a different school, Emily or Emma or Ella. (He probably dated a girl by each of those names that year.) Anyway, he said, "So what do you want to do tonight?"

She went, "I don't care. Whatever you want to do."

He was all, "Want to go out to eat?"

She said, "Sure."

"Where do you want to eat?"

"I don't care. Wherever you think."

Sweeney told me later that apart from how much she put out, it had been like dating himself.

JoBell was never like that. She always had an opinion about what she wanted to do on a date or about what the United States should do about the war in Iran. Well, about how fast the military should leave Iran. She wasn't too bossy or anything. She'd just been raised to be passionate about her ideas, and that passion kept things interesting. Except for when she was complaining about Montaine or the Battle of Boise, I liked it.

I sat parked outside JoBell's house early Friday morning, relaxing and waiting for her to come out so I could drive her to her student council meeting before school.

"*Hey, soldier, your . . . National Guard armory is calling,*" said Digi-Hank.

I looked around for something to punch. "Damn it! What the hell do they want now!?"

"Sorry, partner. Should I ignore the call? Maybe you'd . . . like to listen to some of my greatest hits from your playlist instead?"

Drill was Saturday and Sunday, and Sergeant Kemp had already got in touch with me on Tuesday with his usual leader's call, reminding me to get a haircut and make sure my uniform looked good. He had also asked if I wanted to volunteer for full-time state duty. They put out these requests sometimes, asking for soldiers to help fight a wildfire or flood. I turned him down. I'd had more than enough extra National Guard duty.

"No, Hank," I said. "Put the call on speaker."

"No problem," said Hank. *"You're a great American."*

"Hello," I said. "This is Wright."

"PFC Wright, this is Sergeant Kemp."

I felt a wave of relief. Better Sergeant Kemp than Staff Sergeant Meyers. Definitely better than a call starting with the code "rattlesnake." "Go ahead."

Kemp sighed. *"Bad news. I'm really sorry for the late notice, but I was just notified of this myself. Drill has been changed to a MUTA-Five. Formation tonight is at eighteen hundred hours."*

This was bullshit. Most drills were only MUTA-Four, meaning one Saturday and Sunday a month. They couldn't just change everything the Friday before drill and make it a MUTA-Five. "I can't make it. I have a game tonight," I said. "Can I split train at least for tonight?" Sometimes a Guardsman could make up time before or after drill if he had something really important going on.

"Sorry," said Sergeant Kemp. *"Commander says everybody attends, no exceptions. Some big training exercise."*

I bit my lip for a moment, wondering if I should ask what I wanted to ask, but I didn't need to. Sergeant Kemp went on, *"Don't worry.*

This isn't another Boise. We're heading out to the woods to practice dismounted infantry tactics or something. I'm sorry you have to miss your game. I'll see you tonight before our eighteen hundred formation." He tapped out.

"Damn it!" I punched the center of my steering wheel, sounding the horn. I'd signed up for the Guard to serve part-time. Now it was taking over my whole life.

JoBell came out of her front door and practically skipped down the stairs from her porch. She opened the passenger door with a big smile on her face. "Hey, I was hurrying. You didn't have to honk." She climbed in. With her bag on the floor, she strapped in, her comm in her lap.

"*Great minds discuss ideas. Average minds discuss events. Small minds discuss people,*" her comm said. "*Perhaps you would like to discuss several updates to news stories you've been following.*"

"Not right now, Eleanor," JoBell said.

Her fingers were already sweeping and tapping her comm.

"*I understand. Please let me know if I can be of further assistance.*"

"Hey, I have to tell you something," I said.

"Me first!" she said.

"No, this is really important." She would be pissed when she found out drill had been changed to MUTA-Five. I knew I was mad.

But JoBell didn't look up. "Eleanor, can you bring up the document that I was looking at last night?"

"*Certainly, JoBell. I'm happy to help.*"

"Can you put that thing away for one second!?" I said.

JoBell frowned for a moment, then closed her comm's cover. "Sorry, baby. I really want to show you this —"

"Sergeant Kemp called a minute ago. It's total bullshit, but they're changing drill so I have to go in tonight instead of tomorrow. It's an overnight thing. I'll be gone all weekend."

She froze with a worried look on her face. "Is something happening?"

I reached over and squeezed her hand. "Naw, it's only drill. Some training exercise. One weekend a month and two weeks a summer, right?"

"Plus wars." JoBell looked out the window.

"But I'm not deployable until after I finish my job training, and then it will be a while until my unit ships out again, because they're over there right now. So they won't be sending me to Iran for a long time. It's fine, I promise. It sucks that I have to miss football, though. Coach will be pissed. I know I am."

"Well —" She turned back to me and grinned. "I have something you might find interesting."

What? I'd expected her to be a lot more disappointed about drill. We were planning on partying after the game and spending some time in the Beast on the Abandoned Highway of Love. The thought of it had kept me going through the week. "If it's more bad news, I'm really not in the mood."

She tapped her comm. "No, this is great!" She read whatever she had on-screen. "Dear JoBell. Congratulations! It is my pleasure to offer you admission to the College of Liberal Arts and Sciences at the University of Washington. After reviewing your strong academic record, blah blah blah . . . At the University of Washington, you will join a group of students eager to pursue academic excellence, etcetera, etcetera." She leaned over the center console and hugged me. "I got in! Just like that, the next phase of my life is all set up."

The University of Washington? In Seattle? When had she decided to go to U-Dub? We didn't really talk about college much. I knew she'd always wanted to go, but for a while, she had talked about going to the University of Montana at Missoula, only three hours away. Seattle was, what? At least a five-hour drive?

I fired up the Beast, but something was a little off, a weird low growl under her normal engine noise. Something I felt instead of heard. I'd have to check it out next time I was in the shop. Why would JoBell want to leave? Why hadn't she told me she applied to U-Dub?

"Well," she said as I drove down the street. "What do you think?"

"It's . . . That's . . . You know, far away."

She folded her arms. "How about a congratulations?"

"Well, yeah, obviously. Congratulations." I couldn't even look at her. "I didn't know you'd applied there. You could have told me."

"I guess I didn't tell you because I was worried you'd react like this."

"Like what?"

"Like mad."

"I'm not mad," I said. "Well . . . I'm pissed about drill. That's all."

"You *are* mad. At me. I know you way too well by now not to be able to see through your lame attempt to cover it up."

First the drill change, then this news. I didn't trust myself to say anything, so I drove on in silence. But JoBell wasn't one to keep quiet.

"I know that you've had a lot on your mind lately besides college applications, but I think you should apply to U-Dub too. It would do you some good to get out of this old town. You know? Get out and see something new."

How could she say that? Freedom Lake is where we grew up. Where all our friends lived. Where we fell in love. "I've been to Seattle before."

"This would be different, and you know it." JoBell rubbed my arm. "Okay, this has come as a shock, but think about it for a while. We could go to Seattle and get a brand-new start. It could be really great. Plus, you know, we wouldn't live in a state where the National Guard was sent out to murder innocent people."

Always back to that. I couldn't think straight. I blurted out the first excuse that came to mind. "I doubt they'd take me with my straight Cs."

"Your grades aren't that bad," JoBell said. "You have all year to bring them up. And even if they don't accept you right away, you could still do a semester at Seattle Junior College until you had the grades to get in."

She was living in a fantasy world. I didn't want to go to Seattle Junior College. Shouldn't she know that about me by now?

"We're seniors, Danny. We have to start planning for the future."

"I do have a plan," I said. "Schmidty will want to retire soon. I'm going to buy him out of the business and run the shop myself. I'll take some good auto tech classes at North Idaho Community College and —"

"Babe, that shop isn't making much money."

"It will when I update it, when we can do more work on natural-gas hybrids and solar tech."

"You could find more advanced and interesting work with machines with something like a mechanical engineering degree. Why just change the oil on old cars when you could design new ones?"

"I do a lot more at the shop than oil changes," I said.

She slid her hand down my arm and squeezed my elbow. "I know that. But I —"

"Anyway, I can't leave Mom. She needs me."

"I know she needs you, Danny," said JoBell. "But you need to live your own life too."

"I can't abandon —"

"Hear me out," JoBell hurried on. "We both know that even though she has problems, she is a strong woman. She doesn't handle abrupt changes very well, but she does adapt in time. You had to start really slow with rodeo and football, remember? She got used to it."

She had a point. I let her continue. "When we go to Seattle, we'll come home every weekend at first. After she handles that okay for a while, we'll drop it back to every other weekend. Then once a month. Then every few months like normal college kids. I know she'll be okay. I would never do anything that would hurt her. I love your mother. You know that."

She made it sound like it would be almost easy. But I knew I wasn't college material. I didn't have the grades or the smarts to go to some big university to become an engineer.

I parked the truck in the school lot and leaned forward against the steering wheel. I felt JoBell's warm hands sliding up and down my back. When I faced her, she leaned over in this great, low-cut sort of wrap shirt, and she smiled with the morning sun shining on her golden hair. We kissed for a long time. Amazing how that always made everything feel better.

She touched her forehead to mine. "I need to get out of this town, Danny. And you may not realize it yet, but you do too."

⌁—• I'm standing in a field off the southeast-bound side of Highway 84 over Snake River, where the Idaho National Guard has been mobilized to set up this checkpoint behind me. As you can see, Guardsmen are searching all traffic coming into Idaho, apparently in an effort to make sure no outside soldiers or law enforcement agents enter the state from Oregon. Civilians are free to come and go as they please, but while the soldiers are moving rather quickly with each car they search, this is obviously causing some difficulties with inbound traffic. Earlier today a number of small law enforcement watercraft patrolled the river, stopping at this checkpoint to fuel up before •—⌁

TABBY CHORCRUST ★ ★ ★ ★ ★

Someone want to explain to me how these Idaho border stops are NOT a violation of the Constitution?

"The right of the people to be secure in their persons, houses, papers, and effects, against unreasonable searches and seizures, shall not be violated, and no warrants shall issue, but upon probable cause, supported by oath or affirmation, and particularly describing the place to be searched, and the persons or things to be seized." Fourth Amendment, US Constitution

★ ★ ★ ★ ★ This Post's Star Average 4.65   [Star Rate][Comment]   58 minutes ago

SARAH RICHLEY ★ ★ ★ ☆ ☆

The Fed has given them probable cause by trying to arrest Idaho's governor. Plus, they aren't singling anyone out, only searching everyone for weapons or to see if they're a Fed agent.

★ ★ ★ ☆ ☆ This Comment's Star Average 3.00   [Star Rate]   32 minutes ago

---

⌁—• those of you just joining us here on KRPK 780 AM the Rock, northern Idaho's number one Christian talk station, I'm Mike Veenan. Welcome to The Call, *the show where we do our prayerful best to answer your questions or offer prayers for whatever your concerns*

may be. Please feel free to give us a call at 1-800-555-ROCK, that's 1-800-555-7625. Let's go straight to the phone lines. Hello, Cindy from Sandpoint, Idaho, grace and peace to you through our Lord Jesus Christ. What's on your mind today?"

"Mike, I've been following what's been happening lately in the news? With these checkpoints? And the people shot in Boise? And I . . . I don't know, but I'm really scared. How are we as Christians supposed to respond to all this? I mean, I've been praying for America and for peace and all, but, I mean, I don't want to sound crazy, but this almost seems like the end-times."

"Cindy, of course you're doing the right thing by praying. And you do not sound crazy at all. Our Lord Jesus Christ tells us in Matthew chapter 24 verses 6 and 7, 'You will hear of wars and rumors of wars, but see to it that you are not alarmed. Such things must happen, but the end is still to come. Nation will rise against nation, and kingdom against kingdom.' Now this is Jesus telling his disciples, telling us, about the signs of the end-times. I think you are absolutely right to wonder if recent events are the beginning of the end, but remember, our Lord tells us to see to it we are not alarmed. So . . . Spiritually prepare yourself? Certainly. And maybe we need to begin to stockpile shelf-stable food and bottled water, to make sure we have enough fuel in case •—∿

EIGHT

That evening I stood with my platoon on the armory drill floor, waiting for First Sergeant Herbokowitz to call the formation to attention so that our commander, Captain Leonard, could address the company. A lot of guys in the company were missing, but that was mostly because a bunch of them were already on state duty. I checked my watch. The first sergeant was taking a long time to get things rolling. Formation was supposed to be at eighteen hundred, but they were already ten minutes late. That never happened.

Finally, Herbokowitz came out of the orderly room onto the floor. He faced us and stood at attention. "Company!"

The platoon sergeants standing in front of each platoon turned their heads and yelled, "Platoon!"

But the regular routine was interrupted when Captain Leonard marched out on the floor. "Top," he said to the first sergeant, "just skip it." He held his hands up in the air, waving to us in a "come here" gesture. "Huddle up." We all looked at each other for a moment before we crowded in around the commander.

Captain Leonard stood with his hands on his hips. He bit his lip for a second before pursing his lips and blowing out a deep breath. "These have been difficult times for the 476th Engineer Company. Most of our soldiers are deployed to Iran, and most of the rest of us had a rough time in Boise." He paused and swallowed. "Being a soldier means dealing with tough stuff and helping your fellow soldiers deal with tough stuff." He was quiet for a long time.

Luchen elbowed me and shot me a look like, *What's going on?* Sparrow's expression was unreadable.

The CO continued. "Maybe I should have done a better job helping my fellow officers cope. Now we're all going to have to help each other get through this." He stood up straighter. "It is my sad duty to report to you that Second Lieutenant Chad McFee took his own life with a sidearm this afternoon."

A noise somewhere between a groan and a gasp came from the group, and I felt dizzy.

"He was twenty-three years old, a fantastic and dynamic trooper," said the commander. "A good officer."

McFee had killed himself? I thought he hadn't looked so great the last time I saw him. And what had I done to help him? Nothing. I'd allowed one more casualty from the Battle of Boise.

"Please join me for a moment of silence." A cutting quiet fell over the group. "Now, we recently had our annual mandatory suicide prevention briefing, so I'm not going to make you all sit through that PowerPoint again," said Captain Leonard. "But the chaplain will be around at drill if any of you need to talk to him. I encourage you, I beg you, if you are having trouble, talk to someone. Anyone. And all of us need to remember to be there for our fellow soldiers. Now. We have a lot of work to do, and as hard as it may be to focus on our duty, let's remember that we are always 'mission first.' Let's go to work!" He turned to Herbokowitz. "First Sergeant, take charge."

We didn't waste any time. Our squad and team leaders had everybody pack for a weekend in the field, checking to make sure we had everything we needed.

"Hey, Wright, I finally figured out what PMCS stands for," Luchen said later when we were looking for leaks or other mechanical problems on our five-ton truck.

He was winding me up for a joke, but I wasn't in the mood. "Preventative —"

"Preventative Maintenance Checks Suck!" He snickered with that idiotic laugh of his.

"Good one," I said.

Luchen's smile faded. "About McFee. Do you think it was our fault?"

My throat burned with that acid feeling that came right before I puked. Why did he have to ask me this? It wasn't our fault. It was *my* fault. I'd started the whole mess that had torn McFee up bad.

"Clear your fingers," Luchen said right before he slammed the truck's hood closed. "Because I was thinking that maybe if we'd tried to —"

"Damn it, Luchen, what did I tell you about thinking?" Sergeant Meyers's big form rounded the front of the truck next to ours. "The lieutenant killed himself because he was a coward. He didn't have the guts or strength to deal with life. Now, I don't want to hear any more of this kind of talk. Get this truck ready. We're rolling out in fifteen minutes!"

I had always kind of disliked Staff Sergeant Meyers, but now I hated him. Enlisted soldiers never got to know officers very well, and I had known Lieutenant McFee even less than most. But it wasn't hard to see that he'd been devastated by everything that had gone wrong at Boise. He must have wondered what he could have done differently to prevent the bloodshed. He actually cared about the people who were hurt there, couldn't get the images of the blood and the memory of the screams out of his mind. It was cutting him up inside, burning in his dreams. Wanting to find a way to end all that pain didn't make him a coward. It made him human.

I felt a hand on my shoulder and turned to see Specialist Sparrow. "You okay?"

"He wasn't a coward," I said quietly, struggling to keep myself together.

Sparrow gave my shoulder a squeeze. "I know he wasn't," she said. "Don't listen to Meyers. He's an asshole."

I nodded and we finished up with the truck so we could get it in line for the convoy. I was picked as codriver, riding with my unloaded M4 in the cab with Sergeant Kemp, who chose to drive. We headed out of town and followed the highway as it curved around the north side of Silver Mountain. Then we hooked a left onto Elk Road and headed west for a few miles.

When the vehicle in front of us pulled over, we finally had a good look ahead. On the left side of the road, a brown wooden sign read IDAHO-WASHINGTON STATE LINE. Soldiers were already hard at work on the Idaho side, pounding steel pickets into the dirt and rubble where the highway used to be. Supplies had been stacked on the front lawn of a nearby farm — pallets with more steel pickets, rolls of barbed wire, and stacks of coiled concertina wire.

I'd seen this setup before. We'd had a class about it during my first drill. "They're setting up a wire obstacle," I said.

"Eleven-row concertina," said Sergeant Kemp. "It can stop a Russian main battle tank."

"They're closing the road?"

Kemp pulled over and parked behind the truck that had led us out here. "So much for a simple training exercise."

After we all unloaded, First Sergeant Herbokowitz gathered us around him in a loose cluster near the work site. "Listen up, 476! We've had some difficult news, but we still have to soldier on. This weekend drill is going to be high-intensity and fast-paced." He pulled his comm from the cargo pocket on his thigh and read from it. "Governor Montaine has ordered all Idaho Guardsmen to attend MUTA-Five drill this weekend. The objective is to take all necessary measures to ensure no further armed federal incursions are able to enter Idaho." Herbokowitz put his comm away. "What that means is that the entire border of Idaho is being fortified. That is no small job! We're starting by seizing control of major roadways. Obviously civilian traffic will be allowed through. Only outside military or law enforcement will be forbidden to cross the border. The task of the 476th Engineering Company is to secure Elk Road by wire obstacle with an easily closeable civilian bypass. We will be setting up overwatch positions on the hills that border this valley. Finally, we will bring down trees on our side of the border so that we have some standoff room, so that it'll be easier to spot any federal forces that cross into the state."

This was unbelievable. This was wrong. We were digging in? For what? To get ready for a fight with American soldiers? With our own guys?

Herbokowitz droned on about the plan for work, going over the usual stuff about the need to remember safety and for the leadership to make sure the men drank water. "We'll work until dark. Then we'll go to 50 percent security. So leaders, draw up your guard plan. We'll resume work at first light. Any questions?"

I hadn't been in the National Guard for long, but in the time I'd served, I'd learned some things. The first lesson was, in general, to shut your mouth and do what you're told. I squeezed the barrel of my M4. I knew I should follow that first lesson, but I couldn't help myself. I raised my hand.

Herbokowitz narrowed his eyes. "PFC Wright? You got a question?"

"First Sergeant," I said. "Is all of this even legal? I mean, to tear up a road like this?"

"Damn it, that's exactly the kind of shit we don't have time for!" Herbokowitz's face flared red. "An order has come from our chain of command. It's not up to us to ask if it is legal or illegal, right or wrong. We don't get to make that decision. The lawmakers do. Idaho lawmakers have decided this is legal. Our commanders have ordered us to comply. It's our job to figure out how to obey that order and then to get the job done! You all signed your name on the line and swore an oath, so I don't want to hear no more of that kind of talk. Besides" — he seemed to calm down a little — "we're not being ordered to commit some sick war crimes. We're not killing babies or burning villages or anything like that. We're building a damned wire obstacle and a couple fighting positions. We do this stuff at annual training every summer. The only difference is that instead of doing it on some training ground, we're doing it out here." Herbokowitz put his hands on his hips. "So let's go! We have to work while we still got light!"

Luchen slapped me on the shoulder and shot me a look like, *You should have kept your mouth shut.* Maybe I should have, but this still felt so wrong. First National Guard checkpoints at major road-ways, and now we were digging in using tactics that were designed decades ago when we were preparing for World War III with the Russians. Weren't we taking this whole thing too far? How would Idaho and the Fed ever work out their differences if we were convert-ing our state into a fort?

But maybe the first sergeant was right. We were all sworn to obey orders, and these were the only orders we had. I didn't want to think about what would happen if the president told us to take this wire obstacle down.

"Let's go, Wright! Don't just stand there! Move your ass!" Sergeant Meyers yelled.

I hurried to join the others, who were scrambling to grab pickets and spools of wire. What followed was the hardest, fastest work I'd done in a long time. NCOs shouted orders, calling for soldiers to pound steel pickets into the ground. Then other soldiers wearing wire mesh gloves bounced coils of concertina wire over the pickets, looping each end onto the last picket in the line.

"Move it, ladies!" Sergeant Meyers shouted.

Specialist Sparrow unsnapped her chin strap so she could tip back her helmet and wipe her forehead. "I really wish he would shut up."

Me and Luchen chuckled.

"Stop messing around, Luchen, Wright," Meyers said. "This is a basic combat engineer task. Let's get this obstacle in."

That was easy for him to say. He was only shuffling his fat ass around telling others what to do, and how and when to do it. He knew his stuff and kept us moving, but by the sixth time I had lifted the steel pounder by both handles and slid it over a picket, I was ready to punch the guy.

Shortly before dark, we were allowed to stop, but we only had three rows done. I sat on the ground at the side of the road with Luchen and Sparrow, who, like me, drank madly from their CamelBaks.

"This sucks," Luchen said. "Two more days of this shit. Don't know if I can take it."

Sparrow elbowed him. "Come on, I thought you were supposed to be a tough guy."

"Don't you ever get tired?" Luchen asked her.

"'Course I do," she said. "But I have to hide it more so I don't catch crap from Meyers and you guys."

Sergeant Kemp stepped up behind us. "I just got word that our team is going to be setting up fighting positions somewhere over there." He pointed to the north edge of the valley, toward a hill that was covered in pine trees on the Washington side of the border, but at least partially cleared on the Idaho side. "We may be doing a live demo mission to bring down trees faster, but I doubt they'll actually find us any C4 for that. Anyway, grab your rucks, 'cause we're stepping it out right now. We'll work on it as much as we can before dark, and then finish up tomorrow morning."

"Why are we doing all this?" Specialist Sparrow asked.

"I've decided to stop asking questions like that," Kemp said.

"Let's go, Sergeant Kemp! Get your team up there and get started!" Sergeant Meyers yelled.

"At least we'll get away from Meyers," Kemp said under his breath. Then he added louder, "Oh, and Specialist Sparrow, draw a pack of old field phones and a spool of wire from the back of the truck. We're going to set up some old-school commo."

The march down the lane past the couple farms and then up the hill was no problem. I'd had rougher marches in basic, where the shoulder straps from my ruck felt like they were about to cut right through me. At one point, a civilian rode up on a blue four-wheeler, hauling a little open-topped, single-axle trailer. "Hey, you guys know this is private property?"

Sergeant Kemp approached him. "Yes, sir, we do. I apologize for the intrusion. We have orders to conduct some . . . training operations . . . in this area."

"Looks to me like a lot more than training going on here."

"I'm instructed to ask you to refer all questions to our company commander, Captain Andrew Leonard." Kemp sounded like he was reading a script.

The farmer removed his cowboy hat and shook his head before putting the hat back on. "So it's like that, huh?"

"It's like that, sir."

"Not much point in me asking any questions, is there?" He spat brown tobacco juice. "You boys are gonna do what you're gonna do."

"We're going to set up anywhere from fifty to seventy meters from the Washington border, sir. If you have cattle or anything in that area, it might be a good idea to move them somewhere else."

"Most of my operation is on the Washington side of the border," said the man. "I'm thinking it might be a good idea to make sure it's all on that side."

"I'm sorry, sir."

"So am I," said the farmer. "I've worked hard on this little ranch." He fired up his four-wheeler and headed back down the hill toward his house.

The sun was down but it was still light out by the time Sergeant Kemp got us to the right place. He had specific points marked on a map on his comm where the leadership had decided they wanted overwatch positions. He told me and Luchen to get down in the prone while he and Specialist Sparrow went to find another point farther north.

Luchen and I were in the perfect spot for an overwatch, in a shallow U-shaped crevasse among the moss-covered rocks. The natural rock walls sloped off on the sides on the west end, so that we had a great view of the work site to our left down on the highway. A cliff dropped about ten feet down to a ledge, and then the terrain sloped down another five feet beyond that. Only a few trees blocked our view. From here, it would be easy to spot anyone who came out of the woods on the Washington side of the border, while the overhead branches from a couple evergreens behind us would provide concealment from aerial surveillance.

I lay down, grateful that my knees, belly, and elbows would be padded by the thick layer of long pine needles that carpeted the ground here. Luchen moved to the back of our pit, where the rock walls pinched toward each other to make a three-foot-wide passageway, the tops so high they reached a couple feet above his head. "Hey, this could make a good latrine back here."

"It will not," I said. "I do not want to smell your nasty shit. We're gonna be right here all weekend."

He shrugged and came back to join me, sitting down on the pine needles and leaning back against the gentle slope of the north rock wall. He pointed down to the road. "Better here than with those sorry picket-pounders down there. I only hope they don't expect us to dig into this rock to make a foxhole. We'll need more than our e-tools for that."

I laughed. The entrenching tools, our little fold-up shovels, were definitely not equipped to cut through the solid rock here. "No, but we could stack rocks or logs to get some more cover."

"Yeah, but cover from what?" Luchen said. "What are we doing here?"

We were digging in to prepare for attacks from American soldiers — from our own guys. I knew this, but I didn't want to believe it, and I didn't want to talk about it. I stood up and slung my M4 across my back. "You keep watch. I'll go find some rocks to start building a wall for cover."

I walked around the hillside, picking up big, round stones and carrying them back to close the west end of our bowl and make a barrier between us and the state of Washington. When it was too dark to see, I finally stopped.

Sergeant Kemp showed up shortly after dark with an ancient field telephone, wire trailing behind him from a spool. "Okay, we're keeping comm and radio use in the field to a minimum. The light from the screen can give away our positions, and command is worried that comm-to-comm and even radio communications might be intercepted. So, we have these antiques — battery-powered TA-312 field telephones." He showed us how to crank them to make a call. "Sound like something you can handle?"

"Sounds like something a brain-damaged chimpanzee could handle," I said.

"Good." Kemp laughed. "Then you two might actually be smart enough to make it work. They want us on 50 percent security with half of us awake half the night and half of us awake the other half of the night, but that's crazy. We'll each pull a two-hour guard shift. Just kind of walk around with your night vision glasses on and make sure the brass doesn't come up here to check on us. If they do, hurry up and wake up half of us."

"Yes, Sergeant," we said.

The next morning we were up shortly before sunrise. After shaving and brushing our teeth in cold water that we squeezed out of our CamelBaks, we had field chow. But this was no ordinary field chow like we used to get at basic, with the preprocessed food packs that the cooks simply boiled and put into insulated pans for us. This was something completely new.

"Hope you boys appreciate this chow," Sergeant Gravis, our mess sergeant, said. "I got orders to hold off on using the T-rats and UGR-As. They actually sent me to town to buy all the ingredients for my cheesy ham potatoes."

"This is some good shit, Sergeant Gravy," said Sergeant Hyde from second squad.

He was right. This was real ham, not spongy imitation stuff. And the real cheese on the potatoes stretched out into delicious strings, not like the cheese sauce the Army usually slopped on.

"Yeah, well, you guys better be shitting me up some more privates for KP, cause this shit's going to take a lot longer to cook and clean."

"I might have the answer to that," said Captain Leonard, who had come up from the TOC, the Tactical Operations Center tent. Behind him were about twenty civilians dressed mostly in jeans, heavier long-sleeved shirts, and work or cowboy boots. Most of them looked to be a little older than me, in their early to mid-twenties, but a few seemed to be in their thirties or forties. A couple guys showed quite a lot of gray.

"Listen up, men!" Captain Leonard said. "We have to finish chow and get to work. There's a lot to do today, so I'll skip the formation. Governor Montaine wants to add some jobs to the Idaho economy, and he wants the Idaho National Guard to have all the help it needs for the big border security job ahead. That's why he and the legislature have passed a law creating the Idaho Civilian Corps, a group of unarmed workers who will be helping the Guard with logistics, supply, communications, and other noncombat roles." The commander motioned to the group of civilians, who must have ridden in on a five-ton this morning. "So this is our first group of workers from the ICC. They're here to help, and they will be treated with respect. A lot of them will be helping to build the obstacle, but your leadership will assign others to different tasks as well."

There was some grumbling. Sergeant Gravis raised his hand. "Sir?"

The commander pointed him out. "Yes, Sergeant Gravis, I'll make sure a few of them get put on KP."

A cheer went up from a bunch of soldiers. I'm not gonna lie. I joined in.

First Sergeant Herbokowitz stepped out from behind the captain. "If I hear one more soldier cheer about these civvies in the Corps filling in for shit work details, I'll make sure that soldier does that detail himself. Got it? Squad leaders have the plan for the day. Now get moving!"

My squad spent the morning gathering rocks to build walls in front of our fighting positions. I kept quiet about it, but I was sure glad they brought this new ICC in to pound pickets for the obstacle. After working for hours, we finally took a break at about ten thirty.

"Make sure you all stay hydrated. It's a warm enough day and this looks like plenty of work." Chaplain Carmichael walked up to join us. On one tab of his collar he wore a captain's insignia, and on the other was a black cross. The cross on his patrol cap was shiny silver. "What are you all working on up here?"

Luchen took off his patrol cap and rubbed the sweat from his brow. "We're building fighting positions, sir. Any chance you could ask God to miracle all these rocks into place?"

The chaplain sat down by us on the rock barrier we'd made at the west end of our position. "I'll ask Him," he said with a smile. "But He might want to offer you soldiers the pleasure and dignity of a job well done all on your own. I'll tell you what, though. If you'd like, I'd be honored if you'd be willing to join me for a word of prayer."

Specialist Sparrow stood up. "Sorry, sir, I'm not really one for praying." She walked back toward the crevasse on the east side of our rock bowl.

Chaplain Carmichael nodded. "No problem."

Sergeant Kemp returned with a wooden crate that looked heavy. He carefully placed it on the ground and then sat down on top of it, following the chaplain's lead in taking off his cap and bowing his head. Me and Luchen did the same.

"Lord, Heavenly Father," the chaplain began, "thank You for this new day and for the opportunity to serve others. We thank You as well for those with whom we serve, and we ask, Lord, that You bless every one of us and help us to support each other. Lord, we ask You to accept the soul of Lieutenant McFee into Your Heavenly Kingdom, and we ask You to help all of us cope with the sadness that comes with his loss. Thank You for sustaining us through these difficult times, and we ask You to please help us avoid open conflict. We pray for Your guidance and help in the days and weeks to come. We ask that You please strengthen and protect each and every one of us, so that we may continue to do our duty. In the name of Jesus Christ, our Lord and Savior, we pray. Amen."

"Amen," I mumbled with the rest of my team.

"Thank you, Chaplain," said Sergeant Kemp.

"It's my pleasure."

He didn't sound super pleased about our situation in his prayer. He must have felt that something was really wrong, like I did, like McFee had. "Sir?" I asked. "What should we do?"

"What do you mean, Private?"

"Sir, we're building fighting positions and putting in eleven-row concertina wire so we can keep federal forces out. All of a sudden we're making up this Idaho Civilian Corps thing, so we can get these jobs done a lot faster. They're gearing up for a fight."

The chaplain hesitated before he spoke. "This is . . . a training exercise. We need to have faith that this will remain just a training exercise."

"Fine," I sighed. "But what if fighting breaks out? I'm sworn to serve America *and* this state. What's the right thing to do if they start fighting each other?"

"Lord, to whom shall we go?" the chaplain muttered. "Then, Private, I think all we can do is pray, and search our hearts to see where our loyalties lie."

Nobody said anything for a long time after that. Finally Luchen shook his head. "Uh-uh, no way. It won't come to that."

"I pray you're right, Private." Chaplain Carmichael stood up. "I wish you good luck with all your work. If you'd like to talk more, let your chain of command know. I'm here to help." He headed down the hill toward camp.

I stared down from the cliff where we'd set up, down into the tree line on the Washington side of the border. Would the Americans there really become our enemies, only because they were on the other side of the line? Would we really fight over an ID card? I thought again of the Battle of Boise. It wasn't all simply a matter of an ID card anymore.

"Well, guys, check this out," said Sergeant Kemp.

He opened the wooden crate he'd brought up. It was full of green, plastic-wrapped, one-and-a-quarter-pound sticks of C4 plastic explosive. "I was wrong yesterday," Sergeant Kemp said. "We did get C4. Apparently we're clearing the trees along the border as fast as possible, and it'll take too long to use saws to cut them down one at a time. We're bringing them all down at once."

"Awesome! We're blowing them up!" Luchen said.

"I won't be much use," I said. "I haven't been to AIT. I'm not fully qualified as an engineer, and I'm not allowed to handle explosives."

Kemp looked doubtfully at the crate. "Well, apparently the chain of command doesn't care if you've never had the training with C4. You're going to help rig it anyway. I asked specifically about you, and they're calling for every soldier slotted as a combat engineer to do the work."

Staff Sergeant Meyers and Sergeant Ribbon led our squad's other team to our position. They carried more wooden crates — maybe more explosives or the detonators or something. "Well, boys, seems like we got ourselves a little live demo mission," Meyers said.

Meyers explained that our squad was responsible for clearing trees and large shrubs from the Washington border back thirty yards into Idaho. The border was already marked with bright orange spray paint. Our team leaders would guide us through the placement of the explosives, he said.

A few minutes later we took a path down the rocky cliff and ran the ring main of explosive det cord out on a long walk around all the target trees. Then my team went south while the other went north, looking for trees to destroy.

"If the trunk's diameter is six inches or more, we need to drill halfway through it," Sergeant Kemp said. He handed me a heavy-duty cordless drill.

"Sergeant Kemp?" Luchen said. "What's diameter?"

Specialist Sparrow rolled her eyes, but looked amused. Sergeant Kemp stayed serious. "Relax, Luchen. Try to stay with us. I'll work out the math." We stopped at our first big tree. "Here you go, Wright." Sergeant Kemp handed me a tape measure. "Measure around that tree for the circumference."

It was a big tree. I had to have Sparrow hold one end of the tape while I brought the other end around. "About seventy-nine inches."

Kemp took out his comm and tapped to bring up a calculator to do the math. "That's a twenty-five-inch diameter. Wright, I need you to drill toward the center of the tree for thirteen inches."

I went to work with the drill. By the time I'd bored a hole halfway through, my arms were getting tired of holding the thing up.

Kemp checked his comm. "This says a twenty-five-inch diameter tree — well, we'll call it twenty-seven inches to make sure we use enough explosives — calls for three pounds of C4. Easy." He pulled a block of C4 out of the box that Sparrow had brought. "The only thing worse than an explosive system that doesn't work, is one that works only halfway."

He held up the green-wrapped C4 block. "This is a huge tree. Most of the others will be smaller and will use less C4." He took out a knife and cut one block in half, handing it to me. He handed another block each to Luchen and Sparrow. The stuff was white and smelled like my mom's nail polish remover. "C4 can be shaped, kind of like playdough, and our job is to work it into a cylinder that we will then press into the hole that Wright drilled."

I waited for a moment to see if he was serious. We were really supposed to form plastic explosives into snakes, like little kids playing with clay? But the other two went to work, so I copied them. I quickly found that even though we were supposed to smoosh it like playdough, C4 wasn't quite as pliable. Still, once I got going with it, it wasn't too tough.

"Hey, Wright?" Luchen said behind me. I turned to face him and saw he was holding his C4 like a long white dick. "Wanna bang?"

"You're sick, Luchen," Sparrow said with a hint of a smile.

Luchen made a hissing sound, while pushing his explosive snake toward Specialist Sparrow's neck. She grabbed his wrist. "First, none of your little snakes are ever coming near me," she said. "Second, you will stop screwing around. You will pay attention and do your job like a professional. Do you understand?"

Luchen nodded.

"Do you under*stand*?"

"Yes, Specialist!" Luchen said.

I made up my mind right there never to mess with Sparrow.

We all went to work stuffing the C4 into the tree. My fingers were a little sore by the time we had the tree primed. I reached for my CamelBak hose to get a drink.

"Careful not to get any of that shit on the mouthpiece. If you swallow enough C4, it will give you the runs," Luchen said.

"Specialist Sparrow, you wanna tie up a demo knot?" Sergeant Kemp asked.

"Roger, Sergeant." She tied a quick double overhand knot. When she was done, she showed it to me. "If this knot isn't really tight, it won't spark hard enough when the charge hits it, so the C4 won't go off."

"Then you have a half-working system," I said.

"The kid's catching on!" Kemp said. We pushed the demo knot into the C4 charge and then ran our branch line back to the main line, where Sergeant Kemp showed us how to tie in with a different knot. "This one needs to be real tight too, and don't ever let one part of the det cord line cross another. Then it will cut itself and you'll get . . ." He pointed at me.

"A half-working system!" I said.

"Bingo," Kemp said.

As the hours wore on, we started figuring it all out and we moved faster. Kemp did the calculations. Sparrow tied most of the knots. Me and Luchen took turns drilling. We all placed the C4.

By about sixteen thirty our squad had finished. Sergeant Meyers and bravo team unrolled the coil of shock tube as they started back toward the wire obstacle on the highway. As a combat engineer who hadn't yet gone to engineer school, I'd heard about explosives a lot, but I'd never seen them set off. As Staff Sergeant Meyers hooked up the M81 fuse igniter — a little green plastic tube with a metal pull ring on the end — everybody gathered around.

"This is going to be so huge." Specialist Stein held up his comm. "Okay if I start recording now, Sergeant Meyers?"

"Yeah, roll it," Meyers said. "Who wants to do the honors?" A bunch of soldiers volunteered. "How about a new guy who's never done it before? Wright?"

I didn't feel right setting off the system without ever having been trained on it. "That's okay, Sergeant. I'm good."

"Come on, Wright. Don't be such a pussy," Stein said.

"Fine," I said. "How do I do it?"

Meyers handed me the M81. "You give this metal ring a quarter twist one way and then the other, and then pull it hard. You can't be a little sissy girl about it."

"It's not that difficult," Specialist Sparrow said.

At first, I thought she was making fun of me, but one look at her told me she was just tired of Meyers like usual. I grabbed the ring, twisted it, and pulled hard.

Up on the hill, a white flash appeared around the base of the trees and a huge gray cloud popped into existence. Everything was silent.

"What the hell?" I said.

A second later, a sound like a million cracks of thunder hit as the shock wave passed by. I could feel it vibrating through me like one heavy bass beat from a badass subwoofer.

"I love that!" Luchen shouted.

Chunks of dirt and wood scattered through the air. Trees wobbled and began crashing down in all different directions. In seconds we had taken down a wide strip of forest.

"Timber!" shouted PFC Nelson from the other team.

We waited for about a half an hour to make sure no secondary explosions were going to go off. Then the first sergeant and Staff Sergeants Meyers and Torres went downrange to search for any unexploded ordnance. When they found none, the ICC charged into action with chain saws, cutting up the enormous pile of lumber. About an hour later, second squad set off a similar explosion south of Elk Road, and for the rest of the day we worked on improving our fighting positions as we listened to the buzz of the saws.

By about twenty-one hundred we had good cover and concealment at our position, even laying newly cut logs as a roof over our stone basin. Staff Sergeant Meyers had our squad gather at my team's position. "Everybody take one of these thermal cloaks and a Rules Of Engagement card." When he'd made sure we all had them, he sat on a rock. "Listen up. Standing orders for whenever we are out here. Starting now, every soldier will wear his thermal cloak between sixteen hundred and zero eight hundred hours. No exceptions. Tomorrow, you will cover the roof of this position with mud, not only to fill the cracks between the logs, but to cover the logs themselves. There will be absolutely no smoking and no fires at the fighting positions. All soldiers will keep artificial light and heat sources to a minimum, and the use of such sources must always be under a thermal cloak, even inside your positions."

I unfolded my cloak. The fabric was stiff, like one of those space blankets they sold in sporting goods stores, but instead of having a silver side, both sides were a dark green. "Sergeant, what are these for?"

"Drones," said Meyers.

"Even the most basic Predator drone has a full night vision and infrared surveillance package. We want to keep these positions and the positions of individual soldiers on patrol hidden from the Fed," said Sergeant Ribbon.

"Speaking of the Fed," said Sergeant Meyers. "Everybody take out your Rules Of Engagement card. Standing orders. Every soldier will keep this ROE card on his person whenever on duty." He held the laminated card up and pointed to the bold letters written across the top. "This here is the number one thing to remember. Your primary mission is to protect the state of Idaho by preventing the unauthorized entry of armed soldiers or law enforcement personnel. Does everyone understand that? Sparrow, that means that no matter how handsome you think some Fed soldier is, you cannot let him enter the state."

Meyers laughed, but Sparrow acted like she'd barely heard him. "Yes, Sergeant," she said coolly.

Meyers continued. "Let's go through the steps of graduated force. It's simple. All you have to do is remember the four S's." He went on to explain, in as lengthy and crude a way as possible, what took me about thirty seconds to read.

A. SHOUT: verbal warnings to halt. "Halt! You are not allowed to enter Idaho!"

B. SHOW: your weapon and demonstrate intent to use it.

> **C. SHOVE**: use nonlethal physical force to control the situation when possible, to include using force to detain the person.
>
> **D. SHOOT** (a warning shot): to demonstrate your willingness to use deadly force.
>
> **SHOOT** (to kill): to eliminate a deadly threat or stop the incursion into Idaho. **When possible, check with your on-scene commander for authorization before firing.**
>
> **YOU DO NOT HAVE TO USE EVERY STEP IF YOU DO NOT HAVE TIME AND IF <u>YOU ARE IN GRAVE DANGER</u>!**

"Any questions?" Sergeant Meyers said when he finally finished reading the ROE card.

"Kick-ass," Specialist Stein said. "The Fed better not come anywhere around here!"

Everybody in bravo team except for Sergeant Ribbon laughed. Luchen thought it was funny too until Sparrow elbowed him. I caught Sergeant Kemp's eyes and knew he was thinking the same thing I was. We were all hoping this situation would remain peaceful. That was looking less and less likely all the time.

⌁—• Mr. President, can you confirm reports of a firefight in northern Idaho between federal soldiers and members of the Idaho National Guard?"

"I've addressed this issue several times already. There was no firefight. It is true that US soldiers were conducting movement in northeast Washington, but the explosion that occurred on the Idaho border was an ill-advised and deliberate effort of the Idaho National Guard to bring down trees. Despite whatever rumors you may have heard, the explosion was absolutely not the result of any armed conflict or missiles fired from Predator surveillance drones operating in the area. In accordance with the Safe Skies Act of 2017, there are absolutely no armed aerial drones operating in US airspace."

"Hart Wibley, CNN. Mr. President, why were federal soldiers on maneuvers in northeast Washington in the first place?"

"I'm afraid the answer to that question is classified."

"Is this a preparation for an armed mission into Idaho?"

"I'm not going to answer that, Hart. That's what classified means."

"Nikki Aberall, Fox News. Mr. President, how do you respond to Senate Majority Leader Griffith's criticism that you are being too lenient with the Idaho crisis? Is this a sign of a larger split in your party?"

"I spoke at length with Senator Griffith this morning. I certainly understand her sense of urgency in resolving this situation. However, I think she misunderstands the delicate nature of what we're dealing with here. Yes, this standoff cannot be allowed to continue forever, but it's important to remember these are Americans we're talking about in Idaho. We cannot simply charge in there, guns blazing. I want to assure you and the American people that I am working constantly toward a peaceful resolution to this *situation. However, if necessary, in order to make sure Idaho is in compliance with federal law, no option is off the table, including the use of force.* •—⌃—

ASHLEY FINNER ★ ★ ★ ★ ★

Whatever your position about the Boise shootings, how does this make sense?

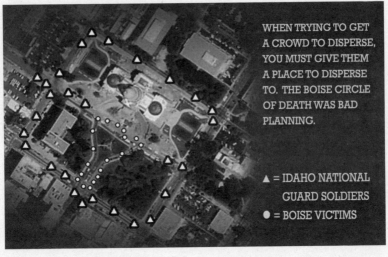

WHEN TRYING TO GET A CROWD TO DISPERSE, YOU MUST GIVE THEM A PLACE TO DISPERSE TO. THE BOISE CIRCLE OF DEATH WAS BAD PLANNING.

▲ = IDAHO NATIONAL GUARD SOLDIERS

● = BOISE VICTIMS

★ ★ ★ ★ ★ This Post's Star Average 4.72   [Star Rate][Comment]   7 minutes ago

CHAPTER

NINE

On Monday morning, everybody was talking about either the football game or the awesome things they'd done over the weekend. Randy, Brad, and Brad's girlfriend, Crystal Bean, walked by. They stopped. "Wright, did you have a good drill?" Brad asked.

I could have told him about the explosives or about how I'd spent all the rest of the weekend helping to build Fortress Idaho. I could have told him about Lieutenant McFee. But I didn't want to talk about any of it. "A boring training exercise."

"That sucks you couldn't make the game. We took Grangeville *down*, bro!"

Randy pulled both hands to his chest like he was snatching a football out of the air. "TJ had this great catch. You should have seen it."

"That's great." I made myself look really impressed so I wouldn't seem jealous. The three of them went off and were lost in the morning crowd in the hallway.

I bit my lip. The problem was that I *was* jealous. Not of TJ — I could handle that idiot. I was jealous of the other guys who had fun beating the snot out of Grangeville at the game, and then afterward making it with their girlfriends instead of being stuck out in the woods. I was jealous of everybody in this whole damned school whose biggest concerns were homework and sports and parties and having fun, while I was trapped in the middle of the so-called Idaho Crisis.

I started walking toward Mr. Shiratori's class. Becca popped out of the crowd and laid her hand on my upper arm. "You okay? I know you have to be down after missing the game. And JoBell said you had to set off some freaky big explosion?"

"JoBell worries too much and then exaggerates," I said. "It was a big boom, but not freaky."

"Oh" — she shrugged and elbowed me — "you just blew up a forest to bring down all the trees. No big deal. You're crazy, Danny. And you know, we all worry about you. Me especially."

"Well, don't. There's nothing to worry about. Drill's over. Things will start to calm down soon."

JoBell came around the corner and started walking alongside us. She took my hand in hers. "Becca! There you are. I've been thinking. We need to get to some of these real protests like the ones they're having in New York or San Francisco. The little local rallies are pathetic. Maybe we could road-trip to Seattle for the big demonstrations there."

Becca put her arm around JoBell. "Gas costs a fortune."

"I know. But I feel so helpless, so disconnected from the people who are trying to end this crisis. And it's important, you know. I want to *do* something about it."

"So study hard," Becca said. "Become a lawyer like you always said you would."

"I will," said JoBell. "And when I'm a lawyer, I'm going to specialize in bringing scumbags like the Butchers of Boise to justice."

I hurried us along to class without saying anything else.

That Wednesday, I was in Mr. Cretis's advanced woods class. The shop was in the back of the school next to the weight room, facing the football field. Not many people made it through the first two classes to take the advanced level. Today there was just me on the belt sander, Dylan Burns over on the drill press, a junior named Chase Draper who never seemed to be able to measure stuff right, and Cal, who was down the hall taking his usual third-hour bathroom break.

Mr. Cretis had two rules for most of his classes. The first was safety. The second was that he would help us with nearly any project we wanted to work on as long as we kept busy and tried to figure out how to do it ourselves first. He'd taught me all sorts of different cuts, wood joints, and finishing techniques. He was a cool guy.

"Danny!" Mr. Cretis yelled.

Except when he was mad. I shut off the belt sander, checked to make sure I'd been wearing my safety goggles, and looked up at him.

"Danny, Mr. Morgan just called on the intercom. You're supposed to go to the office."

I frowned, wiping some powdery sawdust from the hair on my arms. Ms. Pierce, the school secretary, almost always called people to the office on the intercom. If the principal himself had called, this was serious. "Right now?" I asked.

"He said 'immediately.'"

"Sounds like trouble, dude." Dylan started the drill and cranked the lever to bore down into a wooden block.

I shrugged, dropped my goggles on the table, and left the shop, trying to guess what this was all about. Morgan and me had tangled before, mostly after I'd shot my mouth off at some teacher or for peeling out in the Beast in the school parking lot. But with everything that had happened this year, I hadn't given anybody trouble here at school.

The school's shop was down a weird little back hallway. As soon as I entered the main hall, someone slammed into me and shoved me back the way I'd come. It happened so fast, I couldn't see who it was, but I pushed him off me and cocked my fist back, ready to go.

"Dude, chill," Sweeney whispered, holding up his hands.

"What the hell are you doing?"

The bathroom door opened and Cal came out. "Hey, guys. What's up?" The stench that rolled out of the bathroom after him was powerful.

I pulled my T-shirt up over my nose. "Damn it, Cal, what have you been *eating*?"

"Quiet!" Sweeney hissed. "Come on, follow me."

"I have to go to the office. Morgan called me," I said. "What's going on?"

Sweeney put a hand on each of our shoulders and led us back toward the shop. "I was in chorus, and you know how Mrs. Henderson hates using comms for our music, and says the glow from the screens looks bad during performances —"

"No, 'cause I'm not lame enough to take chorus," Cal said.

"Shut the hell up!" Sweeney said. "All the girls are in chorus. How's it lame to be getting all the girls? Anyway, Henderson tells me to go have some music copied in the office." He stopped us outside the door to the shop, but kept looking back toward the main hall. "I get in there and there's all these guys in dark suits. One flashed a badge, mentioned the FBI. He had a gun holstered under his jacket. They told Morgan to call you to the office."

"Oh shit." My stomach felt cold. "So much for things going back to normal."

"It's a setup, Danny," Sweeney said. "They know."

"Know what?" Now Cal was keeping watch down the hall.

"Later." Sweeney pulled Cal back to us. "Right now, we gotta get out of here."

"Maybe I should turn myself in," I said. "Maybe I've been too chicken, you know. Selfish."

"What did you do?" Cal asked.

Sweeney shot me a look like, *Can I tell him?* I nodded. "You have to swear you won't tell anyone about this," Sweeney said. "That shooting in Boise? The one that's been all over the news? Wright was there. He was hit in the face with a rock and his gun accidentally went off."

"Whoa," said Cal. "Did you —"

"I don't know," I said, knowing what he was about to ask. "All I know is I only fired one round. Total accident." That gave me an idea. "Maybe if I go and explain that to them, they'll —"

"No way," said Sweeney. "You give yourself up now, within an hour you'll be on a flight to DC. Who knows if you'll get a fair trial or even a trial at all? And do you even know if they're after anyone else? What if you're the only one they've identified?"

"It ain't fair if you have to be punished and nobody else does," Cal said.

We were wasting time. It didn't take this long to walk from the shop to the office. They would have figured that out by now and come to check on us. "Okay, I can work out whether or not to turn myself in later. Right now, I have to get out of here. How many agents are there? Do you think I can get to the Beast?"

"We're not taking the Beast. That gas hog will never outrun these guys. Here." Sweeney flipped me his keys. "You're a better driver. We'll take the 'stang."

"You guys aren't coming with —"

"We're in it together," Sweeney said.

Cal gave me a light punch on the arm. "'Sides my dad, who's always on the road, you guys are the only family I got. I'm coming with you. My dirt bike's in the shop. We can go out through the garage door."

"This is all kinds of jacked up," I said.

"No shit," Sweeney said.

We headed back into the shop. "Be cool," I said. "Act like nothing's up."

Mr. Cretis looked up from the tape measure he'd taken to something Chase was working on. "Danny?"

"Oh, Mr. Morgan wanted us to move Cal's bike." I said quietly to Sweeney, "Get the door," then louder to Mr. Cretis, "This will only take a second."

"Why do the two of you need to help Cal?" said Mr. Cretis. "Eric, where are you supposed to be?"

Sweeney threw the garage door up. I let out a little breath of relief when there were no federal agents right behind it. Mr. Cretis put the tape measure down. "Danny, did you even go to the office? Mr. Morgan called down here again just now."

Cal mounted the bike and started the engine. Sweeney climbed on behind him. That left only a very little bit of room for me. "Yeah, he probably wants us to hurry with the bike," I said as I hopped on. Then I tapped Cal on the shoulder. "Go, dude, go!"

Cal eased the bike out through the door, then hooked a hard left and gunned it to speed down the back service road to the senior parking lot. "Damn, I forgot my helmet," he shouted back to us.

It felt good to laugh. Helmets were the least of our problems. I kept checking all around us. A black car was parked halfway in the grass down the highway from the school. It might be trouble, might not. So far, though, we were in the clear. Cal pulled to the edge of the lot under a maple tree right next to Sweeney's black Mustang.

I pressed the button to unlock the doors and rushed to the driver's side. A car pulled up right behind us. If it was the FBI or whoever, they had us. I spun around to see Becca driving with JoBell in the passenger seat. They parked and stepped out of the car.

"You guys cutting class without us?" JoBell said.

"What are you two doing here?" Cal asked.

"We were volunteering over at the elementary," said JoBell. "These cute little second graders were working on reading this story and —"

"What's the matter?" Becca said.

I went to JoBell and kissed her, squeezing her close to me. If this went wrong, this might be the last time I could touch her. That alone was reason enough to run from these guys. "I gotta go."

"What's going on?" JoBell asked.

"Wright! Come on, dude!" Sweeney called from the passenger side of the Mustang.

I started toward the car, but JoBell held my hand. "Danny, you have to tell me. Please."

The school door opened and three men in dark suits rushed out. One of them had drawn a revolver.

"We're on the run from the FBI," I said.

"Be serious," said Becca.

I pointed at the federal agents, who had spotted us and were running our way. "I am serious. Bye."

JoBell took one look at the men and ran after me. "Oh no. We're coming too." She pushed the driver's seat forward and scrambled into the back.

"There's no reason for you girls to get mixed up in this," Sweeney said, even as Becca shoved him aside and climbed in the back after Cal. Me and Sweeney slid in and I fired up the car. Its engine absolutely roared.

"Daniel Wright!" the gun-toting agent shouted. They were two rows of cars away from us. "Stop right there. We need to talk to you."

"He got a gun. Just wants to talk," Cal said.

"Talk to the squealing tires." I hammered on the gas and the Mustang's wheels screamed. We shot ahead so fast, I almost dumped it in the ditch next to the driveway. "Which way?" I asked when we were on the road.

"Away from the cop!" Sweeney yelled. The car parked halfway in the grass had started flashing red and blue lights in its windshield. It was one of those sneaky cars-that-don't-look-like-a-cop-car types of cop cars.

Becca leaned forward from the backseat. "No, no, they'll have cars everywhere. Head south. Get around that cop."

"You guys better strap in!" I laid on the gas and we shot off fast. Fifty, sixty, seventy . . . "Hold on!" The black car was trying to block the road. He was halfway across the centerline when I reached him. "Gonna bite a little shoulder here!" The wheels hit loose gravel on the side of the road and I felt the car skid like some shaky, rocket-powered sled. I relaxed on the wheel for a second to regain control before easing it back onto the road and gunning it again. Eighty, ninety . . .

My grip on the wheel was so tight that my fingers ached. I stared straight ahead, barely even risking a look in my mirrors at the two screaming cop cars that now followed us, keeping focused on the road. Biting my lip to concentrate, breathing deeply through my nose to try to calm my racing heart, I pushed the gas pedal down farther.

"You gotta go faster, dude," said Sweeney. "They're gaining on us."

"But this is a Mustang," said JoBell. "They're driving plain Fords, like my mom's work car."

"The cops pack a lot more power under the hood than your mom's grocery-getter," I said. "Sweeney, remember all those times I said no when you asked me to disable the speed governor on this thing?"

"Yeah."

"Sorry about that." A bead of sweat trickled down my forehead. I didn't dare take my hands off the wheel to wipe it. It went in my eye and I blinked it away. "Can someone switch on the air conditioner?"

Ahead, an oncoming semi filled the other lane, and a little Honda pulled up to the edge of a driveway. If he pulled onto the road in front of us, we'd have nowhere to go, and we were cooking along way too fast to slow down in time. "Don't do it. Don't do it," I said to him.

The Honda pulled out several car lengths in front of us. "You son of a bitch!" If we'd been going normal speed it would be no problem, but we were flying. "Damn it! Hold on, everybody!"

I whipped the car into the left lane to pass the Honda and put the pedal to the floor.

"Truck!" JoBell screamed. The semi straight ahead blew its air horns and flashed its lights.

"I got it. I got it." For a second, I thought the cold terror down in my gut would make me lose it in my pants. I'd misjudged the vehicle interval. There was no room.

The second we passed the Honda, I cranked the wheel back to the right. A sound like a gunshot went off and sparks shot up by my window. The car shook, but kept going.

The semi had clipped the driver's side mirror. My heart pounded. I checked the rearview mirror and saw the truck and the Honda pull over as the cops drove by. "Sorry, Sweeney."

"And that, friends, is why you make room for emergency vehicles," said Sweeney. "Well, that's why other people should pull over. You focus on driving, Wright."

"I have a map." Becca held her comm out between Sweeney and me. "We're coming up on that Y intersection. If we go right, we'll stay on Highway 41. Or we can hook a little bit sharper turn onto Highway 54."

I risked a glance in the rearview mirror and saw JoBell look at the comm. "Take 41," she said. "There are way more roads that we can use to lose them."

"Except I bet the cops will have the road blocked at the Y intersection," Becca said. "Check this satellite view. There's tons of trees to the right, so we can't go around the roadblock to stay on 41. But this looks like an open grassy field at the corner of this road and 54. We might be able to drive across that to skip the roadblock."

The speed governor kicked in and I could feel the tension going out of the accelerator. "Ladies and gentlemen, we are cruising along at about a hundred fifty miles an hour. This is as fast as this baby can go. Do we have a plan?"

"I'm with Becca," said Cal. "Hit the grass, not the trees."

"You try to drive onto an open field at this speed and you'll roll it," Sweeney said.

"Maybe there won't be a roadblock," JoBell said.

But I could already see red and blue lights flashing up ahead. There must have been a dozen cars sitting on the road. As we approached, I spotted police, regular uniformed guys, not the suited federal agents that had been at the school.

"They have guns," JoBell said.

I'd seen that too. This was stupid. What if they opened fire? What if I couldn't keep control when we drove through the grass field? What if there was no grass field? I could get my friends killed here. "Maybe we should give up." The cops behind us were closing to within three car lengths. "There's no way we can get away."

Sweeney hit his head back against the headrest. "Dude, we've been over this. If you were just going to give up after all, you should have done it back at the school, *before* we were doing one-fifty and running from the FBI."

We were coming up on the barricade fast. I could see a clearing on the left side of the road, which looked like the open field Becca had mentioned. But those satellite images were crap. What if there were tons of rocks or a big ravine or something else to tear us apart?

JoBell squeezed my shoulder. "Whatever this is all about, I trust you. I believe in you."

"Yeah," I said. "We really need to talk about that. Hold on, everybody. This is a Mustang, and we're about to ride it like a rodeo."

"I so don't like the sound of that," said Sweeney.

As soon as we reached the open field, I cranked the wheel to the left and we launched off the shoulder down a little drop into the grass. The back tires slid and we fishtailed for a moment. The girls screamed. Sweeney screamed. Hell, I think I might have screamed. In the next second, I spotted a gentler-looking part of the embankment, and if not for my seat belt I would have flown up out of my seat when we jumped up onto the other highway.

"You did it!" Cal shouted. "One cop car spun out in the grass. He slowed way down before he came up on this road."

When I'd steadied us on Highway 54, I checked my mirror. The police at the barricade were scrambling to their cars to follow. The two black FBI cars pulled out ahead of them and were after us again.

Sweeney slapped the dashboard. "Dude, let's head onto one of these county highways. We can make two or three turns onto other back roads before they've made their first. We'll lose them."

"Sounds good," I said. "Hold on." I eased on the brake to slow down enough to make the corner. But right as I approached the intersection, about six police cars pulled out from behind the trees on the left to block the road. "Oh shit!" I stomped on the brakes hard, and we skidded out of control. We were going to slide right into the police. I yanked the emergency brake lever back and cranked the wheel hard to the left again, this time sending the Mustang into a sliding three-sixty spin.

"We're gonna die!" Cal screamed.

"These tires are so expensive," said Sweeney.

I bit my lip and held the brake and the wheel. There was nothing more I could do. We would crash or we wouldn't.

Finally, we stopped. I opened my eyes, though I hadn't even realized I'd squeezed them shut. Then I sat back in my seat and unclenched my fingers from the steering wheel, grateful I hadn't killed us all. I let out a sigh of relief.

"Get out of the car!" An officer tapped my window with his .45.

TEN

"Oh, now we're in trouble," Cal said. He ran his hands down his face.

The black FBI cars pulled up, followed by the other police from the first barricade. We were surrounded now. "I'm sorry, guys," I said. "I'm really —"

"Get out of the car!" the officer yelled again. At least now he wasn't pointing the .45 at us. We all climbed out. Tension rocked through my whole body. It was like being all tight with my fists, ready for a fight, only with no way to let loose all the adrenaline. I couldn't fight all these cops.

The FBI agents piled out of their cars and drew their weapons right away — a mix of nine mils, .38s, and .45s. The police all around us hoisted their weapons. Most of the cops had guns like the FBI's, but some had shotguns, and several were packing AR15 assault rifles. They were all tense, ready to shoot. Did they think we were packing?

The officer who had come to my window took two steps closer and raised his .45. "Don't move! You're under arrest."

I slowly raised my hands in the air to show them I was unarmed.

"He said, don't move," Sweeney said out of the side of his mouth.

"Bill," said the officer to another behind him, "get these kids in my car."

"Let's go," said a voice behind me. I felt a firm grip on my shoulder pushing me back behind the barricade. He opened the back door of one squad car and motioned for us to get in.

One of the FBI agents lowered his weapon and gestured for his fellow agents to do the same. "Thanks for your help." He smiled at the lead cop. "You can handle the other kids with whatever you want to charge them with, but I need to take Daniel Wright with me right away." The lead cop remained completely serious. The Fed agent frowned. "Is there a problem?"

The police officer nodded to the other uniformed police. "Now, boys."

Suddenly a dozen cops rushed the FBI men, grabbing their weapons and slapping them in handcuffs. The Feds struggled a little bit, but stopped when the cops showed them their guns.

"I guess you didn't understand me," said the lead cop. "I'm Sheriff Nathan Crow, and you men are the ones under arrest."

"You can't do this!" the FBI agent said. "Who the hell do you think you are?"

The sheriff didn't move. "Like I said, I'm Sheriff Nathan Crow. Governor Montaine sends his regards." He motioned to another officer standing by him. "Get these men loaded and take them back to the lockup at Freedom Lake." He stepped out into the middle of the small army of policemen. "The rest of you, get out on patrol. See if these Feds brought any of their friends along."

The sheriff laughed when he saw us standing outside his car. "Well, don't look so surprised. What? Did you think I was arresting you?"

"I *was* driving one-fifty in a sixty-five zone, Sheriff Crow," I said.

"Recklessly," Sweeney added. I elbowed him.

"Please, call me Nathan." The sheriff reached out his hand and I shook it. "You probably don't remember me, Danny, and of course now it's been a long time, but your father and I were good friends. You sure have grown!"

My father didn't come up in conversation that much, so when he did, it always threw me off. Sheriff Crow was right — I didn't remember him — but if he had been friends with my dad, he must be a good guy.

"I'm glad we were able to catch you!" The sheriff slapped me on the shoulder. "I thought the first barricade would have been enough to rescue you, but I've never seen moves like yours, 'cept in the movies. No wonder you made it past them."

JoBell looked from Sheriff Crow to me and then back again. "Wait a minute. Why is the governor involved in this? What's going on here?"

"She doesn't know?" Crow asked.

I shook my head. Governor Montaine must have told him why these FBI guys were after me.

"No, I don't know." JoBell glared at me. Tears were welling up in her eyes. "But I just risked my life on the run with you, so I better get some answers soon."

"This is supposed to be kept secret," Crow said.

"What's supposed to be kept secret?" JoBell asked. Then she gasped. "Oh no." She wiped her tears with one hand. "You mean, you . . . You didn't stay home to help your mom that Friday night, did you?"

Becca put her arm around JoBell's shoulders. "It's okay."

JoBell's tears were rolling down her cheeks now. "Why didn't you tell me?"

"Sheriff, is there some place me and my friends can go to talk in private?" I asked.

"Sure." The sheriff shrugged. "You're free to go, if you're okay driving home. I ask that you remain vigilant, and keep an eye out for more Fed agents."

"Come on, Jo. Let's get in the car." Becca gently led JoBell back to the Mustang.

Sheriff Crow handed me a slip of paper. "Here's the governor's personal comm number. He wants you to contact him as soon as you can." He gave me another slip. "Here's my number. If you have any more trouble, if you need anything at all, feel free to contact me. I mean it. Your father and I were real close. I take friendship very seriously. You need help, call."

"Thanks," I said. "I will. Do you know what the governor wants?" I snuck a peek toward JoBell and my friends back at the car. JoBell was still crying.

Crow patted me on the shoulder. "He didn't tell me. I'm only a sheriff." He nodded toward JoBell. "But it seems to me you have more important people to deal with. The governor can wait." He held out his hand, and I shook it. "You're a good kid. A good man. You got guts, and I have a lot of respect for you. Hang in there."

"Thanks," I said. "For everything."

Sweeney let me drive again, saying I'd earned it after that crazy chase. As I steered us back toward Freedom Lake, this time at an easy sixty miles per hour, nobody spoke for a while. I think we were all trying to take in what had just happened.

"You know," Sweeney said after a long time, "I know we were almost caught by the FBI and we almost crashed and everything. But still, you have to admit, that was . . . kind of awesome." He gave me a light punch to the shoulder, and then hit a fist bump with Cal, who was riding in the middle of the backseat. "Dude, you whipped us into such an awesome spin! How did you know how to do that?"

I bit my lip to hold back my smile.

"Eric," Becca said. "Not now."

I caught a glimpse of JoBell's tear-soaked face in the rearview mirror. "I don't feel like going back to school right now," I said. "Everybody cool if we head out to Party Bridge?"

"Yeah," Cal said. "I don't even want to be in school on a normal day. After all this? Forget about it."

"Sounds good," said Sweeney.

"Yeah," Becca said.

JoBell stayed silent.

I drove around the ROAD CLOSED sign on the Abandoned Highway of Love and then steered slowly down the middle of the road, veering into the right lane at the point where most of the left lane had long since fallen into the river.

"Party Bridge," Cal said after everyone had climbed out of the car. "Too bad we got no beer."

"It's twelve thirty in the afternoon," Becca said. She watched JoBell duck under the I-beam to walk out on the bridge. "Hey, Cal, Eric. We better make sure the Mustang is okay after that chase. Help me check it out, okay?"

"Wha —?" Cal did his thing where he tilted his head to the side and screwed up his face with his left eye closed. "Wright's the mechanic. He's the one —"

Becca grabbed him by the elbow and pulled him over to the car. "I think *we* should check it."

She winked at me and I mouthed the words *thank you*. I put my hands on top of the I-beam and vaulted over.

JoBell was leaning against the guardrail in the middle of the bridge with her arms folded. I sidestepped a hole in the pavement as I approached. The gurgle of the water rushing around the rocks below would cover our voices and give us some privacy.

"Oh yeah!" Cal called out from behind me. "Yeah, the three of us better check this car out to *make sure it's okay*."

"Would you shut up?" Becca hissed at him.

"Cal's a pretty rotten actor," I said when I stepped up to JoBell.

She finally looked up at me. "You're a great actor. You fooled me."

The tears were welling up in her eyes again. I couldn't stand to see her cry. I slowly reached out for her hands, grateful when she took mine and rubbed them with her thumbs. Maybe I had a chance of keeping her. "I wanted to tell you right away. Only Governor Montaine said —"

She pulled her hands away. "I don't give a damn what Governor Montaine said."

"It's not only that," I said quickly. "I tried to tell you that first Monday before school, but I could hardly get a word in, and you were flashing my photo on your comm. And every time I see that photo, I remember that girl. Makes me want to —"

"That's *you* in that photo?" JoBell stood up straight and backed away from me a couple steps. "I can't believe . . . you were there. You're one of them."

"You have to understand. It's not like —"

"Did you . . ." She waved her hand to fan her reddening face. "Did you . . . kill her?"

"JoBell, no." I reached for her again but she backed away. Tears rolled down her face. What was she thinking? Did she hate me? Was I nothing more than one of the Butchers of Boise to her now? "Let me explain."

"You're one of the shooters?"

When she put it like that, it sounded like she was asking if I was a murderer.

"It's not that simple. It's not like I —"

"Just answer the question!" She held her hands tight to her sides.

A spark of hot anger lit up inside me. Why wouldn't she listen to me? She was trying to lump me in with whoever had fired all those shots, with whoever had killed so many people. But then she sobbed more, and I knew I couldn't be hard on her. She'd been so wrapped up in everything about the Battle of Boise. Learning that I was a part of it had to be a huge shock. I bit my lip.

"I'll tell you everything," I promised.

And I did. I told her the whole truth, from the moment Sergeant Meyers dropped the code word *rattlesnake* to that morning in shop class. All the details about the whole sorry mess.

"You have no idea what it's been like. Seeing that girl in my nightmares. Hearing the shots in my dreams." I wiped my eyes. "I'd do anything . . . anything to get that bullet back. I'm so sorry."

Slowly, she stepped up close to me and pressed herself to my chest. "It wasn't your fault, Danny. You shouldn't have been called to that mission in the first place. Then it was an accident, and afterward, you even tried to help people." I hugged her, and she slowly slid her arms around me and put her head on my shoulder. "You could have told me, you know. I would have understood."

I smoothed her blond hair. "You were so mad at all us soldiers. I was afraid that if I told you the truth, you might . . ."

"What?" she asked, looking up into my eyes. "What?"

"I just love you so much," I said. "I don't want to lose you."

"Danny," she sighed. Then she put her hand to my cheek and we kissed. Nothing in the whole world, not home, not my friends, and if I was really honest with myself, not even church made me feel as good, as safe, as I felt with my JoBell. "This whole stupid situation with the Battle of Boise and everything? It's going to pass." She put her hand on my heart. "You and me? Forever."

"Forever," I said.

She smiled. Then she looked down. "Gosh, you've been going through hell with all this, and I've been a total bitch to you."

"It's not your fault." I leaned so close to her that I could feel the heat of her lips on mine. "You're passionate about stuff. That's what I like about you."

Then we kissed hot and deep for a moment before I swept her up in a big hug and swung her around. JoBell kicked her legs, threw her head back, and squealed. "Danny! Put me down! Put me down!"

"Hey, you two, can we stop pretending to fix the car now?" Becca called out.

I put JoBell gently back on the deck of Party Bridge and waved the others over. "Yeah, come on, guys."

They walked out to join us, and Sweeney held out a shiny steel flask. "Anyone want a nip?"

JoBell snatched it from his hand and held it up to him for a second before taking a drink. As soon as she swallowed, she squinted her eyes, shook her head, and blew out through pursed lips. "Wow. What is that?"

"The finest cheap bourbon whiskey that I could get my cousin to buy for me."

"You keep that on you all the time, do you?" Becca asked.

"Under my seat in my car."

Becca grabbed the flask, took a drink, and then kind of coughed her words through the burn. "You're so going to get busted."

"Naw," said Sweeney. "Sheriff Crow won't bust us, and if he does, Danny can call the governor to get us out of it. By the way, Danny, I kind of told Becca and Cal everything."

"It's cool to know what I risked my life for," Becca said. She took out her comm.

"Well, now that I know why we were on the run, are you sure we did the right thing?" JoBell asked. "The governor has kept everyone in the dark about what really happened. Who was shooting at who. Maybe if you explained it to the FBI, they'd back off and leave you alone."

"Or maybe they wouldn't," said Sweeney. "Twenty-one people were hit. Only three guys in Danny's squad were missing bullets after it was over, and then they were only down eight rounds. That's a whole lot of bullets flying, and they'll never figure out who was shooting. Why should Wright be the only one to pay?"

"Plus, they're really pissed about this," said Cal. "All these protestor people want someone to be punished." JoBell lowered her eyes. Cal whipped a pebble into the river. "Danny didn't do nothing wrong, but the president might want to lock him up just to calm people down."

"That's my point, though," said JoBell. "They . . . A lot of people, even me a few minutes ago, don't know that Danny didn't do anything wrong. If we talked to the FBI or whoever, maybe they'd understand."

"I think Cal might be right." Becca looked up from her comm.

Cal had climbed up on the side rail, holding the vertical post in the truss. "What? Seriously?"

Becca held the comm so we could see the video of a riot the previous night in Oakland. Some people were flipping cars while others were looting or setting fire to stores. Most were shouting in the streets. There was no sound on the video, but when she tapped the screen to enlarge it, we could see a few of the signs the rioters were carrying. Among the usual signs that bitched about taxes or the military, a bunch of them read JUSTICE FOR THE IDAHO 12, and YOU'RE NEXT, IDAHO GUARD, or ARREST THE SOLDIERS NOW.

She flipped to a news site where the headline read RODRIGUEZ VOWS BOISE SHOOTERS WILL BE PUNISHED "TO THE FULL EXTENT OF THE LAW." Below that was another headline: SPECIAL FEDERAL PROSECUTOR PLEDGES TO PURSUE CIVIL RIGHTS VIOLATION CHARGES FOR BOISE SHOOTERS.

Becca snapped the cover over the screen. "The Internet is flooded with this stuff. People arguing back and forth on both sides. It doesn't matter what Danny did or didn't do in Boise."

"People are looking to make someone pay for this," Sweeney said.

Becca reached out and squeezed my arm. "And I think maybe this is all out of control, bigger than the issue of figuring out who shot who that night."

It was my turn for a drink. It burned so bad that my eyes watered. "Well, obviously the Fed knows I was there in Boise and maybe that I fired a round. I wonder who else they're after." I hoped they wouldn't release our names publicly. The less people who knew about this, the better. I took another slug of the whiskey. "Thanks, everybody, for coming with me today."

Cal jumped down off the railing, and I swear the bridge shook a little. "We're your friends, man."

Becca held out her fist for a bump. "With you all the way."

"And while all of this is really touching," Sweeney said, "and I'm glad we didn't get killed in the chase today, I know that neither the sheriff nor the governor could keep Coach Shiratori from killing us if we miss football practice tonight. We better head back. I'm driving."

We piled into Sweeney's Mustang, and I started back to school with the greatest friends and girlfriend a guy could have.

CHAPTER ELEVEN

We rode in silence for a while. Finally, when we were about halfway to the school, JoBell put her head in her hands. "Oh, we're going to be in so much trouble."

"Um, about that." Becca reached into her pocket and pulled out a pack of gum. "Everybody chew this, so we don't show up with alcohol on our breath." She held the gum out to me. "Any chance the governor can get us off the hook with Mr. Morgan?"

"Relax," I said. "If we didn't get in trouble for that chase, they won't touch us for skipping class. I think I can get Montaine to square things away with the school." I hoped I was right.

"How?" Sweeney asked. He wasn't doubting me. He sounded genuinely curious.

I pulled my comm and Sheriff Crow's scrap of paper from my back pocket. "Governor Montaine sent me his personal comm number."

"Bullshit!" Cal smiled. He grabbed the slip right out of my fingers.

JoBell took it from him and handed it back to me. "Oh, 'cause *that's* so unbelievable after everything that's happened today."

"Well?" Sweeney said. "What are you waiting for?"

"What do you mean, what am I waiting for? Yeah, I've been to the governor's mansion, but I was there along with my whole squad. It's not like we're best buddies. You're talking about calling the governor. That's a pretty big deal."

"Do it!" Sweeney shouted.

"Hank, I want to add a new contact," I said.

"*My stars, you're . . . a popular guy. You got it, buddy.*"

I tapped Governor Montaine's comm number into my contacts list. Sweeney looked over from the driver's seat. "Get him on video," he said. "I want to see him."

"Hank, will you get me a video call with Governor Montaine?"

"*Whooooie! You got friends . . . in high places. Calling now. Would . . . you like to hear one of my great country songs while —*"

"Make the call, Hank," JoBell said.

We waited for a long time. Montaine was the governor. On a normal day he was probably busy signing forms and attending meetings. Today he'd just ordered the arrest of seven FBI agents. I said, "He's gotta be way too busy to —"

Wobbly live video popped onto the screen. Governor Montaine looked down at me. Behind his head was a white ceiling. He must have had his comm lying on his desk. "*Private,*" he said, "*it's good to see you're safe. When my people got word that the FBI were making a move on your school, I knew they must have been after you. Sheriff Crow came as fast as he could but . . . Well, I heard about what happened. I'm glad you were able to get away.*"

"Gross, you can see his nose hairs," Cal whispered.

"Yeah, not his best angle," whispered Becca.

"I can't believe he's actually talking to the governor," Sweeney said quietly.

Montaine sat up straighter. "*Is there someone there with you?*"

I guess Sweeney hadn't been quiet enough. I hope he hadn't heard Cal. "My friends, sir. They were with me in the chase. They helped me get away."

"*Private, I told you not to tell anyone about what happened.*" Montaine's jaw trembled a little, as if he was trying to hold in his anger. "*I can't keep you and the others safe if too many people find out about this.*"

"I trust them with my life, sir, and I won't be telling anyone else."

The governor pressed his lips together for a moment. I could tell he did not approve of me letting my friends in on the situation. Tough luck for him. *"Well, I don't know how much longer we can keep it a secret now that the Fed has identified you."*

"Ask about help with Morgan," Becca whispered.

"Sir, I know you're busy, but I wanted to thank you for sending the sheriff and his men to help us today, and I'm . . . well . . . We were wondering if you could pull some strings with the principal at Freedom Lake High School, you know, because we did skip classes today."

When Montaine laughed, the creases around his eyes deepened. *"I expect I can do something about that. In the meantime, for the safety of you and others, Private . . . kids"* — JoBell and Sweeney frowned at his use of the word *kids* — *"I expect that nobody else will know about this or about what happened at Boise. We're doing our best to keep you safe, and I'll be stepping up local law enforcement, but you still need to be alert and be on the lookout for anything out of the ordinary."*

That was almost funny. Since Boise, nothing had been ordinary.

"Wilco, sir," I said. "Thanks for your help."

Governor Montaine nodded. *"We'll be in touch."* He tapped out of the call.

The five of us went back to school, trying to act like everything was normal.

That night's practice was rough. It was hard to focus after what had gone down, and I could have done a lot better. Still, for the most part, it felt great. Football. Normal, hard-hitting football. What fall during my senior year was supposed to be all about.

By the time I made it home, I was shaky and tired. Mom would arrive in a few minutes, so I put my comm and truck keys on the kitchen table and set the kettle for tea. I'd probably have some too, to calm myself down after an insane day.

One thing was sure: In a small town, the best way to make sure everybody knows something is to try to keep it a secret. The FBI had showed up at school asking about me, and a bunch of people had been in the office along with Sweeney. Nobody kept their mouths shut. All afternoon people shot me nervous or curious looks in the halls. Some of the guys on the team flat-out asked me what it was all about. I didn't answer, but how long would it take for people to start figuring out the truth?

"Danny?" Mom called from the living room. I hadn't heard her car roll into the driveway. Good. I'd fixed the belts and must have done a good job.

"In here, Mom." My chair scraped the linoleum as I pushed it back to stand up.

"Hey," she said when she saw me, reaching out for a hug.

I hugged her and felt her kiss on my cheek. She squeezed me close and held on for a long time. Longer than normal, anyway. This could be trouble.

When I finally pulled away, I smiled to let her know that everything was all right. "I'll have some tea on for you soon. Water should be boiling any minute. Why don't you sit down in your chair?"

"I'm okay," she said, leading me to the kitchen. "I'll join you." She took a seat at the table and motioned for me to sit down across from her. "You've been so busy lately with school and football, plus drill or work at the shop on weekends. Then when you *are* home, you've been so quiet, up alone in your room all the time. We never get to talk. Let's talk."

"Sure, Mom," I said. She was right. We used to share everything, but lately, I'd kept my distance. "I mean, I have a lot of homework to do, but I have a little time." This was at least partially true. I did have English and government homework, but I would probably just copy that from JoBell or Becca tomorrow before school.

Mom frowned and tipped her head back a little in that way she had that told me she didn't believe me. "What's new with you?"

"Nothing much," I lied. "Football's going great. Rodeo this Saturday."

She shook her head and started picking the skin next to her thumbnail. "You know I hate you doing that rodeo stuff. At least in football you wear a helmet."

The kettle began to whistle. Perfect timing. I stood up and went to take it off the stove, slipping one bag of chamomile tea into each of our cups before pouring in the boiling water.

"The thought of you being trampled by a bull in a rodeo or of you getting a concussion or worse in a football game makes me so nervous —"

I sighed. "Mom, I'll be fine. I've played dozens of games and been to a bunch of rodeos. I'll always be fine."

She held up her hand. It was shaking a little. "As I was saying, I get nervous about you in those dangerous sports, but I know you'll be okay. And I'm fine, mostly, knowing you're involved in them."

I took a sip of my tea. It burned the tip of my tongue. What was she getting at?

"I have my moments, but I can handle more than you think I can."

"I know that, Mom."

"Which is why I wish you'd tell me what really happened that last Friday in August."

I almost spit out my tea. Some of it dribbled down my chin, and I quickly wiped it on my arm. What did she know? How did she find out? Maybe she was just bluffing, like she thought something was up, but she wasn't sure what it was. "What do you mean? I went with Sweeney and the guys —"

"You went with some guys, but Eric wasn't one of them," she said. "Come on, Danny. The National Guard sent you to Boise, didn't they?"

I hated lying to her. She looked mostly calm now. Her hands weren't even shaking that much as she sipped from her cup. Maybe the tea was helping.

"Okay," I said. This secret was getting harder and harder to keep locked down, but it was probably better she get the truth from me instead of some guy on the news. I slid my comm over from where I'd dropped it when I came in.

"Hank, silently bring up the CNN coverage from the August 27 Boise shooting story."

The story came up with that horrible image as the lead photo. Could Mom handle seeing this? I could barely stand to look at it. I tilted the comm so the image would rotate right side up for her to see it.

"This is me, Mom."

She gasped and put her hands over her mouth.

"I didn't kill this girl. I was there trying to save her, but it was too late."

I watched her carefully. Her hands shook even more when she lowered them to the table. Her breathing was level, though, and that twitch hadn't started in her eye. The edges of the shadow were creeping in, but she hadn't been overtaken yet.

"Let me tell you the truth," I said. And I did, all the way up to a watered-down version of the car chase.

"Are you okay? Is JoBell and everyone else all right?" Mom said.

"Yeah, we're all fine."

She reached over and took both my hands together in hers. "I'm glad you're not hurt."

My muscles relaxed. Now that everyone in my closest circle of family and friends knew what had happened, knew what I'd done and didn't hate me for it, I felt free. Like that feeling I'd get when the snow was all melted near the end of the school year, and the freedom of summer was near.

"I only hope I did the right thing," I said.

"What do you mean?"

I took down a gulp of tea. Then another. "If I hadn't fired that shot —"

"But you did," she said. "That's over."

"I know, but I feel like this ongoing argument . . ." I pointed to the comm. "This Idaho standoff . . . is my fault. The president wants to arrest me. Maybe I could end a lot of this chaos if I give myself up and explain what really happened."

Mom put down her teacup with a thud so loud, I thought it would break. "Now you listen to me." The shaking was gone now and her eyes were a deeper blue than I could ever remember them being. "You owe those people nothing."

"Mom —"

"Nothing! Do you hear me?"

"I swore an oath to obey the president and —"

"Has the president given you any direct orders? Has President Rodriguez activated you to federal duty under his command?"

"Well, no, but —"

"No buts, Danny. I've lost a husband to the Army. You've been without a father since you were eight years old, and I miss him every day." Tears welled up in her eyes. "But I do know something about how all of this works. The governor is right. I don't know about his other politics, and I don't care, but he's absolutely right in protecting you and the soldiers who were with you."

She leaned back in her chair, wiped her eyes, and took a deep breath. "Oh, Danny, I might not look it, and I don't always handle stress very well, but there is still strength in me. And if you give yourself over to those men in Washington, they better get ready, because I will be coming to get you back." I laughed a little, but she didn't. She was completely serious. "Even if the president did order you to turn yourself in, there's more to life than duty, Danny. Remember that."

"What about you?" I said. "You always do your duty as a mom."

She leaned forward with her elbows on the table and a smile on her face. "That's something I *choose* to do. Not out of duty. Out of love."

⌒⌒• Welcome back. I'm Sam Harrison. On the panel today, seated on my left, is Kathy Perkits, regular commentator for the Huffington Post and author of the book The Religious Right Is Wrong. *On my right is a contributor to the conservative website* Reclaim America *and the author of the book* The Myth of Liberal Tolerance, *Emily Leckesh. Welcome, ladies. Let's get started. Yesterday, seven FBI agents attempted to arrest Idaho Guardsmen who were allegedly involved in the Battle of Boise. The names of those soldiers have not been released, and the attempt to detain them failed when the FBI agents were arrested by Idaho law enforcement on orders from Governor Montaine. Many Republicans are criticizing the president for worsening an already tense situation by sending in those FBI agents. Some have even said this might lead to open violence. Is that a valid criticism? Kathy, we'll let you answer first."*

"Sam, this is Republican politics as usual. Republicans and conservatives are trying to stir up baseless fears in the American people so that no one will want to challenge Governor Montaine. The president is well within his rights to take efforts to make sure these soldiers are brought to trial. If anything, the president is being too patient with these criminals in Idaho —"

"Excuse me?"

"Yes, Emily, if I can be allowed to finish my sentence —"

"It's the Democrats and your precious president who are the criminals here, sending FBI agents where they are not allowed! He's already been warned —"

"The federal government doesn't need permission to arrest —"

"— not to send armed soldiers or law enforcement into the state. Now whatever disagreements he may have with Idaho's governor or state legislature, he should know that this is a delicate situation, and he shouldn't be recklessly endangering civilian lives by risking an armed conflict."

"— criminals! It's Montaine who is risking armed conflict! He's trying to hold this country hostage."

"Hold the country hostage? What does that even mean?"

"Whoa, easy, ladies. Is it possible that both sides of this issue are at fault?"

"Any mistakes the president or Democrats have made have been forced on them by Montaine and the Republicans."

"Oh, please. This is another example of liberal bias and distortion in the name of their big-government agenda. •⌁

⌁• certainly an embarrassment for the president and the Justice Department. Attempts have been made to arrest Governor Montaine, and now to arrest at least some of the soldiers alleged to have been involved in the Boise shootings. Both of these attempts have failed. The president has a large personal stake in these issues. They've become a major part of his policy, and so I think it will be some time before another arrest attempt is made. He does not have the option to fail again. It would be a political disaster. •⌁

TWELVE

After a tense week, Friday night football was just what I needed, with an away game against the Bonners Ferry Wolves. We were 2–0 and planned on improving our record. Bonners Ferry was a tough enough team, but their starting quarterback was out on injury, and they had a sophomore filling in who wasn't supposed to be so great. That was too bad for Bonners Ferry. Our defense was hungry.

Most of us were suited up and waiting in the locker room. Sweeney had our usual pregame music pumping, and the room was electric. Coach would be out of the office soon to go over some last-minute strategy and get us fired up. I couldn't wait to cut loose on the field. It was going to be an awesome game.

"I will *crush* that kid." Cal punched his fist into his other hand. "Little punk sophomore quarterback gonna wish he never filled in second string tonight."

"That's what I'm talking about!" TJ slapped Cal five.

"Sweeney, what is this?" Dylan reached up on top of the lockers and took down the comm playing music, flipping it around to show its purple back cover. "We're trying to get ready for a game here."

"Shut up, Dylan. My comm was out of power. I borrowed JoBell's. It still plays music fine."

Dylan shrugged and put the comm back.

The music cut out. *"Anger is one letter away from danger, JoBell,"* said Digi-Eleanor. *"Since you've sounded angry when calling for articles about the Idaho Crisis, I thought perhaps you'd be interested in this breaking news story. The names of some of the Boise shooters are being released."*

"What the hell? I'll put the music back on." Dylan stood on the bench and looked on top of the locker at the comm. "NPR News alert?" He looked at me, confused. "Hey, Wright, it's got your name." He reached up to tap the blinking red box on the screen.

"Dylan, don't!" Sweeney shouted.

"What?" Dylan said.

A deep male voice came on. *"This is an NPR News alert."*

Then a woman's voice continued, *"From NPR News, I'm Alicia Seeve. The White House at this hour has confirmed that despite Governor Montaine's efforts to prevent federal law enforcement from entering Idaho, the first arrest has been made in connection with the late August shootings in Boise. Twenty-year-old Specialist Tony Stein of Coeur d'Alene, Idaho, was taken into federal custody and moved to a detention facility in Washington, DC. An arrest warrant has also been issued for seventeen-year-old Private First Class Daniel Wright of Freedom Lake, Idaho. Both are currently charged with depriving victims of civil rights under the color of law. The Justice Department says more charges will likely follow.*

"Idaho governor James Montaine said in a prepared statement, quote, 'I regret failing to protect one of my soldiers from an unwarranted and illegal arrest. I do not know what President Rodriguez hopes to accomplish by publicly releasing the name of an innocent seventeen-year-old boy in connection with the Boise incident. I remain committed to protecting —"

Coach tapped the mute button on the side of the comm. Nobody spoke or moved. I kept my gaze focused on the floor, but I could feel all the guys staring at me.

"We have a game to focus on." Coach's voice echoed through the silent locker room. "I don't know why you're listening to the news to warm up anyway, but whatever you just heard doesn't change anything. We still have to bring four quarters of hard-hitting football, and we're still a team. We're heading out on that field in a minute, and for the next hour, hour and a half, two hours, all that matters to *all* of us in the whole world is this football game. Is that understood?"

"Yes, Coach!" the guys yelled weakly.

Shiratori slapped a metal locker door. *"Is that understood!?"*

"Yes, Coach!" we shouted again. I'd seen him angry before, but not like this.

"Wright, you played great in our first game. There's nothing different about tonight, understand?"

There was nothing different except now I had formal charges leveled against me and someone from my squad was in a prison cell. I didn't know Stein all that well, but he was still one of my guys, and it could have been me.

"Wright!" Coach yelled.

"Yes, Coach! I got it!" I yelled as loud as I could, but somehow it wasn't quite the excited, answering-an-angry-Army-drill-sergeant type shout I knew I should give.

We stood on the thirty-yard line with our helmets off, facing the American flag behind the end zone, as the Bonners Ferry band played the national anthem. Before, as I held my hand over my heart and listened to the music, watching our flag flowing in the breeze, I felt a sense of pride so great it made something ache in my chest. My dad had died for that flag and the freedom it stood for. But tonight, I didn't have that sense of pride. Tonight, after that news alert, I felt betrayed and in danger. And I had to face the sad truth that not even football could make things right, could get me back to my normal life again.

It didn't take long to figure out that the Wolves had heard the news about me too. The whole pack had it in for me. Early in the first quarter, the play called for me to run a little slant route, ahead two yards and then angling toward the inside. Sweeney hit me with a quick pass, but two linebackers sandwiched me and dropped me. A second later, a third piled on top hard, but still quick enough to avoid a late hit penalty. He punched his elbow into my gut, then his face mask ground into mine. "My cousin was shot at Boise. Might not be able to walk again. After tonight, neither will you."

It was only the first of many dirty shots. By the fourth quarter, I was hurting way worse than I usually would in a game.

"Murderer," one of the opposing players said as I stumbled back to our huddle, trying to shake the pain after the jerk cleated my leg.

It was third and fifteen on our own thirty-five-yard line. Sweeney might have completed a pass to TJ, who was wide open since they were stacking the coverage on me, but a couple Wolves busted through the line and sacked him for a loss of seven. Skylar Grenke came out to punt.

"You okay?" Sweeney asked as I made it back to the huddle.

"Great. You?" I said.

"That was a rough hit, but nothing like you've had all night," he said. "They're all over you."

"They heard the news," I said. "And they're pissed."

Skylar reached the huddle. "Deep punt," he said to Sweeney.

I grabbed Sweeney's shoulder. "Remember our first game, when you helped me get back into things?" He nodded. I stepped closer so only he could hear. "I need something like that again. Fake this punt. They won't hate me enough to double up coverage when they could be going to block the punt."

"You're crazy," said TJ, overhearing. "We're down by six and have terrible position. If you don't catch it, they'll take over right here and be ready to score."

"So you go long too," I said. "I don't care who gets it. I just want to stick it to these bastards."

"We have to hurry!" Brad said.

"Let's do it," said Sweeney. "Deep punt on one. Break!"

We ran to the line. I shot a look over at TJ on the other side of our formation. He shook his head. Coach would make us run until we puked for this stunt, but if it worked, it would be worth it.

The ball was snapped and I shot ahead, spinning off a linebacker and running into open field. Only two defenders were between me and the end zone. They split to go after me and TJ. Sweeney fired his pass a second before they took him down. "I got it!" I yelled to TJ, who ran toward me.

"Drop it, murderer," came a stranger's voice from behind me.

But I caught it and ran like mad. TJ took out the last defender right in time. Then I went on ahead for the touchdown. TJ followed me in and slapped me five.

"That was stupid," he said with a smile.

"Thanks," I said.

Our two-point conversion put us ahead, and the rest of the quarter was a defensive battle. Cal came unglued, shooting through the line for three sacks. That backup quarterback was hobbling around, looking pretty pathetic by the time the game was over.

When we went though the line to shake hands and say "good game" over and over, every third or fourth guy would call me a murderer or worse. To those assholes, I'd say, "You lost." It helped a little bit.

The celebration in the locker room was all loud screaming metal, snapping towels, and the guys laughing and talking about different great plays from the game. A bunch of them slapped me on the back or punched my arm, saying "good job" for my catch. Even Coach Shiratori said it was a beautiful play. "But if you guys try a stunt like that again, I'll make you run until you die," he said. I couldn't tell if he was joking or not. The little victory party was exactly what I needed.

Finally, after we had all showered and dressed, Coach announced that the bus was waiting to take us home, and we should pack our gear and get moving.

"I can't believe we pulled off that fake punt," Sweeney said, walking beside me toward the door to the parking lot.

Cal stepped up on the other side, clapping his hand on my aching shoulder. He wore jeans and a T-shirt with the sleeves cut off, showing off his muscles, which were bruised in at least three different places. "You got balls of solid rock, Wright. Not only the fake punt, but the way you stayed in the fight even with all those assholes gunning for you. All those extra cheap shots and dirty hits they were throwing on you just pissed me off. I think it helped me play better. I hit every one of those sons-a-bitches twice as hard."

"Glad I could help." I shoved the bar across the middle of the outside door to push it open. The cool breeze felt good after the dank, steamy locker room.

Everything lit up bright.

"Daniel Wright, what is your response to being publicly named as one of the shooters from the Battle of Boise?" a woman with a microphone shouted.

A man with a large gut stepped closer, a cameraman following right behind him. "Why did you shoot that night?"

Hundreds of cameras flashed so that I could hardly see. Another man tried to push Sweeney aside to get closer to me. "Private Wright, who gave the order to fire?"

Sweeney wedged back in front of him. A blond woman stood a few feet away in front of a camera that shined a blindingly bright light. "I'm here live on the scene, and this is Battle of Boise shooter

Private First Class Daniel Wright's first public appearance since his role in the massacre has been confirmed," she said into the lens.

Cameras and lights were everywhere. Through the glare and the flashes, I spotted our bus parked thirty yards away. At least a hundred reporters crowded the parking lot and kept surging toward us. A small helicopter camera drone hovered overhead. There were almost more media people wedged in between us and the bus than there had been fans for both sides at the game. The questions started blurring together.

A Bonners Ferry police car had pulled up behind the crowd. Its red and blue lights kept spinning past the brick school wall and across Sweeney's and Cal's worried faces. One cop struggled to push through the crowd, trying to restore order. "You people need to get back! Clear the area!"

"Daniel Wright, I'd like to interview you for *People* magazine!"

"Can you give us the names of any other shooters?"

"What are we going to do?" Brad Robinson had come out of the locker room behind us. "They got us blocked off from the bus."

Coach Shiratori joined us outside. "You have to let us through. I have to get these boys home!"

Another woman held her comm up, shooting video. "Mr. Wright, how many people did you kill in Boise?"

The bright light, the hundreds of questions flying at me, the accusations. It all froze me where I stood. Like the nightmare at Boise all over again, the noise and the pushing mass of bodies.

"I just . . . wanna play football," I said. "Can't you leave me alone?"

"What was that?" "What did he say?" "Something about football." "Can you repeat that, Danny?" "Was it a confession?"

"All right, screw this!" Cal shouted. He shoved me back behind him. "Form up! PAT formation, now! We're moving to the bus."

Coach blew his whistle and the guys started taking their positions for the Point After Touchdown formation. Sweeney grabbed my arm. "Stay with me, dude. We'll get you out of this."

"Get out of the way!" shouted Brad at center. "Come on, boys. Shoulder to shoulder. Nobody gets between us." He started walking forward, and the whole line moved as one. The linebackers and second stringers made a wall to protect our side. Slowly, we pushed our way through the crowd of reporters and cameramen.

"Who gave the order to fire?" "Was it Governor Montaine?" "What were your rules of engagement for the mission?"

"Danny!" JoBell shouted from somewhere in the back of the crowd. "Danny!"

I shielded my eyes from the bright lights. Finally, I spotted JoBell and Becca trying to push through the army of reporters.

"Girls, you'll have to meet us at home," Coach Shiratori shouted. Then he pointed at the struggling cop. "You have to call for backup."

"They're on their way!" the cop said. "Get on your bus."

"Can you confirm reports that some of the protestors were armed?" "Did you yourself sustain any injuries that night?" "Is it true that one of the soldiers in your squad is a member of a white supremacist group?" "Was race a partial motivator for the shootings?"

We were about six feet from the bus door now, and the last few reporters in our way were starting to back up.

"Danny, wait!" JoBell was halfway through the crowd now. A photographer held up his comm with a special camera unit attached. Without looking, he elbowed JoBell to get a better shot. "Hey, watch it!" she said. Then she tripped or someone knocked into her and she fell down into the mass of bodies.

"JoBell!" I called.

"I got you!" Becca shouted, ducking down after her.

I leaned close to Sweeney and spoke quietly. "I have to get her out of there."

"Get on the bus," he said. "We'll get her."

"No way, man. This is my responsibility." I pushed through the line of our guys and rushed toward JoBell. "Excuse me! Excuse me!" I tried to wedge my way through the press.

A man with short, ragged red hair and the scraggly beginnings of a beard shoved people to the side. A couple reporters fell to the ground. A big camera broke on the cement, but the guy had made an opening. JoBell and Becca stood and ran through it to reach me.

"Thanks," I said to the redhead, already moving to the bus with both arms around the girls.

He wrinkled his nose in disgust and pushed me back into my guys. JoBell screamed. I risked a look to make sure she was okay. "Get on the bus!" I shouted. She shook her head and tried to stay with me. "Sweeney, get her out of here."

"Come on, Jo." Becca took her arm and pulled her onto the bus.

The redhead reached inside his light jacket. "Hey, Wright! This is for Allison!" He pulled out a .38 snub-nosed revolver.

"Gun!" Sweeney shouted. He pushed me past our linemen onto the steps in the bus. Brad grabbed me by my belt and shoved me up near the driver's seat. Norm the bus driver ducked. Cheerleaders screamed and hid down in the seats. I stood up to protect JoBell and Becca in the aisle, and the man pointed the gun at me through the front windows.

Then Cal tackled him, and the gun went flying. The man hit the pavement hard on his back. Cal cocked his right arm back and brought his big fist crashing down. I could hear the crack as the punch landed and the man's head hit the cement. A thick stream of dark red blood arched back when Cal brought his fist up again. His eyes were wide, his teeth bared, his face wrinkled in pure, shaking-hot anger.

I ran down the bus steps to try to help, but TJ blocked me, pushing me back up. "Out of my way!" I said.

"You don't want to be out here!" TJ said through gritted teeth. "You want to fight me about this? Fine. But you'll only make everything worse by coming out here."

JoBell stepped up behind me and grabbed my shoulders. "Stay here."

Coach Shiratori, Coach Devins, Brad, Dylan, and Randy all grabbed Cal and pulled him back toward the bus door. Cal accidentally smeared more blood all over his face when he tried to wipe the splatters away. Red splotches dotted his white T-shirt. He yelled at all the cameras, "You come after my friends, you get the same! Just leave us alone."

A small fleet of police cars tore onto the scene, and then dozens of cops were pushing people back. The first cop pointed at Shiratori. "Coach, get your players onto the bus!"

We moved quickly into our seats. Sheriff Crow came up the stairs and stood by the bus driver. "Danny Wright? Are you okay? I'm sorry we were late getting here."

"I'm good, Sheriff," I called from my seat in the far back.

"No." Crow shook his head. "Let's not have you sitting all the way in the back next to that big window in the emergency exit door. Come up here and sit in the middle."

I closed my eyes for a moment, wishing this was all a bad dream, that none of these precautions were necessary. Then I stood and limped up the narrow lane toward the front of the bus. Timmy Macer gave up his seat behind Samantha Monohan.

Sam wiped tears from her eyes. "I'm glad you're okay."

"Listen up," said Crow. "I'm sorry this all happened tonight. We might have to ask some of you questions about the gunman, but right now I want to get this bus moving. You'll have a police escort all the way back to Freedom Lake, so don't worry. We'll keep you safe, I promise. Does anyone need any immediate medical attention?"

Cal held his left hand up. Our athletic trainer, Jaclyn Martinez, was in the middle of bandaging his right one. She'd cleaned all the blood off his face. Crow raised his eyebrows at him. "No, I'm fine," Cal said. "But . . . the other guy, is he . . . you know?"

"Don't worry, son," said Crow. "He's busted up pretty good, but he'll live. We have him in custody, and we've recovered the weapon. That was quick thinking. Good work. Okay? Let's get this thing rolling!" He stepped down out of the bus, and old Norm reached out a shaking hand to pull the lever that closed the folding doors.

In a few minutes the bus was finally moving, the lights and sirens from police cars leading and following us. Other squad cars moved to block traffic at intersections, so we rolled through a red light on our way out of town.

I called Mom to let her know I was okay in case she'd been watching the news. She warned me that reporters were everywhere outside the house. After I calmed her down and said good-bye, I sat in the dark next to JoBell, her head on my shoulder and her hands in mine. Nobody said anything the whole way home. I listened to the howl of the sirens and the sniffles from some of the cheerleaders and tried to ignore the faint sound of the news reports from people's comms.

Football was my thing. Looking forward to it was half of what had kept me going through basic training. The thrill of the game and that awesome feeling I got when I was with my team — that's how I'd been holding on to normal life since that night in Boise. Now that was fading fast.

Randytron: 17 y.o. kid sent on riot control? No wonder it all went bad. #angryamerica #BoB

16 hours ago   Reply - Shout Out

MichiganMan: @Randytron 17 y.o. kids are all ID Guard has left after Pres. deployed so many ID troops. #BoB

15 hours ago   Reply - Shout Out

Chrissykins: Tony Stein & Daniel Wright are murderers! Arrest them now #occupy #BoB

4 hours ago   Reply - Shout Out

JASON FELLER ★ ★ ☆ ☆ ☆

If you don't stand in support of Daniel Wright and Tony Stein, you're sick and unAmerican! Wright is only 17. What would any of you have done if you were 17 and stuck in that situation? The protestors deserved to be shot. If you disagree, you deserve to be shot too!

★ ☆ ☆ ☆ ☆ This Post's Star Average 1.17   [Star Rate][Comment]   46 minutes ago

DESEREE DILSEY ★ ★ ★ ★ ☆

People who don't agree with you deserve to be shot? Your sick.

★ ★ ★ ★ ★ This Comment's Star Average 4.95   [Star Rate]   40 minutes ago

AMIE ROBLIN ★ ★ ★ ★ ☆

I support the troops, including most of the guys at the Battle of Boise. If some of them did wrong, we need to know. That's why we need an investigation. To find the truth! Threatening to shoot people doesn't help anyone!

★ ★ ★ ★ ☆ This Comment's Star Average 4.25   [Star Rate]   39 minutes ago

MIKE BROWN ★ ★ ★ ☆ ☆

Is anyone else sick of all the news coverage of this stupid Idaho thing? 24 hours a day of people talking about a situation that never changes. There are other things happening in the rest of the world.

This Comment's Star Average Unrated   [Star Rate]   52 seconds ago

ᐱ—• *grossly irresponsible move on the part of the administration. Even from the sketchy available video coverage of the Battle of Boise, we can tell there were more than two shooters. And it is about impossible for these two soldiers to have injured and killed so many people on their own in the limited time they had. What does the president hope to accomplish by releasing the names of the alleged shooters? Mob justice? I'm afraid that's what he might get.* •—ᐱ

ᐱ—• *Police have not yet released the identity of the gunman who attacked Daniel Wright, and there is no word on what charges will be filed against him or if charges will be filed against Wright's eighteen-year-old friend who beat the alleged gunman. The White House released a statement condemning, quote, "vigilante justice."* •—ᐱ

ᐱ—• *Calvin Riccon, believed to be one of Daniel Wright's best friends, can be seen clearly in the footage brutally assaulting the gunman long after the gunman was subdued. The would-be shooter survived the incident, but it does raise questions: Was Wright influenced by his incredibly violent friend, and could that influence have caused him to open fire on that horrible night last month?* •—ᐱ

ᐱ—• *A lot of the residents of Freedom Lake have been reluctant to talk to the press, so it has been difficult to find someone who might offer some insights into what kind of person Daniel Wright is, but I'm here in Portland, Oregon, with a CNN exclusive interview with Bill Mann, a former classmate of Wright's. Bill, you were in school with Daniel Wright. What can you tell us about your experiences with him?"*

"I went to school with him through third and fourth grades when I was living with my dad in Freedom Lake. I'd say he was a good guy for the most part. We all used to get together to play Army with toy guns."

"I see. Were you close to Wright?"

"It was a long time ago. I remember we got into some kind of argument over toys or something, and he was kind of mean to me after that, but I wouldn't —"

"So he bullied you? He was a bully?"

"He wasn't a bully. We were kids. I probably did something mean to him too."

"I know this is tough, Bill. Lots of times victims of bullying blame themselves —"

"I'm not a victim. I just meant —"

"Thank you for telling us about this, Bill. So there you have it. Daniel Wright playing warlike games at a young age, possibly making him more prone toward violence, and we now know that he has a history of bullying. The question remains, how did that history cause him to bully the people that fateful night in Boise? More, when Adam Coleman Twenty-four Seven continues." •⁓

The mob of press waiting for us back at the high school was so big, it made the group at Bonners Ferry look like chicken change. The bus could hardly get into the parking lot with the sea of news vans, photographers, and reporters in the way. Plenty of parents were wedged in with their cars running, probably terrified after the shooting attempt, waiting to pick up their children and get them out of there. The sheriff and a bunch of other police started clearing an area between the bus and the school so that we could get in the building to put our stuff away.

"Okay, everybody, we're going to get off the bus and run inside," Coach said. "If your parents are here, we'll have them drive their cars up one at a time between the bus and the school. Just let me talk to them on your comm and I'll fix it with the police." He flashed a weak smile. "We'll get you out of this. I promise."

An endless strobe of camera flashes nearly blinded us as we ran from the bus to the boys' locker room. It was weird, all of us, including the cheerleaders plus JoBell and Becca, being packed in there, but Coach wanted us to stay together for safety. We all stowed our gear and then everybody started making comm calls.

JoBell slipped her arm around me and rested her head on my shoulder. "It stinks in here," she said.

"*Beautiful young people are accidents of nature, but beautiful old people are works of art,*" said Digi-Eleanor. "*Speaking of beautiful old people, JoBell, your father is trying to reach you for a voice call. When you're done with that, there are many updates on the Battle of Boise story you've been following."*

"Dad already sent me half a dozen texts asking if I was okay," JoBell said. "He's probably out there waiting to drive me home, but I want to go with you." She squeezed my hand. "Eleanor, go ahead with the call." She spoke into her comm. "Hi, Dad. No, I'm fine. He's fine too. We're all okay. Yeah . . . yeah. Well, I was hoping to get a ride home from . . . What?" JoBell was getting upset. "It can't be that bad. That was just one crazy guy." I put my hand on her arm. "Hang on a sec," she said to her dad. She looked up at me. "Yeah?"

I leaned close to JoBell and spoke quietly. "Hey, just go with your dad tonight."

"But I —"

"I'm going to go on my own, try to draw away some of the media. Once I'm gone, the crowd will die down here, and everybody else will be able to get home." I looked around. Coach was busy trying to sort out what to do next. Becca had gone to her locker to get some books, Cal was messing with his gear, and Sweeney was chatting up the cheerleaders. This was my only chance to make a move like this. Lucky for me, senior football players always got the best parking spots by the outside door to the locker room.

"Danny, you can't," said JoBell. "You'll never make it out of the parking lot."

"The Beast can make it through anything." I kissed her. "You like watching the news? Watch this." I took my keys out of my pocket and ran for the door. Coach and Sweeney called from behind me, but I didn't stop.

As soon as I came out of the locker room, a million cameras flashed again. "That's him!" "Daniel Wright, can you answer a few questions for us?" "Is football an outlet for the same aggressive tendencies that made you fire on the protestors?" "Can you tell us the names of other soldiers who were in Boise that night?" "Did the announcement in the media about your involvement in the Boise massacre affect your performance in tonight's game?"

"No comment!" I shouted, elbowing one reporter to the side and pushing two ahead of me like I was stuck in a mad stupid football game. Finally I reached the door to my truck. When I was behind the wheel, I tried to close the door, but one guy stood in the way. I put my foot on his chest and shoved him back enough so I could close and lock myself in. Firing up the engine and shutting off the muffler, I revved her up about as loud as she'd go. A few of the vultures actually backed off. I pulled ahead, driving over the little cement tire barrier and onto the grass in the area the police had cleared.

Then I turned toward the street, slowing down when I reached the crowd of reporters. I let the Beast idle-drive ahead, creeping forward to force them to move or be run over. Quite a few looked like they were going to try to stand their ground, but when they figured out I wasn't stopping, when the Beast was physically pushing them back like a bulldozer, they moved out of the way. At least three-quarters of the media people rushed to their vehicles as soon as they realized I was making my escape.

When the Beast bumped down off the curb onto the street, I hammered the gas, turning my muffler back on now that I wanted to be quieter and ditch the press. I'd have to do more than that to escape, though. At least a dozen news vans and cars were chasing me.

"Hey, partner, you got yerself a video . . . call coming in . . . from JoBell. Do you want —"

"Hank, shut up and put it on-screen!" I shouted at my comm on the passenger seat.

JoBell appeared on-screen. "Danny, you cleared out most of the media at the school. It will still be a pain to get out of here, but we *can all manage it now. The only problem is you're never going to ditch those reporters. Check this out."*

An insert image popped up in the lower right corner. It was a live feed from CNN, an aerial shot of the Beast rolling down the street. I tapped my brakes to slow-and-go at a stop sign. Two seconds later, the brake lights on the Blazer in the video lit up.

"You've got a drone tailing you. You might be able to lose it if you turn right onto West Street and then cut through Harper's Field. There are a ton of evergreen trees there that might hide you. And shut your lights off! You know the town!"

"That's my girl," I said, doing as she said. She was right. The drone lost me when it was forced to go above the trees. The CNN feed switched to a street view from one of the vans behind me, but when I jumped the curb and cut through the vacant lot JoBell had mentioned, I started to put some distance between me and the camera.

"That did it!" JoBell said.

At the back of the lot, a rocky slope covered in scrub brush stood between me and Third Street at the top of the hill. I stopped just long enough to shift into four-wheel drive. About four vans had driven into the field after me, their reporters and cameras already dismounting.

"What are you doing?" JoBell said through the comm.

"Let's see these bastards follow me now." I patted the Beast's dash. "Come on, girl!" I hit the gas and she roared as she drove right up the slope, throwing back rocks and dirt toward the reporters. At the top of the hill I stopped, switched back to two-wheel drive, and hooked a right onto Third Street.

JoBell laughed on the comm. *"You are seriously incredible. I think some of whatever your truck's kicking up actually hit one of the NBC cameras. But listen, I'm watching about six feeds right now,* and a bunch are broadcasting from the front of your house. You better head down the back alley and, I don't know, park in the backyard or something."

I headed for home, taking the most stupid indirect route to get there to keep the reporters off balance. "You really think they won't be out back?"

"No way to tell. There has to be fewer of them back there, though. It's your best shot."

She was right. When I drove down the alley behind my house, all the reporters' lights made it look like daylight was coming from the front yard.

A dark shadow crossed the alley in front of me and I hit my brakes. Then more lights lit the alley. More cameras and reporters. I drove around the reporter I'd almost hit, and sped up to drive through my yard. For a moment I thought about parking by the back door and heading in, but I didn't want to leave the Beast exposed out where anyone could mess with her. If I parked in the driveway in front of our single-stall garage, at least she would be protected on two sides, and I could keep a better eye on her from my bedroom window. I drove across the lawn around the back of the garage — too late, I thought, to save my mom's flower garden.

Around front, the press were pointing fingers and cameras at me like my truck moving was the most important story in the world. Some scrambled out of the way as if they were scared I was about to charge down the driveway to the street. Good. They deserved to be frightened. "Thanks," I said to JoBell. "I wish we could have hung out tonight. This is all —"

"Stop talking to me and get in the house! Don't sit there on camera giving the next crazy a chance to take a shot at you."

"I love you," I said.

"I love you too. Now get inside and take care of your mother."

I tapped out of the call and ignored the questions from the reporters on the street and sidewalk as I pushed my way to the front door and slipped inside.

"Danny!" Mom threw her arms around me as soon as I came in. "Danny, oh my gosh, Danny, are you okay? I saw everything! That man tried to kill you. The press has been after you!"

I locked the door. "Mom, why was the door unlocked? It's not safe. It could have been anyone barging in right now."

Mom pointed to the screen. CBS had video on like a two-second delay, showing our front door slamming behind me. "I knew it was you. I watched you come in. Danny, what are we going to do?"

I guided her to her chair. "I'm fine, Mom. Everything's fine. Living room screen, turn off!" The screen went dark. I flopped down on the couch, reaching out to take her hand. "It's okay, Mom. We're going to be okay." I had said these same things to calm my mother countless times over the years. Tonight, I needed to hear it just as much. "Let's leave our screens off, so we don't have to deal with that."

"They found my number somehow. Three different networks called, and call waiting was beeping the whole time. I finally shut my comm off."

Mom's COMMPAD was an even older and slower model than mine. It was still running a first-gen digital assistant. Pretty useless. I pulled my comm from my pocket. If they had already found Mom's number, they'd find mine soon enough. "We'll get you a new comm," I said to Mom. "It might be expensive, but it will be worth it. We'll see if we can get you a new comm number too. That might throw them off."

"What will we do about all the reporters outside?" she said.

"We won't talk to them. We'll do our best to live our normal lives."

"Hey, Mr. Big Shot, you got a video call . . . request coming in from CNN. Wait! Now MSNBC wants to talk to you too. Also . . . another . . . two more requests from —"

"Hank, be quiet!" I shouted. How had they found my number? "Hank, block all calls and messages from anyone not in my contacts list or from anyone I have not sent a call to myself."

"That's a shootin' tootin' idea, partner! Should I leave . . . a message for blocked callers?"

Shootin' tootin'? What did that even mean? I shook my head. "Tell them, 'No comment.'"

"You got it!"

I turned to face Mom, who still looked worried. "We won't talk to the press. We'll tell everyone we know not to talk to the press." Mom nodded and reached out to squeeze my hand. I looked around the living room. All our lamps were off, but so much light flooded in through our thin drapes from the media setup outside that we could easily find our way around. It would be tough sleeping with all this going on. "I might buy some new curtains, or even hang blankets over the windows. I'm sorry it's like this, Mom. We'll get through this. I promise."

The leeches from the press stayed out there all night and still crawled all over Saturday morning. Over a dozen news vans with tall satellite antennas raised above them were parked on the street outside our house. At four a.m., reporters stood on the sidewalk, probably starting so early so their pieces could air first thing on the East Coast. What could the reporters be talking about? Were they standing there saying, "This is the home of Danny Wright, who you heard about last night. Absolutely nothing is happening. Wright hasn't said anything to us"? Why couldn't they get bored with the nonstory and get the hell out of here? I slept on and off until seven, when I gave up and went downstairs.

"Danny, I don't like this," Mom said, coming up behind me where I was peeking through a tiny gap in the blinds. Dark circles had formed under her bloodshot eyes. She was trying to be strong, but I doubt she got any sleep at all. "I've been thinking. Maybe you shouldn't try to go on with normal life like you said last night. Maybe you should stay inside. Hearing about that shooter nearly gave me a heart attack. Now with reporters following you everywhere, how will you be able to look out for someone else who wants to hurt you?" She put her hand on my shoulder, and I could feel her trembling.

"Mom, that was one wacko guy last night. They arrested him. I can't hide away from this forever. Anyway, I'll have to leave the house on Monday at least. I can't miss school." Actually, missing school sounded great, but all that education crap was important to Mom, so I figured I'd play that card. What I left out was that before the world had taken another turn for the crazy at the game, JoBell, Becca, the guys, and me had agreed to spend time together this afternoon for a little rifle target practice and then the rodeo. It was going to be our attempt at getting life back to normal, and the hell if I was going to let these reporters stop me. If I could calm Mom down about me going out, I could tell her that I was working late tonight. Then I just had to figure out a way to ditch the media. I had an idea about that.

"It will be fine," I said to Mom, making sure I looked relaxed. "I have to go to work. It's no problem. Trust me."

She took a deep breath. "Be careful."

"I always am." I hugged her quickly, and then headed upstairs to my room, punching up a vid call with Sheriff Nathan Crow on the way.

"*Danny!*" said the sheriff when he first appeared on-screen. He was in his squad car. "*How you holding up? The phone at the station is ringing nonstop with all these reporters. I went out on patrol to get away from it.*"

"I'm fine. A little sore from the game last night. They really had it in for me after they heard the news."

He pressed his lips together. *"I'm sorry about that. Wish I knew how the Fed found out about you. Anyway, how can I help you?"*

"It's like you said, with these reporters. The street in front of my house is almost completely choked with news vans. I need to get to work, but I don't think they'll let me through."

"Right. Don't you worry about it. I've been working on getting the mayor and council to change your street to no parking either side so we can start towing their vehicles, but until then, I'll take care of the press." He reached for something offscreen, and I heard a siren wail. *"I'm on my way."*

A short time later, four squad cars pulled up.

"Danny, what's going on?" Mom shouted.

"It's okay, Mom. I called the sheriff asking for some help getting away from the press. Everything's fine. Safe, even. You can relax."

At the front door, I put my hand on the doorknob to head out, but Mom stopped me, pulling me into a warm hug. Neither of us spoke for a long time, and when she finally let me go, she locked her gaze with mine. I nodded, took a deep breath, then pushed open the door and headed out to the Beast.

"Daniel Wright! Can I ask you a few questions?" said a woman.

"Can I get you to make one statement?" said another.

As much as I hurt from the punishment of last night's game, I kicked my pace up to a jog. The reporters followed, but were stopped by a wall of police officers who rushed up to block their way. When I reached my truck, I smiled. He'd done it. Nathan Crow and his men had the press all boxed in. I was free to go.

Then a two-foot-square black box with a small propeller spinning above it rose up into the air from one of the news vans and flew over to my truck, hovering twenty feet in the air. Another camera drone. Great. Crow could never stop that.

"Someone want to land that flying robot, please?" the sheriff called out to the news crowd.

"We have every right to fly our camera," said a reporter. "The people deserve the news!"

Crow spun around and pulled his .45 from his holster. He aimed and fired eight heavy rounds into the drone. Sparks and smoke burst from it before it crashed to the street. He holstered his weapon and then faced the crowd. "And this boy deserves his privacy."

He waved me on my way. I took my cue, climbed up into the Beast, called Mom to let her know what the gunshots were, and drove off to work. News vans were following me in seconds.

The street in front of the shop was almost as packed as the one outside my house. If only we could get this much traffic from people who needed car repairs. As I approached, leading the line of other news vehicles, reporters and cameramen stirred to life. I slowed down. The junky old school bus that had been sitting at the side of the shop for years had been driven or towed across the driveway to block the street view of the bay doors. I drove up the first part of the driveway to the sidewalk and honked at the reporters who blocked my way, pulling very slowly forward until they moved. Then I parked in the space between the bus and the shop.

"Daniel, can we please have a quick word with you?" "Does the National Rifle Association sticker in the front window of your shop office mean that you or David Schmidt are members of the NRA, and was the shooting a statement for gun rights?" "Can you describe your relationship with JoBell Linder?"

I stopped for a moment and almost confronted the reporter who'd asked about JoBell. They better leave her out of this. But I thought if I said anything, it would be like dumping gas on a fire.

I entered the shop by the office door. The bay doors were closed, which was unusual in good weather. The radio was playing *Best of This Week on the Buzz Ellison Show*. "Schmidty?" I called out. No one answered. The crusty old coffeemaker that he used every day but never cleaned had a full hot pot on. His coffee mug with the phrase "How About a Nice Cup of Shut the Hell Up" on the side sat half empty on his desk.

I touched the cup. Still warm. Where was he? Sometimes on a Saturday morning he'd go to the Coffee Corner to eat way too much bacon and eggs. But as psycho as he was about the electric bill, he wouldn't take off and leave the radio and all the lights on.

"Schmidty?" I checked in the parts room. Nothing.

Back in the corner of the shop, I sat on his desk. Where was he?

Outside, the reporters kept shouting questions from the sidewalk. One asked something about the federal government.

That's when it hit me. I stood up and went to the wall to grab a heavy wrench. What if the Fed had come looking for Schmidty? Would they use him to get to me? Why not? If the reporters had figured out I worked here, the government easily could. There had to be half a dozen safety and environmental regulation violations in this place. That would be all they needed to bring him in.

If federal agents were still in the area, maybe they were watching the shop. They could be coming for me any second. Standing there in the middle of the bay, I tightened my grip on the big wrench, ready for anything.

"What the hell are you doing?" a gravelly voice came from behind me.

I spun around with the wrench in both hands, cocked back like a baseball bat. "Schmidty." I sighed. He scratched his stubbled chin and flicked ash from his cigarette into the rusted coffee can on his desk. "Where were you?"

"You gonna hit me?" he asked.

"What? Oh! No . . . I . . ." I lowered the wrench and tried to act casual, like it was no big deal that I was getting ready for a fight in the middle of the shop. "I'll put this back."

He rolled his eyes. "Bad enough I got all these pricks from the media up my ass, now I almost get brained in my own shop. Come on. I'll show you where I was." He led me toward the back of the building. A brand-new closet had been built over the floor hatch that led to the basement. It was finished with drywall and painted and everything. There were even brownish grease stains in various places.

"You built this?" I said. "How did it get dirty so fast?"

"No, it built itself." He coughed and then cleared his throat. "I smeared on some grease so it would blend in. Don't want it to look brand-new. It would stand out too much." He opened the heavy metal closet door. Inside, several old one-piece overalls and a few coats hung from a bar. Tools and some junk parts littered a high shelf.

"I don't get it. Why would we need a new closet?"

"Damn it, but you are pretty stupid sometimes." He shook the clothes on their hangers. "This shit's all just camouflage. See?" He bent down — too quickly to spare me the sight of his nasty ass crack, unfortunately — and pulled up on a metal ring in the front corner of the floor, opening the hatch to reveal the steps down into the basement. "It won't look like a trapdoor if it's the entire floor of the closet. Now come on." He breathed heavily as he walked down the stairs.

"What?" I followed him. "Why'd you have to do all that to hide this gross —" I stopped.

The dank old basement that all my life had been filled with junk, spilled automotive fluids, and wastepaper was gone. Instead, the place was totally clean. The floor had been swept, mopped even, and the cobwebs had been brushed away. The stained, dented cardboard boxes and oily car parts that had been stored down here on metal shelves had disappeared. In their place at the other end of the basement were six green Army cots complete with fresh bedrolls. In a corner near that, a cookstove with its own propane tank and four reserve tanks was set up next to a small wooden table. A big black safe stood in the corner of the room.

Schmidty slapped his hand on one of the metal shelves. "I'm still chasing down some deals on more shelf-stable food, MREs, and survival packs and stuff. Prices on all that are way up." He pointed his cigarette at the hatch we came down. "You can lock the closet door from the inside. Plus I reinforced the hatch with some heavy-duty locks. If anyone figures out the floor of the closet is a door, they'll have a hell of a time getting it open." He took a drag on his cigarette. "Oh, and I installed an air circulation and filtration system. I still have to run a duct underground so the vent can come out of that slag heap in the vacant lot next door. Brand-new toilet under the stairs, hooked up to the sewer and everything, but if the water supply gets cut off, there's a bucket version. When this place is ready, you should be able to hide out here for months if you need to."

I tried a joke. "And when the toilet bucket's full?"

Schmidty wasn't biting. "If the damned reporters ever leave, a guy I know, a guy I *trust*, is going to help me dig and reinforce a tunnel to the slag heap. That way you won't be trapped down here if something happens upstairs. Plus you'll be able to crawl out and dump your shit in the creek back there."

Not long ago, if Schmidty had shown me all of this, I would have thought he was turning into one of those survivalist nuts — the guys who spent fortunes and way too much time building bomb shelters and preparing for the end of the world. But after the gunman last night, Specialist Stein's arrest, and everything else that had happened, I was glad to know there was a place like this for me.

"There's more," Schmidty said. "Come on."

"Where you going?"

"Just follow me, damn it," he said, trailing a small cloud of smoke after him.

He led me to the large black safe in the back. The thing was at least four feet tall, with an old-fashioned spinning dial combination lock and a big steel lever. "What's in there?"

He looked at me, annoyed, then leaned forward to examine the dial closely, rotating it so far to the right, all the way around to the left, then a short move to the right. With a grunt, he pulled the lever to the left and yanked open the door.

Schmidty reached in and took out a rifle like my M4 at the armory, but longer. He pointed the barrel at the floor and pulled back the charging handle, checking to make sure there was no round in the chamber. Then he handed the weapon to me. I immediately checked it the same way. One of the holiest commandments in the Army was that the very first step upon receiving a weapon was to clear it.

"An M16?" I said.

"What?" Schmidty bent to reach down into the safe. I closed my eyes, wondering why he even bothered to wear a belt. He stood up and slapped six fully loaded, thirty-round magazines on top of the safe. "No, check the fire selector lever. No auto or burst. It's an AR15."

"Aren't those illegal?"

"The federal government claims it has the authority to take our guns away because the Constitution gives it power over interstate commerce. Idaho is one of a bunch of states with a law that says that as long as the weapon is manufactured, purchased, and remains inside the state, then interstate commerce and federal gun control laws don't apply. This beauty was built down near Boise only last year." He leaned on the safe. "Besides, what's legal or not is starting to matter less and less. So listen. I know you still have your father's nine mil. You got ammo?"

I shrugged. "Maybe one fifteen-round mag for the Beretta. I don't know. It's my dad's. I'm not old enough to have it or buy anything for it."

"Here." He pushed a box of fifty nine-mil rounds into my hands.

"What am I supposed to do with this? I don't think —"

"No, you're not thinking, and that's your problem. He shook his head. "Go down to Post Falls or Coeur d'Alene tonight and buy four more."

"But I'm not old enough."

"Yes, you are. You can't own a handgun or the ammo for it until you're eighteen, but you can buy the magazines."

"Why would I want magazines if I can't —"

"This isn't a damned game!" I jumped a little. Schmidty yelled all the time, but usually at the radio or some frustrating car part he was working on. "Today everybody's still pussyfooting around. How long before the bullets start flying for real? How long before you're gonna need some real protection?"

"This is insane," I said. "It's out of control."

"And that's why you need to keep that Beretta loaded at home. Keep it in your closet or under your bed or some place you can get to it quickly." He grabbed the AR15 from my hands. "People are out of work and pissed off. They don't know if the retirement funds they've invested in their whole lives will be worth a damn. They can barely afford gas or food for their families. Now Idaho and the Fed are at each other's throats. Folks are scared and looking for someone to blame. That man who tried to shoot you last night blames you.

Others may blame you for the shootings or who knows what else. You need to be ready."

"This" — he held up the rifle and then put it back into the safe — "will be down here." He pulled a piece of paper from his pocket and handed it over. A set of three two-digit numbers was written on it in ink. "This is the combination. You get yourself in trouble and you need a weapon, you know where to find it. You need a safe place to stay" — he swept his hand to indicate the basement — "you can come here."

"Thanks, but I don't think I'll need it. I mean, I hope I won't."

Schmidty scratched his big belly. "You believe that, you're an idiot." He took a drag on his cigarette.

I ran my hands along a row of cases of MREs. There weren't even this many rations in my whole armory. "I know this all looks really bad, but this whole crisis or whatever they're calling it is a bunch of political crap. This is America. We've worked things out before. We will this time." I only partly believed what I was saying.

Schmidty put everything but the nine-mil shells back into the safe and locked it. He went to what I guess was the kitchen area and groaned as he sat down on a metal folding chair next to the table. "You know, the assholes in DC are always saying that America loves peace. But I'm fifty-seven years old, and even in my lifetime, this country has been at war for all but . . ." He looked up and squinted his eyes as if trying to figure it out. "All but about twenty-eight years. Half my life. Six different wars. And I'm not even counting when we sent troops to Panama or Bosnia, or when we send our drones or missiles flying in to kill people in Pakistan, Syria, Yemen, Somalia, and half a dozen other places. If they're so committed to peace, but have failed so miserably the last fifty years, the last *century*, what makes you think they're going to figure a way out of this mess without fighting?"

That was different, I thought. America had been forced into all those wars. Things had been wrong somewhere in the world and our soldiers went to fix it. This was the United States. My squad had screwed up and fired in Boise. None of what happened meant that there had to be any fighting. "Things will get better," I said at last. They had to get better. "You'll see."

Schmidty shook his head and stubbed out his cigarette on the bottom of his boot. "Come on. We have some work to do. I want to put some improvements in on the Beast. Reinforce the body and frame."

"What?"

He stood up. "Will you just let me do this? What I gotta do will take a few days, probably, so in the meantime you can borrow my Dodge Stratus."

"Oh, come on, Schmidty, I'll be lucky if that old rust bucket even starts. It has no balls."

"Yeah, but it ain't been on the news like your bright red Blazer. You might trick a few reporters by switching vehicles. More important, I have to fix up your truck in case you're messing with your girl in there some night and another crazy shooter shows up. You may think *you're* invincible, but at least let me help make JoBell safe."

I hated arguing with Schmidty. Worse, I hated when he was right.

⌁—● You're listening to Weekend on National Public Radio. I'm Renae Matthews. By calling a special weekend session of the Idaho state legislature, Governor Montaine has demonstrated his strong support in his own state government, and his skill at quickly passing legislation. Montaine's Freedom from Drones Act goes into effect at the end of the month and outlaws the use of unmanned aircraft in Idaho airspace except by the Idaho military and law enforcement communities, and then only with a warrant and for very specific reasons. The American Civil Liberties Union has long advocated for such privacy measures, but an ACLU spokesperson says she worries about the implications of this law in light of the Idaho Crisis. For more on this story ●—⌁

⌁—● here in the Coffee Corner, a popular café here in Daniel Wright's hometown. I'm with retired farmer and lifelong Freedom Lake resident Herb Rebley. Herb, thank you for agreeing to talk with us."

"I didn't. I'm trying to enjoy my morning cup of coffee. You just sat down at my table and put that camera in my face."

"Oh. Well . . . Can we ask you a few questions about Daniel Wright?"

"You can ask whatever you want."

"How long have you known him?"

"Known him all his life."

. . .

"And what can you tell us about him?"

"What do you want to know?"

"What kind of person is he?"

"Good."

. . .

"Why do you think he fired on the protestors in Boise?"

"Don't reckon I know that he did. You don't know either."

"I see. Well. Is there anything else you'd like to say about this?"

"I'd like you people to leave us alone, to stop asking so many questions, and to leave Freedom Lake."

"Back to you, Tom." •⌁

⌁• here at CBS have had a look at Wright's FriendStar page and found at least one post in which he bragged about receiving an expert rifle marksmanship badge at Army basic training. So we know he is an excellent shot, certainly capable of shooting many people at Boise. He also has a number of violent action movies in his Amazon wish list, including fantasies like The Avengers III and more realistically violent movies about the military and war. Has Daniel Wright embraced a culture of death? What bearing did this have on him at the Battle of Boise? •⌁

⌁• This exclusive KREM 2 video footage was recorded earlier from the KREM 2 Eye in the Sky. Here you see Daniel Wright opening the door to his vehicle. Now, please excuse the crude picture. The shakes and sparks you're seeing are the result of Sheriff Nathan Crow, who fired eight shots to destroy our cam drone. This video was recovered from the wreckage, and our computer experts recon-structed it digitally. The sheriff's office hasn't returned our phone calls for •⌁

⌁• Most people we've talked to have had only good things to say about Wright, saying he's a nice, clean-cut athlete and something of a cowboy. But some of Daniel's classmates, who spoke to our reporters on condition of anonymity, said that everything might not be as perfect as it seems. There are reports of a rivalry between Wright and his classmate Travis Jones, who is rumored to have a crush on Wright's girlfriend, JoBell Linder. Travis at least frequently posts on JoBell's FriendStar page. Travis, thank you for taking the time to speak with me. Is it true that you and Miss Linder have had a secret relationship? Could Daniel Wright's jealousy have had an effect on his actions in Boise?"

"Absolutely not! JoBell and I are friends."

"But the rivalry between you and Daniel Wright —"

"Danny and I are friends. We're both starting wide receivers on the football team. I threw a block to help him score a touchdown only last Friday. You people need to leave us all alone."

"But, Travis, if I could just ask . . . And he's stormed off in an angry rage. As you can see, emotions are running high all over town. April Lindelson, ABC News, Freedom Lake, Idaho. •⌇

FOURTEEN

Later that afternoon, JoBell called and made me delete about everything I'd ever posted online. Then she walked me through closing out my FriendStar, Shout Out, Amazon, and about every other online account I ever had. She said the news was using all that stuff to make me seem bad. At least I didn't have to delete my playlists. Still, the whole process took forever.

After I'd practically gone Amish, I left the shop in Schmidty's stupid brown Stratus, driving across the grass through back lots to come out on a different street. The car smelled like a nasty old ashtray, but switching vehicles threw the media off for a little bit, until their curiosity about any vehicle leaving the shop made them catch on. I tried to outrun them, but when I laid on the gas in the pussy four-cylinder Stratus, the engine would whine real loud as the car made a pathetic attempt to speed up.

"Come on, you piece of shit!" I slapped the dusty dashboard as I headed toward Becca's, whipping tight corners on streets I knew better than the media did. When I finally reached the highway that led out to Becca's farm, I thought I'd be free, but they followed me out there too, snapping photographs as they passed me in Schmidty's weak, slow, worthless car. Finally, I lost them on Becca's gravel driveway, closing the gate behind me and leaving my pursuers back on the road.

Becca's family owned a ton of land, the perfect place to take a break from all the cameras and reporters. Years ago, her dad had bulldozed a berm in the back wooded part of the property and set a plank up with an empty fifty-gallon barrel under each end. All we had to do was stick a few bottles and cans on the plank and we had the perfect shooting range.

When I arrived, JoBell was getting ready to shoot her dad's awesome semiautomatic Springfield Armory M1A Scout Squad rifle that he'd bought back before assault rifles were outlawed. The thing had a twenty-round magazine and fired a 7.62-millimeter round, the same type of bullet used in the Army's M240 machine gun. Becca and Sweeney sat on a log about a dozen yards behind JoBell. Becca had disassembled and was cleaning the parts of her dad's .45. We were just missing Cal, who was at work at the lake.

I stood off by myself, leaning against a boulder. I knew what my friends were trying to do in insisting we come out here today, and I was grateful that they cared, but as much as I loved shooting and rodeo, I doubted their efforts to get us back to our normal lives were going to work.

"What's the matter, Wright?" Sweeney said. "You love shooting. We thought this would cheer you up."

"Would you all shut up?" JoBell shouted back at us, keeping her rifle aimed downrange. "I'm trying to concentrate."

Becca smiled, but didn't look up from her work. "Like you need us to be quiet so you can shoot."

From the standing position, JoBell fired off five quick shots, and one-two-three-four-five, cans went flying off the plank almost all at once. She went down on one knee and fired off ten rounds with almost no hesitation. Ten bottles exploded. She lowered herself to the prone position, careful to keep the rifle out of the dirt, and quickly shot down five more cans. Then she dropped her magazine and cleared her rifle before she stood up. "We're going to need a tougher range," she said.

I clapped as JoBell took a little bow. "You're a better shot than any of my drill sergeants."

JoBell waved my compliment aside and looked down at her rifle. "Please, you all only qualified with wimpy little M4s. You need a real weapon like this baby."

"You know, for as liberal as you are, you sure do like guns," Sweeney said.

She started back to us. "Don't box my politics. Besides, even though my father and I disagree on more and more lately, we've had shooting in common since I was old enough to hold my first BB gun. We go to the range, and all our arguments fade away. There's only him, me, our weapons, and the targets." She put the rifle back in its case.

"It is not fair to ask of others what you are unwilling to do your-self. I am willing to show you some news alerts that have come in, JoBell," said Digi-Eleanor. JoBell reached for her pocket.

"Don't!" Becca said. "You promised. No news. No politics. Today it's just shooting and then the rodeo."

"Come *on*," she said. "I want to see if there are any developments about that psycho shooter last night —"

"Sorry, babe," Sweeney said, pulling a pop from the cooler. "You promised."

JoBell pressed her lips together and blew out through her nose. "Eric, you call me 'babe' one more time, and I swear I'll put a couple seven-six-two rounds through you."

Becca had the .45 back together. She carried the pistol and a mag-azine up to the shooting line and slapped the magazine in. She pulled back and released the slide to chamber a round, then widened her stance and aimed the gun with her left hand over her right to steady her shot. Firing the ten rounds in her weapon's magazine more slowly than JoBell had, Becca shredded seven cans before dropping the mag and clearing the handgun.

"Guess I need more practice," she said.

Sweeney, who never shot much, took his turn next, trying out JoBell's dad's rifle. We loaded him up with ten rounds. He hit four cans.

"You have another magazine for that rifle?" I asked JoBell.

She handed me the M1A, which I immediately cleared before she gave me a twenty-round magazine. "Good luck," she said.

I couldn't hide my grin as I walked to the firing line. This was a sweet rifle, and I hadn't gone shooting since basic training. I hoped I wasn't too rusty. Slapping in the magazine and chambering a round, I started from the standing position. I centered the front sight post on a bottle, breathed in, exhaled, *in and hold*. I squeezed the trigger and the bottle shattered. I aimed at another and fired again, missing. I might have jerked the trigger too hard that time, pulling my shot off. I focused on my shooting fundamentals again and fired, dropping another bottle. I relaxed and kept taking out cans and bottles, loving that feeling of smooth unity with the weapon, that power to hit anything.

When I fired off my last round, I listened, as I always did, for the satisfying sound of my shot echoing into the distance. Instead I heard the rough sound of helicopter blades chopping the air.

"Danny, stop!" Becca yelled, pointing up to the sky above the clearing. "We've got company."

A copter-cam drone hovered there with its camera pointed right at me.

How could I have been stupid enough to think we were free from the press? "Damn it! Why can't you just leave me alone!" I shouted.

A woman's voice rang out from a speaker on the drone. *"We'd be happy to leave you alone if you'd just answer a few questions for ABC News."*

"You've got to be kidding me," Sweeney said. "They want to do an interview via drone?"

"*I'd be happy to talk to you in person.*"

"This is private property," Becca shouted up at the machine. "Get out of here!"

"We should just shoot it down," Sweeney said quietly.

The copter-cam descended a little. "*Oh yes, please. Shoot up this drone. That would make such a great story!*"

I dropped the magazine and cleared the rifle. JoBell stepped up beside me to whisper in my ear. "They have footage of you shooting. They'll get a whole story out of that. We should get out of here."

I hated that we were in this situation, but she was right. I nodded and then held my finger over my lips. Becca and Sweeney got the message. We packed up and went back to clean and lock up the weapons at Becca's house. The copter-cam followed us the whole way.

"Maybe we should just skip the rodeo, guys," I said later while we all sat on Becca's screened-in porch. "The media will be all over it, just like with everything else."

"Come *on*, man!" Sweeney said. "Becca called the rodeo association. They aren't letting reporters on the grounds, and the canopy over the whole arena ought to keep out cam drones. It will be great. Even if the reporters do get footage, they'll have to run the story of the wholesome, all-American cowboy kid."

"Or else they'll report on the animal rights abuser," JoBell said.

Sweeney stood up from where he was sitting. "It won't be like that. This will —"

"Can we just do this?" Becca cut in. "Please? After the car chase and the guy who tried to shoot Danny last night, I need something good, something normal." She looked intently at me. "*You* need this."

Becca can be persuasive, so after the news drone had given up and flown away, we helped her get her horse ready and loaded, and then her dad drove us to the arena. If I'd had the Beast, I would have towed the horse trailer myself, but that Stratus couldn't tow so much as a Radio Flyer wagon.

Me, JoBell, Sweeney, and Mr. Wells took our seats on the wooden benches as the sun dipped below the mountains beyond the arena. Becca was back at the trailer with her horse. Sweeney and Becca had been right. The rodeo grounds were huge, and the North Idaho Rodeo Association was a private organization, so once again I got a break from the media.

The announcer came on. *"Howday, folks. We're fixin' to get started with some rip-roarin' rodeo action as soon as our cowgirls are in place for the grand entry. I want to remind you all, ladies and gentlemen, if you have not had the chance to mosey on over to Eddie's Bar-Be-Cue, you need to giddyup and git yerself some. It's the finest eatin' in all of Idahayew."*

Sweeney laughed. "Is this guy for real?"

Almost everyone I ever met in Idaho talked normal, like the people on the news or on the sitcoms. No accents. But Rick Hayes somehow managed to come up with a hick backwater voice all his own every time he announced a rodeo.

Hayes went on, *"I also want to remind everyone that this is a private club rodeo, and the NIRA asks all members of the media to report to the announcer's booth for a press pass. Any reporters or photographers working without a pass will be politely escorted from the premises. Rodeo is about family and fun, not trying to snag a story."*

I was relieved to hear that.

The grand entry started as the first girl rode in and circled the arena, holding a flag for Dinkins Family Dentistry as she galloped around the ring. The girl rode okay, but bounced a little in the saddle. This didn't bother Sweeney at all.

"She's a beauty," he said.

"Lot of muscle in the flank," Mr. Wells agreed. "Could be a good barrel horse."

"She's got a lot of jiggle in her," Sweeney said. "I like that."

Mr. Wells frowned and looked from Sweeney to the horse and back. Then he shook his head. "Eric, did I ever tell you never to date my daughter?"

Sweeney gave a little chuckle. "Several times, sir."

Mr. Wells nodded. "Good."

One girl after another rode out, each displaying a different flag for the sponsor she was promoting.

"*Ladies and gentlemen, next up is Becca Wells, carrying the beautiful dark blue flag of Idahayew, proudly displaying our state motto* Esto Perpetua, *which is Latin fer 'Let it be forever.'*"

Becca and Lightning came out of the gate and rode around the arena at a fast gallop, but unlike a lot of the other girls who bounced around and sometimes lost their hats, she rode smooth and fluid. She smiled the whole time, with her belt buckle shining and her reddish-brown hair and that big Idaho flag both fluttering in the breeze. She went through the center of the sponsor line and stopped her horse a few paces in front.

"*And Idahayew will be forever, ladies and gentlemen, no matter what problems this great state may face. Idahayew will be forever because all of us as the people of Idahayew will continue to work to make this state great. That's why we take this moment to salute all of Idahayew's brave men and women, and all of America's brave men and women who are serving in our armed forces tonight. Whether they are serving in Iran, Pakistan, or right here at home, they are fighting fer our freedom, so that we all might live our lives as we wish. They make it possible fer us to enjoy the heritage and traditions of our wonderful sport of rodeo, and so, as Miss Layna*"

Thompson enters the arena carrying Old Glory, our American flag, won't you join with me in standing and removing yer hat, as Layna's sister Laura sings fer us our national anthem."

The girl in the announcer's booth sang sweeter than I'd heard our anthem in a long time, even without music to back her up. As I listened, I wanted to get back to that pride I'd felt when I first enlisted, but the memories of Fed troops trying to arrest the governor, of being chased by the FBI, and of Schmidty's secret war bunker and all those things that he'd said kept creeping into the back of my mind.

I tried to shake off these thoughts and enjoy the rodeo. After the calf roping ended, JoBell stood up. "I'm going to see if Becca needs help getting ready."

I watched her go, admiring her butt in her cowgirl jeans.

"Hey guys." Cal sat down with a Mountain Dew in one hand and a paper plate with a massive cheeseburger in the other.

"Whoa!" Sweeney said. "Got yourself a double, big guy?"

Cal put the plate on the bench beside him. He took a swig of pop and then belched, covering his mouth with his hand. "A double is my single. Triple cheeseburger here." He took a huge bite and chewed for a while. "Big day at the lake. The boss let us all have one last flight in the seaplane. He even let me take the yoke for a little bit once we were up. Then we cleaned and put away the kayaks and everything for the season."

We watched the saddle bronc riding and the steer wrestling events. After a long while I closed my eyes and took in a deep breath of that smoky, earthy rodeo smell.

"Having fun?" Sweeney asked.

I opened my eyes. "Yeah. This is good."

"You deserve it, buddy."

Finally it was time for the barrel racing. "Becca's second in the order," JoBell said as she sat down next to me again and took my hand. "I love the barrel racing. Definitely my favorite event. Plus it's like the only one that's all for the girls."

The first cowgirl rode into the arena and then kicked her horse into a gallop past the starting line. She circled her horse around the barrel to her left, then rode over and went around the barrel that had been to her right.

"She cut that too wide," Mr. Wells said. "She's losing time."

As the rider's horse rounded the third and last barrel, it stumbled a little, disqualifying her from the event. She trotted back slowly toward the gate.

"Becca's up now," JoBell said.

Lightning trotted through the gate into the arena with Becca smiling in the saddle. She leaned forward and patted the horse's neck, whispering something into its ears. Then she kicked her horse into a gallop, riding smooth like in the grand entry, but even faster. She guided Lightning through a tight loop around the left barrel and then they shot off to round the second.

"Come on, Becca," I whispered. "Come on. You got this."

JoBell squeezed my hand as Becca and Lightning circled the last barrel and bolted toward the finish line.

"Thatta girl! Go, go, go!" Mr. Wells shouted. Everyone cheered as Lightning crossed the line and trotted out of the arena.

"Well, folks," said the announcer. "Becca Wells is the blazing-fast cowgirl who takes the lead in tonight's barrel racing with a time of seventeen point five nine seconds. Outstanding."

I stood up and stretched. No use watching the rest of the barrel runs. Nobody was beating that time. "I'm going to go help Becca get Lightning brushed down and everything. You guys coming?"

"I want to watch some more of this," JoBell said. "Tell her I said good job."

Sweeney and Cal waved me off.

I left the arena and headed off into the shadows by the rows of horse trailers. Becca was nowhere to be seen, but Lightning was tied to the side of her trailer with the saddle already off. As I approached, I could hear Becca messing around inside the trailer, putting stuff away.

She stepped out of the little side door near the front and wiped her hands on her jeans before she leaned back against the trailer. "You did good tonight, Lightning. Real good." She stroked the horse's forehead. "That was a good ride. I wonder if he'll notice."

"If who will notice what?" I asked.

She jumped and Lightning jerked her head up. "Danny," Becca said. "What are you doing sneaking up on me like that!? You about gave me a heart attack."

"Sorry," I said.

Becca smiled. "No, you're not."

"You're right. I came to see if you needed any help, and to tell you that was an awesome ride."

"I've had better rides," she said. "It's not my best time." She shrugged and looked down, and I'm not gonna lie, but with her little pout and the way the light from the arena shined on her red-brown hair, Becca looked really pretty. Not for the first time, I thought about setting her up with somebody. She should have someone. It was too bad Sweeney was . . . well, the way he was.

She tossed me a brush. "I'll get the bridle off, if you want to brush her down."

I started brushing Lightning's rump, while Becca took out the horse's bit and removed the bridle.

"I'm going to take this all apart so I can clean it better," she said as she unhooked the bit from the bridle, dangling the metal piece by the reins. "Are you nervous about your bull ride?"

"Naw," I answered. I never really got too nervous until I was in the chute getting on the bull. Then during the ride, there was no time to be worried or to be thinking about anything. I straightened my lucky cowboy hat on my head and said something that had been creeping around at the edge of my thoughts all evening. "But I don't know, Becca. I don't know if I'm very into this tonight. I'm not so sure it's a great idea for me to get back on the bull."

"But you're so good at it," she said.

"I hope you're right. It's just, we're seniors now, and I was already feeling like this was our last chance for all of us to have fun together, here where we all grew up, I mean. Now with all this stuff that's happened since Boise, maybe we've already missed our chance. Maybe it's been stolen from us." I rested my head against Lightning's flank. "I wanted to live my life, you know? But now . . ."

I felt her arm around me and her hand rubbing my shoulder. "You're going to be okay, Danny," she whispered. "We're your friends. We're here to help."

"You Danny Wright?" said a deep voice behind me.

I lifted my head and turned to face three guys, two in full cowboy getup, hats, boots, and all. The third, in a ratty T-shirt with a baseball cap on backward, stood with his arms cocked back a little and his fists at his sides. I'd been in enough fights to know this was trouble.

"Yeah," I said. "What do you want?"

Baseball Cap elbowed the others. "See? Told you it was him." He took a step closer to me. "Lot of people are dead 'cause of you."

"You weren't there." There was a coldness churning somewhere deep inside me, and my heart began pounding. It was a lot like the feeling I had right when I first climbed up on a bull. "You don't know shit."

"Why don't you guys leave us alone?" Becca asked.

The taller of the two cowboys stepped up. "Bitch, shut up and stay out of this."

I threw my fist and cracked that bastard in the nose. Blood splattered everywhere, and my left hook sent him spinning to the ground. When Baseball Cap launched at me, Becca whipped the horse's bit around by the reins, snapping him hard in the nuts. He groaned, grabbed his crotch, and dropped.

Short Cowboy connected with a hard right jab that put spots in my vision on my left side. Another shot crunched into my gut. My hat fell in the dirt. I could hardly breathe. I managed a little shove to get him off me. Tall Cowboy rose to his hands and knees, but I kicked the toe of my boot into his ribs.

"Think it's fair to kick a man while he's down?" Short Cowboy shoved me back into Lightning. The horse whinnied.

Becca swung the bit around over her head to hit Shorty's face. Blood arced from his mouth as his head spun away from the impact. "Think it's fair to gang up three to two?" she said.

I had most of my breath back now. "You done?" I asked as Shorty wiped the blood from his mouth. He put up his fists and took a step forward. I shook my head. "Guess not."

I ran straight at him. My fist connected hard, sending tingles up my forearm. Shorty dropped to the ground, a bloody nose to go with his bloody mouth.

"Now you're done," I said as I picked up my hat, dusted it off, and curled the brim a little.

Baseball Cap held up his hand as he slowly stood, still bending over from the pain. He helped the other two up, and they walked off, but Baseball Cap stopped when they were about ten yards away. "This ain't over, Wright."

"I'm right here," I said with a lot more guts than I felt right then. I put my lucky cowboy hat back on and put my hands on my hips. "You guys get a couple more of your friends together, then maybe you can give me and this girl a fair fight."

"This girl?" Becca said when they'd walked off into the shadows. "You say that like you think it's a bad thing."

"You know I don't think that way," I said, rubbing the heat from my jaw where Shorty had punched me. "But those guys do. Or at least they did before you crushed that guy's balls."

"Where'd you learn to fight like that?"

"Oh, freshman year, Sweeney and me were nervous about starting high school, so we promised that no matter what happened, we would have each other's back. Problem is 'Sweeney' sounds a lot like 'weenie.' Then, like an idiot, Eric decided that he'd fight anyone who called him that. So, of course, I'd have to join in. We were in so many fights that year — half the time with juniors and seniors, even."

"I remember." She laughed. "I thought you two were going to be expelled. Or killed."

"We got our asses kicked plenty of times, but we won more than a few. People finally stopped messing with us sophomore year."

By the time we finished cleaning up Lightning, it was time for the bull riding to start. I was fifth in the order. The first three riders were good. All of them made it eight seconds and had decent scores in the mid to high seventies. The fourth rider looked strong coming out of the chute, but his free hand hit the bull when it switched directions on him.

Then it was my chance. I slipped on my gloves and climbed up on the wooden fence around the chute.

"Next up, ridin' a bull named Revolution, is one of our own, seventeen-year-old Daniel Wright." As soon as he said my name, the bleachers erupted in cheers and boos. *"He's active not only in Idahayew rodeo, but also in the Idahayew Army National Guard."*

The hysteria in the stands was building. One man flipped me off. A bunch of people clapped. Rick Hayes didn't seem to know what to say for once. A couple guys started shoving each other, almost getting into a fistfight until others broke it up. A bunch of people were running their comm cameras to record it all. I realized they were probably reporters who had snuck in. They were dressed a little too nice for rodeo. I sighed. Bull riding was hard enough at the best of times. All this chaos was the last thing I needed.

A horrible shriek of microphone feedback blasted out of the speakers. *"Now listen up, folks,"* Rick Hayes said. *"Daniel Wright is a soldier who has promised to put his life on the line for our freedom, and part of that freedom is the right of innocence until proven guilty. What's more, as cowboys, cowgirls, and fans and friends of rodeo, we may love a rough sport, but we are, at heart, ladies and gentlemen. If yer not gonna act that way, I'm gonna ask you to leave."*

Gradually, people sat back down on the bleachers.

"That's better," Hayes said. *"Now more than ever, we have to remember that we are all Americans, all proud of our home, and proud to take part in Idahayew rodeo! So let's get that cowboy ready and ridin'."*

I started to climb down onto the bull, but Short Cowboy came up on the fence right next to me. "I been slapping this bull around. Poking at him. Pissing him off. You're gonna get bucked and then stomped. This bull's gonna kill you, Wright."

I flicked the guy in the nose where I'd punched him before. He winced and backed up. "You got a little swelling there," I said. "You're gonna wanna ice that."

Then I pushed my lucky hat down secure and dropped onto the bull, grabbing the bull rope. Revolution breathed deep beneath me, shifting the tension in his huge packs of muscle. I gripped the rope hard with my right hand and held my left up as my free hand. This was what it was all about. Eight seconds in an eternity of intensity. This was rodeo.

When the chute opened I watched Revolution's head. He was looking straight ahead. He'd buck straight. He lunged forward, landing on his front hooves before throwing his hind legs up in the air. I stayed centered over my riding hand. Revolution jumped up with all four legs off the ground, his back twisting in midair. He landed hard and I clamped his sides even tighter with my legs. He puffed out through his nostrils. He was pissed. He spun to the right, and I shifted an inch. Not good. I tried to recenter myself, but my hand slipped on the rope. Revolution bucked one more time, his front legs high in the air, and I could feel the heat of the friction as my glove slid along the rope. I flew off, crashing hard to the dirt and scrambling to my feet to get clear. His hooves stomped down a few feet away, and he seemed to glare at me, his big black eyes zeroing in with rage.

Then the clown came, shouting and distracting Revolution to drive him away from me. I grabbed my cowboy hat from the dirt and ran for the edge of the ring.

"So close. About seven and a half seconds. Let's have a hand fer Danny Wright, ladies and gentlemen," the announcer called out.

I climbed over the arena fence, trying not to notice Short Cowboy clapping and whistling behind me, then walked off into the shadows away from the crowd. I'd been bucked off before. Every cowboy has, but I used to get absolutely pissed about it. After disqualification, I'd keep my cool until I was out of the arena. Then I'd cuss up a storm and kick at the dirt.

Tonight was different. Even though this was the first time I'd been bucked off in years, the first time ever while wearing my lucky cowboy hat, I wasn't very mad. Tonight bull riding felt like building forts in the woods as a kid: huge fun back then, but not so important now. Rodeo used to be a big part of my life, but now I knew it was part of my old life. And after everything that had happened, after the fight tonight, I knew my old life wasn't coming back.

Eventually I found my group out by Mr. Wells's truck, which is usually where we met up after events. JoBell put her arms around my neck and kissed me. "Sorry, baby. But hey, you haven't been in a rodeo all summer. It's bound to take a while to —"

"Get back in the saddle?" Sweeney asked. Cal and Becca groaned.

"Well, yeah, I guess," JoBell said. "If there were saddles in bull riding. Still, you must be bummed."

"I'm okay." I shrugged. "There'll be other rodeos."

Then JoBell took a closer look at my face. She frowned. My cheek stung as she touched it. "When did you get this?"

"It's nothing. Don't worry about it. I got it in the bull ride."

"Danny, I think I would have noticed if you hit your face." She stepped back and folded her hands over her arms. "Trust me, nobody is watching your bull rides as closely as me."

Why couldn't she ever leave anything alone? If I told her what really happened she would make a big deal out of it. Maybe try to find the police to arrest those three idiots. Who knows? The thing about guys is that most of the time a good fight settled everything. Whatever issue had caused the fight was over when the fight ended. JoBell had always said that that system was barbaric, but it sure seemed to beat the way girls would drag every conflict out through a long battle of words and gossip for months and months.

"Well?" she said.

"We got in a fight," Becca said. "These three cowboys —"

"Total jackwads," I said.

"— were mad about the Boise thing. They tried to jump us out here when Danny was brushing down Lightning."

"Whoa, you and Becca took on three guys?" Sweeney asked.

"Aw, man, awesome," Cal said.

I couldn't hold back my smile. "Yeah, Becca swung Lightning's bit and nailed one of them right in the nuts!" The guys laughed, and even Becca and her father looked amused. JoBell did not. "What?" I said to her. "What were we supposed to do? They attacked us."

"It's not that. I wish you would have told me."

"I was going to —"

"When?"

"I don't know." I threw my hands up. "Sometime when you wouldn't get all mad about it."

"I'm not mad about the fight. I only —"

"You sure seemed pissed to me."

Sweeney took a step forward. "Hey, you two, can you —"

"I'm tired of being kept in the dark about everything, Danny!" JoBell shouted. "You just tried to lie to me again about how you hurt your face, and I'm tired of being the last to know what's really going on. How long did you wait before you told me about Boise? Who else knew before I did? Now this? I mean, what other secrets are you hiding?"

"Nothing! I didn't want to tell you about it because I knew you'd act like this!" I yelled.

Becca put her hand on my forearm. "Danny, it's okay. There's no need for everybody to get so upset."

I shook my arm out of her grip and took a step closer to JoBell. "I'm tired of you being mad at me about this Boise shit!"

JoBell opened her mouth like she was going to say something else, but she stopped and pressed her lips together, blowing out through her nose. "That's *so* not the point. I'm done with this right now." She started for Becca's dad's truck.

"JoBell, come on," Cal tried.

"I . . ." She waved her hand behind herself as she walked away. "Not now."

◇—• Look, the bottom line is that the federal government has enough evidence to prove that Daniel Wright was involved in the Battle of Boise. Now yesterday he and his friends were practicing shooting military-style semiautomatic assault rifles, a weapon presumably purchased before the assault weapons ban was passed. He threatened to shoot at a news copter-cam! This kid is clearly dangerous, and this has gone on long enough. If the news media can find Wright wherever he is, what's keeping federal authorities from bringing him in? Are Idaho border checks that effective in keeping Fed agents out? It's funny, Idaho is a state that traditionally resists a lot of background checks for the purchase of firearms, and yet the state has now instituted its own background checks for weapons purchases to make sure any undercover FBI agents can't get guns. So, some credit might go to Montaine's effort to obstruct justice, or as he says, to protect his soldiers, but I think one of the main factors holding up these arrests is that the president is simply afraid to fail again and further complicate this situation. •—◇

◇—• passed the Texas House and now it looks like the measure might narrowly pass in the Senate. With us on ABC's Sunday in Washington are Speaker of the House Jim Barnes and Senate Majority Leader Laura Griffith. Mr. Speaker, Senator, it's an honor to have you with us today. Thank you for joining us."

"Thanks, Rachel."

"It's a pleasure to be on the show."

"Mr. Speaker, with the ongoing crisis in Idaho, what will it mean for America if Texas votes to nullify the Federal Identification Card Act?"

"That's an excellent question, Rachel. As you know, I voted for the act, but the version of the bill favored by me and by most of my

Republican colleagues was different in key ways. The law as it was passed was a result of bipartisan compromise, and most of the components of the law that Idaho and Texas are objecting to were added by Democrats. Am I entirely happy with the law? No. Do I believe that nullification is the answer? Absolutely not. But what are we as Americans going to do about this situation that the president has allowed to drag on for so long? Look, like I promise in my campaigns, I believe in commonsense solutions, and I think the commonsense solution here is to delay implementation of the law while Congress comes up with revisions that are more manageable, that help restore unity. Now the Republicans in the House already have a plan for —"

"Excuse me, Mr. Speaker. Senator, you're shaking your head. You disagree with Speaker Barnes? Why am I not surprised?"

"I do agree with the Speaker that nullification is not the answer. Let me make this absolutely clear. Nullification is unconstitutional and illegal. It is a dangerous crime that threatens the way this country works, the way it was designed to work over two hundred years ago when the Framers wrote the Constitution. It will not be tolerated. It is really insurrection, and should be treated accordingly with all due swift and immediate force. But I'm telling you right now that I will resign my Senate seat before I allow any compromise legislation to pass the Senate."

"Proving Democrats are impossible to work with!"

"Spare me your partisan cheap shots, Mr. Speaker. The federal government does not change its laws at the behest of state legislatures. It's the other way around! I will not allow any state to hold us hostage by throwing a little nullification fit. I trust Texas will come to its senses and stop this nonsense immediately. And I have a message for Governor Montaine. You do not have infinite time, Mr. Montaine. You will comply with legal federal demands, you will obey the law, or you and the members of the Idaho legislature who are cooperating with you will face serious penalties."

"In the spirit of compromise, I hardly think threats are in order. This is exactly the sort of Democratic heavy-handedness that got us into this mess in the first —"

"That is not a threat, Mr. Speaker. That's a promise. •⌒

FIFTEEN

I'm not gonna lie. Me and JoBell had had fights before. Show me a good couple who hasn't. That's what love is, still loving each other even when we both were mad. I wouldn't have cared if JoBell was angry enough to hit me in the head with a ball-peen hammer. I would've still loved her. By Sunday, I was already missing her, but when I tried to call or text her, Digi-Eleanor wouldn't let my messages through.

Weirdly enough, missing JoBell made me think about how she was constantly tracking news updates, and that made me check to see what was going on. The coverage, if not the mob of reporters outside the house and all over town, actually backed off the Idaho Crisis for a while on Saturday night, after the Iranian military hit US troops with a surprise attack in some place called Birjand. Maybe the attack reminded everyone that we were supposed to be fighting Iran, not each other, or maybe the seven Idaho soldiers among the forty-six killed made the "hate Idaho" crowd remember that we were all still Americans. I was just relieved that none of the casualties were from my unit. I guessed the deployed guys from the 476th Engineer Company were stationed closer to Tehran.

The governor seemed to be doing his best to make sure that Specialist Stein was the last Idaho Guardsman that the Fed could get its hands on. The Freedom Lake cops and the state police drove by the house a lot to make sure everything was okay. Good old Nathan Crow was living up to the promise he'd made. My father would have been proud. Crow became truly aggressive, arresting any reporters who trespassed on private property. Then he convinced some of his friends on the city council that the public sidewalk in front of my house was unsafe and needed to be torn up and replaced. While it was torn up, reporters weren't allowed to use that sidewalk space to film their stories. Even better, he made sure there were always plenty of cars and trucks parked on my street so that news vans couldn't get near my house. He had even arranged to have my mother moved out to her nursing conference undercover, driving her in his own car to Spokane. Despite all his efforts, though, the media still swarmed all over Freedom Lake.

On Sunday night, Schmidty finished the upgrades to the Beast. He'd worked overtime all weekend to weld two-inch steel pipes inside the doors and fenders and under the hood. The normal windows had been replaced by glass that was rated to withstand 7.62 rounds. Where he found that, I'll never know. A heavy steel-pipe push bumper had been welded to the truck's frame and wrapped the grill in a cool sort of cage. He'd even put a false bottom in the back behind the seats, raising the carpeted floor and toolbox to make a small hiding place back there. All of this made the truck even heavier and cut down further on gas mileage, but it would be safer if I ran into another crazy shooter like the one after that football game. It felt great to be up in the driver's seat of the Beast again.

On Monday morning, I was relieved to see the school had hired private security to keep the parking lot clear of the media mob. After ignoring the reporters shouting questions from the street in front of the school, I moved quickly and quietly, hoping to avoid detection. I had a very serious mission, though it made me grin like a dork. When I reached my destination, I was in with a few quick spins of the combination lock, and I let out a little breath of relief. I would pull this off without being caught.

"Hold it right there," said a voice from behind me.

I froze in place. I'd been so close, only to be stopped now.

"What do you think you're doing?"

I turned around to face JoBell and held out the bunch of roses I bought for her the night before. "I was trying to sneak this into your locker as a surprise. I thought you had a student council meeting this morning."

"We wrapped up early." She smiled and took the flowers. "They're beautiful. Thank you." I had hoped for a warmer reaction than that after our fight, but that would have to do. She held the flowers up to smell them. "What's the occasion?"

"No occasion." That was only partly true. "Just . . . Well. I'm sorry. I should have told you about the fight at the rodeo right away. I thought it would be better not to worry you about it, but I was wrong." I'd been practicing that speech over and over all the way to school. "And with everything that's been happening lately, I was thinking about how much I . . ."

It felt weird saying it, right out in the open hallway. Dylan was messing with something in his locker a few doors down. He'd have some jackwad comment at practice if he heard me getting all mushy.

JoBell looked down at the bouquet. "How much you what?" she said quietly.

I wanted to touch her, to hold her, but she stood a few steps away, and oddly enough, the roses were between us. "I'm a lucky guy," I said. "To be with you, I mean."

Her expression brightened a little, and that gave me some encouragement. "Thank you," she said. "For being man enough to apologize. And I'm lucky too." She smelled the flowers again. "I'm going to go put these in the office so they'll get some water and won't get all crushed in my locker. Thanks so much for this." She spun so that her hair whipped out behind her and headed off down the hall.

"Smooth move with the roses, Wright," Dylan said as he closed his locker. "That's a slick trick. You're a master."

What guys like Dylan Burns would never understand was that it wasn't a trick at all. I loved JoBell and liked to see her happy. She liked flowers and nice surprises. I only wished that this particular surprise had made her happier. It hadn't gone as well as I hoped it would, but at least we were talking again. Sort of.

The halls were beginning to get crowded. Samantha Monohan and a group of cheerleaders taped up signs on lockers for the JV football game this Wednesday. A freshman girl hurried by with an instrument case. A group of kids copied a worksheet that was probably due first hour. They wrote down the answers in a big hurry.

I sighed. All of these different parts of high school life used to seem so important. I remembered scrambling to get some sort of assignment ready for my teachers and liking the way the locker posters signaled I was part of the team. Now half the country wanted me in jail or worse, and the other half seemed to talk about me like I was some kind of hero. I had never liked school that much — hated the assignments and couldn't stand a lot of the teachers — but I had belonged here. Now this place was like the rodeo. I felt my old life slipping away.

Becca found me in the hall on the way to government. "Hey, cowboy, you still sore from the weekend?" She grinned and elbowed me.

"I'd be a lot worse off if not for you helping me with those three idiots," I said. "I bet that dumb bastard's balls are still in a sling. Without your help, they'd probably have put me in the hospital or something." I shrugged. "I'd have gotten more behind on my schoolwork. Flunked all my classes. Failed to graduate."

"Golly, I'm glad I saved you then."

"I wouldn't say you saved me, but you definitely —"

"I *saved* you! And good thing, because your grades are bad enough."

"Ouch!" I said. "Keep talking, Wells. Just remember our bet."

Becca stopped walking, her eyes wide. "What bet?"

"You remember when we were in, like, third grade, at your brother's graduation, and you had to explain to me what the valedictorian was?"

"I do remember that. You kept pronouncing it valley doctorian." She narrowed her eyes and pressed her lips together. "Hmm. And I *think* I was your 'girlfriend' " — she flashed air quotes with her fingers — "for that whole weekend."

"Oh yeah!" I said, remembering. "You dumped me the following Monday." I grabbed Becca's arm. "But don't try to get off topic. At that graduation, you said you were going to be our valedictorian, and I bet you a hundred dollars that you wouldn't be."

"Hey, cut me some slack." She gave me a little push, and we went on toward class again. "I was in third grade!"

"A bet's a bet. What are you ranked, sixth in the class?"

She gazed at the floor for a moment. "Eighth." Then she fixed me with that look that said she had an idea. "I seem to remember you were a pretty fast runner back then."

"I'm still a fast runner!"

She shrugged. "You said if I was ever a faster runner than you, you'd kiss me."

I laughed, though my cheeks felt a little hot. I knew where she was going with this. "You cut *me* some slack. I was in third grade!"

"I seem to remember beating your time in the open eight hundred in track last year, so, um . . ." She stepped close to me. "A bet's a bet."

I didn't know what to do. I looked at Becca, with her green eyes and the sprinkling of a few freckles on her nose, her red-brown hair and the purple butterfly hair clip she always wore. A tingle shivered up my spine.

Her lips passed less than an inch from mine as she leaned forward to whisper in my ear. "*You owe me.*"

Then she hurried into Mr. Shiratori's room. I followed her into class, trying to fight back the disappointment at being faked out like that, trying to fight back the guilt over that spark of disappointment.

Mr. Shiratori paced the room and tapped his stick on the floor. Step, step, tap. Step, step, tap. "We've finished our study of Article One of the Constitution. Your test on this material will be on Wednesday." He stopped for a moment and finally looked up at us. "In case any of you were interested."

He went back to tap-walking. Sweeney looked at me like, *What's he doing?* I shrugged.

Mr. Shiratori drew in a long breath. "Your homework for the weekend probably didn't require much writing. Four or five short paragraphs at the most. But it did require a lot of thinking. What was your assignment for the weekend?"

Oh crap. The assignment. I'd forgotten all about it. I slid down in my seat a little.

JoBell raised her hand, as usual.

"Someone besides Ms. Linder for a change," Mr. Shiratori said. "How about Ms. Monohan?"

Samantha sat up straight in her chair the way she did whenever she answered a question. "We were supposed to write a paragraph for each section of Article One that had significant . . . relevance . . . to . . . circumstances . . . being reported in the news."

"Thank you, Ms. Monohan, for that well-memorized verbatim reply," said Mr. Shiratori. "I've been thinking . . ." He loved dramatic pauses. ". . . about what is fair." He looked right at me, and I knew I was doomed. "I think after the events of this last Friday night, some of you might have been a little shaken, and you might need more time to write and revise your essays. Also, in your papers, I want you to imagine how some of the things happening today might develop in the future, and how those events could become relevant to issues regarding Article One. So I expect this assignment in my inbox before we take the test Wednesday, whether or not you are in school that day. No late work when you can easily wire it in on your comm."

I sighed with relief and sat up a little. One more chance. That was good, since my grade in this class was already not so hot.

"ATTENTION. PRIORITY MESSAGE." A deep robotic voice blasted out of my comm. "ATTENTION. PRIORITY MESSAGE . . ."

I jumped up in my seat, scrambling for the mute switch. I swear I had switched off the sound when I got to school. I checked it. It was shut off. How was it still making noise?

Mr. Shiratori pointed the Stick of Power at me. "Mr. Wright. You just bought yourself a detention."

"It's not even Hank! I turned the sound off! It's off right now!" I said. Normally I wouldn't dream of giving Mr. Shiratori back talk, but this wasn't fair. The screen read:

INCOMING VOICE CALL REQUEST
LIEUTENANT COLONEL RICHINGHAM
UNITED STATES ARMY
ACCEPT • DECLINE

"ATTENTION. PRIORITY MESSAGE. ATTENTION. PRIORITY MESSAGE . . ."

"You're testing my patience, Mr. Wright."

"Mr. Shiratori. It's the . . . Army calling. I think I need to take this one."

I kept my eyes locked on him and tried to ignore the stares from everyone else. The hardness went out of Mr. Shiratori's face. "Oh. Well, then. Go ahead. Why don't you step out into the hallway, Mr. Wright?"

When I was alone, I tapped to accept the call.

"Hello, sir. This is PFC Wright."

"Private First Class Daniel Wright." The voice somehow threw extra emphasis on each individual word, almost as if it were spitting them. *"By order of the president of the United States of America, you are hereby requested and required to report for active duty service at Fairchild Air Force Base no later than zero eight hundred hours Wednesday, September 29, for an initial period of service not to exceed seven hundred and thirty days."*

I backed up until my back pressed into the lockers and slid down the cool metal until I sat on the floor. Now the Army was calling me in the middle of class to try to trick me into giving myself up? This couldn't be happening.

"Private Wright, are you there?"

I licked my lips. "Yes, sir."

"Your official orders will be in your inbox later today. You'll need those orders as proof that you're on active duty. Report to the main gate at Fairchild Air Base, and the personnel there will direct you to your duty station. Uniform is MCU. Do you have any questions?"

"Sir, I can't serve. I was involved in . . . I started . . . the shootings at Boise. There's a warrant for my arrest."

"I know who you are, Private Wright. You think they have a lieutenant colonel calling every single member of the Idaho National Guard? No. I have a gymnasium full of lieutenants here calling Idaho Guardsmen and ordering them to active duty. I'm instructed

to inform you that the soldiers involved in the Boise incident will receive a full pardon upon completion of their active duty service. All you have to do is come and serve your country, and then you won't be caught in the middle of this circus anymore. If there are no further questions, I have other calls to make. If there's a glitch and your orders don't come through by this time tomorrow, call me back at this number. You're expected on duty by zero eight hundred hours Wednesday. Richingham, out."

The call ended. A pardon? They were finally giving up on punishing us for Boise? Could it be that simple? Could I trust them? Even if I could, it would still mean as much as two years of full-time Army life. JoBell and me had enough problems without a big separation to deal with. And how would Mom cope with me being gone for so long? I put my head back against the lockers.

Mr. Morgan came out of the office, and of course he spotted me right away.

"Daniel? What are you doing out here?"

I rubbed my eyes and held up my comm. "Call from the Army."

Morgan straightened his tie. "Yes, well, I trust it was something important."

What did he expect, that the Army called in the middle of the day for no reason? What an idiot. "I've been ordered to active duty," I said. "I'm supposed to report to Fairchild Air Force Base Wednesday morning."

"Oh. Well, surely they'll understand that you are still a high school student. I'd be happy to contact them to explain the situation."

"That was some hotshot officer personally calling me to issue my orders. I'm not sure they're interested in listening to a high school principal." Then, realizing I probably pissed him off, I added, "No offense. I think every soldier or at least most of the soldiers in the

Idaho Guard are being activated. Probably to leave Governor Montaine with no Guard forces to protect him."

"Well, maybe that's for the best," said Mr. Morgan. "Put this all behind us."

Before he said that, I might have felt that way, but hearing the idea come out of his weasel mouth made it sound sickening. Nobody wanted things in America to go back to normal more than I did, but after the FBI had almost run us off the road trying to arrest me, after Governor Montaine did everything he could to protect us when the president wanted us in jail, after all that, I was supposed to go to their side? I was supposed to leave home and school and my friends and JoBell and report for Army duty? I was supposed to trust that after I gave them two years of my life they'd pardon me? At least Governor Montaine had given us a choice when he called for volunteers to work full-time Idaho National Guard duty.

But then another part of me remembered that I had sworn an oath to obey the president, and these were the first direct orders he had sent me. And if he was serious about the pardon, maybe this was my only way out of all this.

"Daniel?" Mr. Morgan said. He fiddled with his tie tack. He was real fidgety about his ties.

If he had been talking, I hadn't been listening. Morgan was the kind of guy who was easy to tune out. I shook my head and focused on him. "What did you say?"

Mr. Morgan put his hands on his hips. "I said, if you're through with your Army call, you should go back to class."

Why not? It was better than hanging out here in the hallway with this clown. I stood up and started back to class.

"Hey, partner! You got a big conference call coming in. You wanna check this out?" Digi-Hank.

Mr. Morgan huffed. "The Army again?"

I checked the screen and shook my head.

"Well then, Daniel, if it's not urgent, you know school policy is no calls during —"

I held up the comm to show him the screen. "It's the governor calling." As often as I had wanted my involvement with the standoff between the governor and the president to be over, I was glad right then to show this pencil-pushing jackwad that he wasn't the highest authority in the world. Morgan frowned and took a step back. A message came on-screen when I tapped ACCEPT.

> CONFERENCE CALL LOADING PARTICIPANTS
> *PLEASE STAND BY FOR AN IMPORTANT MESSAGE*
> *FROM GOVERNOR MONTAINE*

"He put me on hold?" The direct line to the governor was spoiling me.

Mr. Morgan stood up straighter. "Well, why don't you take that call in private?" He led me down the hall to his office and closed the door behind me, leaving me alone.

If I was going to have to wait in the principal's office for this call, I might as well make myself at home. I went and sat down in the high-backed swivel chair behind Morgan's big wooden desk. "Comfy." I put my feet up, crinkling some of his papers under my shoes. He'd be pissed if he saw me like this, but what was he going to do, kick me out of school? I had to be in the Army in two days anyway. Mr. Morgan could deal with it.

Finally my comm beeped. The message disappeared and the screen went black. Then an image came on-screen. The governor stood behind a podium in the entryway to the governor's mansion. I could see the staircase behind him.

"Soldiers and airmen of the Idaho Army and Air Force National Guard. Greetings. I'm James Montaine, governor of the great state of Idaho. I'm told that about 73 percent of you are watching this announcement live, but for those of you unable to join us at this time, as well as for those who may wish to watch this broadcast again, this announcement will be recorded and available in your inbox at the conclusion of my remarks.

"By now, most of you have received or are about to receive orders to report for federal active duty in the United States Army or Air Force. To be sure, this is a legal order, effectively signed by the president of the United States. But at this time, I would ask each of you to consider why the president is issuing these orders. President Rodriguez has a disagreement, not only with me, but with the entire state of Idaho.

"First, despite the fact that both houses of the Idaho state legislature strongly voted to nullify the Federal Identification Card Act on the grounds that the act represented an unconstitutional invasion of privacy, the president insists that his signature law be implemented everywhere. Given his way, he would do away with government by the consent of the governed and force us all to live under his new surveillance program.

"Second, he has demanded the arrest of Idaho Army National Guardsmen who committed no crime except to obey lawful orders given to them by their chain of command. He wants to punish those soldiers, your comrades in arms, for doing their duty.

"Third, in order to force me to sell out and surrender honest, loyal Idaho Army National Guardsmen, the president has repeatedly demanded that I release those soldiers' identities. As a veteran of the Battle of Fallujah in Operation Iraqi Freedom and as governor, I will never betray soldiers under my command. I will do all I can to support Idaho's men and women in uniform. With the help of the state legislature, I made sure that Idaho Guardsmen deployed in Iran would not experience a pay freeze due to the recent federal government shutdown amid their budget dispute. In Idaho, we take care of our own!

"The president could not accept this, however, and despite my best efforts to protect those involved in the Boise incident, some names of soldiers at Boise were leaked. The president then sent federal operatives in an attempt to arrest them. That attempt was foiled when I directed local law enforcement to detain and deport the armed federal agents. The president may try to act like he has your best interests at heart, but why then do aerial drones — some of them possibly armed, in violation of the law — constantly monitor Idaho Guard positions? And would a president with his soldiers' interests in mind order FBI agents to risk one of his soldiers' lives in a deadly high-speed chase, as he did with seventeen-year-old Private First Class Daniel Wright?

"Fourth, under the mistaken belief that removing me from Idaho will cause the people to give up their love for freedom and their respect for their rights, the president has broken the law as set forth by the Idaho state constitution and sent armed forces into this state in an attempt to arrest me, as well as the Idaho Guardsmen who were involved in the incident in Boise. You men and women have already worked hard to construct a barrier to prevent further such incursions, and I thank you for it.

"The president has made no effort to explain to you soldiers and airmen why he is calling you away from your homes and loved ones. There is no pressing threat to national security. There has not been a simultaneous federal activation of every member of a particular state's National Guard forces in over sixty years, not since President Eisenhower federalized the Arkansas National Guard so that

Arkansas soldiers wouldn't be used in defense of school segregation. The Idaho Guard has not been called upon for any such evil purpose. On the contrary, you've been hard at work, protecting our freedom at home and abroad. The president would seek to stop that work, and by his attempt, he has shown that he has no concern even for Idaho's need to maintain a force to help the state in the event of dangerous floods or deadly wildfires.

"The president is not being honest with you, but I promise you that I always will be. President Rodriguez is calling the entire Idaho National Guard to active duty and ordering you out of the state so that he may send in soldiers from other parts of the country or possibly even foreign troops — to illegally arrest me, certainly, but worse than that, to force Idaho to comply with his unconstitutional mandate.

"The media has dubbed this situation 'The Idaho Crisis,' but I say there is nothing wrong with Idaho! The crisis is with a president and a federal government that have overstepped their bounds and assumed more power than the Constitution allows. It is the president and the federal government who have committed crimes by passing laws in opposition to the highest law of the land, and, therefore, any effort to resist those criminal laws cannot be illegal.

"However, soldiers and airmen, without your support and defense of the Constitution, without your belief in and dedication to freedom, we will lose this most important struggle and there will be no end to federal tyranny.

"I meant what I said when I promised to be honest with you. I will not force you to actively serve against your will as the president is attempting to do. As governor of the state of Idaho, I, James P. Montaine, hereby activate the entire Idaho Army and Air Force National Guard for state duty. However, realizing that these are difficult times, realizing that you have sworn an oath to obey both the president and your governor, and realizing that you are good and true soldiers and airmen who take your oaths seriously, I offer the following choices.

"First, you may report for federal duty as the president ordered.

"Second, if you are too conflicted by this decision and do not wish to choose one option over the other, you may be released from the service, hand in any weapons or equipment you've been issued, and go on with your lives at home.

"Third, if you believe in freedom. If you love your friends and neighbors and wish to protect them from gross invasions of their privacy and from federal tyranny. If you support the state of Idaho and the good things this state stands for, then I ask you, I implore you: Report for duty to the state of Idaho. Support your governor and your state legislature by saying NO to the president and the federal government. No! We will not allow you to unconstitutionally force surrender on us! No! We will not allow you to ignore the Constitution and our freedoms! No! We will not allow you to invade our state, our communities, and our homes with armed federal or international forces.

"Now, I want to take a moment to address those members of the Idaho National Guard who are deployed to Iran or Pakistan at this time. I have received word that some of you have expressed a desire to return home to serve your state, and that some of you have considered refusing to perform your duties abroad. I appreciate your loyalty, patriotism, and sacrifice. However, given the critical nature of your missions in fighting terrorism and preventing Iran from further developing or obtaining nuclear weapons, I am suggesting — and I would issue orders if you were currently under my command — that you continue to obey the orders from your federal chain of command. I can only hope that the president will consider this a reasonable gesture and reciprocate by allowing you all to return when your scheduled tour of duty is over. Deployed Idaho National Guardsmen, my prayers are with you.

"Good soldiers and airmen in the state of Idaho, you have a difficult decision to make. I'm sorry that the federal government has forced this decision upon you. But I know I can count on each and every one of you to make the right choice, and I promise you, the state of Idaho will enact no penalties against you regardless of what you choose. To make your decision, please reply with a call to this number, and officers will assist you.

"Thank you for your time and thank you for your service. May God bless you, the state of Idaho, and the United States of America."

The screen went blank. I sat back in Mr. Morgan's chair, staring up at the brown water stains in the ceiling tiles. For a moment, I thought Morgan's swivel chair was spinning. Then I realized it was just me.

SIXTEEN

Football practice did not go well that night. First, although all I wanted to do was get out on the practice field to get ready for our next game, Coach kept us all in the locker room for a long time right away, talking to us about the gunman last Friday and the ongoing problem with the press.

"So while I cannot order any of you not to speak to reporters about all of this, I want to make it clear that if I find out that any of you have been in contact with the media, I'm going to wonder if you are truly focused on the upcoming game. I might not be able to start a player who is so unfocused."

TJ stood up from the bench. "Coach, I didn't say anything bad about —"

"But you saw how they twisted everything you said!" Coach yelled. "It makes you look bad. It makes your team look bad."

"Yes, Coach." He sat back down, keeping his eyes on his feet.

It felt good to see TJ shut down like that, especially after his idiot stunt with the reporters, and I was really glad that the guys all seemed to agree not to talk to the media, but the good times didn't last. When we finally got on the field, I kept screwing up the plays and running the wrong routes, and I missed about every pass thrown to me. In tackling drills, I got knocked on my ass at least three times. I tried to focus, I tried to give a hard practice like I always did, but I couldn't stop thinking about the fact that depending on what I chose to do, I might not play in this Friday's game. I might never play football again.

Finally, Coach Shiratori pulled me aside. I felt sure he was going to yell at me, make me do laps around the field, something horrible. "Listen, Wright," he said quietly. "Mr. Morgan told me what that comm call was about. I watch the news, and I know what's going on. Why don't you take the rest of the night off? Go home and get yourself sorted out. Make plans and things."

"That's okay, Coach. I'm fine. I just want to play football. That's all I've ever —"

"This isn't really a request," Coach Shiratori said. "Take the night off."

"You're kicking me off the team?" I asked. "Coach, I've done everything you asked. I've had a good season so far."

"This is bigger than football, Mr. Wright." He clapped a hand on my shoulder pad. "Bigger than either of us."

As I walked toward the locker room, the team went back to running our offense. I stopped for a moment at the edge of the field as Sweeney launched a pass. Not one of his best. It wobbled a little. TJ caught it, and even dodged out of the way of three defenders.

"Thatta kid, Teee Jaaaaay!" Randy shouted.

I was so pissed I could have thrown up.

I was sweaty from practice, but I didn't even bother showering. I changed into my jeans and T-shirt, went out to the Beast, and threw on my cowboy hat. Coach had said "Go home," but that was the last place I wanted to be. With Mom away at her conference, the place was too quiet, too lonely. With the mufflers switched off, the roar of the engine sang to me. So I drove all over, finally ditching the two news vans that had tried to follow me. I ended up at the Abandoned Highway of Love. Maybe that was ironic. Hell, I didn't know. I missed that vocab word on my last English test.

I slowed the Beast down a little as I steered around the collapsed left lane. Why was it that when I felt depressed, I would put on depressing music or go to lonely, quiet places? I should've been trying to cheer myself up. How? I didn't know. Maybe I should have gone to a pet store or something. Seen the puppies.

I got out of the truck and went out onto Party Bridge. The dark water of Freedom River churned around the rocks below. A cool breeze whispered through the pines on the riverbank. I thought back to all the parties we'd had out here the summer after sophomore year. Cold beer and a good fire. A few cheap cigars with the guys. Girls in bikinis splashing around down there when the water was warm. Now those parties were over. I'd missed all of them when I went to basic training this last summer. Then summer ended at Boise. Maybe my life ended there too. I hadn't thought about that until now.

"I've been looking for you," JoBell said as she ducked under the I-beam barrier and came out onto the bridge. She put up the hood of her blue-and-white Minutemen sweatshirt.

"Welcome to the party," I said, looking out at the water.

She stood beside me without saying anything for a long time. I wished she'd take my hand or rub my back like she used to do when I was facing hard times, but I guess that was too much to hope for. At least she was giving me some quiet time. I was grateful for that. I didn't feel like talking about the situation. I was tired of it. Tired of talking and thinking about it.

"Volleyball practice was fun tonight."

"Good," I mumbled, watching a fish skip out of the water downstream.

"Cassie Macer was in a really good mood."

I raised an eyebrow. "Did Sweeney and her —"

"Yep."

"This last weekend?"

"Sunday night. He convinced her to come over to 'study,' I think."

"JoBell," I said, finally looking at her. I didn't know where to begin.

She put her arms around me and drew in for a kiss. After that, she squeezed me close and rested her head on my chest. "You're going to be okay, Danny."

"I wish I knew how."

"Let me call the others." She held up her comm. "We'll figure this out together."

About fifteen minutes later, Cal, Sweeney, and Becca showed up, and I explained the whole thing so they had the full details, not just the little bit I told Sweeney at lunch. "So that's it," I said. "Those are my choices." I shook my head. "And I have no idea what I should do."

"I know you probably won't want to hear this," JoBell said. "But you've been talking about how you want this all to be over. You want things to be normal. *Quit the military.* It solves everything. You can go back to football and hanging with us and school, which is what you really need to be focused on, so we can get your grades up for your college application."

"It's not that simple," I started.

She took both of my hands in hers. "Babe, what if it is? What if it's exactly that simple? You've been given your way out. This can all be over."

"I signed my name on the line. I swore an oath to obey the president. To obey the governor."

"Exactly." JoBell flipped a strand of hair back behind her ear. "And the governor said you can get out of the military with no penalties, so *do* it."

"But the federal government is expecting him to show up at that Air Force base Wednesday," said Sweeney. "If he doesn't, it's a crime or something, right?" I nodded. He went on, "The federal government has thought he was guilty of a crime for a while now. I don't know, maybe it would be a good idea to go federal and get that pardon. On the other hand, even without a pardon for Boise, and even if they're pissed that he doesn't show up to federal duty, it's not like they can come and arrest him. The Idaho Guard won't even let them into the state."

"Bingo." Cal spoke through a belch before crushing his empty Turbo Juice can. "What's he supposed to do? Act like it's all good while the National Guard protects him?" He pointed at me. "While they put their asses on the line, you're just going to sit around and watch? I say go state all the way, man. You don't owe the Fed shit. They tried to arrest you. They almost killed us all, trying to run us down in the car. If you go to that Air Force base, they'll probably bust you right there. You're insane if you think the president is really going to give you that pardon. He already proved he ain't trustworthy by accidentally-on-purpose leaking your name to the news. The governor's right. The only reason they're calling you to active duty Army is so they can come into the state and arrest Montaine, and that guy is the only one who kept you out of jail after that whole thing went down in Boise. He helped you. Now you got to help Idaho. Someone has to stand up to these guys."

I don't know exactly what the others were thinking, but they had to have been as shocked as I was. That was the longest, clearest speech Cal ever gave, better even than his classic sophomore-year English-class presentation, "Why Brittany Mavis Is the Best Actress and Singer and She Turns Me On."

Finally, JoBell shook her head. "That's illegal. That's rebellion!"

"Whoa, whoa. Easy, guys." I didn't need my best friends fighting about this.

"It's the damn Fed that's breaking the law." Cal threw his can into the river. "The Idaho Guard is only protecting us. It's not rebellion. It's self-defense."

"It's suicide," Becca said quietly. She had this way of getting everyone's attention without having to yell. She didn't always talk much, but when she did, her words mattered. "If it comes to an all-out fight? Idaho against the full Army, Air Force, and Marines of the United States? Suicide."

"It won't be a fight if the Fed stays out of Idaho," Cal said.

"What if they don't stay out? What if they storm the state? They don't even need to come in. They can fire cruise missiles or drop bombs or something," Becca said. "I'm sorry, but Idaho doesn't have a chance. Not in a million years."

"Hey," I said. "The Idaho Guard is just as well trained and —"

"They're going to get killed," Becca said. "You know it's true."

"But they won't take it that far," said Sweeney. "What president would order the total slaughter of his own people? He'd never be elected again."

I put my head back and pressed my fists to my eyes. "This isn't getting me anywhere. If I obey the president, I have to leave home for two years."

"Or maybe longer," JoBell added.

"Or maybe longer," I agreed.

"Or probably go to jail." Cal folded his big arms. "And you'd be selling out your state."

I leaned against a steel girder in the bridge's truss. "If I stay with the Idaho Guard, I'll probably end up getting killed."

"Not necessarily," said Sweeney.

"And you'd betray your oath to the president," said Becca.

"But if I drop out of the military entirely," I said, "I'd be a traitor to both."

JoBell took my hand.

"Dude, I don't know what you should do," said Sweeney. "But I'll support you no matter what you decide."

"Thanks for coming out here, guys," I said. "It means a lot. Tomorrow's only Tuesday, right? The Fed doesn't expect me until Wednesday, so I can sleep on it."

Cal slapped me on the back. Becca put one arm around Sweeney's shoulders and the other down around Cal's waist, and we all started back toward our cars, parked in a line on the Abandoned Highway of Love.

With Mom gone, I could dodge the reporters by parking in the garage, but JoBell had to park over a block away and then sneak through backyards on foot to escape notice. I let her in, then went upstairs to shower and change into clean clothes, but when I came down to the living room, she wasn't there.

"Jo?" I called. Someone reached around from behind and grabbed me. I spun out of the grip and pulled my fist back, ready for a fight.

She stood there, smiling and wearing my cowboy hat.

"Whoa! Sorry. Bad idea," she said.

I breathed deeply to still my pounding heart. I had been ready to crush whoever was behind me. "Don't scare me like that," I said quietly. I never would have been like this before everything had fallen apart. JoBell slid her hands up under my T-shirt and pressed them to my bare chest. My breath seized up. "Whoa, ice-cold," I said.

She cupped her hands over her mouth and blew to warm them with her breath. Then she rubbed her palms together before placing them on me again. "Better?"

I kissed her and tried to put my arms around her, but she slipped away. "I'm hungry."

"So am I." I grinned.

She giggled and headed for the kitchen. "I'm hungry for *food*. Show me what frozen delights you have for us tonight."

She put on a playlist of our favorite songs, and I showed her my master chef skills in cooking the perfect fish sticks and fries. Before we sat down to eat, I found a couple candles from the junk drawer, lit them, and put them on the table.

"Poor man's romantic feast." I pulled out JoBell's chair for her.

She bowed. "Thank you, sir," she said in a rich-sounding accent before sitting down.

I sat down across from her, and we clinked our wine glasses filled with grape pop together. Then we settled in to eating. The food may have been cheap and crappy, but I couldn't remember a better meal.

"I was feeling pretty miserable today." I dipped my last fish stick in the little dish of ketchup between us, holding it up afterward. "But being with you makes everything so much better."

"I'm glad I can help." She grinned. "You're going to be okay, Danny. You're strong enough to handle all this. That's what I've always loved most about you. It wasn't your looks —"

"Hey!"

"— or your choice in music. But I've always loved how brave you are. Pulling off that fake punt in football. The bull riding. Even your courage to enlist and go through basic training with all those mean drill sergeants. You're strong . . . and brave." She pushed her empty plate away and looked at me. In her eyes I saw her other hunger. "And yeah, it actually was your looks too."

She rounded the table and sat on my lap, straddling me, taking my head in her hands. Her tongue explored my mouth.

"I think," she gasped after a bit, "that we should go upstairs."

"To my bedroom?" Had I been in a condition to think straight, I might have said something smarter.

She got up and slipped her sweatshirt off so that she stood there in a little T-shirt and jeans. She held out her hand. "Come on, babe."

As soon as we entered my room we were on each other. She backed me up to the bed and then pushed me down onto my back before climbing on top of me to kiss me more. All my concerns from earlier in the day, all the problems in the whole world, melted away. The universe was only JoBell and me. And it felt so good.

Hours later, with the blankets pulled up over us, we lay there in the dark, so close that we breathed each other's breath. I'd never felt so . . . *with* someone, so much a part of someone else. When we'd been together before, it had always been hot and steamy, but that night it felt warmer, safer, than anything I'd ever felt before. I wanted to stay there forever.

"Danny," she whispered after a long time. "Danny, please don't go. Please don't leave me. Forget everything I said earlier today. Forget politics and laws and duty. Just stay. For me."

I squeezed her. Of all the arguments that everybody had made this afternoon on the bridge, what JoBell had said right now made the most sense. What was the point of being in an army that was almost ready to fight itself? What was life without JoBell? I didn't want this closeness to end.

After a long time, I began to fade into sleep. She slipped out from under my arm and moved toward the edge of the bed. I caught hold of her hand. "Where you going?"

"Home." She smiled.

"No," I whispered, stretching my arms around her waist to pull her back. "You are home. Stay here."

"I can't," she said. "My dad would kill us both. You know that."

I did know that, and I let her get up. I also knew that I loved her, and the feeling was so intense that it ached in my chest. I knew then what I had to do.

"Hold on," I said when she had her shoes on. My heart beat heavy in my chest as I pulled on my jeans and went to the drawer in my nightstand. I swear my hands were shaking so much when I approached her that I thought I'd drop the black box hidden behind my back.

"What are you doing?" JoBell said. "I have to get going."

Was this the right time? Was I being stupid? I ran through all the arguments in my head again. Was proposing to JoBell any crazier than everything that was happening in America lately? No. This was right. That much I knew. I switched on the bedside light and went down on one knee, opening the box to show her the ring. I hoped the lamplight sparkled right on the diamond.

JoBell gasped.

"JoBell Marie Linder, I love you," I said. "I love you more than I could ever love anything or anyone. Will you marry me?"

She froze with her mouth dropped open. Then she pressed her hand to her chest and took a step back, bumping our rodeo picture off the shelf. She made a clumsy grab to catch it, but missed, and it clattered to the floor. "Oh, Danny." Tears welled in her eyes.

I smiled. She was so happy, she was crying.

"Oh, Danny," she said. She pressed her fist to her mouth, biting one knuckle.

My knee was getting a little sore, kneeling like this on the hardwood floor. "I want us to be together forever."

"So do I." She nodded as a tear ran down her cheek.

I stood up and moved toward her. "Then you'll —"

"Not now, Danny."

I felt almost like someone had punched the wind right out of my gut. "What?"

"I want to be with you forever too, Danny, but we can't be engaged in *high school*. Even if our parents would let us, we're still too young. There's college coming. I'm going to the University of Washington in Seattle and I want you to come with me, but you'll probably . . ." She paused.

I snapped the ring box closed.

JoBell went on. "But even if you come to U-Dub too, who's to say we'll be the same people there as we are now? Who's to say we won't change?"

I squeezed the box to keep myself under control. "This . . ." I stopped and swallowed back the stinging feeling in my throat. "My love for you won't ever change."

She ran to me and kissed me full on the lips. She put her hands around the box and pressed it between our bodies, over our hearts. "Keep this," she said. "For when the time is really right."

"How will I know —"

She pressed her finger to my lips. "You'll know, Danny." She kissed me again, and then hurried from the room.

I followed her downstairs to the kitchen, where she went to the back door. She stopped there for a moment and looked back at me. Then she slipped outside and the door slammed shut behind her.

·

SEVENTEEN

I stood in the kitchen for a long time watching that closed door. Then I made myself a drink of lemonade from water and a powdered mix along with some ancient vodka that Mom had forgotten at the back of the cupboard, going over everything that had just happened. JoBell said she loved me, said she always would, and that she wanted us to be together. If that was true, then what did she mean with all that stuff about going to college and changing into different people? Did she think we'd meet people at college that we liked more than each other? Did she think she'd take some classes and learn that she didn't love me anymore? No way. I took a sip of my vodka lemonade and shook my head as I went into the dark, lonely living room. I'd mixed my drink way too strong.

Maybe it was time to admit to myself what JoBell had almost said tonight. I probably wasn't going to college in Seattle or to any other big university. Yeah, I wanted to stay closer to home, but it was more than that. I wasn't flunking out of high school, wasn't in danger of not graduating, but my grades weren't that great. So far this year, with the bad dreams about the Battle of Boise and even about Lieutenant McFee's death keeping me awake all the time, and the waking nightmare of everything that had happened, I had not been able to focus on my schoolwork at all. What's more is that I simply wasn't able to make myself care about homework and grades. Never could. Is that why JoBell had turned me down? Because I wasn't smart enough? Because she knew I wouldn't be going to college with her?

I didn't *need* college. I had my plan, my perfect plan, to take over the shop someday and raise a family here in Freedom Lake with my JoBell. What was the good of any plan if it didn't include JoBell?

I pulled the ring box from my pocket and squeezed it in my fist against my forehead. Why had I asked her tonight? She was right. We were still in high school. Nobody got engaged in high school! That's why she'd said no. None of that other crazy stuff mattered. Me and JoBell were good. Good for each other. Meant to be together. Soul mates or whatever.

I took a drink, the ice cubes clinking against the glass in my shaky hand.

I had asked her to marry me because everything else in my life was falling apart. I was afraid that I would have to leave, and I didn't want to lose my girl in the process. I only wish . . . How was I supposed to come back from a rejection like that? I'd tried to put our relationship on a higher level and she'd shot me down. What happened to us now?

Later, I did my duty as a good son and called Mom in Spokane, even though I really didn't want to talk to anyone right then. She said she was fine, but I could hear the shadow in her voice, and my call log showed me she'd already tried to call me a couple times tonight while I'd had my comm on silent. Luckily, the conference had set her up in a nice hotel with room service that offered chamomile tea. She said I shouldn't worry about her at all, but I'd been worrying about her my whole life.

The next day was worse than Monday. I still had the deadline for reporting for duty, but now I had a touch of a headache from last night's drink, and I had to face JoBell. By the look on Becca's face when she saw me, JoBell had told her about the flop proposal from the night before. At lunch, when I asked JoBell to come over that night, she made an excuse and then went to the bathroom. Becca would hardly look at me. She said quietly, "Give her a little time. It'll be okay."

So Tuesday night I sat alone on the couch, flipping through feeds on the living room screen to see if there was something live that was good. Of course, there was nothing worth watching, and I didn't feel like catching old shows on the Internet. I sighed. "I'm bored enough to actually do homework," I said to nobody.

The doorbell rang and I jumped up, thinking it better not be a reporter. I was pissed enough to finally give them a statement, and it wouldn't be one they would like. I opened the door a crack so I could slam it shut if it was trouble.

And there Becca stood on the porch, smiling and holding a foil-covered pan.

I hadn't expected to see her and had no idea what to say. "Um, hey."

She laughed a little. "Can I come in?"

Reporters out in the street started taking photos. "Oh." I opened the door and rushed her inside. "Yeah. Sorry. Sure. What's up?"

"I know that your master plan was to eat frozen pizzas or canned soup all week." She went to the kitchen, put the pan on the counter, and leaned over to start the oven. "But since my parents are on vacation in Florida with Eric's mom and dad, I thought I'd bring you some real food." She peeled the foil off the dish. "My famous lasagna. Won a blue ribbon at the 4-H fair freshman year."

"You didn't have to do this. I'm good with the frozen pizzas, really. Plus I have some fish sticks."

"You're good with that stuff, but it is not good for you. Plus, it's too late. I've already made this. Now I have to bake it, and then we can eat."

"But . . . That's a pretty big pan. I hope you're really hungry or counting on leftovers because I don't think you and me —"

She leveled her gaze at me. "Relax," she said. "The others are on their way over right now. If you *are* going to report for federal duty tomorrow, and this is your last night at home, we thought we'd send you off in style." She reached up to unclip the shiny butterfly from her hair. "And no matter where you go, I want you to remember that you have friends back home who care about you." She held the hair clip out to me. "Take this to remind you of that?"

Except when we were little babies, I'd never seen her without that clip. She'd told me once that her older sister had given it to her on the day she died of cancer, asking Becca to keep it to help her remember.

"Becca, I can't take this," I said quietly.

She grabbed my hand, opened my fingers, put the butterfly in my palm, and closed my grip around it. "Yes, you can." She kept my hand in both of hers. "No matter what you choose. No matter where you go. I don't want you to forget me. Forget us."

"I could never forget you guys." It was silent for a moment. Then I smiled. "And what if I stay home?"

She laughed and pushed my hand away. "In that case, I'm going to want that back."

"Hey, you two didn't start without me, did you?" Sweeney came in carrying a duffel bag that was obviously packed with some sort of box. "When the folks are away, the kids will play! My old man won't miss a few beers."

JoBell and Cal arrived next. JoBell shut the front door. "Damn it, Eric, why don't you shout that a little louder? I don't think the reporters or the cops heard you. Or do you want me to just call them and ask them to bust us?"

Believe it or not, a grumpy JoBell yelling at Sweeney actually made me feel better, closer to normal after the awkwardness from last night. She followed me into the kitchen, where we were alone, and kissed me on the mouth. When she pulled back, her face was still close to mine and her fingertips slipped down my cheek for a moment, sending tingles through me.

"You okay?" she whispered.

I took a step back from her. Somehow her concern bothered me. I'm not gonna lie, having my marriage proposal rejected last night hurt, but being treated like a wounded little puppy didn't make me feel any better. "Yeah. I'm fine," I said. "You know, forget about last night. I was an idiot."

"No." She put her hands on my upper arms. "Danny, it was beautiful, it's —"

"Yeah, I know. It's cool. I get it." I broke free from her grip and went to join the others in the dining room.

As I came into the room, I heard the welcome *crack-hiss* of a beer being opened. "So my parents are gone," Sweeney said. "Becca's parents are gone, conveniently to the same Florida resort. And maybe this will influence your decision about tomorrow, buddy." He tossed me a beer — a good, expensive one, Wild Moose, brewed in Montana. "I'm thinking I'm going to have to have a party at my house on Friday. A big party. Epic. An off-the-hook stupid party."

"Hell yeah!" said Cal. He chugged half his beer. "Samantha's kind of been giving me the eye in government class. I think this weekend could be it."

"Down, boy," Becca said. "Sorry, but Sam is so not into you. I happen to know that her and Chase Draper were —"

"Wait. Hold on. Quiet," JoBell said, turning the volume up on the living room screen. President Rodriguez was giving a speech, sitting behind his desk in the Oval Office.

"Oh, will you shut that off?" said Sweeney. "Better yet, put on some music."

JoBell stared at the screen and held up her hand. "Shhh."

President Rodriguez spoke sternly, looking directly at the camera. "*. . . have every hope for a peaceful resolution to this crisis. However, Governor Montaine has produced an intolerable situation by* *posting Idaho National Guard soldiers along all the borders of Idaho in an illegal effort to block the entry of federal military and law enforcement personnel. I cannot wait any longer to take action in reply. That is why, effective immediately, all federal financial aid to the state of Idaho has been cut off. Furthermore, I have given orders to the United States Army to create a blockade that will allow anyone to leave Idaho, but will not allow any people or materials to enter. All flights into the state have been canceled."*

"He can't *do* that! That's totally illegal!" JoBell shouted.

"Shhh," Sweeney said. He wasn't messing around either, but really listening.

"I appreciate the cooperation of the governments and people of Washington, Oregon, Nevada, and Utah. I've been in touch with the governors of Montana and Wyoming. They have met in emergency session with their legislatures and agreed that they don't want the dangerous situation that Governor Montaine has created spilling into their states. They have also asked that besides normal business at existing federal military outposts within their states, no additional federal troops be assigned for blockade operations. Instead, the Idaho borders with Montana and Wyoming will be closed and patrolled by state police and National Guard personnel from those two states. The end result will be the same. As of this moment, the Idaho border is closed."

"Bastard's gonna try to starve us out," Cal said.

"If Governor Montaine and the members of the Idaho state legislature who voted for nullification truly support the people they claim to represent, they will stand down their soldiers and surrender themselves to federal authorities."

"Now Idaho representatives are arrested for voting like morons?" JoBell said.

"If they start arresting every elected idiot, there won't be anyone left," said Sweeney.

"In the meantime, I fully expect all members of the Idaho National Guard to report for federal duty by zero eight hundred hours tomorrow as ordered. Any member of the Idaho National Guard who does not report at that time will be deemed as guilty as Governor Montaine and those select members of the Idaho legislature.

"The Idaho Crisis has gone on for far too long, and now, unfortunately, unprecedented measures must be taken to restore order and the rule of those laws duly passed by the legal representatives in the United States Congress. Further announcements will follow. May God bless the United States of America."

The screen went black for a second and then went back to the CNN newsroom. A gray-bearded man sat motionless for a moment before snapping alert. *"Welcome back to the CNN Idaho Crisis situation room. I'm Al Hudson. We've been monitoring large-scale troop movements in the northwestern part of the United States all afternoon, and there's been much speculation about what those movements could mean, but it seems now we have our answer. For any of you joining us now, and for those of you who saw the president's announcement and are as shocked as I am, let's review what the president of the United States just told us."*

The screen went dark. Becca was holding the remote control. The look on her face made it clear that she wasn't listening to any arguments about turning it back on. A tear ran down her face, but she quickly wiped it away. She looked to Sweeney and me. "Our parents are trapped out of state. We need to talk."

Becca's comm rang.

"JoBell, a call labeled urgent is coming in from your father," said Digi-Eleanor.

"Breaker one nine! Hey Cal, Daddy Big Bear is squawkin' for you. Come back now, ten four," said Cal's Digi-Trucker John.

"*Mmmm, Eric, baby. You got a call coming in, you big hot stud.*" The voice from Sweeney's comm was breathy and hot. "*Come get it, big boy.*" Sweeney picked up his comm. I saw the naked brunette in the bottom right corner pop-up video. "*Yes! Eric, I want your fingers on me. Touch me all over! Tap in to that call. Tap me hard, Eric.*"

"*Hey partner, your mama's calling. You gonna take this?*" said Digi-Hank.

Everybody knew their worried parents were calling, but nobody tapped in yet.

"*Ooooh, Eric, tap me! I can't wait any longer!*"

"Okay, Trixie," said Sweeney. "Calm down, baby." He seemed to notice us staring. "What?"

"Really, Eric?" JoBell asked. "What if someone calls while you're at school?"

"No problem," said Sweeney. "As soon as Trixie gets near school, she puts her clothes and glasses back on and becomes Hot Librarian Trixie. She's the best digi-assistant ever programmed."

"We don't have time for this," I said. I ran upstairs for privacy. If Mom was having an attack, I didn't want to parade it around in front of the others.

"Mom?" I said when I tapped in to the call.

"Danny? Oh my gosh, Danny, are you okay? I saw on the news . . ." Her breathing came in a wheeze. "They said . . . they said the border was closed. They're not going to let me go home, Danny. They're not going to let me come home. What are we gonna do?"

"Mom?" I tried.

"How are you gonna get by all alone? *I'm* all alone. When this conference is over, I can't afford to keep paying for a hotel."

"Mom."

"Can't afford an apartment." She coughed. "They say you've all been ordered to federal duty. But if you go, they'll arrest you, Danny.

You can't go. What if they don't arrest you, but send you to war? They could stick you in Iran, Danny, and all those Idaho boys were killed there the other day."

"Mom!"

"Oh, Danny!" There was a sound almost like retching.

"Mom, listen to me!"

"Oh. Oh, don't yell at me, Danny. I don't know what to do!"

"Shhhh. Mom, it's okay. You're okay. Breathe. Force the air in." I heard her breathe, shaky, but deep. "Now exhale." I could hear her breathing. There were little sobs, but we'd get this ironed out. "And breathe in, deep as you can. And let it fall out. Have a seat in the chair if you've got one there."

We sat there like that on the phone, breathing, for about five minutes. I was out of time for debating my options. I had to make some decisions and I had to make them now.

"Danny." She seemed calmer now. "What are we going to do?"

"Okay, I'm not going to report for federal service," I said. That was the first decision I made.

"But then they'll call you a criminal like the governor and —"

"They're already calling me a criminal, but they can't get in here to arrest me. So relax about that."

"Oh, Danny." She sounded like she was going to cry again. "Maybe I should rush home right now. Maybe I can make it across the border before the soldiers can really stop anyone from —"

"No, Mom. You know, stay in Washington for now. Carry on with your conference for the rest of the week. Anyway, this is probably going to blow over soon." I squeezed my eyes closed, praying I wasn't talking a lot of false-hope gibberish. "The government will get this mess straightened out in no time, and the president will at least have to let normal Idaho people come back home."

"But what if —"

"If it drags on longer, I'll look online for a place for you to stay. I'll take out a loan and buy you an RV. Something."

"You're only seventeen, Danny. They're not going to loan you —"

"Then I'll have Schmidty take out the loan for me. I'll take care of you, Mom. I promise. Whatever it takes, I'll make sure you're okay." There was silence on the line for a long time. "Mom?"

"You're a good boy, Danny," she said sadly. "Well, a man really. I don't know when you stopped being a boy, but I'm proud of the man you've become."

I talked to Mom a little longer, trying to get her mind off the fact that she couldn't come home, trying to keep her calm. Eventually, after we agreed to check in every day, I tapped out of the call.

Downstairs, the earlier party mood had vanished. JoBell's dad had insisted she come home right away, but she had argued that she needed to have one last dinner with her friends. Her dad gave in, but he got in touch with everyone else's folks, and he promised to check up on the rest of us from time to time. Sweeney's folks didn't seem as worried as he thought they should be. They seemed to think it was like a longer vacation. His dad let him know how to tap certain emergency funds he had set aside. Becca's parents worried about their farm and wanted to make sure she'd be able to continue to take care of the cattle, but they seemed reassured when we all promised to help her.

Cal surprised me. He wiped his eyes, turning away from us so we couldn't see.

"What is it, Cal?" JoBell asked, sitting down beside him and putting her hand on his shoulder.

"My old man," he said quietly. "He's out on the road. On the way back from a lumber haul to Minneapolis." The last part of his sentence sounded a little choked.

"I'm sorry," JoBell said.

"Even if he can't get back home," I said, "his rig has a big sleeper. He can keep trucking. He can still make money. When this is all over, he can —"

Cal faced us. His eyes were red and watery, but he was smiling. "He was calling from the parking lot of the Lookout Pass resort, right inside the state line. He said the Montana Highway Patrol closed the border about two minutes after he crossed into Idaho." He held up a fist in front of his chest. "Good old Dad. Always brings the rig home right on time." A tear rolled down his cheek. "Oh hell, give me another beer."

I laughed as I handed him another round. Cal was so big and tough that I sometimes forgot there was more to the guy than partying and busting heads in football. His old man was a real a-man-needs-to-take-care-of-himself type guy, and he left Cal on his own a lot while on trucking runs, so I was happy he'd be able to make it home now.

Later we gathered at the table to enjoy Becca's lasagna and the Wild Moose beer. Becca served us each a big square, and then sat down with her own. Cal grabbed his fork, stabbed right into it, and was about to take a huge bite when Becca held up a hand.

"Wait a second," she said. "How 'bout we say grace first?"

"What?" Cal said with the steaming mass of cheese and pasta in front of his open mouth. "Oh yeah."

We all bowed our heads. Becca led the prayer. "Lord, thank you for this food we are about to eat. Please help us and help our parents as we go through this difficult time. Thank you, Lord, for letting the five of us be together tonight. Thank you for this friendship. Amen."

"Amen," we all said.

I reached out for JoBell's hand and she squeezed mine. I looked at Sweeney, who took a drink. Cal had stuffed down that huge bite of very hot lasagna and was holding his mouth open, breathing heavy, trying to avoid burning his mouth. Becca laughed at him, and then her eyes met mine, and she flashed the warmest, kindest smile I'd seen in a long time.

Becca was right. We should be grateful to all be together. Silently, I thanked God for my friends. That night, though, they felt like more than that. Closer than that. More like family.

"I love you guys," I said.

"Oh, Danny." Sweeney spoke in a high-pitched voice and dabbed a napkin to the corner of his eyes in big, exaggerated movements. "That's sooooo sweet!"

JoBell laughed until her face was red. "That's what you get for trying to get mushy around these lunkheads."

"Hey," Cal mumbled with his mouth full. "Ahm na a lunhea."

I pointed my fork at Sweeney. "Nobody likes you very much."

He held his beer up to me in a mock toast.

Glass shattered in the living room. We heard a thud on the floor and squealing tires and a horn honking from outside. My fork clattered to my plate and I was up and sprinting toward the front of the house.

"Danny, wait!" JoBell yelled. "It could be dangerous."

I was glad I had my shoes on, because the living room floor was covered in glass. I ran out the front door, jumped off the porch, and bolted to the street as fast as I could, but I only caught a glimpse of the taillights of a car as it whipped around the corner down the block.

I stood in the middle of the street, marveling in the quiet. Most of the media circus was gone. There were only three news vans and maybe about a dozen reporters or camera people. They'd finally found a bigger story to go after.

I heard a camera click, and I spun around to face one of the last reporters in America who was not covering the blockade right now. He started snapping photos of me in front of my busted front window.

"Thanks for warning me," I shouted at him. "You get a picture of that guy for the news?"

The prick gave me the thumbs-up and then went back to taking pictures of me. Others joined in, rolling video and shooting photos.

"I know this is a stressful time," said a woman, "but could I ask you a few questions? Getting your side of the story out might help people understand you better. It might prevent stuff like this from happening in the future."

Cal and Sweeney were right behind me. "You see the license plates?" Sweeney asked.

"Nope," I said. The girls were looking out through the spiderweb of cracks in the front window with a two-inch hole in the middle. "Nice job the governor's extra security is doing, huh?"

Cal stepped up to the first photographer to shoot pictures that night, a skinny guy maybe in his early thirties. Cal's upper arm looked about as big as the reporter's waist. "Cool comm," Cal said. The reporter took a few steps back, but Cal grabbed the comm out of his hands. "Where's the pics? They go up to your cloud? Pull 'em up!"

"Take it easy," said the reporter.

"Cal, knock it off," I said.

Cal held the comm out in his left hand and cocked his big right fist back. "Pull up the photos!"

Other cameras were rolling, getting video of the whole thing. The footage would make Cal look like a monster, and the press would have a field day with that.

With shaking hands, the man did what he said.

"That's the first smart thing you've done." Cal tapped the screen a couple times. "Dumb bastard has no pics of the car or the rock throwers or anything." He fiddled with the screen more. "There. All the pictures of me and my friends deleted. And in case this is one of those weird old-fashioned comms with a hard drive and you have any more copies saved to it —"

"Cal, no!" Sweeney shouted as he and I ran to stop Cal from spiking the comm on the street.

"What?" Cal said. "We can't keep letting them —"

"This isn't helping me." I took the reporter's comm from Cal and handed it back to its owner. "They're just going to make some terrible distorted story out of all this."

"Let's go," Sweeney said.

· We all went back inside, where Becca had started sweeping up the glass. JoBell handed me the rock. It was wrapped in paper tied with string. I ripped off the string, unfolded the paper, and dropped the rock to the floor. "Let's see what these bastards have to say."

> *We know who you are. We know what you did. The governor might have pardoned you but we don't. Your responsable for this whole mess. We are going to make you pay. Like the people you killed in Boise. Sleep careful. We'll be back.*

"What?" JoBell asked.

I gave her the note, then went up to my room. I had thought Schmidty was kind of crazy with his guns and survival bunker, but now he was starting to make sense. From under my bed I pulled out Dad's nine-millimeter handgun — my gun now. I picked up its empty magazine and the box of shells, wishing I'd taken Schmidty more seriously and gone to buy more mags already. I went back to the others, put the gun and ammunition on the coffee table, and grabbed my comm.

"You're going to want to hide the beer," I said to Sweeney. "Hank, get me a voice call with Nathan Crow."

"You got it, ace! How'd you like to listen to —"

"Shut up, Hank," I said.

"Hank's still better than Eric's porn assistant," said JoBell.

"Hey, you'll hurt Trixie's feelings," Sweeney said. "She's very sensitive."

"Danny Wright!" said Sheriff Crow when he picked up. "Good to hear from you. Did you see the news? How are you holding up through all this?"

"Not good," I said. "Somebody threw a rock with a death threat through my front window. I'd like to press charges if you can catch the guy, but more importantly . . ." I looked at Sweeney. "I'm going to be staying at a friend's place. I need someone to keep an eye on my house. Can you spare anyone?"

"For you, Danny, I'll keep eyes on the house around the clock. I'm sorry I didn't have my man watching this evening. The problem is, as you can imagine, with everything going on, we've been very busy. Traffic's all backed up with a bunch of cowards trying to get out of Idaho as fast as they can. I can't spare any officers, but I do know some men I trust like brothers. I'll send one of them to keep watch. Don't worry. Go do what you have to do. Your house will be safe."

"Thanks, Sheriff." I tapped out and looked at the others. "I'm going to join the Idaho Guard full-time."

"Yes!" Cal said.

"Danny, you can't," JoBell said. "What about school?"

"I'll have to see about classes online. Maybe just get the GED."

She put her hand on my arm. "That will never be good enough for the University of Washington. You have to get your grades up and —"

"JoBell, you and I both know I'm not going to some big, fancy university. That's part of what you were thinking last night, wasn't it?"

"This has nothing to do with last night."

"Last night?" Sweeney asked, but Becca elbowed him.

"Okay," I said. "Never mind about that. This is something I have to do. I swore an oath to protect my home." I swept my arm in a gesture to all of them. "To protect the people I care about. Now this asshole president has locked down the border."

"Montaine was doing the same thing!" JoBell said.

"He was keeping outside military out. The president is keeping out civilians. There's a difference. My home is in trouble, and I've got to help."

"By going to war against your own country?" JoBell asked.

"Nobody's fighting," said Cal.

"I'm going to help keep the state from being overrun by the Fed until they can work out some kind of agreement," I said. "If nobody goes to back up Idaho, the Fed will send in the Army and arrest me and the other guys in my squad in a heartbeat, and then they'll go after Montaine." JoBell was about to interrupt, but I cut her off. "Whatever you think of the governor, he hasn't let me or my Guard guys down. He's stuck by us and done his best to protect us. I owe him at least that much." I brushed a few shards of glass off the couch and took a seat, then opened the box of bullets and started snapping rounds into the magazine.

"What are you doing?" JoBell pointed at the gun. "It's against the law for you to have that thing."

"It's against the law to chuck rocks through someone's window and threaten to kill him." I held up the weapon. "I'm just leveling things out."

↗—• president assures us this is not a prelude to open military conflict, despite the fact that a blockade of this nature hasn't been in place in this country since the Civil War in 1861. In response to human rights concerns about the distribution of food, medicine, and needed supplies, the White House said merely that any difficulties resulting from shortages within Idaho are the result of Governor Montaine and the Idaho state legislature's irresponsible policies. Exactly how much of its own food does Idaho produce? For more on that, we'll talk to an agricultural expert from •—↗

CRYSTAL LEESLAN ★ ★ ★ ★ ☆

Mom, I can't get a call through to you. I have the comm set to redial, but it keeps saying the server is over capacity. Even the old landlines are jammed. I'm with Jake. I-84 heading into Idaho is completely gridlocked, both lanes. There're coils of like razor wire, soldiers, and tanks everywhere. Bright lights on towers. We watched a bunch of people get beat down with clubs when they tried to run on foot across the border. We're going to go back to Jake's friend's house in Tremonton. We're okay. Scared but safe. EVERYONE, if you are reading this, do NOT try to cross the border! The Utah/Idaho border is not safe! If you know my mom Nichi Leeslan, please give her this message.

★ ★ ★ ★ ★ This Post's Star Average 5.00   [Star Rate][Comment]   34 minutes ago

---

ADAM LEESLAN ★ ★ ★ ☆ ☆

Hey cousin, my dad's driving over to see your mom right now. He'll let her know what's going on. Hang in there. Stay safe.

★ ★ ★ ★ ★ This Comment's Star Average 5.00   [Star Rate]   28 minutes ago

---

↗—• CBS News has unconfirmed reports that shots were fired when an unknown person attempted to drive around a checkpoint on eastbound Highway 270 in Washington, on a stretch of road between Pullman, Washington, and Moscow, Idaho. The vehicle was trying to enter Idaho when it was reportedly fired upon and

disabled. Again, this is an unconfirmed report, and we're trying to get more information on that situation. If this has happened, we have no information as to whether anyone was injured or even who fired the shots. •⟋

⟋• live in the news chopper with aerial footage of an unprecedented deployment of federal troops and combat vehicles along Idaho's borders with Washington, Oregon, Nevada, and Utah, with Montana and Wyoming state police and National Guard troops along their own borders with Idaho. Easily several thousand troops, if not tens of thousands. In this live picture, you can see people leaving Idaho after a brief inspection by federal troops, but nobody is being allowed to enter the state. This has traffic backed up for miles. Oh my word — Can we get . . . Do we have . . . Can we get a shot of that, Rick? Ladies and gentlemen, we're being intercepted by a military aircraft. A well-armed helicopter gunship of some kind. We're getting a signal. I'll try to patch it through."

"CIVILIAN AIRCRAFT, YOU HAVE ENTERED A RESTRICTED AIRSPACE. YOU WILL LAND IMMEDIATELY OR WE ARE AUTHORIZED TO OPEN FIRE."

"Rick, land. No, no, don't turn back. Just land somewhere. Anywhere! Ladies and gentlemen, I can't imagine that the US Army would fire on an unarmed news chopper, but then again, yesterday I would never have imagined a blockade like this. My pilot will try to find a —"

. . .

. . .

. . .

"Ladies and gentlemen, that was Roy Greptis in our KREM 2 News Chopper. We don't . . . Excuse me. We don't know what has happened, but certainly the video you've just seen is disturbing.

Again, we cannot stress enough, do not attempt to approach the Idaho border. We do not believe it is safe."

"Okay, we've received a call from Roy. They are okay. They were forced to land their helicopter, but before they could even begin to descend, Roy says, their audio and video transmissions were jammed. We don't know who jammed that signal, but that's a powerful transmitter on our news chopper. We can only speculate at this time that perhaps the signal was somehow interrupted by military forces in the area. We have more reports that ●⎯⋏⎯

EIGHTEEN

The next morning I slept in. Why show up on time when I wouldn't even be going to class anymore? With the big blockade story to cover, there were a lot less reporters around town, making it much easier to get where I needed to go. When I finally rolled into school between fourth and fifth hour, I marched down the hallway in my MCUs, my tan combat boots clomping on the floor. Lots of conversations dropped to a whisper when I passed.

I'd come to school to officially drop out. All that meant was I wouldn't be able to walk at graduation with the cap and gown. So what? The one person who would appreciate seeing me do that would be my mother, and right now the federal government wouldn't even let her come home.

I probably should have gone to the office first, but I didn't want to deal with Mr. Morgan. Instead, I went to Mr. Shiratori's room. He was a great coach and the best teacher in the school, about the only one I could really stand. I couldn't take off without saying anything to him.

No students were in the room, so it must have been his prep period. When I walked in, he sat slouched in his chair facing the screen. Some teachers had their screens on a lot before or after school, watching their favorite shows or listening to music while they graded assignments. Mr. Shiratori usually only used his screen to show us historical videos or for maps, charts, or graphs. But today he'd split the image into six different news feeds at once.

"*In a televised address, Governor Montaine assured the nation and Idaho residents that he has been in touch with Idaho agricultural authorities and was confident that, although some items consumers are accustomed to would be scarce or unavailable, the nutrition needs of Idaho residents would be met despite, quote, 'the president's attempt to starve us out.' The governor also announced plans to tap the deposits of silver found last year in the mountainous Payette National Forest region in order to compensate Idaho National Guard personnel with newly minted silver coins. The governor said, quote, 'Idaho's rich wealth in silver and other precious minerals is more than enough to pay the Idaho National Guard.'*"

I stood by the door for a moment, waiting for him to say something, to even look at me. He didn't. "Mr. Shiratori?"

He switched the sound to a different feed. "*The president is on very shaky legal ground here. He's relying on the precedent established by President Lincoln in 1861, when Lincoln ordered a blockade of the Confederate states by proclamation and without the express authorization of Congress. Despite facing heavy criticism suggesting that he has been too patient and lenient with the Idaho Crisis, after his strong action yesterday, the president's poll numbers have actually dropped.*"

Mr. Shiratori muted the sound. "Do you know why I teach American history and government, Mr. Wright?"

Did he really want an answer to that? It sounded like one of those questions he was about to answer himself, but he waited so long in silence that I thought I should say something. "Um, because they pay you?"

"Hmm." He snorted and spun in his chair to face me. "I could make a lot more money doing something else. No, I have taught history and government here in this school for over fifteen years because I *believe* in America. Oh, don't get me wrong. This country has made her fair share of mistakes. My great-grandparents were forced into internment camps during World War II. But even with his family imprisoned, my grandfather enlisted to fight in that war because he, like my father, like me, *believed* in America, in the philosophy behind its Constitution, in the purity of what America was supposed to be, what it could have been." He waved his hand around in the air in front of him. "You know, equality and a decent chance to work hard to make something of your life."

"It can still be that way," I said.

"It looks like President Andrew Jackson was right way back in the 1830s. 'Nullification means insurrection and war.' We're about to find out."

"It won't come to that," I said.

"Really? You say that, and yet there you are in uniform, running off to serve in one army or the other."

I dropped my duffel bag to the floor, unzipped it, pulled out my Minutemen game jersey, and held it out to him. He made no move to take it from me.

"I'm going to support the governor," I said. "The Feds have trapped my mom plus Eric's and Becca's parents outside the state. Someone's got to stand up to them. We can't just let them trample our freedoms."

"That's a slogan, Mr. Wright. We are heading into a war. No matter what slogans help you march into it, if you're lucky to survive long enough to hobble back out, it might be hard to remember what the slogan even meant, much less if it justified all that we've lost in its name."

I stood there for a minute. Finally I put the jersey down on his desk. "Well, you've been a great teacher and coach, Mr. Shiratori."

He stood up quickly and shook my hand with a firm grip. "Thank you, Mr. Wright. I'd try to talk you out of this if I thought it would do any good. So instead I'll wish you luck, and I'll be praying for you."

I nodded and then headed for the door.

"Oh, and Danny," he said, just before I walked out of his room. "I have the feeling this is going to get really bad. Be careful who you trust."

I went to the office to sign out of high school. For once, Mr. Morgan didn't lecture me too much. He didn't even ask which side I was joining. He said that since the district hadn't ever had a student unable to finish high school due to military service, he would have to review my situation with the school board to determine the next step. He said he'd do his best to help make sure I at least got my diploma. The guy was still a total jackwad, but I was impressed that he could be decent for once.

I went out to the Beast, started up the engine, and drove out of the parking lot for the last time. I'd called my Guard unit last night, and a female specialist whose name I didn't recognize told me I could either report directly to the border checkpoint all the way on the other side of the mountain or wait at the armory for a truck to shuttle me out there at eighteen hundred hours. No way was I going to wait around all day. It was close to lunchtime, so I decided I'd stop by the Coffee Corner to eat before heading out. It would be cool having my own vehicle out on duty. Maybe some nights if there wasn't much for me to do, they'd let me drive back into town to see JoBell.

The Coffee Corner was a crappy diner down on Main Street, the kind of place where old-timers and farmers stopped by after morning chores to have coffee, talk work and weather, and tell jokes. JoBell worked there sometimes. Alice seemed to work there all the time. She looked up from the comm she'd been reading. Everybody always checked out whoever came in, and today a couple reporters followed me in. That meant a lot of eyes on me. The conversation quieted.

"No media," Alice called out. "Owner's policy. You'll have to wait outside for your story. Get out, or I'll call the sheriff."

When the reporters left, some people clapped.

"There he is!" said a farmer in overalls who sat with his friends at a table.

"The hero of the hour," said a big man with a beard. He saluted.

I quickly sat down at the last stool at the counter. I didn't know what they were making such a big deal about or why they were so happy, but I'd had more than enough attention.

"Sorry about that," I said to Alice after she'd put a glass of water in front of me.

"Oh, no bother. We're used to it," Alice said. "No school today, sweetie?"

"There's school, but I have to report to my National Guard unit."

"Hey, Alice, whatever the soldier wants, it's on me," said another of the old-timers.

"That's not really necessary," I said to Alice.

"Well, they're excited, and I can't blame 'em." She motioned to the room, her thick plastic bracelets clicking. "Look at this place. Everybody is in here ordering food like we ain't gonna have none tomorrow. And now with this blockade on, my brother finally found work. You know they've cut down so many trees on the border that the sawmills can hardly keep up. They're running extra shifts, and my brother was hired on."

"I told you, Alice," said the man in overalls. "Montaine is a different kind of governor. When he said he was going to bring jobs back to Idaho, he knew what he was talking about."

"And these guys are laughing all the way to the bank," Alice said to me. "Food prices are up already. They're saying potatoes are worth their weight in gold." I raised an eyebrow. She patted my arm. She was real touchy-feely like that. It was weird. "Not really, of course, but they're making some good money."

"They say the state legislature rushed through some special zoning and funds to get another factory going in Boise, building even more electrical equipment," said a red-haired guy sitting next to me. "So the construction business will be booming. They're talking about starting something like that up in Coeur d'Alene too. I guess they can get a lot done without all the federal red tape holding them up."

Was anyone going to just let me get lunch? "Cheeseburger basket, please," I said to Alice.

A guy with shaggy black hair and three days of stubble slapped me on the back. His breath reeked of coffee and cigarettes. "I have to shake your hand," he said. I reached out and shook his rough hand. "I know this has been tough, the way they blamed you for all them deaths in Boise, and then chasing you around the state, but I got to tell you, we's all proud of you."

One man's chair scraped the floor loudly as he pushed it back and stood up. "I can't listen to any more of this garbage." He stormed out of the diner.

"Forget him," said Mr. Coffee and Cigarettes. "Most of us is right behind you. You got this whole thing started so we can finally stand up to them bastard crooks in Washington."

"Um, thanks, I guess," I said, finally freeing my hand.

A man who went to my church — I'd forgotten his name — leaned forward at the counter. "He's right. You're a real hero, Danny. Oops. I mean, Private First Class Wright."

Why couldn't these people leave me alone? I was no damned hero. I'd failed to maintain control of my weapon and it had started a nightmare. I pretended to check my comm for the time. "Hey, Alice, can I get that burger to go?"

A short time later I was back in the Beast, eating my lunch on the road. I was surprised when the news on the radio actually stopped and the theme music for the *Buzz Ellison Show* came on.

Greetings, greetings, fellow patriots! Welcome to the Buzz Ellison Show, the beacon of freedom, shining the light of truth as we broadcast live coast to coast — despite the president's blockade — from Conservative Central Command in downtown Boise, Idaho. It's a new day in America! A landmark day in the struggle against big government. The number to call if you want to be on the program today is 1-800-555-FREE, that's 1-800-555-3733.

Well, he's finally done it. El Presidente Rodriguez has closed the border for anyone wishing to enter the state of Idaho. And it's ironic, isn't it, that part of the reason behind this standoff is the federal government's ridiculous unconstitutional spy card act? One of the benefits that the president has claimed this card offers is that it will supposedly reduce illegal immigration. If he had sealed the US border the way he's sealed the Idaho border, we wouldn't have had any illegal immigrants to worry about in the first place!

But, oh, where to begin today, folks? Students at colleges and universities across the country walking out of classes, protesting for peace, calling for an end to the blockade, calling for talks. Food riots already in Brooklyn and Harlem. New York National Guard running patrols to maintain order. And there's not even a shortage out there yet! People are simply scared of the food supply being interrupted. Food riots in Detroit. A couple people have been hospitalized after fights broke out there. Though in Detroit . . . Buzz laughed. *I don't know how they'd tell that apart from an average day. There* are even unconfirmed reports that someone in northern Oregon took shots at federal soldiers stationed on the border there with Idaho.

Texas is about to vote to nullify the Federal Identification Card Act, and polls show that such a measure is a runaway favorite to pass. Oklahoma is expected to follow along. What will Rodriguez do, enforce sanctions against those states too? That would be rich — Rodriguez closing Texas's borders with the rest of America, but leaving the Mexican border wide open!

Still, a lot of people here in Idaho are worried. Worried about food shortages, about shortages on everything. Police, National Guard, and Idaho Civilian Corps people have had to stand guard at stores to prevent total chaos. But I want you to take heart, fellow patriots, and listen to the Buzzman as I assure you, we're going to be okay. The president won't be able to stop us from trading with Montana and Wyoming. And he . . . Buzz chuckled. Do you know he's asked Canada to post troops at their border with Idaho, but they've refused? They'll only enforce the blockade at their regular checkpoints on two highways. Folks, Idaho's border with Canada is maybe fifty miles long, but it includes some of the most wild, mountainous, wooded lands on the continent, perfect for smugglers. We're going to be getting plenty of goods in from Canada. Canadians up there are probably thrilled at this new business opportunity.

Now, I know . . . I've been getting a lot of messages from listeners who think that this handful of Democrat congressmen calling for amendments or repeal of the spy card act is cause for a lot of hope. Some of you think that Rodriguez is going to come to his senses on this, but listen to *the threats from Senate Majority Leader "Lazy" Laura Griffith. She says, quote, "The state of Idaho, in refusing to comply with the law, and in refusing to allow the entry of soldiers, has become a rebel state, and rebellions must be ended quickly, by whatever means necessary." End quote.*

Woo! Now I know Lazy Griffith wants people to think that she's tough even though she's a woman. Now, now, don't misunderstand me. Women can be plenty tough. Just ask my ex-wife! But for some reason women politicians seem to have more to prove, and so they say things like this to try to carry through the tough image. But seriously, fellow patriots, Idaho is a rebel state? That's absolutely absurd. The president's cut off all the money coming into Idaho, but you notice he didn't say anything about money going the other way! So we in Idaho are still paying way too much money in federal taxes, though hopefully Montaine will do something about that soon. Plus, over a thousand soldiers from the Idaho Army National Guard are on federal duty, serving in Iran right now. That's before El Presidente tried to activate the rest of them. Which, by the way, only about 2 percent of remaining Idaho Guard forces reported for federal duty.

"At least I won't be alone," I said to myself. Somehow I felt better about my decision, knowing so many others had chosen the same.

Most of them are in lockstep with the governor. As they should be! Everybody should be supporting the heroes of the Idaho National Guard and Governor Montaine as they take a long-overdue stand against federal tyranny!

The show cut out to silence for a moment. Had the Fed shut him down? What about free speech? Then some music played, followed by an announcer.

> *This is an ABC News special report: Live from Washington, here's Chris McCormick.*

A different voice came on.

> *Moments ago, Vice President Aaron Henke officially announced his resignation. He has become only the third vice president in American history to ever resign from that post. In a brief statement to the press, Mr. Henke said he, quote, "refused to take any further part in one of the most dangerous situations in American history." End quote. There is no word yet on who President Rodriguez will appoint as the new vice president, but a White House spokesman says that the president is spending a great deal of time and thought on the issue and hopes to have a selection before the end of the day. The reaction from —*

I switched the radio off and drove on in silence. Everyone I talked to and everyone on the news had a different take on the standoff. Now the vice president, like Lieutenant McFee, was getting out of it. Not for the first time, I wished I could too.

The next four weeks of Army life were good for one reason. Most of the time, we were cut off from the news. The little news we did get went around the ranks quickly. That Laura Griffith woman became the next vice president. Some of the guys were worried about that because she'd been demanding the Fed get tough with Idaho, but we soon got word that President Rodriguez and Governor Montaine were videoconferencing to work out a possible compromise — something about tinkering with the stupid ID card law. Montaine sent a message to all of us, promising that he wouldn't agree to any deal that would allow Idaho Guardsmen to be punished for the shootings at Boise, or for their service in the Idaho Guard during the standoff. I hoped the talks would work so we could end this and all go home.

We also heard that enough pissed-off Idaho voters had signed a petition that the state would have to have a recall vote on November 2. If Montaine lost, he would be out of office and the lieutenant governor would take over. I didn't know who that was, but I did know that we were screwed without Montaine. If he was removed from office, the Fed would come in here and arrest every soldier who had been at Boise or refused to obey the president's activation call. Sergeant Kemp was real into politics, and he said he didn't think the recall effort would work, because not only would the majority of special election voters have to agree to recall the governor, but the recall votes had to exceed the number of votes for Montaine when he was first voted into office. He'd won in a landslide, and a lot of the

Montaine haters had left the state after the blockade started. Still, it was one more big political thing to worry about.

It seemed all the more important as Fed soldiers set up their own checkpoint across the state line from our wire obstacle. They dug in their own fighting positions and gouged a big anti-vehicle trench in the road. A large dirt berm behind the ditch made it impossible to drive through and would provide cover for Fed troops.

My team's job was to stand guard at the position Luchen and I had started building weeks before. Shortly after I showed up to duty, we stacked more rocks to build the west wall up higher. Then we pressed mud into the cracks between the rocks to harden up the barrier. After that we used some of the wood from the trees that we'd brought down to put on a log roof. More mud sealed up the gaps and mostly kept the rain out. Mostly. It didn't keep out the cold, though, and the temperature dropped further the deeper we got into October.

There were four soldiers in our team, and we pulled guard duty in pairs, twelve hours on, twelve hours off. At least one of the two soldiers on duty needed to be awake at all times. Me and Sergeant Kemp got stuck with the night shift, and twelve hours is a long time to be awake through the night, so we took turns staying up to keep watch. Still, even with our ever-present thermal cloaks, it was tough sleeping out on that cold cliff, and boring sitting through the night watching the Washington border through our night vision glasses, shivering and waiting for the sun to come up over Silver Mountain.

The only major duty we had besides sitting there and staying awake was weapons maintenance. Every time the shift changed, the guys coming on had to remove the 7.62 ammo from the M240 Bravo machine gun, strip the weapon down, clean the parts, put it back together again, and then perform a functions check to make sure it would fire if needed. After that, we had to do the same to our M4 rifles. The whole process took over an hour if we did it right, but after a while our team came to the agreement that the 240 only needed to be taken apart and cleaned once a day. We alternated that duty.

We also killed time cleaning our personal weapons, which the Idaho Guard allowed us to carry. They weren't strict with how often we performed personal weapons maintenance, but they did tell us we had to do it at least once a week. A lot of guys cleaned their weapons more often than that because they liked to get them out and show them off. Specialist Danning had his own Barrett 82A1 .50-caliber rifle. The rounds for that sucker were each about five and a half inches long, and he had two ten-round magazines, plus a wicked scope. The whole setup had to have cost him way over ten grand. Me, I was good with my standard-issue M4 and my dad's nine mil.

Staff Sergeant Meyers hadn't reported for duty, meaning he had either stayed home or sold us out and joined the Feds. Our new staff sergeant was named Shane Donshel. They'd tried promoting Kemp, but he refused, saying he preferred to stay with his team. That was lucky for me. He was in charge, but he was also one of us. Best of all, Sergeant Kemp allowed me to bend the rules on using comms on the line so that I could call my mother.

She was getting along okay, staying in the guest bedroom of a nurse she'd met at the conference, but she was rapidly using up all the vacation days she'd saved for several years. She worried that if she couldn't get back to the clinic soon, they'd have to let her go, and then we'd be in serious financial trouble, as we had a mortgage, car payment, and other bills that had to be paid. I was getting paid from the Idaho Guard — real silver coins with a picture of Idaho on one side and a Revolutionary War soldier on the other — and we had some income from the shop, but a PFC didn't make much, and with gas supplies cut off, people weren't having work done on their cars.

I could hear the shadow creeping into Mom's voice more and more as time went on.

"*I can't take it, Danny,*" she said one night. "*I want to go home. You don't understand. I need to go home.*"

"Mom, you're fine where you are. I know you'd rather be —"

"*I've heard rumors that the Army doesn't have every part of the border completely guarded, so people can sneak across into Idaho. Maybe I could do that, Danny. I used to do a lot of hiking when I was younger, and if I try it before the snow comes, it might not be that hard.*"

I stood up without thinking and hit my head on the low ceiling in our bunker. "No, Mom. Listen to me. I've been on border duty for a long time now. If the Fed doesn't have a camp somewhere, they are running patrols or scouting the border with drones. They would find you."

"*But —*"

"It's too dangerous for now, Mom. But these talks between the governor and the president seem like they're going well. I'm sure you'll be able to come home soon."

"*Oh, I hope you're right, Danny.*" She did not sound convinced.

Each time we talked, it seemed like it took longer to get her to calm down and stay where she was. As I sat up nights looking out into the darkness on the Washington border, I worried about Mom a lot.

One Thursday night, Sergeant Kemp was conducting our nightly nineteen hundred hours shift change team meeting. "Good news and bad news," he said. "The good news is we're going to get some leave time tomorrow. The bad news is it's going to be really short. So they're going to let each one of us go home for half of our shift. That's six hours off, and that includes travel time. Do not be late getting back because you'll be screwing over the next guy. You have one major order while you're at home: Gather all your civilian cold-weather gear. Hats, gloves, snowmobile suits, long underwear, whatever you got. It seems the Idaho Central Issuing Facility doesn't have close to enough gear for everyone. They have to outfit us and the ICC."

"What? The civilians?" Luchen said.

"Get used to it," said Specialist Sparrow. "I hear they're thinking about arming the ICC and putting them through some training."

"That's bullshit!" Luchen shouted.

"Maybe," Kemp said, "but that's the way it goes. Wright, tomorrow you can go home starting at nineteen hundred. Be back shortly before zero one. I'll take the worst shift off."

"Are you sure?" I asked, like I wanted him to take the best leave time. Like it was no big deal.

Kemp laughed. "You're a bad actor, Wright. Just shut up and take your shift before I change my mind."

The next day when my time came, I drove back to town, telling Hank to call JoBell over and over. Every time the call went straight to voice mail. Where the hell was she? My plan had been to call her same as I had every few days, acting like I only wanted to talk, but this time I'd be calling to figure out where she was. Then I'd show up there and surprise her. So far my plan was falling apart.

"Hank, call Becca, and don't ask me if I want to listen to any damned songs."

"*You got it, partner.*"

"*Danny?*" Becca said. "*Oh my gosh, how are you?*" There was a lot of loud talking and laughter in the background. Was that music playing?

"Hey, Becca. What's up? You at the game?"

"*All the games have been canceled due to gas rationing. Danny, hang on, I can hardly hear you. Let me step outside.*" A moment later the background noise died down. "*We're all at Cal's. His dad has* been making trucking runs for the ICC, picking up supplies from somewhere. He brought back, like, a pallet of beer for himself, and we didn't think he'd miss a few cases. I wish you were here. I miss you. I mean, you know, we all miss you."

"JoBell there and everything?"

"Um . . . Yeah." There was sort of a long pause. "Should I put her on?"

"No, no." Bingo. Found her. "I'll call back later. My sergeant is yelling at me to go do something. I have to go."

We said our goodbyes and tapped out. I cranked up the radio, switched off my mufflers so the Beast would be loud as hell, and drove on toward Cal's. Although it was against uniform regulations, I even put on my cowboy hat. It was my night off and they had a party going and everything. The night was starting to look a lot better.

A short time later, I'd parked the Beast, sprinted across the gravel lot by Cal's trailer home, and jumped up the wooden steps to his door. I could already hear the music thumping inside. Forget knocking. Nobody was going to hear it anyway. I rushed inside, threw the door closed behind me, and stopped when I saw JoBell.

She and TJ were sitting on the stairs that led up to the kitchen. TJ was leaning toward her, saying something real quiet-like so nobody else could hear. JoBell threw her head back laughing and playfully elbowed him.

"Oh, you gotta be kidding me," I said.

JoBell saw me and stood, her eyes wide in shock.

"Danny!" Becca jumped up from the faded plaid couch where she sat between Cal and Sweeney. Brad Robinson waved to me from the cracked vinyl recliner in the corner. Becca ran up and hugged me. I squeezed her once, but then gently pushed her away.

JoBell was right behind her. She kissed me quickly and then hugged me. "Danny, what are you doing here?"

"Yeah? Surprised? Didn't expect to see me?"

Her smile faded. "Of course I didn't expect you. I thought you were on duty."

"Why is your comm shut off?"

"We made her keep it off so she wouldn't be checking the news all night," Sweeney said.

JoBell frowned. "Are you okay?"

I'd waited, like, a month to see my girlfriend again, and when I finally had a chance for a couple hours with her, I walk in to catch her with that jackwad TJ. "Why don't you ask him?" I asked.

JoBell saw who I'd nodded at. "You mean . . ." She folded her arms. "Oh, come on. We were just talking."

"Keeping your comm off so I can't call you —"

She put her fists down by her sides. "Oh, I'm sorry, I didn't realize I was on twenty-four-hour standby in case the Guard happens to allow you a few minutes to use your comm!"

TJ stood up. "Hey, Wright. Seriously, it's no big deal."

"You can shut the hell up or I will beat your ass, TJ." I took a step toward him. Even though we were still a good six feet apart, Brad and Cal were instantly on their feet between us.

JoBell stepped up and shoved both of the guys out of the way. "I think that uniform and all that macho weapons bullshit have gone to your head. Why don't you calm down so you don't ruin everybody's good time? Have a beer."

"I can't drink. I'm only on a pass. I have to go back on duty."

She threw her hands up and let them drop to slap on her thighs. "It's always something. I told you not to enlist in the first place, to get out when the governor —"

"You know . . ." This was one of those times when I knew JoBell was half drunk and probably didn't mean what she was saying, when I knew in my head I should just be quiet, but in my heart I was really pissed and I couldn't stop my mouth. "You know," I said, "I'm getting sick of you bashing on my service. I swore an oath, okay?"

"Words, Danny! Just words!"

"Come on, you two," Sweeney said.

"Damn it, it's more than words! I promised God I would do my duty."

"So did the killers at Boise!" JoBell shouted.

"Whoa," Brad said. Becca tried to take JoBell by the arm, but JoBell shook her off.

"That's what it really comes down to, isn't it?" I said. "You've acted all fine, but you still blame me for that! I told you —"

"No! I was talking about other soldiers at Boise, Danny! We've been over this! I'm not blaming —"

"— I fired by accident! One shot."

"— you for any of this!"

Cal stepped up to me. I brought my fists up, ready to fight. He held his hands up, open palmed. "Come on, Danny. Calm down."

"You know what?" I shouted. "Forget this. I don't need this shit tonight. See you around!"

Throwing open the door, I took the steps two at a time and hurried across the lot toward the Beast.

"Danny, wait!" Becca called from behind me. She caught hold of my arm right as I reached the driver's side door. "Danny."

"What?" I was shaking mad all over, and half of me wanted to storm back into that trailer and knock TJ on his ass.

"Hey." She gripped me by both shoulders. "Hey, look at me. Come on." She looked up at me with those deep green eyes. "She's been crying, Danny." I gave her a look like, *Yeah, right.* Becca nodded. "She's been crying a lot. She's worried about you. She misses you. Told me so." She cocked her head back toward Cal's trailer. "Why don't you come back inside?"

I thought about it. I kind of wanted to, but decided against it. "Naw. I don't think I could deal with TJ right now, and it would make more drama if I went back in. I need to get some cold-weather gear and get back to the Guard." Becca seemed so sad right then, looking down and shivering in the cold in her little Hank McGrew T-shirt. "You're freezing," I said. I rubbed my hands up and down her arms.

When she met my eyes again, a tear trailed down her cheek. "I miss you too."

I gently wiped the tear away. "You're so cool," I said. "Always so, you know, understanding or whatever."

She put her arms out for a hug, and as we came together, she leaned her face forward so that for a moment I thought she would kiss me. I stopped, then moved forward again, but this time *she* stopped. We laughed and finally simply hugged. She squeezed me tightly. "Goodbye, Danny," she whispered in my ear. "Be careful."

I pulled away from her and opened the door to the Beast, then took one last look at the trailer, wondering if I should go in and try to work things out. I decided I better not. I gave Becca a little fake punch to the shoulder, climbed in behind the steering wheel, and drove away from a disastrous night.

With my one and only chance to be with my friends totally jacked up, I figured the least I could do was get something good to eat, and the Bucking Bronc bar on Main Street had the best tenderloin sandwiches in the world. When I stepped inside, though, I was surprised to see the place so empty on a Friday night.

"There he is," said a man with a beer at the bar. "The kid who started all this."

Great. Why couldn't I go anywhere without people giving me shit?

"Leave him alone, Gary," the woman behind the bar said.

A woman sitting at the end of the bar played video poker on an old bar-top game console. "Oh, he's just messing around." She spun on her stool to face me. "You Idaho Guard boys keep up the fight, hear?"

"Well, there's really no fight, ma'am," I said. "We're making sure they leave us alone."

"Yeah, well, can you make sure they allow some beer through?" the guy said. "I'm a Budweiser man, and I can't find one single can or bottle anywhere."

The bartender tossed back her bleached-blond hair. "I ordered as much as my cooler would hold as soon as the blockade started, but they only brought half my order. Anyway," she said to me. "What would you like? We're out of most everything, and I'm thinking you might not be twenty-one."

"Can I get a tenderloin?" I said.

"Sorry. Ran out last week."

"Hamburger?"

She shook her head. "I can get you a fish sandwich. I might have some chicken nuggets left. Maybe one of those frozen pizzas. That's about it."

I had the fish, but once again ordered it to go so I wouldn't have to listen to people talk about me or the standoff with the Fed.

As I neared my house, the street was mostly empty. The last few reporters must have finally given up after I went to the Guard full-time. But one strange pickup was parked on the street in front, its back bumper covered in stickers. DON'T TREAD ON ME, PROTECT THE SECOND AMENDMENT, and one that was a simple drawing of a white eagle. Someone was in the cab.

Right away I reached under my seat for the nine mil. I had been asking my chain of command for a holster since I came on duty, but they hadn't found me one yet. I checked to make sure the safety was on, then slipped the gun into my cargo pocket.

Parking a few car lengths behind the pickup, I climbed down out of the Beast and closed the door quietly. If this was someone who wanted to mess me up, I didn't want him to know I was here. Should I come up to him with my gun drawn? Ignore him, go inside, and wait to see what he would do? In the end, I knocked on his window. The guy inside jerked awake, and the next second I had a .38 revolver pointed at me.

I jumped back and started to reach for my nine mil, but the guy was out of his truck and waving his gun like I should get my hands up. "Who the hell are you?" the man asked.

Damn it, how could I have been stupid enough to get stuck like this? There was no hiding my identity. I was in uniform with my name tape on my chest, after all. "Private First Class Dan Wright."

"Oh!" The man put his gun back in his truck. "Sorry, man. It was dark, and I couldn't see you, and you kind of snuck up on me there." He held out his hand, and after a moment I shook it. "Jake Rickingson. Wow, it's an honor to meet you. I was wondering if I'd ever get the chance."

Why was this guy honored to meet me? I was just a kid with a cold fish sandwich who really wanted to go inside and take a long, hot shower.

"I've been pulling the first night shift for a couple weeks now, keeping watch over the house. I'm really sorry, but one night I was coming off a long shift at the mill, and I kind of dozed off in the truck for a minute. Next thing I know, these punk kids were up on your porch about to spray-paint something on your house. I fired a warning shot in the air right away, and they ran off, but they left that one little dot. Dab of white paint will cover that right up."

"Thanks," I said. What else could I say? "You're one of Sheriff Crow's friends?"

"Yep. We're real close. Nathan and me go way back. Anyway, he says you're one of his friends, so that makes you one of mine. I sure appreciate what you've done and what you and the Idaho Guard keep doing every day."

"I have to get some things from the house, clean up a little, and then I have to go back to the line," I said.

"Oh, sure, I don't mean to keep you."

I thanked him and went inside. The house felt cramped and stuffy. I wished I had time to air the place out. I left a trail in the dust on a shelf in the living room, running my finger past a bunch of photographs. There was Mom and Dad's wedding picture, a family photo of me and her taken shortly after Dad died, a picture of us at a rodeo last year, one of me in my dress blues Army Service Uniform at basic training graduation, and a photo of me in that uniform standing with Mom. She was looking at me instead of at the camera in that last picture, and she looked so proud.

I video called her, hoping she was okay.

"Danny!" she said when she popped up on-screen. "It's so good to see you!" She tilted her head like she was trying to look past me. "Are you at home?"

"It's good to see you too, Mom. I have a pass until midnight. I came home to get a few things."

"Is everything all right? Are you okay? Are you safe?"

"Oh yeah, Mom, I'm great!" If I didn't fake a lot of happiness, she'd worry more. "Everything's fine. The Army is taking good care of me. How are you?"

"I'm okay. Delores has me using my sick days now. They're doing all they can for me, but if I can't get back soon . . . Well, they say I'll have a job with them as long as I want one, but I'm worried they're going to let me go. I've looked for jobs around Spokane, but there's nothing going. Everybody I talk to says so many people were out of work even before the blockade, there were people lined up just to apply for an opening at McDonald's." She wiped a tear from her eye. *"I really think I ought to come home."*

"Mom, you can't. Soldiers have the whole border blocked off on both sides."

"But I've been looking at some maps. There's a store here in Spokane that sells nothing but maps. I think I've found some places where I can sneak across."

I rubbed the bridge of my nose with my thumb and index finger. "Mom, we've been over this. It is not safe to try to cross that border. People have been hurt. The Fed will stop you. I don't know, maybe arrest you."

Tears sprang to her eyes. *"But I can't stay here, Danny. I have bills to pay, and . . . and I miss you. I want to come home."*

"I miss you too, but Mom, you have to try to relax. I can take care of stuff over here. They'll probably be promoting me soon, and I'll be making more money then, so I can pay for some more stuff. I have a little bit in a savings account too."

She smiled, but not too happily. *"When did you grow up so much? You're only seventeen."*

"Me and you, Mom. It's been that way for a long time. We'll figure this all out."

"I worry about you, though." She bit her fingernail. *"Things are scary here in Spokane. At the fairgrounds and at different places around the interstate, there's lots of Army stuff. Trucks and tank-looking things. It's like the whole town has become an Army base."*

"I'm sure they're only rotating troops in and out of the blockade."

"Maybe. But a few nights ago, someone set off a homemade bomb and messed up an Army Humvee. Now they're talking about ordering a curfew here."

If things were that bad in Washington, it was only a matter of time before people started getting hurt. But I didn't dare say that to Mom. "That's nothing for you to worry about. Get some rest and, you know, have some fun maybe. There has to be some cool things to do in Spokane. I'll take care of everything. I promise."

We talked for a while longer, even though neither of us had much more to talk about than we did the last time I'd called her. The blockade had everything stuck. After we tapped out, I ate my crappy sandwich and soggy fries. Then I was grateful for enough hot water to take a shower for as long as I wanted, unlike the usually half-cold showers we had once a week at camp when the hygiene trailer came around. After that, I gathered some coats, sweatshirts, hats, gloves, and blankets and headed back to the Beast. I had another hour or two before I had to report back to duty, but what was the point?

As I drove, I thought about the night. If I was honest with myself, I'd have to admit that I'd acted like a jerk back at the party. The problem was that even if JoBell didn't want a relationship with TJ, I knew that prick wanted *her*. Everything in my whole life already felt like it was slipping away, so to walk in and see TJ sitting next to JoBell was like all those rumors the media had been kicking around brought to life. It was too much to take.

And if I was *really* honest with myself . . . Yeah, like I said before, all couples fight, but I don't know. Maybe . . . Maybe me and JoBell hadn't fought enough. When we were both yelling at each other at Cal's, it felt like we were saying a lot of stuff that had been on our minds for a long time — stuff we'd been holding back since the Battle of Boise. I don't know, maybe something had been building up between us even before that horrible night. We never talked about it. I never wanted to think about it. I sure as hell didn't want to think about it now.

A cop was parked outside the Gas & Sip when I pulled up to the pump. As I was opening my gas cap, he stepped out of his car and approached.

"Evening, soldier," he said, loud and friendly. He leaned against the gas pump. "What're you doing?"

What the hell did it look like I was doing? I put on a smile and answered. "Getting some fuel." I noticed the price display on the pump. "Whoa. Ten ninety-nine a gallon?"

"Did you check with the attendant inside with your ration card?"

"What?"

The cop rubbed his nose. "The pump won't work until the attendant activates it. For that you have to show her your ration card to make sure you're allowed to buy the gasoline. Then it's prepay only."

"I don't . . . I mean, I never got a ration card. I've been on the line with the Idaho Guard."

"You look familiar," said the officer. Oh no, not again. "I've seen you on the news or something."

I tapped my name tape on my chest. "I'm PFC Danny Wright. I have to buy some gas so I have enough to get back to my duty post before mid —"

"Oh yeah! I thought I recognized you. Listen." He took a card out of his wallet. "Law enforcement has their own cards, and we charge the fuel for our cars to the state. I was given a nice promotion and raise after the guy in charge of me freaked out about the blockade and left. I owe you big." He was about to swipe his card, but I held out my hand to stop him.

"No thanks." I'd had enough handouts and special treatment lately. Cheating on a rationing system didn't seem right. "I have enough gas to get out there and back. I'll get the ration card later and buy my own gas."

He looked confused. "You sure?"

I told him I was, and then climbed up in the truck to drive back to my post, praying all the while that I really did have enough gas for the trip.

I returned at about twenty-one hundred to find Sergeant Kemp at the fighting position. Instead of leaving right away, he stayed on watch and let me get some sleep. Shortly after midnight, though, he woke me up and left. I was alone then, on duty until zero seven, watching over nothing.

Back when I'd enlisted, the Idaho Guard had issued me layers and layers of cold-weather gear. Long underwear, poly pro undershirts, a Gor-Tex jacket, an Army field jacket, leather gloves, wool glove inserts, and stocking caps. That night, as I waited for Sergeant Kemp to get back from his pass, all of that, along with my Freedom Lake High School sweatshirt, extra-big mittens, and the anti-drone thermal cloak was simply not enough. The M240 Bravo machine gun that used to look so tough was now a lump of cold, boring metal, and my M4 was an uncomfortable pain in the ass that I had to have with me at all times, even when I went to the latrine. A sharp cold front had come in and a fierce, freezing wind whistled through the valley. I wouldn't have been surprised if it had started snowing.

By zero five thirty the contour of Silver Mountain was coming into focus out of the dark as the eastern sky began to lighten. I took off my night vision glasses and rubbed my tired eyes. Soon I could put them in my pocket and stare at the nothingness without them. An hour and a half left of my shift. Impossibly long. Way too tired. I bit my lip to try to stay awake.

My head jerked up. It was brighter out now. Crouching down behind the wall to keep the light from my comm out of view, I checked the time. Zero six fifteen. I slapped myself in the face. I couldn't be falling asleep like this. Guard duty was boring, but it was important, and the most holy commandment of guard duty was "Thou shalt stay awake." I squeezed my eyes shut and then opened them wide again to fight sleep.

Something moved down in the valley. Or at least I thought I saw something move. Sometimes when I was this tired, my mind started thinking nonsense thoughts or I would need sleep so bad that I would see things that weren't there.

But whatever I thought I'd seen moved again. There really was someone down there. Cold dropped in my stomach and spread all the way through me. My heart beat harder, and I was awake now.

It was a soldier. He put up a hand signal. Someone else crept out of the tree line on the Washington side.

"Oh shit," I whispered. Fed troops. They were coming. I squeezed Becca's butterfly hair clip in my pocket, hoping for some extra strength and courage. "Why? Why now?" I threw my mittens off, ran to the shitty field phone, picked up the receiver, and turned the crank as fast as I could. "Come on, come on . . ." Nothing. I cranked some more. "Pick up the damned phone, you sleeping bastards!" They didn't answer.

I dropped the phone and ran back to the gun port on the bunker. It was a whole squad, moving in a file across the clearing. We must have done a great camouflage job on our fighting position, because they hadn't spotted me yet.

Using my teeth, I yanked both gloves off so I could better use my fingers. I wasn't cold anymore anyway. Then I went to the handheld Motorola radio they'd assigned to this bunker. We were supposed to use it as little as possible. Batteries were precious, and it wasn't a secure frequency. It could be easily monitored by anyone willing to drop sixty bucks on another radio at Walmart.

I keyed the mike and spoke quietly. "Rattlesnake base, rattlesnake base, this is position three, one, alpha, over." I had identified myself as the fighting position for third platoon, first squad, alpha team. Why weren't they answering? Were the batteries still good on this thing? I spoke louder, hoping the squad below wouldn't hear me. "Rattlesnake base, this is position three one alpha. Pick up the damned radio! Over!"

"Three, one, alpha, this is rattlesnake base. Go ahead, over."

It was Specialist Crocker, the idiot who worked the comm back at the TOC near the wire obstacle. Great. "Rattlesnake base, be advised I have eyes on at least a squad-sized element moving across the border from Washington into Idaho. They're armed with standard squad weapons, but I think at least one of them has an AT4 rocket launcher. Request instructions. How copy, over?"

"That's a good copy. Wait one, over," Crocker radioed back.

"I can't wait one, damn it," I whispered. Soon the Fed squad would be up tight against the cliff where I couldn't see them. Then they could go anywhere. Sneak around behind us. Lob grenades up at me. I didn't have time for Crocker to wake up the first sergeant or whoever he was going to go get. By the time they were on the radio, it would be too late.

"Get ahold of yourself, Wright," I said. I was a trained soldier. I could handle this by the book. What did my ROE card say? My primary mission was, basically, to keep the Fed out of Idaho. Four S's. "Shout, Show, Shove, Shoot," I said. What did the card tell us to shout? Oh, who cared about the stupid example on the card?

I went to the machine gun. I bet anything that shouting and showing came really close together. We'd been over and over the procedure for loading the M240, but could I remember? What was first? I couldn't think of it. I flipped the cover up. Obviously, I had to get the belt of rounds onto the feed tray. Holding the rounds in place, I closed and locked the cover. Then I pulled the cocking handle to the rear to lock the bolt back before easing the handle forward again. The weapon ought to be ready. I prayed I wouldn't have to use it.

I lifted the machine gun and pointed it out the gun port. "Hey!" I yelled. The Fed soldiers stopped where they were, and suddenly I remembered what the ROE card told us to shout. "Halt! You are not allowed to enter Idaho!" Then I added, just in case they hadn't spotted me, "I've got you all covered with an M240. Get back on your side of the line. Now!"

The first soldier motioned them ahead and ran toward the cliff. Shoving was out of the question. Was it time to shoot? I had my orders. I could not allow these soldiers to enter the state. I'd fire, not to hit anyone, but enough to show I meant business and to scare them back into Washington.

I aimed the weapon for what I hoped was a point about ten feet in front of the lead soldier. I had maybe a minute before he'd be too close to the cliff and under cover. I had to fire. I had to shoot now. *Now.* "God forgive me," I whispered. I pulled the trigger.

Nothing happened. "Damn it!" I clicked the safety to fire, aimed, and squeezed the trigger. The weapon jerked as it blasted rounds downrange. Puffs of dust popped up where the rounds impacted, a littler closer to the squad than I had hoped. I squeezed the trigger again, walking the impact back from the squad, but making sure the rounds hit close enough to scare them away. The noise was deafening inside the bunker, the tracers making red-hot streaks through the air. "Get back on your side of the line!" I yelled over the roar. "Get back! Get back! Get back!"

I let off the trigger. The machine gun was supposed to be fired in three- to five-second bursts to save ammo and so the barrel wouldn't overheat and melt. Some of the federal soldiers had run back to the tree line and were firing at me. Muzzle flashes sparked back in the shadows under the trees. Their bullets cracked against the rock wall in front of my position, rock chips flying everywhere.

But their lead soldier was rolling around on the ground, screaming and holding his leg. I'd hit him. Oh God, I'd hit him. More shots rang out from the trees. This time, like an idiot, I ducked. Could they see me? Could they get a good shot? If I got the machine gun back up in my firing window, would they have me pegged?

The lead soldier kept screaming. Another crawled out across the clearing. "Hang on, buddy, I'm coming!" he shouted.

"Get the hell out of here!" I yelled as loud as I could, putting the machine gun aside and grabbing my M4. I could aim and control the M4 a lot better. "Get back on your side!" I sighted the rifle, aiming about six feet in front of the crawling soldier. I fired. The crawling soldier covered his head. I let go three more rounds, walking each shot in a little closer until he started crawling back.

Another machine gun opened up from their side of the woods. I could see the flash, then suddenly I was in the snare drum from hell as bullets pelted my bunker. How long before some of these rocks cracked and the wall began to crumble? Would those logs overhead come crashing down on me? I couldn't let that happen. I grabbed the 240, jumped into the firing window, and opened up, aiming for where I thought the machine gun had fired from.

Forgetting the barrel, I kept the trigger squeezed, and the end of my ammo belt approached. I had another, but it would take forever to reload with no other cover fire. Then I saw puffs of dirt and dust shoot up from the ground on the Washington side of the border, and twigs and small branches started falling off the trees there. The other half of my squad must have finally woken up and started shooting.

I fired off the rest of my belt, concentrating on the tree line but keeping my eye on the crawling soldier and the wounded guy.

Wounded Guy was still moving, but not as much, and he didn't seem to be yelling anymore.

When my ammo was gone, I grabbed the second belt, but in the pause between the other team's bursts of fire, I could tell the Fed was no longer shooting back. Instead, I heard the moans from the wounded man.

These guys were idiots for crossing into Idaho. If that soldier weren't already bleeding, I'd want to punch him for making me have to shoot. But he was still an American soldier, just like me. He had sworn to protect his country, he had a family somewhere, and he was bleeding bad. I could see the redness from up here. I thought of that girl lying dead on the ground in Boise and how I had been too late to help her. I couldn't let that happen again.

I grabbed the radio and keyed the mike. "Three one bravo, this is three one alpha. Cease fire! Cease fire! I'm going down there! Three one alpha, out."

"*Negative, three, one, alpha.*" It was PFC Nelson on the radio. "*Do not go down in that valley. Maintain position, over.*"

Nelson could stuff it. No way was I going to sit up here and watch that soldier bleed out. I dropped the radio, slung my M4's strap over my right shoulder, grabbed our medkit and an extra Freedom Lake sweatshirt, and ran out of my bunker to the path below, scrambling down the steep embankment. I waved the white sweatshirt above my head. "Cease fire! Cease fire! I have a medkit," I yelled as loud as I could, hoping they could hear me all the way back in those trees. With my weapon slung and no cover, these guys could pick me off easy.

A couple shots went off, and shards of rock hit me as the bullets struck nearby. I dropped to the rock face, skidding and tumbling the rest of the way down. I pulled out my M4 and pointed it at the trees, stupidly standing ready for a fight I could not win.

When no shots came, I ran to the wounded soldier. Another soldier ran from the Washington trees, waving a white rag over his head. "Medic! Medic! Don't shoot! I'm a medic."

When I reached the wounded man, acid burned in my throat as I looked at him. A pink-white bone flashed through the torn flesh of his leg, and deep-red blood soaked the dry grass around him. I could see he was slipping out of consciousness. Bleeding out.

"Come on, buddy, stay with me," I said, ripping open my medkit and pulling out a field dressing. "You're good. Breathe and stay with me." We'd been over combat field medicine in basic training a hundred times. Now I had to do it for real.

When the other soldier skidded to a halt next to me, I looked up only long enough to catch sight of his rank. If this specialist wanted to shoot me or capture me, I was in trouble, but right now all I cared about was saving this guy if I could. "I'll try to stop the bleeding," I said.

"I'm going to run an IV."

I ripped off the paper and spread out the gauze pad. "Sterile side to the wound," I mumbled.

"Can you handle that?" said the medic.

"Yeah, I got it, damn it. Get the IV in him."

The wounded soldier coughed and rolled his head around a little, floating on the edge of consciousness.

"Hey, buddy, stay with us," I said. I wrapped the green cloth bands around the back of the leg and brought them up to cross over the center on top of the white bandage pad. Then I looped both straps again and tied the ends. "We need you to stay awake. We're going to get you fixed up and back to a hospital. No problem." If the bleeding didn't stop, I'd have to apply a tourniquet above the wound to stop the blood flow. If I did that, this guy might live, but he'd lose his lower leg.

The bright crimson blood soaked into the bandage, dulling to a sort of brown, but that was to be expected, right? Doing this stuff in training was a lot different from doing it in real life. "Here." I stood up and held out my bloody hands to the specialist. "Let me hold the IV bag. Can you check this bandage? I can't tell if it's stopping the bleeding enough."

The medic handed me the bag before inspecting my bandage. "You did a pretty good job." He straightened my ties a little. "I think this is going to work. I think he's going to make it."

I closed my eyes and let out a sigh. He'd live. I wouldn't have his death on my conscience. I smiled. I knew I was right. Soldiers are soldiers, and America was still united enough for me and this medic to save this guy's life.

"No thanks to you."

"What?"

I opened my eyes to see the medic with his nine mil drawn.

"Oh shit," I said. "You gotta be kidding me."

He kept his weapon aimed at me and wiped his nose with his free hand. "You're under arrest for shooting my squad leader. And I'm sure my chain of command will be happy to hear we finally have PFC Wright in custody."

"I wasn't even aiming at him, you dumb son of a bitch! I was just trying to scare you guys, make you go back to your side. If you'd stayed over there, he'd be fine."

The specialist shook his sidearm. "Slowly lower your weapon to the ground."

I bit my lip and tried to focus, tried to keep my legs from shaking. I was glad that the soldier I'd shot was okay, but I still felt like a moron from one of those zombie apocalypse movies who wanders off alone and foolishly trusts some desperate psychopath in the woods. Stupid mistakes like that always end up getting people hurt.

"I'm not joking!" the specialist shouted. "Put your weapon on the ground or I'll shoot you right here."

"Hey, Wright! You okay down there?" Luchen called down.

The medic risked a look up. I grabbed my rifle by the end of the barrel and swung it like a baseball bat into his wrist. His nine mil went flying. I gripped the rifle barrel with both hands and jabbed it at the medic hard, crunching the stock into his nose. Blood exploded from his face and he fell backward. "Luchen, cover me!" I shouted as I ran, picking up the medic's sidearm and the first soldier's M4 before scrambling up the steep rocky path to my bunker.

Safely behind the cover of our fighting position, I sat in the dirt and rested my head back against the rock wall. While I was in the valley, my whole team had crammed into the tiny space, along with Staff Sergeant Donshel, First Sergeant Herbokowitz, and Captain Leonard. We watched the line until the bleeding medic carried his wounded comrade back into Washington.

"What happened?" Captain Leonard asked, and I told him the whole story.

After I finished, the first sergeant frowned. "Next time, don't try to be a hero. Someone says not to go down there, then you damn sure better stay up here. Got it?"

"Yes, First Sergeant," I said.

"You stopped an incursion, saved that soldier's life, and captured two good weapons." Captain Leonard smiled at me. "Good work, Wright." He patted me on the helmet as he walked out of the bunker with Herbokowitz.

"Why don't you take some downtime, Wright? Come with me. We'll make sure you get some chow and plenty of water." Donshel held out his hand to help me up. I took it and followed him away from our fighting position down toward the TOC tent near the wire obstacle.

"The commander is talking about organizing a Quick Reaction Force that would always be on standby to back up any fighting position if something like this happens again. I'm sorry you were on your own like that, Wright. I'll make sure someone has your back from now on, I promise."

I didn't answer. I was still so hopped up on adrenaline that I barely trusted myself to speak.

Donshel put his hand on my shoulder. "Hey, you need anything?"

I licked my lips. "Like to use my comm," I said. "Make a call."

"Yeah, sure. There's a charging station inside the TOC if the power's low."

"Thanks, Sergeant," I said.

Donshel nodded. "But I meant what I said. Chow first, and drink at least one CamelBak of water. Then you can make that call."

About twenty minutes later, I climbed up into the Beast to call Mom in private. When the audio connected, though, it wasn't Mom's voice on the line.

"Danny?" said a woman.

Where the hell was Mom? Had the Feds arrested her for some reason? "Who is this?" I said. "Where is Kelly Wright?"

"Whoa, relax. Is this Danny?"

Even if this was a trick, there was nothing the Fed could gain if I confirmed what they already knew. "Yeah, this is PFC Wright."

"I'm Sarah. Your mother has been staying with me for a while. Your mom's fine. She's in the shower."

"Why do you have her comm?"

"Listen, I'm sorry if this is freaking you out, or if this is an invasion of privacy or something, but I think we have a problem. It's your mother."

"Is she okay? Is she having an attack?"

"She's fine! She's fine. But . . . Danny, she's packing her bags. She's paid someone to drive her up near the Idaho border. She's going to try to sneak across the line."

"What!? Don't let her!" Anything could happen if she tried that. The whole border was lined with anxious, trigger-happy soldiers. Idaho Guardsmen could mistake her for the Fed. The Fed could figure her for a smuggler or a Guardsman. My uniform was still stained with the blood of soldiers who had tried to cross the border this morning.

"That's the thing. I don't think she should try to cross the border by herself, but she also can't stay here. It's not good for her being trapped over here, Danny. She can't handle it. Wait. Here she comes. Danny . . ." Sarah became very quiet. *"You gotta do something. You've seen the news. People get arrested, shot, trying to cross —"* Her voice picked up. *"Hey, Kelly, your son's calling! It was nice talking to you, Danny. Here's your mom."*

"Danny?" Mom said.

"Hey, Mom," I said. "How're you doing?"

"Are you okay?"

"Yeah, Mom. Fine." No way was I going to freak her out with the story of this morning's shoot-out. "They gave me a little time to make a call this morning, and I thought I'd check in. How are you?"

"I'm good!" she said. *"Better than I have been in a long time. Danny, I'm going home. I've paid a friend to drive me to the border, and I think I know a good place to sneak —"*

"Mom, no."

"But Danny, I can't handle —"

"Mom, you can't —"

"— being away from home any longer. I need to get home. I need to get back to work. I really think I have it worked out and —"

"Mom, listen to me! Be quiet and listen! Be quiet!" I closed my eyes and pressed my comm to my forehead, taking deep breaths to calm down. I could hear her sniffling on the line. She was crying. "It's not safe for you to cross the border. You'll never make it."

"*I'll never . . . make it if I . . . if I have to stay here,*" Mom choked out her words through heavy sobs. "*You don't understand, Danny. I have to come home. I have to.*"

Neither of us said anything for a long time. I pressed my fist to the side of my head, trying to figure out what to do.

"Okay," I said. "Okay, fine. You need to come home. I get it. But I'll come get you, Mom. I'll bring the Beast and I'll pick you up. I've been working the border for weeks, and I know how to get you across safely. Okay?"

It sounded stupid even as I said it. Leaving Idaho was easy. Trying to sneak through the Fed blockade and back across the border into Idaho was nearly suicidal. But what choice did I have? I couldn't let my mom try this alone and on foot. She'd have a better chance with me in the Beast.

"*Really, Danny?*" she asked. "*I don't know —*"

"Stay where you are for now. I'm on my way to get you. I'll bring you home, Mom. I promise."

A few hours later I was approved for a three-day pass. I hadn't screwed around putting in a leave request and waiting for it to go up the chain of command. I just called Governor Montaine directly and told him I needed a few days to settle some things at home now that my mom was trapped in Washington. He bought my story, sent the leave orders to my unit, and ordered my chain of command to give me a gas ration card. I know I pissed off the captain and first sergeant by jumping rank, but I didn't care. I'd do anything to protect my mother.

I told the truth to Sergeant Kemp, though. A guy learned real quick not to talk about too much personal stuff in the Army. Lots of times, the other guys had a sick sense of humor and would give you a lot of shit about your family or girlfriend if you were stupid enough to tell them about it. But Kemp seemed like a guy I could trust.

"You really think you can get over the border and back?" he said.

"I'm going to try," I said.

"As your team leader, I should let the chain know what you're up to. They'd put a stop to it. I doubt even the governor would approve your leave if he knew what you were really planning to do."

"No way you or anyone else can stop me, 'cept if you put me in handcuffs or something. I have to do this."

Sergeant Kemp clapped his hand on my shoulder, and I spun away, thinking he meant to keep me from going. But he smiled and pulled his hand back. "I know we couldn't stop you." He held out his hand. "So I wanted to wish you good luck. Bring her home safe."

"Thanks, Sergeant. I will." I shook his hand. "And keep your comm on, will you? In case I need a little extra help getting back."

"You got it," he said. "Give me a call when you're coming home."

Having said my goodbyes and leaving my Guard-issued M4 with my unit, I climbed into the Beast and started her up. Then I drove down the highway to begin my most dangerous mission yet.

⌁—• A spokesman for Governor Montaine's office has confirmed earlier reports of hostilities on the Washington-Idaho border in northern Idaho. Montaine claims that early yesterday morning, a small group of federal troops crossed the border into Idaho. The troops were repelled by soldiers from the Idaho National Guard, including Private First Class Daniel Wright, who is already wanted by the federal government for his alleged involvement in the shootings in Boise. The White House admits that one federal soldier is recovering from wounds received in this action, but declined to comment further on the incident, particularly on the squad's reason for crossing the border. •—⌁

⌁—• Thank you for joining us on NPR's Weekend. I'm Renae Matthews. It's been twenty-six days since President Rodriguez announced the federal blockade of Idaho, and while there have been several incidents of violence between federal troops and civilians trying to run the border to return home or to smuggle goods, yesterday was the first time that an open firefight has broken out between Idaho and federal forces. With us this morning is one of NPR's top Idaho Crisis correspondents, Richard Arwell. Richard, the White House seems to be downplaying the recent border skirmish. What is the real significance of these events?"

"I'm afraid this could be fairly serious, Renae. First, word of this firefight is bound to increase anxiety in both federal and Idaho troops, and that's going to lead to trouble. Second, I can't imagine that this incident will help the negotiations, which were finally beginning to show some progress toward arriving at a conclusion to this crisis. If Idaho and the federal government are going to come to any sort of an agreement, it simply won't work for either side to be negotiating under the threat of violence. •—⌁

CHAPTER
TWENTY-ONE

By the time I got home, I had been awake for the better part of a day. I was fried, and even though I had to fight to avoid thinking about this morning's firefight or Mom's trouble, I fell asleep almost as soon as I flopped down on my bed.

The next morning, dressed in regular jeans and a sweatshirt, I drove down to the shop. The news was playing on the radio. Word of the "border skirmish" was already out. Schmidty looked up from the engine of the little Honda he'd been working on. "Danny. It's good to see you."

That wasn't the greeting I'd expected. Coming from him, that was downright cheerful. He lit up a cigarette from a pack on his desk, squinting a little as the smoke wafted up in his eyes. "You just can't seem to stay out of trouble, can you?"

"I . . . almost killed a guy yesterday, Schmidty. I wasn't aiming at him. Suppressive fire, but . . ."

Schmidty blew out smoke. "You did what you had to do. Like I did one day in Gulf War One. Wish I could say it gets easier."

"Maybe I need to find a way to make it easier. Or . . . not easier, but so I can deal with it better. I went down to help the guy I'd wounded, and after I saved his life, a Fed medic tried to arrest me. I guess I should have —"

"Known you can't trust the Fed." He flicked some ash to the floor. "Not anymore. They're talking on the news about working

312

this all out real peaceful-like. But this situation is a lot like Vietnam or the second Iraq war. Once blood is spilled, we're stuck in the fight for the long haul, because if we quit early, if we work out a compromise, then what was the point of those casualties?" He took a long drag on his cigarette. "We're all too deep in this now. It's going to get a lot worse before it gets better. If it ever gets better. Ain't no running away from this."

"I'm not running away," I said. "I only wish there was something I could do to make things right."

"Nothing you can do to fix this mess." He put his hand on my shoulder and led me out to the driveway. He pointed at the faded old American flag fluttering in the breeze. "See, way I reckon, this country is like its flag. When troubles hit the country like the weather on that flag, people got different ideas about how to fix that trouble. They start arguing about it. Folks getting madder and madder at one another, pulling apart in different directions, until, like that flag, there are little threadbare spots, small tears. Finally, something comes along that's too much, and those little worn spots rip open, leaving the flag, like this country, in tatters."

Schmidty was making a lot of sense, but it felt weird hearing him all serious like this. "That's real poetic of you," I said.

"W'd'ya shut the hell up?" He led me back into the shop.

"Sorry," I said with a smile so he'd know I didn't mean it. "Anyway, I'm here because I'm going to go bring my mother home from Spokane."

I heard footsteps on the pavement behind me, and I reached under my belt for my gun.

"Hey, babe."

It was JoBell. I turned to face her. She ran to me, throwing her arms around me and pulling me close for a hungry kiss.

"I missed you," I said. "I'm sorry —"

"I'm sorry about what happened at Cal's. Let's not fight any-more?" she whispered.

Behind us, Schmidty hacked and then spat on the floor. I stepped back from JoBell. She brushed a strand of that golden hair out of her eyes. "Saw your truck out front. I couldn't believe it at first, but here you are. I thought you had to go back on duty."

"You really gonna do it?" Schmidty asked loudly, as if to make a point to JoBell. "Jump the border?"

JoBell's eyes went wide. "What?" She pressed her palms to my cheek and made me look at her. "Danny, what is he talking about?"

"I got to," I said. "You know my mom. She can't handle being trapped over there much longer. Says she's going to try to sneak back into Idaho. After what went down yesterday morning, I can't let her do that on her own."

JoBell took a couple steps away from me and looked down at her comm. She tapped away.

"What are you doing?"

"Texting the others. Telling them to get over here."

"I don't know if that's a good idea." I made a halfhearted grab for her comm to stop her, but she twisted away from me. "I mean, I can see them when I get back."

JoBell shook her comm up above her head. "Maybe they'll talk some sense into you."

"You're high if you think you're going alone," Sweeney said after he arrived with Becca and Cal.

"I am going alone." I paced to the other end of the shop, squeez-ing my hands tight into fists. "I mean it. I'm not putting you guys in danger again. It's not your problem. You don't have to do this."

"Nobody has to do this," said JoBell. "Nobody's jumping the border."

Cal put his arm around JoBell's shoulders. "Oh, come on, JoJo, Danny's mom is totally cool. We can't leave her trapped over there."

She was too upset to even bother complaining about the nickname. "I know she's great." She pulled away from Cal. "I love that woman . . ." She paused a moment, then smiled and added, "and her son. Which is why we shouldn't encourage either of them to take the risk of trying to run the blockade."

I was both happy to hear what she said about love, and sad that I would have to disagree with her again. "I'm sorry, JoBell," I said. "But I am doing this no matter what you say. I'm going alone. None of you are coming with me."

"Yes, we are, Danny," said Becca. "We're your friends. Besides, it will be great to have the whole group back together."

"No, it won't!" Schmidty was coming up the stairs out of the basement, blinking against the cigarette smoke in his eyes, carrying the AR15 in his hands and its spare loaded magazines under his arms. Gross, I thought. The magazines would be funkified by Schmidty's nasty, sweaty armpits. "It won't be great. This ain't the damned senior prom. If you try to travel on paved roads into Washington, the Feds will stop you all and arrest Danny on sight. So first you'll have to find some way to hide him, or else try to cross in the woods somewhere. The way back will be even harder. You have spooked-out, pissed-off soldiers on both sides of the state line. Be real easy for y'all to end up in the crossfire." He held out the rifle to me. "Here. It's what you came for, right?"

I cleared the rifle, slung it over my shoulder, took the ammo, and then held up the magazines to show them what my life had become. "Schmidty's right, Becca. That's why I'm going alone."

"You won't make it by yourself," Becca said. "Anyway, if you try, we'll just follow you in one of our cars. You won't be able to stop us. So we're with you — or *I'm* with you — no matter what."

The argument dragged on for an hour. Eventually I had to give in and agree to let them come. I believed them when they said they would follow me in their own vehicles whether I wanted them to or not. Even JoBell changed her mind, figuring she got along real good with my mom, and she might need JoBell's help.

We thought getting out of Idaho would be the easiest part, provided the Feds didn't find me. I'd ride on the floor behind the backseat until we approached the border, when I'd wedge myself into the storage space under the false bottom that Schmidty had installed. Sweeney already had a fake ID, but he made new ones for everyone else so the Fed couldn't recognize their names and link them to me. For the return trip, Cal said he knew a tiny dirt logging road near the Canadian border. If the Fed had that blocked, we'd off-road up into Canada and come back down into Idaho on one of the smugglers' routes.

"Cal," I said, "you think you can drive? If the Feds find out I'm hiding back there, you'll have to whip the Beast around and get us back into Idaho fast."

Cal folded his big muscled arms over his chest. "You kidding? I'm the son of a long-haul trucker. Driving's in my blood."

"The problem is gas," I said. "I finally got one of those ration cards, but I don't have enough money, really, to fill up the tank."

Schmidty blew smoke in my face. "See? While everyone else was playing grab-ass and wondering, *Oh, is the governor going to play nice? Will the president let this go?* I was getting ready. Buying ammo, buying a dozen cartons of cigarettes."

"Twelve cartons?" Sweeney said. "That had to cost you . . ." He poked around in the air like he was doing calculations.

"Cost way too much! What's it to you?" Schmidty growled. "They cost about twice as much now, and you can't find any."

"Yeah. Smart," Sweeney said.

"Anyway, my point is I also have two hundred gallons of gas in four barrels down in the basement."

"Geez, Schmidty," I said. "You've been smoking down there."

He shrugged and flicked ash on the floor. "You guys will have to use the hand-crank pump to fill the gas cans and then make a million trips to carry it all up."

He was right, but about an hour later we were packed up and fueled. We even changed out the plates on the Beast to make it harder to identify.

"Thanks for all your help," I said to Schmidty.

"Just bring my rifle back." He coughed. "Oh, and buy me some cigarettes while you're over there in the land of plenty."

I nodded and climbed into the back of the Beast, cradling the AR and keeping my nine mil handy. With Cal behind the wheel, JoBell rode shotgun. Sweeney and Becca sat in the back. Becca leaned over the seat and winked at me, then covered me with a blanket. It was time to go.

"I don't care what Schmidty says," said Becca after we'd been on the road for a while. "It *is* great with all of us together again."

"Yeah, buddy. It hasn't been the same without you," said Cal.

They filled me in on everything as I rode along under the blanket in the dim light and the heat from my own breath. It felt weird hearing my friends' voices when I couldn't see them.

Football, volleyball, and cross-country were basically all canceled after the blockade. Schools couldn't afford the gas to travel to other schools for competitions. Instead, Coach divided the football squad into two teams that would play each other.

"It's not nearly as fun. Took all the suspense and competition out of the games," Sweeney said.

"I don't know," JoBell said. "With everything else that's happening, sports don't seem to matter as much as they used to. We're lucky they're keeping the school open at all. Some districts have a bunch of the newer buses that run on natural gas, so they're doing okay, but Freedom Lake only has two."

"Yeah," said Becca. "Buses are only running on limited routes and hard-surface roads. Some kids have to travel pretty far to their bus stops."

"It hasn't all been bad," Cal said. "I finally got a date with Samantha Monohan. She agreed to go with me on my motorcycle. Takes less gas. We were going to go Saturday night, but the movie theater closed down on Thursday, so we stayed in and watched movies online. It was a good time."

"What movie did you watch?" I asked.

"I can't remember," said Cal. "Didn't see much of it."

"Yeah, dude," Sweeney said. "That's the way it's done. She's a cool girl. Don't screw this up."

"I won't," Cal said. "She's really great. I've never had a girlfriend this awesome."

I smiled under the blanket. Cal had never had any girlfriend. It was great to hear him so happy.

"Hey, Becca," said Cal, "who was it that said Sam'd never go out with me?"

"I've never been so pleased to be wrong," Becca said.

I was grateful that my friends knew me well enough to know I didn't want to talk about the Guard or the shoot-out on the border. Instead, we talked like normal — well, normal except that I was hiding under a blanket in the back of a truck — for a long time. Next to what we were about to try to do, maybe that seemed crazy, but it felt right. I needed a dose of school, and sports, and regular life.

Cal flipped on the radio. He tuned it to the country station, and a song I hadn't heard before came on.

"Hank McGrew put this song out a couple days after the blockade started," JoBell said. She hated country music, but for once she was cool about it. I listened to the words.

> Last night I watched the news
> 'Bout trouble out in Idaho
> We gotta find a stop to this
> People are dead, you know
>
> Now a dark fright'nin' shadow
> A divisive creation
> Has turned brother against brother
> And threatens our whole nation
>
> When the times get tough
> Put your faith in God above
> You gotta stand for something
> Trust the ones you love
>
> No matter where you are
> Or what you believe
> We're all still Americans
> As long as we're free

The song went on like that for another couple verses, and I don't know if it was the song or if it was me, but something had changed.

"You know, I really used to love Hank McGrew's music," I said. "But now that 'we're all Americans' line sounds too easy. I *want* McGrew to be right, and I pray every night that we can all just be Americans again, but nothing can be that simple —"

"Yes!" JoBell said. "Finally he gets it!"

Becca giggled. "Digi-Hank will be sorry to hear that."

"You need to get Digi-Trixie," said Sweeney. "She's so hot."

"Gross, Eric!" JoBell said.

We talked and laughed most of the way south, but after we reached Interstate 90, things got quiet. We'd be at the border in no time.

"You awake back there, Danny?" Cal said after a while.

"Yeah." I stretched the best I could in the cramped space. I could feel the Beast slowing down. "Bit of a crimp in my neck. What's up? We at the border?"

"Last rest stop before Washington. We get any closer to the border, they'll see you. You better make the switch to that compartment now," said Cal.

I climbed out the back, dropped the tailgate, and slipped into the tiny dark space under the false bottom. Cal shut the tailgate behind me, closing me into darkness. We drove on.

"We're getting close now," JoBell finally said. I was glad I could still hear her. "It looks like a total war zone out there. Coils of razor wire and concrete barriers all over. Traffic's been funneled into one lane, but there are only two cars ahead of us."

"I see some tanks out here. And some serious machine guns," said Sweeney. "All pointed across the border at each other. I wouldn't want to be around if everybody here decided to start shooting."

"Okay, everybody shut the hell up," said Cal. "Act natural." I could hear the sound of the driver's-side window going down.

"I need to see your IDs," said a voice I didn't recognize. There was a long pause. I hoped Sweeney's fakes were good. "Okay, here you go. I'm required by federal law to inform you that pursuant to the Unity Act, no one leaving the state of Idaho will be allowed to return under any circumstances until such time as the blockade has been lifted. If you wish to turn around and remain in Idaho, our soldiers will guide you through the turnaround route. If you understand these instructions and still wish to leave the state of Idaho, and if you are at least seventeen years of age and are leaving of your own free will, I need a verbal confirmation from each of you. Do you wish to leave the state of Idaho?"

"Yes," Cal said.

There was a little pause. "No, I said verbal!" said the stranger. "A nod of the head won't cut it."

"Yes!" JoBell shouted.

"Yes," said Sweeney and Becca.

"All right. Pull ahead slowly to the next station so they can search your vehicle for contraband. Thank you, and have a nice day."

I heard the window going back up.

"Asshole power-tripping Army prick," JoBell said quietly.

"Well, let's hope that false bottom works," Sweeney said. "If they find you, we're screwed, Danny. They have us totally boxed in with concrete barriers on either side of us. Armed soldiers everywhere. There's a huge machine gun at the guard shack ahead."

"Yeah, Danny, I think we might have really messed up here. I didn't know they would be searching like this going *out* — I thought they just wouldn't let us back in. Damn it!" Cal slapped the steering wheel.

"Just chill," said JoBell. "Be cool. They might not figure out there's any space under there."

It sucked being helpless, stuck in this smelly little hatch in the back like this, walking into another Fed trap, this time with all my friends in trouble too. The driver's-side window went down again.

"How you doing?" said a different voice.

"Fine," said Cal. "Sick of being stuck in Idaho. There's no food, barely any gas. We're tired of it."

"Tired of putting up with Governor Montaine and the Idaho National Guard's bullshit!" JoBell said.

The stranger at the window chuckled. "I hear that. I can't wait until this is all over. Checkpoint duty is about as boring as it gets, you know." My friends laughed, and I hoped not too much.

"Big tough guy like you?" Becca said. "I would have thought they'd have you flying a jet or manning a really big gun."

The soldier chuckled again. "No, I'm only a grunt, stuck on gate duty."

"Bet you wish you could get back to base," Becca said. "Where you from?"

Becca sounded really interested. She was laying it on thick. If we were super lucky, she could get us out of this search.

"Right now," said the soldier, "I'm stationed at Fort Lewis, but originally I'm from South Carolina."

"Sounds like you miss it," Sweeney said.

"Yeah. Searching people and being on guard against other Americans? That's not what I signed up for. As soon as my enlistment is up, I'm going home."

"Well, sorry you have to leave." Becca giggled. "Thanks for your service."

"Well, I appreciate that," said the soldier. "And I'm sorry, but I'm going to have to search your vehicle. Is the back window unlocked?"

"Yeah," Cal said. "You have to pop the Chevy bow tie on the

door and crank the window down. It's kind of tricky. What are you all searching for anyway?"

"We're checking for contraband and persons of interest. Plus we have to make sure that nobody under seventeen crosses the border without an adult guardian."

Then it was quiet for a moment.

My heart pounded as I heard the sound of the back window being rolled down. I squeezed the pistol grip on my nine mil, then changed my mind and hid the gun underneath me. This was it. The false bottom would work or it wouldn't. I was never going to win a shoot-out here, and provoking these soldiers would probably get my friends hurt. If they had me, they had me.

"Got supplies back here?" the soldier said, his voice sounding louder and so close to me now.

"Yeah, not much stuff though," Sweeney said. "The blockade's made life so tough that we had to sell most everything we had."

"Hey, what's the trouble back there, Ortega?" someone shouted from near the front of the truck.

I heard the sound of the window being cranked back up. "There's no trouble. All clear."

"Welcome back to the United States," another soldier yelled. "Drive on ahead. Follow the posted speed limits."

The Beast pulled forward and Cal rolled his window up. "Everybody be cool. Act normal. Wait until we're away from all these Army guys," he said.

In my dark hiding place, I took deep breaths to try to calm down.

A short time later, Cal drove us onto some gravel roads and pulled over so that I could get out. JoBell hugged me. I placed my hand on the back of her head, happy to be free to hold her.

"I was so worried he'd catch you," she said.

"Schmidty did a great job making that little hiding place," I said. "I just never thought I'd have to use it like that."

Becca hit me lightly in the arm with one of two screwdrivers she must have pulled from the toolbox in the back of the Beast. She used it to point to a trailer house set back in the pines. The yard was full of broken-down cars and other junk. "There are probably more cars with Idaho plates driving around the Spokane area than usual, but I don't want to stand out any more than we have to. Eric, help me with this." She tossed a screwdriver to Sweeney, and the two of them crouched-ran through the yard, dodging old farm equipment until they reached a truck with Washington plates.

JoBell grabbed the AR15 from the back of the Beast and climbed up into the passenger seat, keeping the weapon out of sight of the trailer. "Well, if we're in it this far, I guess I'll cover them, in case there's trouble."

Soon enough, Becca and Sweeney came running back to the Beast. I took the keys from Cal as everyone scrambled inside, and we took off down the road, finding a place a few miles away to stop and swap out our Idaho plates for the Washington ones.

"Now, drive normally," Sweeney said. "Don't speed or do anything else that will get us caught and arrested. If we play it cool and don't draw attention to ourselves, we should be able to pick up your mom and get back in no time."

Everything he said was true, but it sounded like he was describing a mission into Iran or North Korea, not a neighboring state and a city I'd been to hundreds of times growing up. Then again, I'd finally accepted that America wasn't going back to normal any time soon, and that more and more, my home was a war zone.

As we rolled down I-90 toward Spokane, we passed Army five-ton trucks, Stryker armored fighting vehicles, and even M1A3 Abrams tanks. We saw tents set up in the mall parking lots and armored Humvees parked on side streets alongside cars. Soldiers were everywhere. We got stuck in a lot of traffic, since so many roads were closed to store military vehicles.

"All of this can't be for the blockade," Becca said.

I checked my mirrors and took care not to speed. "It's not. This city is a staging ground for an invasion force."

"If that's true," said Cal, "Idaho is in deep shit."

"Just like we'll be if we don't get Mom and get out of here." I handed JoBell the piece of paper where I'd written the address of the apartment where Mom was staying. "JoBell, can you have Eleanor give us some directions? Otherwise we'll be stuck driving around Spokane all night until someone catches us."

JoBell keyed in the address. "Got it," she said a moment later. "Exit the freeway in one point two miles."

A little over fifteen minutes later, we were knocking on the door of the apartment. I hoped Mom had listened to me and waited. And even though I knew there was basically no chance that anyone knew I was here, I kept looking up and down the hall nervously, expecting the FBI or Fed soldiers to come running after me any second. I knocked on the door again. "Come on, Mom. Be here," I whispered.

Finally, I heard the jingle of the chain being unlocked on the other side of the door, the dull click of the deadbolt being released. After almost a month, I'd finally get to see my mother. The door opened.

And there stood a hot blond woman in little white shorts and a blue button-up shirt, who couldn't have been more than four or five years older than us.

"Oh wow," Sweeney whispered very quietly right behind me.

"Can I help you?" the woman said.

"I'm looking for my mother," I said instead of introducing myself. I didn't want her neighbors hearing my name and getting ideas about calling me in to the police or the Fed.

"Oh my gosh! Hi! I'm Sarah. We talked before. Come in. Kelly's sleeping, I think, but she'll be so glad to see you!" She led us into the living room of a small, simple apartment with white walls and a wood floor. Then she spoke more quietly. "I'm glad you came when you did. This morning she was talking about making the trip herself again. Anyway, I'll go get her."

Sweeney leaned around me to watch her butt as she walked down the hall. "Dude, check her. I think I'm in love. Saraaaaaah. She's so hot."

"Don't you have a girlfriend?" Becca whispered. "Remember Cassie?"

"Well, we've gone out a couple times, but —"

"You mean *made* out a couple times," said Cal.

"Same thing. But who cares about that? This girl . . . this *woman* . . . Sarah is so beautiful, and I think she kind of likes me. Did you see the way she looked at me? She knows Asians make the best lovers."

"Eric," JoBell said.

"Maybe we should spend the night here instead of going straight home. You know, get some rest and —"

"Eric, shut up!" JoBell growled.

"Danny?" A soft voice came from down the hallway.

I couldn't hold back my smile. "I'm here, Mom. I promised I'd help you. We're here to take you home."

Mom ran from the hallway and hugged me. "Oh, Danny, you made it. Are you okay? It can't be safe for you here. Are they looking for you?"

"Easy." I gently backed her up a step. "They got no idea where I am, and it's going to stay that way."

Sarah followed Mom into the room. "Why don't we go into the kitchen?" Sweeney said, pressing his hand to Sarah's back. "If you don't mind, could I trouble you for a drink? We've had the most amazing journey. Let me tell you about it."

Sarah actually seemed charmed, and JoBell rolled her eyes, but Becca led her and Cal into the kitchen after the other two.

Mom held my face in her hands with her warm palms pressed to my cheeks. She looked older, like instead of being here for about four weeks, it had been more like four years. Tears traced the wrinkles around her eyes. "You really came to get me."

"I promised I'd take care of you, Mom. I always will."

"Was it tough getting here?"

I took her hands off my face, but held them in mine. Her question would have been funny if the whole situation weren't so tragic.

"No problem getting out of Idaho," I said. "Getting back might be tricky, but you're going to have to trust me, okay? I mean, it could be a little scary, but I promise we'll make it."

"I trust you, Danny. You're such a good son." She hugged me again, and I squeezed her back.

"You better go pack your things. We should get out of here as soon as possible."

"We've been thinking, Danny," JoBell said a few minutes later when everyone had come back from the kitchen. "We should do some shopping, you know, pick up supplies that we can't really get inside the sanction zone. We all wouldn't have to go."

"That's a great idea!" Sweeney said. "Why don't you all go get us some real food, and while you're at it, Cal, since you're eighteen, why don't you buy me about three hundred dollars' worth of cigars and cigarettes? We can sell it to guys like Schmidty for three times as much in Idaho." He handed a debit card to Cal and wrote the PIN on the back of an old receipt in his wallet.

"Sure you don't want to come along?" Cal said to Sweeney.

"Ah . . ." Sweeney looked down and lightly kicked his foot back and forth. "I better stay here with Danny and his mom. You know, in case they need any help."

Cal laughed a little. JoBell looked from Sweeney to Sarah and shook her head. "Okay. We'll buy all we can and hurry back. Then we'll go home." She held up her hands. "Keys, babe?"

"Be careful with her," I said as I tossed her the keys to the Beast.

"I should crash that truck." She smiled. "I swear you love it more than me."

"That's impossible," I said.

After they were gone, we settled into that useless polite talk that just fills silence. Sweeney asked Sarah all about her work. He'd never been so fascinated with nursing before, and I knew he never would be again. Finally, he said, "I noticed you have a lightbulb out in the kitchen. Can I change it for you?"

"Sure," she giggled. "If you want. You don't have to."

Once again, Sweeney gently placed his hand on her back and led her through the door to the kitchen. He winked at me before the door swung closed.

"I better get my things ready," Mom said.

"Good idea. Hey, I spotted a gas station down the block. I'm going to go buy a Mountain Dew. There's basically none left in Idaho, and I've missed it."

Mom squeezed my hand. "Be careful, Danny. Hurry back."

Out on the street, I shielded my eyes from the late-afternoon sun. It was still weird to see so many cars on the road. Because of the rationing and the cost of gas, traffic in Idaho had dropped to a minimum. Plus, I'd been living in the woods with the Guard for so long that I'd kind of forgotten what normal roads were like. It didn't seem fair that everybody here, twenty minutes from the Idaho border, was able to live their lives like they always had, while innocent people in Idaho had to suffer.

I stepped into the Gas & Sip and almost started drooling. Candy bars and beef jerky and pop . . . Even milk and bread looked great. Instead of empty or nearly empty shelves, instead of ration signs and increased prices posted everywhere, this Washington convenience store had everything, and signs for discounts. I took my sweet time wandering the aisles.

On the way back to Sarah's apartment, I dumped some delicious M&M'S in my mouth, chomping them like a hog and barely getting them down before chugging some Mountain Dew. Pure sugar! I'd missed junk food like this. It was so good.

My comm vibrated in my pocket. I had Digi-Hank shut off so I wouldn't draw attention to myself if someone called me. I pulled my comm out to see a call from Cal. "What's up?"

"Danny, they got JoBell and Becca."

I dropped my pop so I could hold the comm closer to my ear. "Who?"

"The Feds, man. Soldiers."

"Weren't you with them?"

"They sent me away when I kept picking out Frosted Flakes and Oreos. There's a cigar place next to the grocery store. I was in there when I heard a scream." Cal was whispering, but almost panicked in his breathing. *"When I went out, these Army dudes had 'em."*

"Where are they now?"

"Right around the side of the store. What should I do? I got a knife. Should I go get them?"

"No!" Damn it, what was I supposed to do? I didn't even know where they'd gone. "Do you have the keys to the Beast?"

"JoBell does."

I took off at a sprint toward Sarah's apartment. "Me and Sweeney are coming. Send me your location. Whatever happens, don't let them leave, or else stay with them."

"Yeah, the soldiers don't have a Humvee or nothing. I think they radioed for backup."

"Cal, just keep eyes on them. We're on the way." I tapped out right as I entered the apartment building, rushing up the stairs. "Come on, Sarah, have a car, have a car, have a car," I whispered.

Cal's comm location popped up on my screen. I tapped for directions between us. He was ten blocks away. We'd never get there in time on foot.

The apartment's living room was empty. I rushed to the kitchen. As soon as I burst in, Sweeney jumped away from Sarah, who started buttoning up her shirt. Unbelievable.

Sweeney pushed his hand back through his hair. "Dude, you could have knocked."

"They got JoBell and Becca," I said, adding to Sarah, "You have a car?" She nodded. "Mom," I shouted. "The girls . . . um . . . bought too much stuff. Sarah's going to take us to meet them in her car. We'll be right back. Stay here."

"Danny?" Mom called from her bedroom, but I didn't wait around. No time.

Sarah knew right where the grocery store was, and she drove as fast as she could. I checked my comm. "Cal hasn't moved. He'd follow them if they left. Or he'd call."

"What are you going to do when you get there?" Sarah asked.

I took my nine mil out from under my belt. "I'm going to get Becca and JoBell back. I don't much care how."

Sarah pulled into the parking lot of a strip mall with a big grocery store and other businesses. The parking lot was packed with cars, some wasting gas, stopped with their motors running.

We drove on and sure enough, in the parking lot around the corner, two soldiers stood with M4 rifles next to JoBell and Becca. The girls' hands were bound with plastic zip ties. The only thing we had going for us was that the side lot was mostly empty. Only one car and truck were parked over there.

Sarah drove through the lot until she pulled up in front of the store, out of sight of the Army guys. As soon as she stopped, Sweeney and I scrambled out of the car.

"Listen, Sarah —" Sweeney started.

I pushed him aside and leaned down to the window. "Go back to your place. Tell my mother that we're leaving the second I get back there. Be cool. Don't tell her what's going on. Try to keep her calm." She chewed her nails. "It's okay," I said. "Thanks for all your help. We'll see you soon."

She drove away. Cal ran up to us. He pulled out his pocketknife. "What do we do? You got your gun?"

"We can't shoot them," Sweeney said. "I mean, it's broad daylight. It'll make too much noise. Draw too much attention. Plus, you know, we can't just *kill* them."

I drew them into a huddle. "If the three of us hurry, we might be able to get the jump on them, take their weapons, and maybe tie them up." I elbowed Sweeney to get him to look at me. "But here's the thing. We need to be hard-core on this. Yesterday I gave these guys a chance, saved the life of this asshole Fed soldier. As soon as I helped get him stabilized, the Fed medic tried to arrest me. We can't trust them."

Cal's eyes were hungry. He looked like he was getting ready for a big football game. I knew he was in, but Sweeney looked away. "Hey," I said, grabbing Sweeney's arm. "We have to be willing to do whatever it takes. You with me?"

He nodded. "With you all the way."

"Hell yeah," Cal said. "What's the plan?"

"We rush those guys. Tackle them. Like football," I said.

Sweeney wiped his brow. "I'm the quarterback. I don't really tackle people."

"It's three against two," I said. "Me and Cal will go for the tackle. You help where you're needed. Make sure we get their guns. We only get one chance at this."

I motioned for them to follow. We walked past the storefront until I could peek around the corner. Becca was crying. JoBell was talking to her like she was trying to calm her down. The soldiers were maybe fifteen feet away. That would be a lot of ground to cover when they were armed. We might have only a few seconds from the time they spotted us.

"Here's the play," I whispered. "Tackle some asshole Fed soldiers. On three, on three." The guys signaled that they understood. I made sure my nine mil was secure in my pants with the safety on so it didn't go flying or accidentally shoot me in the leg. I closed my eyes and said a quick silent prayer. Then it was time to do it. "Set, hut, hut, hut!"

I ran faster than I ever had before, right for the bigger of the two soldiers.

"Hey!" the other one called out.

My target spun to face me and started to bring up his rifle. He was too late. I drove my shoulder into his gut, wrapped my arms around the back of his thighs, lifted him while I pushed him back, and dumped him hard on the pavement. Then I scrambled up and punched him in the nose before yanking his M4 out of his hands and standing up.

Cal and his soldier rolled on the ground, each of them trying to pull the M4 from the other's grip. Sweeney ran up and clocked the soldier in the nose, but he somehow kept fighting for the rifle. Sweeney punched him again.

"Come on, man! Hit him harder!" Cal grunted as he kept trying to get the rifle away.

Making sure the guy I'd taken down could see that I had his weapon, I pressed my new M4's muzzle to the other soldier's head and yanked the charging handle back to chamber a round. The loud click of the bolt's action froze Cal's man right there.

"Give him your weapon," I said calmly. When me and Cal were both standing with rifles aimed at the soldiers, I motioned with mine toward the alley behind the grocery store. "Get up. Walk over there. Keep your hands low, but where I can see them. You try to go for a weapon or a radio and I swear I will shoot you."

The Feds stood up, and we all moved together into the alley.

"Danny, thank God," Becca said when she'd followed us to the alley. "It's my fault. I'm so sorry. We were running groceries out to the truck and I was talking about you with JoBell. These soldiers recognized your name and the vehicle description, and they just grabbed us."

"It's okay. Don't worry." To Cal, I added, "Give Sweeney your weapon. Cut the girls loose."

Me and Sweeney pushed the two soldiers — a sergeant and a specialist — up against the wall near a big green metal garbage dumpster.

"What are you going to do, shoot us?" said the sergeant.

"I'm PFC Wright. You have a problem with me, you come for me, got it? You leave my friends out of it." I handed JoBell my M4. "Cover me while I search them."

I patted the guys down, finding more zip ties in the sergeant's pocket. I faced them away from us and bound their wrists behind their backs. The rest of the search turned up the usual things soldiers carried: sunflower seeds, chewing tobacco, cigarettes, and a couple knives. But each of them also carried one smoke and one CS gas grenade. "I'll take these," I said, stuffing the grenades into my pockets. "Never know when they'll come in handy. Now, you boys are going to stay here. Don't try to follow us."

"You're not going anywhere," a voice said from behind me. "Don't move!"

I drew my nine mil as I spun to face this new soldier, just as he pointed his M4 at me. Two more Feds rushed in from the side.

I kept my nine mil aimed at the one who had spoken. He had me in his sights. JoBell was locked up gun to gun with a soldier to my left, Sweeney in the same situation to my right. Cal ran behind us, and out of the corner of my eye, I saw him knock the first two zip-tied soldiers on their asses before they could try kicking us or something.

"I'm Staff Sergeant Kirklin," said the soldier aiming at me. "You folks need to put your weapons down."

"Sergeant," said the specialist on the ground. "It's him. It's that guy from the Idaho thing."

"I know who he is." The staff sergeant spoke like everything was normal — except he kept his rifle pointed at me. "Now, Private, I am prepared to order my two men to put down their weapons if your two friends will do the same. What do you say?"

Only me and him would be armed then. It gave my friends a better chance. I bit my lip. My hand was starting to shake from holding up the gun. I slowly brought my left hand up to brace my right.

"Okay, guys," I said to Sweeney and JoBell. "If those two put down their guns, you do the same."

"Dude, are you sure?" Sweeney asked.

"Trust me on this." My mouth was dry.

I kept watching the staff sergeant as the other two soldiers started lowering their weapons. A stinging drop of sweat ran into my eye and I blinked to keep focused. The rifles rattled quietly as the soldiers and then JoBell and Sweeney put them down on the pavement.

"Okay . . . Good," Sergeant Kirklin said. "Now, Private, you put your weapon down as well."

"I don't think so, Sergeant," I said as I slowly started walking backward. My friends moved with me, but I didn't dare take my eyes off the soldiers. "JoBell," I said. "You still have the keys? Let's head for the Beast."

"Stop right there," Kirklin said. "All of you."

We kept moving. "We're leaving now," I said. "Don't try to follow us." The tense rise and fall of Kirklin's chest mirrored my own. I wondered what would happen if I did stop. Just gave up and surrendered. Maybe I'd get a fair trial, maybe not. But then my friends would go to jail for helping me. And my mother — there's no way she could handle me being arrested.

"I said stop!" Kirklin shouted.

And if I trusted him, if I let my guard down at all, he could just betray me like that asshole medic yesterday. My nine mil was still locked on him. What if I wounded him, shot him in the leg or something? No good. He'd still be able to fire, and Army doctrine was one shot, one kill. If he shot me, he'd probably get a medal and a promotion. I could see the fire in his eyes, the finger tight on his trigger. I kept backing away.

Kirklin moved a step closer. "Private, you and your friends are under arrest."

I had only one option. Could I do it? If I did, there was no going back.

Kirklin tightened his rifle against his shoulder. If he made his move, I'd never know.

I took control of my breathing. *Oh, God, please forgive me.* In and out and in —

"Private," Kirklin shouted, "if you take one more step I will shoot —"

— and hold —

I pulled the trigger. His chest burst blood and pieces of flesh. I fired again. His hand was ripped away from his rifle as he fell to the ground. The other two Feds dove for their weapons, but my guys tackled them. People were yelling. I couldn't tell who.

"Nobody move!" I shouted. "Shut up!" I pressed the business end of my nine mil to one Fed's temple. They both stopped struggling. "Guys, get all the guns," I said. Cal and Sweeney picked up the rifles. Becca and JoBell zip-tied the last two Feds so all four of them were bound tight and helpless on the ground.

I stepped up to Staff Sergeant Kirklin's body. The Army mental health pamphlets warned soldiers against staring at bodies, particularly those of people they'd killed. But I felt like I owed this man enough to look at him, to not try to ignore what I'd done. His body lay crumpled in a big, expanding pool of bright red blood, dust floating on the edges. His arm was thrown back so that he almost looked like he was waving, except above his wrist there were only shreds of meat. Steam rose from his still, open chest and bone fragments jutted out of the deep red cavity. His dull eyes stared up at nothing. It was too much like that girl at Boise, except this time, I had chosen to make this person dead.

When I looked up, I saw JoBell standing in the middle of the alley, her M4 dangling from her hand with the muzzle pointed at the ground. Tears rolled down her cheeks as she stared at me. I met her eyes. What was she thinking? Did she think I was a murderer? Did she understand that I'd had no choice? Did she know I'd done this at least in part for her?

I swallowed and licked my lips. "We gotta go."

Cal motioned toward the soldiers with his M4. "We can't leave these guys and the . . . We can't leave them out in the open. Someone will find them. Find out we were here."

"Someone probably heard those shots already." I started toward the Beast. "We're leaving now."

Back by the Beast, the image of the man I'd killed flashed through my mind again. I felt the acid burn at the back of my mouth. My stomach lurched, and I puked and then dry-heaved before I was finally ready to get into my truck.

When we were all mounted up, we had a truck full of the groceries the girls had been able to load, four M4 rifles, an AR15, my nine mil, four silent people probably wondering what had just happened, and me, PFC Daniel Wright, who, no matter his reasons, would from now on be a killer.

TWENTY-THREE

I told everyone to play it cool as we got back to Sarah's apartment. We needed to keep quiet about everything that had happened so my mom wouldn't freak out. We also needed to hurry. The Fed would be after us soon. It was going to be even tougher getting out of here now.

"Is everything okay?" Mom asked when we all came into the apartment. Sarah was leaning back against the wall behind Mom. She smiled at Sweeney and slid her arm around him. For once, Sweeney wasn't on his usual game and didn't respond much.

I picked up Mom's suitcase and her other bag. "We should get going."

"I'll miss you," Sarah said to my mom.

"I'll miss you too," Sweeney said.

JoBell shook her head. "Eric, will you knock it off?"

But Sarah squeezed his hand. She hugged my mom and we all headed out.

This time Mom rode in the passenger seat. JoBell with the AR15 and Cal with an M4 sat wedged in with the food and supplies in the very back by the toolbox. I'd thought Mom might freak out at the sight of the guns, but she was taking all of this very well. "It's a messed-up world," she said, "when a seventeen-year-old boy and his friends have to carry guns so his mom can go home."

"Amen to that." I put on my cowboy hat and drove out of town, grateful that Mom had no idea about the horrible thing I'd done.

The plan was to cross into Idaho on a tiny logging road way up north, so I headed up Highway 2 toward Mount Spokane State Park. Nobody said much on the drive. The radio was on the country station, but I wasn't listening. I kept going over what had happened behind the store. "Thou shalt not kill" ran through my head again and again. Maybe I hadn't needed to shoot. What if he and I had both put our guns down? Could we have got out of there peacefully? No. Kirklin wouldn't have put his rifle down. He was on the edge of shooting as it was. And even if everyone had put their guns down, we all would have just fought hand to hand, and who knows what would have happened then? One of us might have ended up fighting one of them for a rifle. It could have gone off. Anyone could have been killed. Like in Boise.

Maybe I should have given up and let him take me to jail the way they'd done to Specialist Stein. But then JoBell and my friends would be in jail too, and Mom would be trapped in Washington, where she would slowly go crazy, or make a stupid run for the border on her own. Plus, she'd freak out if I was arrested. She'd already lost my father. I really didn't think she could handle losing me too. And I had promised that I would take care of her.

It all came down to what I'd learned from that Fed medic. I didn't have the luxury of taking stupid, trusting chances. That sergeant's finger was on the trigger. He could have shot me at any time. It would have taken one second. I'd never know what he meant to do, but waiting around to find out could have gotten me and maybe even all my friends killed.

If I explained it to myself like that, it started to make sense, but then in the next second I was full of more doubts. Worse, even when I could convince myself that my action had been necessary, I couldn't shake the hollow, cold, desperate feeling that I had done a very terrible thing.

"You know," said Sweeney after a long time, "a lot of this situation really sucks, but at least I had the chance to meet Nurse Sarah and —"

"Eric, shut up," Becca said.

"What? What's so bad about me finding true love?"

"You find it every day," Becca said.

"Shut up!" JoBell said. I checked my mirror and saw her pointing at two fast-approaching Army Humvees. Red lights flashed on the roofs of the vehicles. "They've found us."

"Everybody hold on. This is going to get rough!" I sped up. With the Feds chasing us, there would be no time to find some forgotten dirt road to get home. I hooked the corner onto the highway that would take me to my Guard company's position. Humvees were heavy, especially armored Humvees, and heavy meant slow. Of course, the Beast wasn't exactly lightweight either. I just hoped they were slower than me.

The crack of gunfire echoed from outside.

"Oh, Danny, they're shooting!" Mom screamed. She was going straight into a panic attack.

I looked in my rearview mirror again. The gunners standing in the turrets at the top of the Humvees were firing the light machine guns on their mounts. I guessed they were M249 SAWs, Squad Automatic Weapons. The Humvees' .50-cal heavy machine guns would have ripped right through us. Their muzzles flashed as they fired again. This time I heard the *thump, thump, thump-thump-thump* as the rounds hit the Beast.

More shots hit the back window, which spiderwebbed right in front of JoBell and Cal. They would be dead now if Schmidty hadn't put in the bulletproof glass.

"What are we gonna do?" Sweeney shouted. "They're shooting at us!"

"We're going to have to shoot back," Cal said.

"Cal!" JoBell pushed his barrel down.

"Self-defense!" Cal yelled.

Another barrage pelted the back of the truck. More round divots in the glass. Cal hit the window hard with the butt of his rifle. "Damn. This glass is tough!"

"Cal, those are American soldiers!" JoBell yelled. "We can't —"

"It's them or us," Cal said. "They've already made their choice. We're in this too deep, JoJo."

JoBell frowned. "I told you before." She pulled and released the charging handle to chamber a round on her AR15. "Don't call me JoJo." She joined him in hitting the glass until it finally gave way. "Danny, your back window is ruined. I'm going to take out their weapons. Hopefully, I won't hit anyone." One-two-three, she fired quick. One of the turret gunners crouched behind his machine gun. "It's hard to hit anything when we're moving."

"I'll keep the Beast steady," I said. "You keep shooting."

Cal opened up too, firing wildly.

"Try to aim at something, Cal. You're wasting bullets." JoBell fired again. While the one turret gunner ducked down, she shot round after round, sparks jumping off the machine guns as she pelted them. I figured that at least that SAW wasn't going to be able to shoot again. The .50-cal was a different story. Those things were like tanks themselves.

The second Humvee caught up to us and brought its front bumper up side by side with my door handle. Then it swerved at me and struck. The two-inch pipes welded inside the Beast's body kept us from being crumpled right there.

The Humvee hit us again. My tires squealed as we were pushed to the side. "Oh, you did *not* just scratch up my truck!" I shouted. I yanked the wheel to the left, slamming into the Humvee and knocking it back. The turret gunner on top lost his balance and struggled to get himself back under control. He reached to unlock the mount on his SAW so he could move it to fire on us.

I rolled down my window and grabbed my nine mil. I didn't want to do this, but I couldn't let him spray us all with 5.56 rounds. I held the steering wheel with my left hand and with my right aimed as best I could across my body at the gunner. Then I squeezed off five rounds, hitting him in the shoulder. He dropped down into the turret.

"Sweeney!" I yelled. "Get on my comm. Call Sergeant Kemp. Tell him we're coming through the checkpoint on this highway in about five minutes, and we could use some help with the company we're bringing."

The Humvee that had been alongside us dropped back a little, but we had worse trouble ahead. Another gun Hummer was coming down the road straight at us, gunner ready. I switched my shooting and driving hands, holding my gun out the window with my left, firing forward wildly and unsupported. "JoBell, we need you up here!"

She scrambled to climb over the backseat, rifle in hand. "Hang on a second."

But we didn't have a second. The approaching gunner completely opened up with his SAW, spraying the hood and windshield with bullets. The Beast swayed all over the road as a hot dagger sliced my left hand. I dropped my gun and shouted in pain.

Then I heard a choking, gasping sound. Mom was flailing around in her seat with a gaping, spurting red hole in the upper right part of her chest.

"Mom! Mom! Someone get a bandage on her! Stop the bleeding!" I swerved to the left to dodge the oncoming Humvee, its armor scraping alongside my truck. "Becca! Somebody!"

Becca had her shirt off and held it to Mom's chest. "You're okay, Mrs. Wright. I'll stop this bleeding, no problem."

"Put more pressure on it!" I shouted. "You gotta put pressure on it!"

"I am!" Becca cried.

We were coming up on the border. I could see our wire obstacle in Idaho and a bunch of soldiers around the new Fed checkpoint on the Washington side. Mom screamed, pressing her blood-soaked hands over Becca's. JoBell slid up between me and Mom, using the big center console as a seat. "Danny, you have to drive. There're soldiers ahead." She knocked out the cracked-up front windshield with her rifle and then opened fire. The Feds scattered for cover. There were dozens of them, though. They'd rip us apart before we ever reached our side of the border.

"Danny," Mom said with a raspy voice.

"Mom, I'm right here. Stay with me. We're almost there."

"Oh, it hurts, Danny."

"I know, Mom." I wiped my eyes and blinked so I could still see through the pain in my own hand.

"Maybe we should surrender." Becca leaned over my mother. Mom's blood had soaked Becca's bra and was smeared up her arms. "Maybe they have a doctor."

She was right. This might be our only chance. And we'd never make it through to Idaho with all those soldiers ready to shoot us up from either side of the road. I let off the gas.

Then two Apache gunship helicopters dove down out of the sky from Idaho. One fired its cannons danger-close to the Humvees. The other tore up the ground right at the edge of the road, providing suppressive fire to keep the Fed soldiers down. Kemp must have come through, probably calling the governor himself to get this air support.

"We'll go to our doctors," I said, pressing the accelerator again.

As the Apaches kept firing, keeping the Fed soldiers distracted, I drove ahead. "Hang in there, Mom. We're almost home. Just like I promised." I could see the little dirt road that let civilians bypass the roadblocks to leave Idaho. We'd use it to get back in.

Then a Fed gun Hummer rolled up to cut us off. The border was completely blocked.

"Oh shit." I looked over at Mom. She wasn't crying, wasn't moving. I looked back at the road. The Fed had piled up that big dirt berm on the highway across from my company's wire obstacle, probably to use as cover in case of a firefight. It was the only way home.

"Everybody get in a seat and strap yourselves in! Now!" I screamed, pressing the gas pedal all the way to the floor. "Hold on to something!" The Beast's engine roared. JoBell scrambled into the backseat.

"Danny, no, don't!" Becca shouted. She must have figured out what I was planning to do. "That stuff only works in movies."

"We're about to find out!" I kept the Beast right on course for the dirt berm. When we reached it, I was knocked back into my seat as we shot up the six-foot, sloped barrier and then into the air over the anti-vehicle ditch.

Out the busted windshield, all I could see was sky. The engine roared louder as the wheels were suddenly free of the road. I fought hard to keep hold of the steering wheel so the tires would be straight when we landed. I let off the gas and put on the brakes instead.

We hit the wire obstacle hard. Two tires exploded at once. A green steel picket burst up through the floorboards, barely missing Mom's legs. I heard metal scraping on metal as the wire wrapped itself around the axles and driveshaft, then the other tires burst. My seat belt dug into my chest as the Beast ground to a sickening, crunching halt. Steam rolled out from under the hood as the engine shut down, the temperature gauge spiking. Something must have hit the radiator. But we were in Idaho territory, and Mom could get help.

I had to push hard against the handle to open my dented door. "Medic!" I screamed. "I need a medic now! Call a medevac chopper!" I high-stepped through the barbed concertina wire as fast as I could to the other side of the truck. I opened Mom's door and reached across her to unbuckle her seat belt. She felt cold and looked so pale.

"Come on, Mom. Hang in there. You're fine. You're fine. Where the hell's that damned medic?" I shouted to the soldiers, who weren't running fast enough. Mom wasn't saying anything. I couldn't tell if she was breathing or not.

I lifted my mother into my arms and carried her, stumbling a couple times in the wire. Finally, two soldiers took her from me, setting her down on the grass beside the road, cutting away her shirt and getting a dressing on the wound. A third medic pulled me back and started wrapping my left hand. JoBell appeared beside me and slid her arm around my back.

I winced as the medic finished bandaging me up. He waved his hand in front of my face to try to get my attention. "I don't have enough gauze to wrap this right. It should stop the bleeding for now, but this is going to need stitches, maybe surgery."

I pushed him aside and stepped toward Mom. The medics were trying CPR, but her eyes . . . They were dull and not focused on anything. She didn't move, didn't breathe.

She was dead. My mother, Kelly Elizabeth Wright, was dead.

I promised I would always look out for her. Promised to bring her home safely. That's all I wanted to do, bring her home. I clenched my fists until blood began to soak through the bandage on my wounded hand.

My mother was dead. The damned Fed had ruined everything.

"They killed her," I whispered.

One medic shook his head. The other looked up at me. "I'm sorry," he said.

"They killed her," I said louder. I rushed to JoBell and grabbed the AR15.

"Danny, no!" JoBell shouted.

Sweeney and Cal were still back by my busted-up truck, yelling for me to stop, but I didn't listen. I ran up beside the wire obstacle, closer and closer to the border, clenching my left fist at an angle above my head, trying to stop the blood that was already soaking through parts of my white bandage. I held the rifle in my right hand, the stock supported under my armpit, as I came to within a dozen feet of the state line. The Feds over there must have been scared of the Apaches coming back. They stayed behind whatever cover they could find. "You killed my mother!" I shouted across the border. "Why the hell can't you leave us alone!"

I opened fire. One, two, three rounds at a cement barricade. Soldiers ducked behind it. Another Fed shot at me from behind a tree. I gave him two rounds, but my shot went wide.

"Come out and fight, cowards!" I shot again and again, most of the Feds staying covered, my adrenaline keeping me moving as a few rounds struck the ground around me. "You want war? We will give you a war!"

Finally, the trigger brought only a dull click as my rifle ran out of ammunition. Idaho Humvees rolled up next to me and soldiers rushed out to stop me. I dropped to the ground, sobbing, feeling as empty as my weapon.

─⋏─• As governor, I did approve PFC Daniel Wright's leave, as he said he needed to settle some things at home since his mother was trapped in Spokane. I did not know about, and I certainly did not authorize, his mission into Washington. The death of Staff Sergeant Kirklin is a tragedy, but it was the result of self-defense, as Wright had committed no crime except for trying to help his mother return to her home when Kirklin attempted to arrest him. Specialist Barlon, the turret gunner that Wright was forced to wound, is in good condition and expected to make a full recovery. The air support assets I deployed to protect Wright were ordered to provide nonlethal cover fire, and I'm pleased to report no Fed soldiers were hurt.

Unfortunately, federal troops did wound Wright. They did kill Wright's mother. His father was killed in action in Afghanistan years ago. Now this seventeen-year-old soldier is without parents. I offer my condolences to Private Wright and to the family of Staff Sergeant Kirklin, and my apologies to Specialist Barlon. We are faced with tragedy upon tragedy as a result of the federal blockade. •─⋏─

─⋏─• More bad news from the New York Stock Exchange today as investors who had been encouraged by recent negotiations between Idaho and the Fed are retreating in light of recent shootings in Spokane, Washington, and on Idaho's borders with Washington and Nevada. Some markets declined as much as •─⋏─

⌁• The president today said that he does not accept Governor Montaine's explanation of the recent events surrounding Private First Class Wright, and demands that the young soldier stand trial for wounding Specialist Barlon and for the death of Staff Sergeant Kirklin. The president said, quote, "In order to honor Specialist Barlon as well as Staff Sergeant Kirklin's wife and two children, Wright must be held accountable for the shooting. Until then, there can be little hope for progress in negotiations between the state of Idaho and the federal government."

NBC News has also learned that Daniel Wright has been placed on special bereavement leave and reduced two ranks to private, the lowest rank in the Army. Governor Montaine insists this disciplinary action is not related to the shooting in Spokane, but instead results from Private Wright applying for leave under false pretenses. •⌁

TWENTY-FOUR

It was a warm day for late October. A light breeze rustled the bare limbs of the trees overhead, but the sky above was the deepest blue I could ever remember. The world all around was bright and fresh.

And completely wrong.

". . . beloved wife and mother, Kelly Wright devoted herself . . ." Chaplain Carmichael droned on beside my mother's grave. JoBell, sitting to my right, squeezed my hand. Becca, on my left, pressed her hand to my shoulder, over the new suit she and JoBell had bought for me.

"Lord, we thank You for sustaining us through these difficult times, and we ask You to please help us avoid open conflict," the Chaplain continued. "We need to have faith that this will remain, just a training exercise."

"Amen," said the small crowd gathered at the graveside.

"Danny." It was Mom's voice. At first I thought it was coming from the coffin, but then I figured I must be hearing things. "Danny, it hurts," the voice came again.

I turned around and saw Mom standing a few feet away. She stumbled toward me, holding her bleeding chest, and I ran to her.

"She's dead," JoBell said. "You can't change that."

"Yes I can! There's still time!"

Mom fell to the ground. I kneeled, and from the cargo pocket of my suit I pulled the field dressing, unrolling it and pressing it to Mom's wound. "Can someone help me!? She's lost a lot of blood. Can someone start an IV?"

The boots of that Fed medic stepped up to me. "It's too late," he said.

I looked up at him, but it wasn't the medic after all. It was the staff sergeant I'd killed in Spokane. Blood leaked from his chest and his mangled stump of a hand. He stood next to the Humvee gunner I'd shot during the chase.

When I looked back at my mother, the redheaded girl from Boise lay dead on the ground next to her.

I jumped up and backed away from the girl, her blood soaking through the legs of my pants. My mom was gone. At the grave, her silver casket slowly descended into the earth.

"I'm sorry, Danny." Becca stood next to me in her rodeo jeans, her shiny "Cowgirl Up" belt buckle shining right below her belly button. She shivered a little in a purple lacy bra and slid her arms around me, her fingers tracing my cheek. We kissed softly at first, but then with more hunger. When she stepped back, her arms and chest were covered in my mother's blood. "I'm so sorry. . . ."

I sat up in bed quickly. Each night, the nightmare was a little different, but it always involved one last phantom chance to save my mother. It had never involved kissing Becca before, though. I was glad I wasn't one of those people who spent a lot of time trying to figure out the meaning of dreams. Though as for that, if dream Becca wanted to make out with me, I would rather have that and skip the horrible funeral.

We'd held the real funeral a couple days after Mom died. After she was shot. After those Fed bastards killed her. After I killed her, trying to get her back.

I'd lived at Sweeney's house in the two weeks since. There were too many memories where me and Mom had lived. Eventually, I'd have to go back there and clean the place out so I could put it up for sale — not that anyone was buying houses in Idaho. Still, now that nothing got into the state except for stuff the ICC smuggled in, good secondhand items sold well, and I could probably make some money selling some furniture, her dishes, and some of her clothes.

I groaned a little as I swung my feet out of bed. I never could manage to get back to sleep after these nightmares. Whenever this happened, I had to go out and take a walk around the lake. I'd been taking a lot of walks lately. My head ached a little after last night's drinks. I pulled on a pair of jeans and a sweatshirt, still a challenge with my bandaged left hand, but less and less so as time went on and my injury healed.

I picked up my new .45 and stared at the gun, squeezing the grip. My friends and I were always taught that guns were dangerous, that they had to be respected, that they were absolutely not toys. Still, guns had seemed so cool, especially after I'd first enlisted. Whenever I held the weight and cold metal of a weapon in my hands, I felt a certain excitement, maybe power.

I stood up and strapped my belt and holster around my waist. I hated guns now, but I never went anywhere without my .45. I needed it for protection.

My shooting of that sergeant had made the news. So had my mom's death. Someone had even put a video online of me carrying her out of the Beast, her lifeless arms dangling as I screamed for help. That video had only been viewed twenty or thirty thousand times. The real viral hit was the video of me holding my bleeding hand up and shooting at the Feds. Someone was even making T-shirts and little flags and stuff with the image of my crooked fist wrapped in a blood-soaked bandage, the red-and-white tail hanging down.

Privately, the governor was absolutely furious at me for my border run and for killing Kirklin. He flat-out told me that he wanted to turn me over to the Fed or prosecute me himself, but that he couldn't "afford the political liability at this critical time." So publicly he still protected me. It was lucky for me then that he survived his recall vote. While the majority of those who voted in the special election wanted to remove the governor from office, that majority still wasn't more than the number who had elected him in the first place. Montaine treated it like a huge victory.

The air was cool and crisp on that bright November morning. Well, I'd slept late — it was more of a beautiful early afternoon. I tried to focus on the trail, on the rocks and trees and the cold clear water of the lake. On anything but all that had happened. But waking or sleeping, I couldn't shake the memories of my mother screaming and bleeding, of the way she'd lain so still on the ground after she'd been shot. The way she'd been so peaceful in her casket. My eyes stung and I wiped away hot tears.

Later, I was walking a low path that ran along the base of a cliff, a few feet from the lake. When I saw someone coming toward me down the slope on the path ahead, I instinctively reached for my weapon.

"Hey," JoBell called down to me.

I relaxed, sat on a boulder, and looked out at the water. I was halfway around the lake. She had walked far to find me.

"Care if I join you?" she said as she sat down next to me.

I took out a small cigar, clumsily clipping the end, working the cutter with my bad hand, and lighting up. The cigar had been a present from Cal, one of only a handful that he'd smuggled on our stupid so-called rescue run. It cost about eight bucks in Washington, but due to the short supply of tobacco, probably sold for nearly thirty here in the sanction zone. I owed him. I owed all my friends, big.

"How you doing?" JoBell finally said.

"Shitty," I said. "Same as always."

A crane or some other large bird flapped its huge wings and took off from where it had been swimming on the lake. Its wings beat the surface for a while, cutting a line in the smooth cold glass, and then it soared off. A cool breeze blew in off the water, sending a shiver through me despite my coat.

JoBell slid her hand up my back and rubbed my neck. I closed my eyes and let the warmth from her fingers flow through me in waves. We'd been together so long that we didn't always have to talk much to say a lot.

"You were right," I whispered.

"What?"

"You were right," I said louder. I covered my eyes with my hand. "I'm so sorry. I should have listened to you, JoBell. If I hadn't gone to Washington to get Mom. If I hadn't . . ." My throat tightened up. "Maybe she'd still . . . Should'a listened to you. You were right. Shouldn't even have enlisted. Now both my mom and dad are dead, both killed because of the Fed. I got no family. I'm alone."

"Shh." JoBell gently touched my cheek and turned me to face her. "Don't talk like that. You're not alone. You have me. You have Cal and Becca and Eric." She wiped away my tears. "And don't apologize to me. That's why I came out here today, Danny. I wanted to say that I'm sorry."

I shook my head. "No, you see, I've figured —"

"Let me finish," she said in her firm no-argument voice. She kissed my cheek and pressed her face to mine. "I've been so hard on you, Danny." She shook her head. "You've been wrapped up in this thing that's so much bigger than either of us. So much has happened that you couldn't avoid, and all I've done is tell you to run away from it, as if it were your fault." She kissed me on the lips. "I'm so sorry, Danny. I've been wrong. And now with everything that's happened, I can't go to Seattle. I'm staying right here. Maybe I'll head down to Boise State after everything calms down. If everything calms down."

Since Mom's death, I'd felt a very real, physical cold weight some-where in my core. Now, hearing this from JoBell, I noticed a little warmth there. I felt like thanking her, almost like celebrating, but I knew that I had to say what was right. "JoBell, you can't give up your dream."

"Like I said, this is bigger than either of us. During the chase, I was firing in self-defense, but the Fed won't see it that way. I'd prob-ably be arrested if I went anywhere near Seattle."

Was that the only reason she was giving up all her plans and dreams? Because my botched rescue had ruined them? I'd passed my problems on to her, made her a part of all of this. I looked down and kicked a rock off the trail.

JoBell leaned down so I'd have to look at her. "I *want* to stay, Danny. I want to be here with you."

Her arms slid around my waist. We kissed, long and deep and warm, like we had before I'd proposed and everything got so weird between us.

Like we had when Mom was still alive. The memory of my mother came on so fast that the tears started before I could even think about trying to stop them. "I'll never . . . never see her again," I gasped. "Never talk to her ever again."

JoBell rested her forehead on mine. "I know," she whispered. "I know. I miss her too. I loved her too."

We stayed like that for a long time.

A while later, as we walked hand in hand along the last part of my lap around the lake, JoBell stopped me. "I have to warn you. I tried to talk them out of it, but they wouldn't listen. Sweeney and Cal think the best way to help you right now is to have a little party tonight."

I sighed. "Well, maybe they're right. Maybe it will help me get my mind off all the horrible things that have happened."

"Really?" She squeezed my hand.

I squeezed back. "No, but I thought I'd try to believe that, since the party is happening anyway."

She laughed a little and leaned her head on my shoulder as we went back to Sweeney's house.

The thing about Eric Sweeney was that his concept of a "little party" was at least twice the size of anyone else's. Close to a couple dozen people packed his house, some playing video games, others watching a movie, some hanging around talking or slipping off somewhere to make out. Almost everybody was drinking. Although I really wasn't in the mood for any of it, I had to appreciate his skill in lining up one of the most insane parties I could remember.

When I asked how he'd done it, Sweeney flashed his million-dollar smile and put his arm around my shoulder. "Priorities, my brother! While Schmidty was crawling around storing gas and whatever in the basement of your shop, I knew there would be a different, much worse shortage. *Beer.* I'm too young to buy it from the store, and I knew the supply would run out fast. So I rushed out and bought up all the home brewing equipment and supplies I could get my hands on. I spent, like, fifteen hundred, and put it all up in the loft above the boathouse. I'll easily make back four times as much selling my surplus beer. In the meantime" — he took a swig from his unlabeled brown bottle — "we won't have to worry. Our parties will be well supplied."

I had to laugh. The guy was a genius. "Okay, give me one of these beers of yours."

"Yeah! That's what I'm talking about!" He reached into a cooler, pulled out a bottle, popped the cap with the opener he kept on his keychain, and handed me my first beer of the night. "Here's to a good party, and some long-overdue fun."

We clinked bottles and I took a drink. It had a nice bite. "Strong stuff."

He drank again. "Yeah, well, if you're too much of a pussy to handle it, you can always drink the pink berry punch with the girls."

I slugged him in the arm.

"I'll have a beer," JoBell said.

Sweeney gave her one. The three of us touched our bottles together.

The party rolled on. Brad must have downed almost a dozen beers. He swayed back and forth with his arm around Crystal as he and Randy yelled, "Nothing is so clear, as when I'm drinking beer" along with Hank McGrew on the living room screen. Someone had either invited TJ or he'd just showed up on his own. He was playing with Sweeney's office putter set, only he whacked the golf ball way too hard, sending it bouncing off the wall so that it flew back and almost hit a window. What a jackwad. Cal and Samantha had disappeared a while ago, so that was one good thing.

Skylar came up and leaned on me. He was one of those guys who acted like he was completely hammered and could hardly walk after only a couple beers. "Wright, I haven't had the chansh ta talk to ya too much lately." He pointed at me. "I jush gotta shay, I saw that . . . video." He held his left fist up above his head and made a finger gun with his right, acting like he was shooting. "You were shooo badass."

"Thanks." My left hand ached. I moved as far from him as I could.

"Hey, babe," JoBell said when I entered the dining room on my way to the fridge in the kitchen. She and Becca were playing beer pong. "Want to play?"

I put on a smile. "Maybe later."

The truth was I didn't want to play anything at all. I knew that half the reason Sweeney was throwing this party was to try to cheer me up, but it wasn't working. I simply didn't feel like being cheered up. It didn't count as having fun if you had to force yourself to act like you were having fun.

TJ had given up golf and came over to the beer pong table. JoBell nailed a slick bounce shot, her Ping-Pong ball plopping down into a plastic cup full of beer. "Awesome shot!" TJ patted her shoulder. Then he said to Sweeney, "It sucks that your parents have to be gone for so long, but in a way it's cool because we get to have fun."

That was it. I put my beer down and rushed around the table, grabbing him by the neck of his T-shirt and pushing him up against the wall. "Yeah, it's so cool that our parents are gone!"

"Danny, don't!" JoBell shouted.

"Dude, I didn't mean that," TJ said. His eyes were wide.

I hit him into the wall again. "Sure you didn't. And keep your damned hands off JoBell."

Sweeney wedged himself between us, pushing me back. "Dude, chill."

TJ stood up against the wall with his hands up. "I'm sorry. I didn't mean anything. It was stupid what I said. I'm sorry."

Sweeney leaned in close so he could speak quietly. "I know you're pissed, and I know you don't like him, but we both know this isn't about TJ. Okay? Chill. Leave him alone."

"There a problem out here?" Cal came back into the room, holding Samantha's hand. Their hair was all messed up.

"No, I was just leaving," TJ said.

"Travis, you don't have to go," JoBell said.

"He does —" I started to shout, but JoBell put her hand over my mouth. At first this made me madder, but then JoBell backed me up against the wall, pressing her body tight to mine and smiling.

"If you calm down and be nice," she whispered in my ear, "I'll make it worth your while."

"How will you —"

She kissed me, her tongue flicking around in my mouth, and she drew in my breath. "Are you cool now?" she finally asked.

I nodded.

She kissed me again real quick. "Good boy. I'm going to get another drink."

When she was gone, I leaned my head back against the wall with my eyes closed. "Wow," I whispered. When I opened my eyes, my cheeks went red-hot right away. The entire party had stopped to watch me and JoBell. Samantha giggled and flashed me a thumbs-up.

"I'm jealous," Randy said.

Becca was down on the floor, wiping up a spilled drink. Her eyes met mine for a second, then she got up and headed toward the basement, leaving a soggy pile of paper towels in the middle of her punch.

TJ stepped up to me and my whole body tensed. "You still here?" I said.

"I'll leave if you want me to since you live here now," TJ said.

"Good." I jerked my head toward the door. "Get the hell out of here."

He nodded. "I know we don't get along, but I want to tell you I'm sorry for what you're going through. Sorry about your mom and that you're caught in the middle of all of this. It isn't fair to you, man. You're really . . . I mean . . . I have a lot of respect for you, the way you've dealt with things. If you ever need my help —"

I folded my arms. "With what?"

"I don't know. A place to crash, a ride or something while your truck's in the shop. A place to hide." He shrugged. "Let me know." He started for the front door.

I wasn't prepared for TJ to act as cool as Cal or Sweeney. For the longest time, I didn't know what to say. "Hey, Travis!" I yelled finally. "Why don't you stay and have another beer. You don't have to go if you don't want."

Skylar shouted from the living room, "Hey, everybody shut up!" He was peeking out through the curtains. "Who's going around outside with a flashlight? There's some guy . . . Oh shit. Cops!"

"Yeah, thanks for the offer, Danny, but I think I'm leaving anyway!" TJ started running for the sliding door in back, but stopped when he saw the police officer standing there, knocking on the glass.

"Oh no," Brad said. "I really don't need to deal with this right now."

I didn't care. They could bust me. I was already in trouble everywhere outside of Idaho. A few charges in the state couldn't make that much of a difference.

Someone shut off the music as Sweeney sighed and opened the patio door. The cop stepped inside.

"I hope you're all of age." He smoothed his mustache. "Otherwise I think a lot of y'all are in real trouble."

Another officer with a big belly came in through the front door. "We have two other squad cars out there, so don't nobody try to run, either."

"Let's go," said Mustache. "Let's see some IDs."

Since I had nothing to lose, I handed mine over first. Mustache looked at the photo, then looked up at me. He frowned. "Hey," he said to Fatty, showing him my ID.

"Whoa," Fatty said. "Sorry. Didn't recognize you." He laughed a little. "Grown your hair out a little since the last time I saw you, er, since you were on the news." He looked down. "Sorry about your mother."

"Yeah," I said.

Mustache hooked his thumbs under his belt. "Listen, Sheriff Crow is a real good friend of ours. He says you're a good guy, someone we can trust. So, tell you what. We came out here because one of the neighbors complained about the noise, said they were pretty sure there was underage drinking going on over here. If you'll keep it down, we'll let them know they should mind their own business."

"Meantime," said the fat one, "don't none of you be driving tonight."

The cop with the mustache rubbed his nose. "Hey, um, you know you all must have spent some serious money on this party. Beer's getting hard to come by. You mind if I take like a six-pack with me?" He slapped me on the shoulder. "I like a cold beer as much as the next man."

Sweeney rushed to get the man his beer. Mustache handed back my ID, and with a nod to his buddy, they both left.

For what seemed like a long time afterward, nobody said anything. My eyes met TJ's. He looked at me like, *What the hell was that all about?* Then everybody started cheering and celebrating.

"Wright, you are the coolest!" Mike Keelin said, holding up his beer to toast me.

Aimee Hartling let out a long breath of relief. "Oh, I so couldn't handle a possession ticket. Thanks, Danny, for whatever you did."

That's the thing. I hadn't really done anything. We all should have been slapped with expensive tickets for drinking under age. Instead, I was being congratulated by everyone. I slammed my beer and then opened another. I thought maybe if I drank as much as I could, it would numb me to everything, to my friends having fun while I felt miserable, to missing Mom, to how much I wanted to kill the damned Fed.

I thought wrong.

"Hey!" Someone shouted from the living room. "Sweeney, something's wrong with your screen. The game just blanked out."

I staggered in to see what was up.

Black letters came on over a gold background.

ABC NEWS
SPECIAL REPORT

"What now?" I said.

"Hey, quiet everybody!" JoBell yelled. "If they're cutting into ESPN, this is something serious."

Sweeney turned up the volume.

"This is an ABC News special report. Live from Philadelphia, here's Brian Logan."

The image switched to a man standing in front of dozens of police cars and other emergency vehicles, all with their lights flashing. Sirens screamed in the background. *"It is my sad duty to report to you that moments ago, President Rodriguez was shot three times on his way into a convention center where he was about to address an audience regarding compromise amendments to the controversial Federal ID Card Act. The shooting has been captured on video, I'm sure by a number of comm cameras. The video we are about to play for you is graphic, and may not be suitable for sensitive or younger viewers."*

They cut to a video of President Rodriguez smiling and waving at onlookers while comms flashed photographs. He leaned down to shake a little girl's hand, stopping for a moment to say something to her. Next to him, a man in a black suit held his finger to his earpiece. He spoke into his microphone, then grabbed the president's arm, yanking him upright, away from the little girl.

A quick blast. President Rodriguez's chest tore open. Another round sliced through his neck. His head slumped sideways, and a third bullet ripped into his face and burst from the back of his skull. Then the video was a blur of people screaming and running around.

"Oh no," Becca said.

"This is not good." Timmy shook his head.

"Quiet! I want to hear this!" said Samantha.

The image cut back to the reporter. *"As you can see from the video, despite the fact that we have no official confirmation that President Rodriguez is dead, there can be little doubt that his wounds were fatal. Other videos that we have seen, but which we will not show you, clearly show extreme damage to the president's head, neck, and chest to an extent that no person could survive. We have no word yet on the apprehension of an assassin or assassins. But the atmosphere here in Philadelphia tonight, and I'm sure around the nation and around the world, is one of fear and deep sadness."*

A woman sitting at the studio news desk appeared on-screen. *"I'm sorry to interrupt you, Brian, but ABC News has just received official word from the White House that President Rodriguez is dead, and, as nearly everyone surmised, was killed instantly from three gunshot wounds. We are also told that Laura Griffith, appointed to the vice presidency in the wake of Aaron Henke's resignation a little over a month ago, is safe aboard Air Force One. For security reasons, we are not being told the location or destination of the presidential aircraft, but we are told that the vice president has taken the oath of office of the president of the United States, and will be addressing the nation shortly."*

Everyone at the party had been watching mostly in silence. I took my comm from my pocket and shut off the living room screen. I hated that guy, but I didn't want him dead. Now that he was, I knew there was about zero chance of Idaho and the Fed working out a deal.

The party tried to go on, but it seemed like everybody kind of felt more like I had been feeling all night. A bunch of people had their designated drivers take them home. I kept drinking with the few who were going to stay over.

Later that night, I staggered into my room. Someone helped me collapse across the bed instead of falling on the floor. Hands were on my ankles, straightening me out and then taking off my shoes.

"Cold'n here," I mumbled.

"I know," said a girl's voice. "Here." Blankets were pulled up to cover me. Then a gentle hand ran back from my forehead through my hair, again and again. "If you get sick, there's a bucket here beside your bed. Go to sleep, Danny."

"JoBell?"

"It's me, Becca."

"Where'sh J'Bell?"

"She had to go home. Her dad won't let her stay over. You know that."

"I *do* know that!" I shouted.

She laughed. "Shhh. Relax."

"I don' wanna dream," I said. "Don' wanna dream 'bout my mudder, 'bout Boise or nothin'." Somehow I reached up and took hold of Becca's hand. "So tired the dreams, Becca." I was able to focus my eyes on her then. A little moonlight filtered in through the window. "You know what?"

"What?" she said, and I swear her hair sparkled in the moonlight. Maybe I was already dreaming.

I pushed out a single finger and lightly poked Becca in the arm. "Ya ev'n really here? Is any a dis ev'n real?"

She smiled, but somehow didn't seem so happy. "It's as real as you want it to be, Danny."

Yes! This was one of those sweet dreams where I made it with the girl. I sat up. "Yer really pretty," I said. My fingers traced her cheek, and she closed her eyes and leaned toward my touch. When I could focus my eyes, her lips looked so soft and warm. I slid my arms around her and drew her to me. "If I wasn't wit' J'Bell, I hope you 'n' me —"

Her whole body tensed up, and she took me by the shoulders and gently pushed me back down to the bed. "Oh, Danny." She leaned forward and kissed my forehead. "Go to sleep. We'll be here for you in the morning."

~~• out of more than twenty presidential assassination attempts in our history, this is only the fifth time an assassin has succeeded. The previous four presidents killed while in office, Abraham Lincoln, James Garfield, William McKinley, and John F. Kennedy, were —"

"Dr. Langethol, I'm going to have to interrupt you there. Word has come into the CBS studio that the Secret Service has been involved in a shoot-out with a man who has not yet been identified, but who was killed in the firefight. The shooter was using a high-powered rifle. Experts have not had time to locate or analyze the bullets that killed President Rodriguez, but certainly it is possible that the president's extreme wounds were caused by such a weapon. One would think it would have to have been a weapon of some considerable power. So at this hour, it is possible that the president's assassin is already dead. Of course, none of that is confirmed yet. •~~

~~• President Griffith, who had been aboard the vice presidential plane on her way to visit her son, a third-year cadet at the Air Force Academy north of Colorado Springs, was in the air at the time of the assassination, and of course as she was sworn in, Air Force Two became Air Force One. We go now to President Griffith in the Air Force Academy Chapel."

. . .

"My fellow Americans, today we are devastated by a national tragedy. I stand before you in this majestic chapel with a heavy heart. A broken heart. We all feel this sadness, suffering a loss that cannot be measured. I have lost a valued colleague and a personal friend tonight, but I know that the death of President Rodriguez is mourned around the world, and that people everywhere share a deep pain with and sympathy for Mrs. Rodriguez and her family. As your president, I promise to do my best. That is all anyone can do.

I ask for your help. And now, if you'll join me in a moment of silence . . .

. . .

. . .

"May God bless President Rodriguez, his family, and the United States of America. Thank you." •⌁

TWENTY-FIVE

The next two weeks were a blur of news and shows about the president. The guy who shot him was identified as Bob Latham Collinder. The bullets in his gun matched the ones that killed Rodriguez, and he left a letter in his Philadelphia apartment, rambling about how the president was destroying the country and how only he could save the world from Rodriguez. He was a world-class nutjob acting alone, but of course FriendStar and tons of other sites were full of people blaming it all on Idaho and Governor Montaine. The governor, for his part, gave a speech saying the assassination was a tragedy and that he appreciated a lot of what the president had done, especially his work in recent negotiations.

They had the funeral a few days after it happened. I didn't watch it. Maybe I hadn't wanted Rodriguez shot like that, and in my head I knew it was terrible he'd been murdered, but my heart wouldn't let me be sad for that son of a bitch who had sent his soldiers to Idaho and gotten my mother killed. I heard Mr. Morgan had brought in grief counselors and everything to talk to everyone about their feelings. I was glad I wasn't going to school anymore. I tried to avoid it all. Instead, after my hand healed, I worked long hours at the shop with Schmidty, making repairs to the Beast after she'd been hauled in on a flatbed trailer.

That Saturday, as I returned from a walk, I came into Sweeney's living room, draped my coat over the back of the couch, and took in the scene. Sweeney was sitting back in his recliner. Cal was stretched out on the couch. JoBell . . . was pacing the living room with her arms folded.

Oh no. This was absolutely not what I was in the mood for.

"You're not doing it! It's insane! Look what happened —" JoBell saw me and dropped whatever she was about to say. She smiled. "Hey, babe."

"Hey."

"Hey, supper will be ready in about twenty minutes." Becca came in through the archway between the living room and kitchen, but stopped when she saw me. Ever since the party on the night of the assassination, she had been acting really weird around me. I couldn't quite explain it, but there was a definite tension. "Oh, hey, Danny. How was your walk?"

"It was . . . good. What's going on here?"

"Burgers and fried potatoes tonight." Then she went back into the kitchen.

"Cheeseburgers?" Cal called.

"Everybody's out of cheese," Becca yelled back.

"Can I get a double?" said Cal.

"Cal, no. There's a shortage of everything. We have to ration," JoBell said.

We wouldn't have any meat at all if Becca hadn't sold her herd, filling two deep freezers in Sweeney's garage with some beef from cows she'd had slaughtered just for us.

"Will somebody tell me what you were all arguing about?" I asked.

"Oh, nothing," Sweeney said. "Don't worry."

I leaned against the back of the couch. "No, really. Come on."

"We have to tell him," JoBell said. "These two idiots want to join the Idaho State Militia."

Last week, the Idaho Civilian Corp had begun arming and training some of its members for combat. Governor Montaine had renamed it the Idaho State Militia. JoBell walked up and put her arm around me. "And we are not getting involved in any of that stuff again. Look what it cost . . ."

Nobody moved or said anything. It was tough. I'd been doing a lot of thinking on my walks. Even though my unit had put me on extended leave after Mom died, I wanted to rejoin the Idaho Guard. When it came right down to it, yeah, Mom might still be alive if I hadn't driven into Washington for her. But I wasn't the one who had shot her. It was the Fed who had attacked us, and for no greater crime than trying to go home. It was the Fed who had killed my mother. It was the Fed who should be made to pay. If I went back to the Idaho Guard, then the next time they tried to invade Idaho, I'd make sure they got more than a warning shot.

"Maybe it's worth considering," I said.

"What?" JoBell dropped her arm. "You can't be serious."

"It's decent money," I said. "And Idaho needs more soldiers."

"For what?" she said. "All of America needs a lot fewer soldiers so we can put a stop to all this!"

Cal stood up from the couch and stretched. "I'm joining, and there ain't nothing you all can say to make me change my mind. I'll either join the fighting ranks of the militia or I'll drive truck for them, smuggling supplies over the Canadian border. I already talked to my dad about it. He thinks it's a great idea. I gotta do something. We can't let the Fed keep pushing us around like this."

JoBell wiped her eyes. "Guys, please. I'm asking you, *begging* you, not to do this."

"I know what you're saying, JoBell," Sweeney said, "but here's the thing. I've always had everything. The best toys when I was little.

A sweet car now. Boats. Snowmobiles. A Jet Ski. I live in this awesome lakefront house that costs a fortune . . ."

"Yeah, everybody knows your parents have money, Eric," JoBell said. "What's your point?"

"My point is that my *parents* have money, or at least they used to have money. Idaho real estate is about the worst business a guy could be in right now. Even if my dad were here, he couldn't work any deals, because the market is flooded with people trying to sell and nobody's buying."

"What does that have to do with joining the militia?" Cal asked.

"I'm getting to it," Sweeney said. He took a deep breath. "All my life I never had to work for anything. I never had any real goals. I always thought I would go to college because that's what my parents expect of me. I'd party there, get with a bunch of girls, learn a thing or two about business, and basically avoid growing up. Then I would come home and go into business with my dad."

"Charming," JoBell said.

Sweeney stood up. "No, listen to me for a second. I'm serious. I'm trying to say I want to do something more important than just partying and chasing women."

Coming from Sweeney, this was big news. I could hardly believe he was saying it.

"Don't take this the wrong way," he said. "But when we were over there in Washington rescuing the girls from the Fed, I was scared and it was terrible, but also I felt . . . alive, like what I was doing really mattered. I want to do something that's real, something important. We're heading toward war, and right now I can't think of anything that matters more than helping Idaho by joining the militia."

"It doesn't *have* to be a war just because bad things have happened," JoBell said. "It doesn't always have to end in violence. If enough people decide to stay out of this, it can work out. You want to do something important, Eric? Then help to convince others to work for peace. Doing something important doesn't always mean doing something violent." She shook her head. "We have like six months of high school left. We've worked this whole time so we could go to college. And when this is all over, you're going to want a high school diploma, a college education. I know things seem crazy, but now more than ever, we need to work for a better world."

"The world has changed," I said. "Everything has changed."

A high-pitched tone went off. It was loud, irritating.

"What the hell?" Sweeney said.

The image on the living room screen had switched from the skateboarding show he'd been watching with the sound muted to the seal of the president of the United States over a blue background.

"Can you stop that sound?" Cal asked.

Sweeney picked up his comm to change the living room screen volume. "It won't turn down. It won't turn off. It's on the comm too."

"Same here." JoBell held up her comm. She tried the power button. "It's stuck."

We all checked our comms. They were all the same way.

"Hang on." Sweeney ran to another room and came back with an old, emergency hand crank–powered radio. He cranked it a little and then switched on the radio, adjusting the volume and spinning the station dials. No matter what station he tuned to, he could only pick up the same high-pitched whine that was coming from everything else.

"It must be playing on everything, everywhere," Becca said.

JoBell moved closer to me and took my hand.

"If someone doesn't turn that sound off, I'm going to start smashing screens and comms," Cal said with his hands over his ears.

The noise stopped. The seal of the president was replaced by an image of the new president herself, sitting behind her desk in the Oval Office.

"*Good evening.*" President Griffith folded her hands on top of her desk. "*This is the second time I have spoken to the nation, and on both occasions, I have done so with a heavy heart under the weight of tremendous responsibility. I did not seek or request this office, and I am keenly aware that you, the American people, have not elected me to this position. Nevertheless, I will not avoid or neglect my duty as required of me by our Constitution.*

"*It is regarding that same document, that foundation of American democracy, that I address you tonight. For the past several months, our Constitution and our nation has faced a crisis the likes of which we have not experienced for over one hundred and fifty years. The governor of the state of Idaho, along with the Idaho state legislature, have taken it upon themselves to disregard Article Six, Clause Two of our Constitution.*

"*This clause, known as the Supremacy Clause, dictates that if federal law conflicts with a law passed by a state, the federal law will be supreme. The state law must be amended or set aside. This basic operating principle is what has allowed our states to remain united for nearly two and a half centuries. Without it, states could determine for themselves which national laws they choose to obey and which they want to disregard. Chaos and disunity would be the inevitable result.*

"*It is the position of the government of the state of Idaho that certain laws recently passed by the United States Congress are not consistent with the spirit or the letter of the Constitution. That opinion is their right, and our democracy allows them the opportunity and a legal process whereby their congressional representatives and* senators can work to pass amendments or even to repeal the laws to which they object.

"However, they most certainly do not *have the right to*, by force of arms, refuse to allow Constitutional authority to take precedence in their state. This is what they have attempted to do, and entertaining arguments toward the legality or legitimacy of this practice only serves to prolong it, escalating the problem.

"I have, therefore, reluctantly been forced to declare the state of Idaho to be in a condition of rebellion, and by the authority vested in me as the commander in chief of the United States military, I have ordered our armed forces to end this rebellion.

"All Idaho military, law enforcement, and militia personnel are ordered to immediately and unconditionally surrender. All Idaho residents are ordered to disarm, remain in their homes, and obey all instructions from federal authorities. These demands are not open to negotiation or debate.

"This is a dark and dangerous time for our nation, but the United States of America has overcome difficult times before. Our people will persevere through this current crisis. We will *be united once more*.

"Thank you. God bless you. And God bless the United States of America."

The screen and our comms switched to the presidential seal for a moment. Then they cut out, displaying the "no signal" message. I fiddled with the setting on my comm, trying to see if I could connect to anything, but it was cut off. No cellular feed was available.

Then the power went out, plunging us into darkness.

I squeezed JoBell's hand.

"My God." I reached for my gun. "They're coming."